A
Tree on
Turtle Island

First Edition
www.atreeonturtleisland.com

ISBN 1-58961-034-2

Hand-colored cover photograph by Leith A. Rohr
Map by Matthew S. Ozmun

Published by Open Passage Press, Inc.
P.O. Box 1047, Evanston, IL 60204-1047
in cooperation with PageFree Publishing, Inc.

OPEN PASSAGE PRESS

EVANSTON, ILLINOIS

10 9 8 7 6 5 4 3 2 1

A
Tree on
Turtle Island

a novel

Sheila Seclearr

Advance Praise for
A Tree on Turtle Island

"Seclearr's multi-generational tale will transport you to another world, one so true and compelling, it delivers an 'Ah-ha!' on every page. *As A Tree on Turtle Island*'s brave women struggle to own up to and embrace their past—the people, losses, triumphs, and landscape that formed them—they remind us that where we've been and what we've done matters far less than what we're becoming."

Carol DeChant, author of
"Momma's Enchanted Supper: Stories for the Long Evenings of Advent."

"Sheila Seclearr is a masterful story teller, weaving the wisdom and struggles of the past into current reality. Her characters living in parallel lives, take us on a rich journey though time, awakening us to the complexities of being human and the liberation of the human spirit. This book touched my soul and heart and caused me to ask what is important now."

Liz Ashling, author of "Pulling on New Genes: The Heart Journey Home"

"A gripping tale of our contemporary chaotic world intertwined with personalities from the distant past. Don't miss this one."

Corinne Edwards, author of "Reflections from a Woman Alone"

"Told through timeless eyes across history and culture, A Tree on Turtle Island powerfully, yet gently takes the reader into the web of life where we can discover we are all connected. Seclearr's characters surprise and delight with their fullness and humanity. She weaves several disparate cultures and themes—early Native American, colonial and Morovian history, modern day America, issues of the gay, lesbian, bisexual and transgender community—without seeming forced or contrived. *A Tree On Turtle Island* traveled into my heart and psyche and took root."

Moonhawk River Stone, psychotherapist and Co-Chair, New York
Association for Gender Rights Advocacy, Albany, NY

For my dad,
Warren H. Sechler,
who taught me about
breaking family patterns

FOREWORD

Before I entered school and even before I knew the word 'history,' I knew about stories. My dad told stories. Everywhere our family went, packed tightly in our sedan, from a Colorado forest to a desolate lava field in Idaho or a tiny farming town in Kansas, he would regale us with tales of the native people or early settlers of the area. As I listened, my eyes would follow his pointing finger to the bluff where a wagon train first emerged into a valley or to the mists of a waterfall where a legend was born.

As a child, I never wondered how he knew these stories or how he remembered them. I never wondered why they were important. I knew that his words held the authority of truth. Later I figured out that the stories were collected in books, rows and rows upon his shelves holding the offerings of many writers and historians. But that revelation came too late for me. I had been immersed as an infant in the stories that were told over campfires, those that held his audience of any size enthralled. While I will always respect textbooks and their authors, my early experience gave me a sense of the world that held stories in its topsoil, legends in the faces of cliffs, myths buried within mountains. Even after my dad was no longer with me, I could still travel anywhere and sense a story lurking.

I've been privileged to meet some famous and prolific authors, but when asked, they admit that they are mystified by the process of writing. I've never met a fiction writer who could explain how characters come alive and take over a writer's plans, but all who experience the phenomenon say it's what makes fiction writing compelling.

My character Maggie introduced me to the Moravians and the backwoods of Pennsylvania. She and her family are completely fictional, but the Moravian history of native missions and schools is based on fact, as is the early treaty work of Benjamin Franklin and Conrad Weiser. Though my account is fictionalized, the book's website includes a reading list for those readers who wish to explore the scholarly texts.

The interesting thing about our natural world is that even when we think we have made a straight line, it is ultimately bent by the curve of the earth's shape or its cycles around the sun. We humans will never change or control that. We may think we are separate, we may think we are on distinct and different paths, but we are always on a long curve toward each other and ourselves.

My father left his alcoholic home in Missouri as a teenager, heading west to create a better life for the family he would later have. It had been several generations since our direct descendants lived in Pennsylvania. Maggie had already led me to Shamokin village on the forks of the Susquehanna River when I received a package of family genealogical information from my aunt. I learned that my father's forebears had helped settle Danville, right across the river from Shamokin only a few years after the time period of my story. On my initial research trip to Pennsylvania, my first stop was in Danville to seek out the old cemetery and honor the graves of my ancestors.

Ancient cultures around the world teach of a sacred tree with roots that nourish and connect all people. In its protective shadow the people find wisdom, healing, power and security. I am grateful to all my fellow explorers seeking the Tree of Peace.

Sheila Seclearr

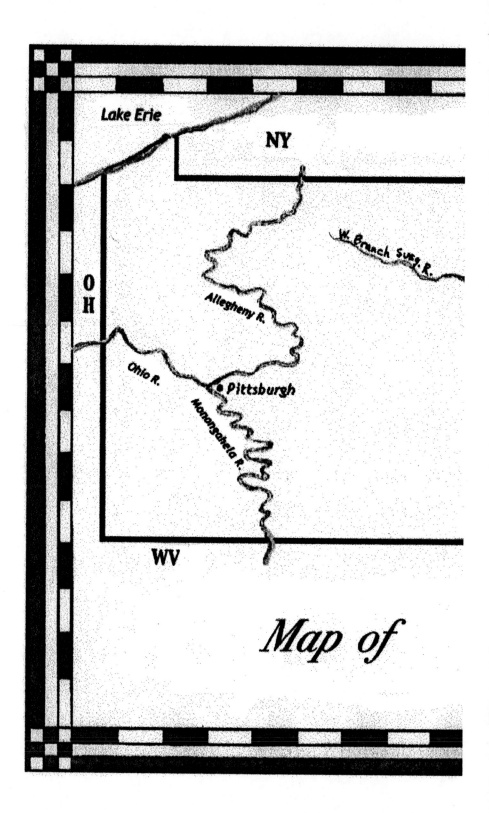

Lake Erie

NY

W. Branch Susq. R.

O
H

Allegheny R.

Ohio R.

• Pittsburgh

Monongahela R.

WV

Map of

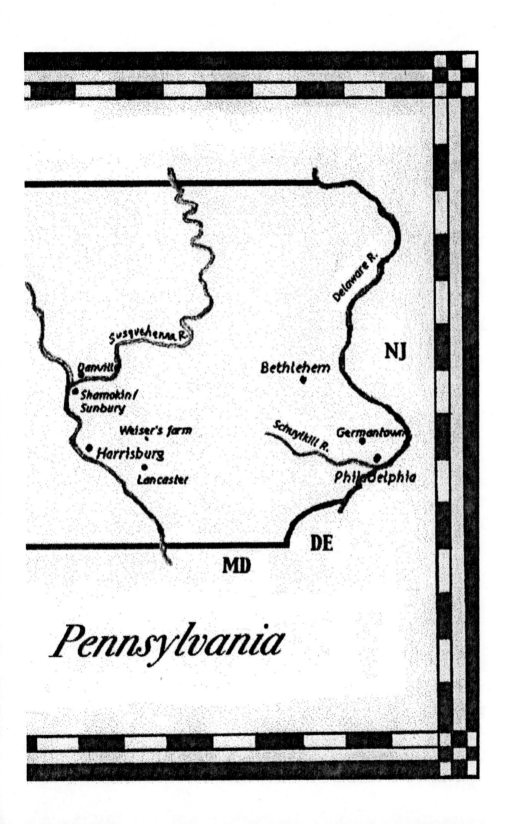

1

Dread was a familiar sense for me, but I suddenly felt saturated. It thumped against my eardrums and blurred my vision of the sunny afternoon beyond the car windshield. A rock mountain jutted up from the golden dry grass hills of southern Pennsylvania, but my only focus was on the gaping hole at its base, the Fort Pitt Tunnel. Two creeping, red lines of brake lights indicated many more delayed travelers alongside us, probably all of them anxious to get through the tunnel to Pittsburgh. I was just anxious to get through the dark belly of the mountain. I rubbed sweaty palms on my shorts, thankful that my friend, Quinn, was at the wheel. I helped her drive from Chicago, but that was before my head began to ache. It's times like this when I sense my mother's hands holding mine. She seemed to be squeezing old memories to the surface.

I was ten years old again, crying in my bed, unable to sleep because of the terrible pressure I felt in my head, in a place I couldn't show and didn't know how to explain. "Point to where it hurts, Reed," my mother whispered as she rubbed my forearms.

I shook my head and strained to speak. "Everywhere, Mama, everywhere." She held my hands and patted them until my eyes closed. She said I must have a gauge in my head, something like our faded brass weather barometer nailed beside the back door that warned me about oncoming storms. Gramama had the gauge, too, she told me. Gramama Inez lived in Mexico and by then I had seen her only once in my life. I fell asleep, feeling no doubt that Gramama Inez would come soon and explain it all to me.

The next day, Mama had a brain aneurysm, or, as I was told at the time, a blood vessel in her head broke and made her eyes stop working. A few minutes after dropping me off at my school, she drove her car into a stone wall. She's been dead now for twenty-five years. Maybe that's the headache connection: approaching a mountain that feels like a stone wall; my mother nearly the same age as I am now. She always picked me up after school, but on that day my teacher pulled me from class before lunchtime to go home with my dad. When I heard Dad's words, the remaining dull sinus pain changed to a stab of heartache and shame. My previous night's agony must have been our warning, I thought, one that I had missed. I should have known. I could have stopped it all from happening.

That feeling, the one about making it stop, lives under my skin like an inflammation. I can feel the heat now just as I felt it then. If I believed in destiny, I'd be worried about the vessels in my own head, but when my heart pounds, I hear the blood whooshing past my ears.

I barely remember Gramama Inez arriving two days later. She was like a cloud that blew before my bleary eyes; I had been sweeping, sweeping, cleaning everything the way Mama liked. My dad's face was puffy and red except for the thin white line of his mouth, clamped tightly so no words could get out. Gramama followed me to my room and sat on my bed, seeming to already know what I felt.

"You see?" she pointed to my wall where a National Parks wildlife calendar showed a picture of a spotted fawn. "People thinks each day comes after the other, plink, plink, plink, just like thees. But you look at old calendars in my country. They are round. The days, they swirl." She made a sweeping spiral with her gnarled pointer finger. "Everything swirls and you bump against next day, feeling bad because you sense your blessed Mama gone, and nothing you can do won't change it. But, Reed, you don't make thees thing happen."

"You know that?" I stared at her swollen hands.

"I know thees feeling for many years. If I could change things, so many times, I would do it." Gramama shook her head slowly. "But we cannot."

I told Gramama Inez that if I had known what the pressure was about, if I had paid better attention and not been a crybaby, I could have warned my mother. She could have gone to the doctor.

"You must listen to me. Your old grandmother knows. I give to you thees vision just as I give you my once-dark hair. You might know something. You might see something. But always, you cannot know what it means. You are responsible for yourself alone." Gramama Inez said this with great and final authority, like her next announcement that I must learn to cook, or the statement made in front of my father that there would be no television in the evenings. The discussion was closed like a fat suitcase. Shreds of fabric poking from the edges were the unasked questions I had for Gramama. But like the evening TV, they were turned off. I filled my head with other things. Great long lists of things. But I continue to berate myself when I don't pay enough attention, which seems to be often. It's exhausting to try to follow everything.

Inside the tunnel, I leaned back against my headrest and sighed. Mechanically, I stretched an elastic bungee cord band on my wrist. I'd worn it following a wrist sprain several years ago and kept a supply of them in my office for clients. Quinn has never been a client. There have been times when she needed physical therapy, but she usually has her own trainer from whatever team or school she's working with. She and I are old friends; known each other since high school. She would scoff at my fears if I admitted them to her. If I said I had a feeling something big was about to happen, she'd nod and listen. But if I told her I was so afraid of its arrival I couldn't move, she'd laugh and tell me to breathe through it, or walk off the anxiety. She's a true girl jock, a basketball player. She says things like that.

Quinn tapped her thin fingers on the black Beetle's steering wheel along with the radio tune. "Amazing," she said loudly, above the music. "You can hear the radio all the way inside the tunnel now." She eased the volume knob. "Wasn't like that when I was a kid. We'd get static, then my dad would turn it off and we'd all be spooked in the dark."

I nodded. The slow traffic was creepy enough. I've been in lots of traffic jams in Chicago, but not inside a mountain. Quinn noticed my shortness of breath and said, "Sunday afternoon. Probably a Steelers game." Quinn's not interested in men romantically, but she knows all about their sports games. If I weren't feeling sick, I'd want to hear her commentary on the Bears' surprising season. She probably knows about the Steelers, too; the radio announced they're winning their division. She says basketball holds the future for women's' sports, but Quinn's favorite sport is the same as mine—baseball. We're two of the many Cubs fans who remain faithful, year after losing year.

We moved ahead in the slow traffic until a distant spot of daylight broadened at the exit and reflected sparks of brilliant color. My hopes of freedom from the tunnel rippled like the little American flags on so many car radio antennas. We picked up speed as traffic emerged into daylight. Suddenly, great shining skyscrapers appeared across the river. I gasped as I stared into a mirror image of our mountain tunnel reflected in shining, high-tech windows.

Quinn shrieked, "God, it's grown and changed so much! Can you believe it?"

"It's the first time I've been here," I said as tears spontaneously streamed from my eyes. I covered them and squeezed the headache at my temples.

Trying to hide my confusion from Quinn, I rifled through my memories for past glimpses of Pittsburgh that could explain how I knew the Monongahela flowed west beneath our bridge. The three river valleys intermingled their familiar curves where the Ohio River was birthed. I was annoyed by the modern buildings blocking my view of the wooded bluffs north of the city.

I had watched a few Cubs games broadcast from Three Rivers Stadium, now a phantom of the new PNC Park, buttressed beside the Allegheny in the span across the bridge ahead. I may have seen sweeping views of the city from the televised games, but I had no conscious recollection of such an intimate view of downtown Pittsburgh.

I leaned to see over the bubble dash of Quinn's Beetle and she noticed my eyes and red streaked face. "What is it? What's wrong, Reed?" she asked, slowing the car.

"Just a little emotional," I said. "The whole place popped up so quickly, you know? We came out of the tunnel and wham! We're right here! In the middle of the city."

"It's the terrorist thing," she said. "Big buildings look different now. They probably will from now on."

"Right." I knew it was more than that. Looking over the bridge railing at swarms of people strolling around the park at the point made me feel squeamish. It was a busy Sunday afternoon, fairly nice weather for the end of October. But I didn't feel like being in a crowd. We'd weathered the initial shock of last month's terrorist attacks on New York and Washington D.C. Lately, the news was full of anthrax stories.

"Quinn, let's go up to your old neighborhood. We can come back to the city when it's less crowded." I knew Quinn's childhood home had been up on the bluffs overlooking the Allegheny from the map she had e-mailed a week ago. Last night, she and I had stayed in a cabin at Raccoon Creek, an hour from Pittsburgh. We left our things there and planned to return after a day of exploring. But I wasn't ready to go from the peaceful woods to the bustling city.

Quinn had grown up in Pittsburgh before she moved to my little southern Illinois town of Metropolis where we met in high school. We had both migrated to Chicago and stayed after college: me to Northwestern in Evanston, she to Loyola with a partial basketball scholarship.

Quinn reached into the glove box for a bundle of papers and slid them into my lap. "Good. You navigate. My memory's not stellar enough to remember back twenty years. Besides, everything has changed. Look at the new stadium." We crossed the bridge by PNC Park and cruised up the river highway. "I know I want Butler Street. Which bridge should I take?" she asked.

I shuffled through the sheets she had printed from Mapquest with pictures and directions, street by street. The second bridge I named elicited a yelp from Quinn. "That's it! I know where we are," she said. We were passing the industrial warehouse Strip District, but were in a part of Pittsburgh that seemed like a movie set from the fifties. The dull, rusty jungle of factory buildings seemed completely different from the glistening city that I saw when we emerged from the tunnel.

"No wonder," I said. "Do you still think everything has changed? It must have looked the same way fifty years ago. Where are the shopping malls, the chain stores? Where's Burger King?"

"I can't believe I'm remembering the streets. I didn't even know how to drive when we left here." Quinn's voice lifted into a song as she cornered the Beetle sharply and headed up a steep hill. Tall oaks and maples shaded the simple, vintage 40s and 50s brick homes, reminiscent of an old Doris Day movie or the "Happy Days" neighborhood. There was no "Fonz," no kids in sight, just colorful flower borders along manicured lawns. After a few Mapquest maneuvers, we were atop the hill and close to Quinn's old home.

"Right down there," she pointed. "Just as I recall."

I gazed at the row of neat brick boxes, two stories and well kept without new vinyl-sided additions or cedar decking. She parked the Beetle by the tallest tree in the neighborhood, a scraggly pine. Most of the tiny yards barely had room for a few trimmed evergreens or an ornamental bush. Quinn shrieked with delight. "It all seemed so big back then!" She glowed as she pointed to her bedroom window and imagined walking me through the house, room by room. "That would be the stairway, the fireplace."

I heard Quinn's voice and felt her happiness, but it was her world. They were her memories. We got out of the car and strolled toward her old house. While she was slipping back into the seventies, I felt a larger slip beneath my feet into even older memories of wild and barren land, before Quinn's house, before the city skyscrapers. I felt like peeling away the asphalt and manicured grass and putting my hands in the cool dirt. I imagined my headache slipping into the ground. I pretended to listen to Quinn, but from where I stood at the top of the hill, I felt the dry October breeze cool my head with each swell of air from the river valley. I saw the brown river in the distance at the base of the steep street. Looking across a neighboring side yard, I saw the river again, flowing in a different direction.

"Is it the same river?" I asked. Quinn dropped her pointing arm and asked what I had said. "The river," I repeated. "You can see it down there and again that way. It seems like the same one. Right?"

"I don't recall ever seeing the river from up here. Can you believe that?" She gazed over the yards and treetops toward the dull ribbon of water shrouded by the afternoon haze. "I ran around on this street every day without paying attention to the river. But, yes. That's the Allegheny. It snakes all around. Now I remember my mother talking about watching the river while she washed dishes." Quinn glanced back at the house. "See, there in front. There's the kitchen where she stood." We wandered around the neighborhood, along the grass lane behind the house and further, toward her elementary school. "Down there's the sledding hill. Look at that big, old tree. We'd nearly kill ourselves seeing how close we could get without hitting it. Somebody always hit it," she said. "We were stupid." Beyond the sprawling oak was a baseball field adjacent to the rear schoolyard.

"Ah, Valley View." She began to tell stories about teachers, classes, walking home for lunch every day for chicken soup and sandwiches. It was a hummed ballad in the background of my thoughts. As we strolled past the dense forest bordering the field, I imagined the mischief my own former classmates would have manufactured in such wild woods. Walking closer, I saw a trail leading down the hill into the forest.

"Let's walk down," I said.

Quinn stopped still. Her hollow-eyed stare had a noise like static, like our signal was lost or we'd switched to a bad frequency. Come back, Quinn. She blinked and slowly formed the first word. "You—aren't serious." It wasn't a question.

"A short walk?"

Quinn started to back away. "I won't tell you the horrible stories. I just won't go, that's all."

I smiled at Quinn. "You just got eight years old, didn't you?"

She turned away, brushing me off with the back of her hand. "Go ahead. I'm going to walk around the school."

I watched her long-legged stride over the baseball diamond then I took a few steps into the shady, steep pathway that wound around large boulders and tree trunks. Cool, musk scented air was dizzying. Trees grew close enough to the trail to grab a trunk or branch for balance. A patch of sunlight revealed a section of path that overlooked the rocky terrain. Out on a ledge of rock, I peered over the six-foot drop and considered how adults through the years had allowed scary legends to fill the school halls. Any means necessary to keep some kid from pitching on his head and suing the school.

I followed the ledge trail to a sunlit patch and stretched my arms in the warming daylight. When I glanced over my shoulder toward the school yard, I saw only trees. Below me was a barren gravel pit, no buildings in sight. There were a few patches of vegetation below in the midst of the rock and gravel, but no trees until the hazy valley of the river. When I swung my legs over the rock ledge, I spotted a glint of shimmering black rock on the ground beside my hand. To pick it up, I had to pry the edge and pull it from the crusty, gray dirt. It was an oval of black rock, perhaps obsidian, nearly the size of a silver dollar. It was flat underneath but rounded and bumpy on the reverse. There were four stumps, like legs, poking from the outer edge.

I leaned back and turned the stone in the center of my palm. My hand was covered with gray powder, like fine ash, grainy between my fingers. Suddenly squeamish at the thought of digging up industrial waste, I heard a rumbling chuckle from behind. I spun and saw a mangy old man duck from behind the rocks and crouch on the ledge between me and the school trail. His glistening black face crinkled as he coughed again, showing a few yellow teeth. I took a step backward, behind the rock. When I peeked, he had moved closer. His eyes were darker and smoother than the stone in my hand. He straightened up and looked out over the valley. The haze had lifted and the river undulated between deep blue and silver sparkles. He pointed a curled finger and said with a scratchy whisper, "Best give care to what'ch you dig up."

I glanced at my hand where he pointed. The stone's bumps seemed more pronounced, the ridges deeper. I cleared my throat, "If you're trying to frighten me, you don't. You might scare children around here. I see a harmless old man." When he was silent, I raised my eyebrows. "Right?"

"Joe."

"Joe. You live around here?"

He nodded, sniffed. "You?"

"No. I live in Illinois. Near Chicago."

He gazed across the river. "West?"

I nodded. "A very long day's drive."

He climbed over on the ledge beside me, sitting with his legs dangling over the edge. "Name?" he asked.

"Reed." I cringed at my spontaneous honesty. I felt invaded by his inquiries. I wanted to leap over him and rush back up the trail.

"You know the meanin'?" His words rasped like a half whisper.

"My mother named me. Two e's, like the plant."

He nodded. He clasped his hands together and pressed them in his lap. "Ah know this plant. Grows by the river. Your mother is Indian?"

I took a breath and felt it flow deeper into my chest. Talking about my mother seemed relaxing. I felt increasingly calm and curious. Though he continued to ask intimate questions, I stayed. I said, "Her mother was Mexican." When he appeared confused, I added, "South of the border?"

"Border? Mmmm. Yes." He focused his watery gaze on the distant horizon. He said, "Everything has a purpose. The reed has a hollow stalk. A pathway for spirits."

I had almost decided that Joe had wasted his brain on cheap wine, but what wino talks about purpose? He didn't smell bad, though his ragged gray shirt was stained around the neck and armpits with progressive rings of yellow. His black head was shiny bald with little tufts of white curls behind his ears and over his collar. Deep crevices spread from Joe's eyes, nose and mouth, then plunged downward, leaving small bags of flesh gathering moist beads. He seemed to prop his drooping skin with a pointy chin, clenched tightly and poking upward. His lips were sealed in a pout.

He nodded up the hill. "The friend who waits. . . number is five." He held up his hand and pointed to each curled, bony finger. "Five," he said at the last. "Healing hands."

I shivered. Five. Quinn. Quint? How did he do that? Had he been watching us, listening to our conversation from the bushes? I looked at my own hand, the one with the rock. I'm the physical therapist, mister, if you must know. "What about mine?" I held up my hand. "Healing hands?"

He shrugged and nodded slightly. "Reed has many ways to raise the earth spirits."

He talked about me as if I weren't there. Probably well practiced at fortune telling, I thought. It must be how he begged his way through life. "Joe, I need to get going. What do you need, man? Food? Money?"

My offer was intended to be compassionate, but it elicited his anger. "You believe Ah came here for your money? Ah let you take the token." He nearly shouted his emphasis on the "Ah." "You think by your own vision you found it? Your world is one of money and things. Ah want nothing. Take it. Go."

"Joe, this is yours? Here. Have it back. I'm sorry." I held the stone toward him.

He folded my fingers around the rock with his cool hands, whispering,

"Still know nothing? Your journey here is solemn. You were allowed to see the token." He tapped my hand. "Earth spirit. . . through Reed, phhht," he whistled, "to sky spirit." He pointed up the trail. "Take it. Back you go." Behind him, down in the gravel pit toward the river valley, I saw a small cloud of dust from a vehicle traveling over a dirt road. When I stretched to look, Joe moved into my line of vision. "Go now."

He stepped to the outside of the trail and I twisted past him to hike back up through the trees. I squeezed my hand around the protrusions of the token, as he had called it. Crazy old guy. I looked back in his direction, but he had vanished. I thought it wise to move along before he got any more wacky. I strained up the steep portions of the trail with trees and rocks as handholds and braces, welcoming the opening where the woods met the ballfield. Quinn ambled across the field through a sparkling ring of humid mist, a welcome vision in straight legged jeans and sneakers. She waved and her nylon jacket flapped in the breeze. She must have forgiven my folly. I wondered if she'd change her mind if she knew about the murky character I had encountered. I didn't know what to tell her so I shoved the stone into my pocket and waved back.

"Not very enthusiastic, Reed. You okay?"

"A little winded, I guess. It's steep!"

"You're pale." A slow grin rounded Quinn's cheeks to ripe apples. She said, "By the color of your face, I was right. It's spooky down there!"

Tossing my hair back, I brushed past her. "It's gorgeous. I found a ledge with a view of the whole valley."

Quinn's glee evaporated and she seemed serious again. "No way. It's all woods."

"You said you'd never been down there."

"I did not," she said quietly.

"Well, there *is* a rock ledge. I'm sure any scary stories were meant to keep you kids away from it."

"I thought they put up fences after Jimmy Sears fell on his head."

"Nope. No fences. They should, though," I added, tugging again on the bungee wristband. "Want to show me your school?"

"No need to humor me. I window-peeked and saw the tiny desks, the short blackboards."

"You mean the ones that used to be hard to reach?"

"They still have the same alphabet letters around the top of the board," she said.

I was already walking in the direction of the car, wanting more distance between us and the old man. "A few things never change. Shall we walk back to your old house?" As soon as we topped the hill, I could see all over the valley, hazy once again.

"You think it's gloomy, don't you?" asked Quinn, following my gaze down the hill to the distant river shore, lined with rusted warehouses, factories and railroad yards.

"Mournful is more what I'm thinking," I said. "But I'm looking at the water. Seems it ought to be more sparkling." I couldn't explain it to Quinn, but I was sure that when I was with Joe, the river was deep blue green and lit up with sparkling lights.

"Ha! You people from downstream always want things to be cleaner. Do you remember when I moved from Pittsburgh to Metropolis? You all stuck your noses in the air for weeks; called me a dirty Pittsburgher. Jimmy Dallburton called me the 'Three Mile Island girl' until the day we graduated."

I grinned. "We're squeaky clean in Illinois, you know."

"Dumb, too. Three Mile Island is near Harrisburg, not Pittsburgh. Besides, Metropolis must be having a race with Paducah, across the river, to see who can choke the last life out of the Ohio River."

"Not true. They're such small towns."

"Small towns add up," said Quinn. "That brown water you're seeing hasn't even passed through Pittsburgh, yet. Comes from all the towns further upstream."

It's true that in Metropolis, the town where I grew up, we had always vilified Pittsburgh as the source of the Ohio's pollution. Seeing the dirty water from further upstream, I realized Quinn had a point. The source of our gripes was broader.

Quinn stopped at the top of the hill beside the car. "I have so much water in my astrological chart that I have to live near it or I'll dry up and disintegrate," she said.

"Me, too, I guess."

She said, "When I was a kid living up here, I must have sensed the river surrounding me. Chicago's lake and rivers are what drew me there. I know it."

I said, "If I couldn't walk along the lakeshore every day on the way to work, I'd be very unhappy." I pictured the giant oaks and grassy park on the Evanston waterfront, imagined the lake's moisture on my face and the familiar faint scent of fish. It occurred to me that in Chicago, at least in the city and north shore, prime property lined the waterfront, not factories. I passed rows of multi-million dollar white-collar mansions on my short walk to town each morning. It was further inland from the lake in Evanston that houses and apartments became more modest and industrial neighborhoods sprawled.

Quinn said, "I think it's river-fed farmland that really gets to me."

Her words jogged my thoughts and I nodded. "Did you ever go to the county fair in Metropolis?" I asked, sighing. "Silver-skinned trout on paper plates. Fresh corn from the bottom lands."

Quinn said, "Okay, let's go get some lunch. Now I'm famished." We climbed into the Beetle and pulled slowly past Quinn's old home then turned down the hill. She said, "I know what you really miss is that giant, full-color statue of Superman in the Metropolis town center. The people who run the museum and the comic book shops convinced me that it's really Superman's home. He brings in the tourists."

"No. The star of Metropolis is the river," I said, laughing. Paducah, Kentucky had the larger population, but Metropolis claimed the riverboat casino and the site of the old fort. "I loved going out to the site of Fort Massac. What a view. Imagine when forts were the inns, the trading posts and the police stations all in one little box."

"Probably the news channel, too," said Quinn. Quinn is a cable news junkie. She turns on CNN for current news, ESPN for sports scores. Even though she's a baseball addict, after watching the Cubs fall from first place in the division, she doesn't even feel like watching the World Series.

My friendship with Quinn goes back to a rainy afternoon when our Junior Varsity track meet was canceled. The team was going out for Cokes, but she had just moved and none of us knew her very well. My girlfriends planned to ignore her and leave when I noticed a towel beside her locker from the nearby country club. I stopped and asked her about it, believing I had found the only other teenage girl in the county who played golf. My dad had been taking me on Saturdays since my mother died. That was the housekeeper's day off. He'd put me in a lesson with a pro then play a round with his pals. I think Quinn and I bonded forever over a green with three sand traps. We both hit from one to the other until we switched sand wedges and popped out onto the green, both laughing.

That was twenty years and five inches ago on my hips. We still make time to go to the Evanston community course a few times each summer. Quinn has to give me a handicap though, because she golfs more often and because I'm angry that she hasn't gained any weight since high school. I'd take a stroke per pound, except that I don't need any encouragement to put on weight.

There are still many things I'm learning about Quinn. Of course, I keep a long list running in my head, both her attributes and complications. Sometimes I find myself staring at her. I watch her hands grasping the wheel as she drives, notice the veins, muscles like taut cords. I'm curious about the ridges in her neck that vibrate as she sings with the radio, her long race horse legs with no ripples or imperfections. I've decided that I simply admire Quinn's health, her vigor, from the standpoint of a physical therapist.

I've seen all sorts of bodies at the clinic. I've worked on very physically fit men, tennis pros, golf pros and many pudgy old guys who are weekend duffers. I've done treatments on quads that felt like steel beams and on calf muscles as big as hams. Many of my clients, though, are very smart men and women at all levels of life who believe their bodies are invincible. They go out on their rare free weekends to test themselves. I see them when they fail. I get to ease their joints back in place or soothe their strained muscles. I see bodies as muscular or skeletal systems, sorting my observations into my mental business files.

My personal files are slimmer. Three months ago, when I turned 35 in July, I vowed to pay more attention to my health. But I walk to work every day, never have smoked, and hardly ever drink. I'm in pretty good shape. My last serious relationship ended a year after college and it's been years since I had an interesting date. I don't mind. I like to keep life uncomplicated. Romance is low on my list of importance.

Quinn says she finally told me that she was a lesbian years ago because she thought I would never ask. She says I never picked up on her subtle hints. But we'd usually get together, just the two of us, and if I asked her about dating, she'd shrug and make a casual, genderless reference. I think we both had to be ready before she told me. One day I mentioned all the good-looking, interesting men she knows from her work and she said, "Once off the playing field, they just don't call the right signals." I still didn't know what she meant until she spelled it out more clearly. I was a bit shocked, but I said it didn't matter; told her I have little interest in my own sex life, let alone anyone else's. I guess since I don't spend much time thinking about sex, it's hard to imagine that it could be important enough to wander so far outside the considered norm. But what she does is her own business. She seems happy, content. Quite remarkable for these days. I don't mind that she's a lesbian, though I suppose she thinks I do, since we rarely talk about it. I'm curious sometimes, but she's right, I never ask questions.

The same year I broke up with my college boyfriend, Quinn was chasing the Italian Basketball League, coming home only after dozens of unsuccessful tryouts. It was unusual to see her so disheartened. As Quinn sped down the Pittsburgh hill, back toward Butler Street, I asked if she ever thought about Italy.

"I probably never should have gone," she said. "I'm not tall. I'm not a dazzling ball handler. They wanted American stars." I recall her moping for only a short time. The next time I saw her, she was working at a summer camp and was as enthusiastic as if she were training the Olympic team. "What I really enjoy is working with kids," she said. "Girls now have grown up with all kinds of women role models. Some of them really believe they can do anything the boys can do. I had a thirteen-year-old come inches from a dunk shot. She probably got it by the time she was in high school."

Quinn had taken referee jobs in city tournaments and leagues until a coaching job came along at a Chicago Catholic high school. It seemed like a good fit for her and I was surprised when she left it after a few years to work for Loyola University. "I should have stayed with the younger kids," she said. "Who knows how long it will be before I'm doing anything more interesting than making reservations and chaperoning college girls on the road."

"This trip is more interesting, isn't it?" I said. I knew she loved being in the college game, even if it wasn't at the level she wanted.

"It's better than my glorified secretarial tasks for the athletic department," she said. "The coach is starting to give me a few more responsibilities."

I once made a comment about her easy job and she pulled out her laptop with scads of files and lists; I conceded to her claim of being a sports detective. She helps recommend which game and player the coaches will go see; only one piece of the puzzle, she says.

This trip to Pennsylvania was somewhat of a break for her, at least in her own mind. She was asked to make recruiting visits to two girls who play in Pennsylvania parochial leagues. Loyola usually recruits from Illinois or neighboring states, but these girls have Loyola family ties and might be good enough to warrant bringing them to Chicago to show them the campus.

As Quinn drove down Pennsylvania Avenue through the Strip District's produce markets, she spotted a little Italian eatery. When we walked through the door, the garlic-scented Italian beef nearly caused me to drool. While we waited for our sandwiches, she reminded me of our lunch in Evanston a month ago when she had talked me into joining her on the trip.

"I'm driving, so I need the company," she had said. "Plus it'll be cheap. The games are in little towns that are too spread out for it to make sense to fly, thank God. I don't think I'm ready to fly yet, after 9/11."

That conversation had been in the latter days of September, after the world had witnessed the terrorist attacks on America. I had continued walking to work, on September 11th and every day after, even when clients canceled their therapy and claimed they were in shock from watching constant replayed images of the burning World Trade Center. One woman said she had to reevaluate what was important. I imagined her sitting in front of the television for days, trying to figure it out.

Quinn must have sensed that I was spending long hours at the center, cleaning the equipment and the space, organizing, doing backed up paperwork. She had shown up there, unannounced as usual. She lives a few minutes south of Evanston in Chicago's Rogers Park neighborhood, but we hadn't seen each other in months. "You always sound busy," she said, "but no more. You must have lunch with your dear old friend." She beamed her impish smile. I recall the blonde highlights in the fine hairs around her face, making her appear distinctly opposite of all the gray, glassy-eyed faces I'd seen for days.

"You look great." My words had an overly thick tone of astonishment.

"Well, I had to break away today," she said. "I keep pooling up with tears and I'm having a hard time keeping my thoughts in order."

When I cocked my head, she defended herself. "I'm not obsessing. I just feel connected. You don't?"

"Of course I do. It was an attack on our whole country." I had been among the crowd in Evanston who lit candles and stood on Ridge Avenue for hours. But I hadn't told anyone how I felt depressed for days before the attack and then was secretly relieved that it hadn't happened in Chicago. Or that no one I knew had died. It's the nerves that spin wildly with my old storm barometer. I kept my guilty thoughts to myself as Quinn and I eavesdropped on neighboring conversations and their ritual telling of whereabouts when they heard or witnessed the terrible news.

As we walked back to the clinic, Quinn explained the Pennsylvania trip's timing. "One of the schools has an early season and an invitational tournament with their rival. The coach wants to see how this girl plays under pressure, but her own preseason banquet and speech prevents her going. The coaching assistants are busy with the startup of practice schedules."

"So you get to make the trip," I said.

"I know the final decision will come from the coach, but I think if I could be instrumental in getting a couple of the girls, watch them grow through the system, I'd be able to devote myself to the nitty gritty stuff that I usually get called on to do," Quinn said. "I'd be excited about going to the games and feeling like a part of it all."

"You really miss playing, don't you?"

"It's hard when you think the most exciting part of your life is in the past."

"You?" I said. "You're excited about everything."

She flashed her gorgeous smile. "I told you, Reed. I'm a good actress. Listen. There are a few days and lots of miles between the games. We can take some vacation days on one end and visit my old hangouts around Pittsburgh," she had said. "Reed, you know you haven't had a vacation in the ten years since you started working at this so-called 'Wellness Center.'"

She had made her point, although it took another week of late night calls as Quinn cajoled, then begged before I agreed. I knew it was a good step for her. She had helped weed through early scholarship admissions' decisions and been involved in recommendations, but most of her work was with statistics, lists and phone calls, nothing hands on. And Quinn is a hands on person. Funny, she wanted me to go because I'm too hands on. She thought I should get away from my office and get a new perspective on life.

Our Italian beef sandwiches gave me a completely new perspective. I wanted to share them with everyone. I wanted to run around Pittsburgh and give them away to people on the street. We bought a couple of extras to take on the road and headed back to the Beetle.

As I reached for the car door, a gray-haired woman stepped up on the sidewalk in front of me. She wore a long skirt and smelled musty; an old hippie, I thought. With a slight limp, she ambled past me, down the street. A breeze whipped through her thin hair, revealing a series of carved symbols on the back and sides of her head. I got in the car as Quinn started the engine and said, "Did you see that hair? Whew, ugly." When I raised my eyes, the woman was standing still, welding me in my seat with her searing look. Her head was tilted back; her eyes challenged me to observe the jagged pink scar tissue up one side of her face and behind her ear. What had looked like symbols were scars from some terrible fate and a botched repair.

"Oh, God. My window's open." Realizing the old woman had heard my insensitive comment, I felt as if my heart had sunk, squeezed tightly through my stomach and dropped to the floor of the car. I slumped in my seat as the woman disappeared behind stacked crates of produce on the sidewalk.

"What is this?" Quinn laughed at my shrinking act. "I didn't see the woman, but if her hair is that bad, it's not the first rude comment she's heard. Or not likely the last. What are you doing?"

"I have to apologize," I said as I stumbled from the car. "She can't be far." The woman was nowhere. I searched both ends of the street, even walked out into traffic as I looked. "You don't understand, Quinn. Scars. I thought it was a funky cut, but it was scars. And the most anguished eyes. They burned right through me." To myself, I thought I'd felt those eyes pry between every knot of emotion I'd ever had.

Quinn's right eyebrow lifted slightly, indicating a concern she usually reserved for perplexing things like menus and maps. I'd managed to upset an amazingly easy-going person twice in an afternoon.

"I'm sorry, Quinn. But the look she gave me—ugh." I rubbed the flesh on my arm and raised the window.

"God, Reed. Now do you understand?" she said. "You've been pushing yourself too hard. You've really flipped out."

"What? Do you think I'm seeing things? I made her up?"

"Aren't you fatigued?"

"Everybody's fatigued," I said.

"Reed," Quinn said as she turned off the car and twisted in her seat to face me. "I've been meaning to talk to you. Don't you think it's ironic that you make a living relieving people's stress, but you have so much? I think your job has created even more tension between you and your father."

"My father! Why bring up my father? Besides, I do more than relieve stress, thank you." I was annoyed with myself for sounding so annoyed.

"You're the one who's always talked about how your father wanted you to be a doctor, like him."

"You know I never wanted that. It took awhile for me to figure it out, but I like my life. It's quiet. I go home at a decent hour..."

"By yourself..."

"But I'm accustomed to it." I didn't want to argue with Quinn. "I enjoy my simplicity," I said.

"That shows. You have a low maintenance hairstyle, a low maintenance wardrobe. You go through life like a whisper so no one will notice you."

"People notice me."

"That's because you have your mother's cheekbones."

We both smiled just a little. Quinn sighed and said, "We should head back to Raccoon Creek. We'll have a simple evening. Build a fire in the pit by the cabin. There should be stars tonight."

"You're not upset?"

"I was never upset," said Quinn. She winked and turned on a CD. Acoustic music riffed us over the highway as we headed out of town, up and down hills, up and down scales of tangled thoughts.

"You know, Quinn," I said, "I see my father once or twice a year, a few obligatory holidays. Before I walk in the house, I tune in, like those car radio memory features, to old conversations in my head."

"What conversations?"

I said, "He's always disappointed. But I don't hear his voice."

"You said there were conversations," said Quinn.

"We had a housekeeper when I was younger, before you moved. Miss North. She did all the cooking, cleaning. She came to live with us after my mom died because there were so many nights my dad worked late. But she always chased me out of the kitchen. You remember that my grandmother wanted me to learn to cook? I never learned until I got my own apartment. Miss North would send me to my room to study. She told me how unhappy my dad would be if I wasted my time in the kitchen. 'You're supposed to be a doctor,' she'd yell. 'Your father told me to make you study.'"

"I told her my mother was a wonderful cook and I wanted to learn. She said my father insisted that we never speak of my mother. He would fire her, she said, if he heard us or if she let me cook. 'Stop wasting time and go study.' She even told me once that my dad wanted me to be a doctor to prove that our family wasn't weak. Said there were rumors that my mother was crazy."

"Reed, you didn't listen to that nut, did you?" asked Quinn.

I shrugged. "Not really. But sometimes she was the only one around."

"So why do you think your dad's not pleased that you're a physical therapist?" Quinn asked.

"He used to always introduce me to his friends as 'tops in her high school class.' After changing programs in med school, he stopped saying that. I think he expected different results from his Northwestern tuition payments."

"You think he sees you as a quitter? Thinks you couldn't cut it as a doctor?"

"PT happens to be what I love," I said. "My father may be disappointed that I didn't follow his footsteps, but growing up with him leaving the house at all hours of the night or his late arrivals after taking care of other people wasn't particularly inspiring."

Quinn accepted my wordless reverie the rest of the hour-long drive to Raccoon Creek. The soft music was a cushion, though I felt strapped with the seat belt into a motionless panic. Trees hung exposed branches over both sides of Highway 30, lining with brittle pointers each curve, each pitch and roll between hills. I had a full range of stomach flutters, more than I could blame on twisting rhythms or the undulating road.

Our progress seemed to be watched with distant forest eyes that followed our little black Beetle's tracks to the cabin. Once there, I felt the fresh air begin to revive me. I relaxed as Quinn bustled around with efforts to buoy my spirits. The cabin was tiny and very rustic. I walked inside to find everything the way we had left it in a hurry that morning. Twin beds on either side of the room had thin mattresses and our sleeping bags. There was only extra room for a chair and an old gas heater, which we were afraid to use. Quinn lit a fire in the truck wheel fire pit outside the door. She waved through the streaked glass panes for me to come outside. Rolling a log stump close, she turned it over and sat, motioning me to the solitary aluminum folding chair.

"Thanks for the fire," I said, as I plopped into the hard seat.

"Raccoon Creek is my dream! It's one of my favorite places of all my memories." She gazed at the slow, meandering creek as a fish jumped and spread tiny rings across the surface. "I know I've told you about camping at the state park. Well, even though I loved our family's little tent, I used to think the people who stayed up here in the cabins were so lucky, fancy even."

"Fancy? In these cabins?"

"Relatively speaking. We rarely went on vacation and if we did, we camped. I didn't stay in a hotel until I was on the road with a basketball team." She poked at the fire with a green stick. "Look at those stars." Her voice drifted up to the sky.

We sat while the fire popped and flickered, protecting us from the crisp October night air. I thought about the old man, Joe, and wondered where he went at night. Overcome with fatigue or, more likely, an intense craving to escape the bizarre day, I begged off the star watch and ducked inside the short doorway, wishing Quinn good night.

Definitely not a fancy cabin, I thought, looking around the tiny room as I undressed. It was made of real logs, but they had been painted shiny brown, giving them the appearance of snap-together toys. The inside walls were dusty. Our duffel bags were propped on wooden chairs between the narrow beds. A tiny kitchen extended like a porch off the back of the cabin. Squeezed in at the end of the main room was a bathroom. When I slipped off my shorts, the little carved token made a soft clatter on the pine floor. I tucked it under the pillow in my sleeping bag before going into the bathroom to bathe. Returning in t-shirt and stocking feet, I hopped across the cool floor to my bed.

Quinn had calmed the fire to a steady orange glow outside. I hardly heard her come in later and crawl into her sleeping bag. Though I had been exhausted, I seemed to teeter on the edge between sleep and wakefulness, aware of the wild scents and the chatter of raccoons rustling the dry leaves outside the window. The smell of mildewed soil under the floor of the cabin seeped into my dreams. I thought I heard digging.

ζ

The hands were dry, wrinkled and brown like the clay soil being poked with a flat rock. Fingers brushed a white strand of hair but then it fell back in front of my eyes. One hand balled into a weathered fist. I smacked an indentation in the soil, set the stone turtle on the ledge, as if guarding the valley. I jumped at a scraping noise nearby. The old man, Joe, teetered awkwardly on a twig crutch, watching me. A yelp escaped from my throat and I sat up in bed.

ζ

I heard Quinn throw off her sleeping bag and fumble in the darkness. "What is it? Reed?" She rushed across the room and sat beside me. "You're shivering. Are you that cold?"

My eyesight hopped around the moonlit cabin. "What a dream. I can't believe I'm relieved to be in this place."

"This place? You think this is awful."

"Sorry, Quinn. I didn't mean it like that."

Everything was quiet in the cabin, but my mind reeled with confessions and excuses for my odd behavior. "Yesterday was a really strange day," I finally said.

"You don't realize how stress has affected you until you start to unwind," she said. "That's why some people never do it—unwind."

"We could talk," I said. "I'll tell you what happened."

"Why don't you try to sleep. We'll make pancakes in the morning and you can tell me about anything you want."

Quinn seemed exhausted and I probably looked worse. She made it easy to put off my admission until morning. That sounded reasonable. I would sleep. I'd tell her later about the old man, the dirt path, the token. She thought I was having a hallucination when I saw the old woman on the street. I hated to think what she would say about Joe—or my dream. I rolled over and reached under my pillow as my eyes closed. The curve of rock fit snugly in my palm. Outside, a light breeze tapped a branch of pine needles against the window and lulled me to sleep.

ζ

My neck spasmed with a rocket flare into my head, like a search party was sending up signals. I tried to track the wild, pulsing lights, squeezed my eyelids and begged them to stop. A message whistled in the distance, a whistling breeze, smelling of pine sap and humidity. I remembered nothing of the day or where I was. Morning. It must be morning with the fresh scent of new mown grass, or was it hay?

If I could look about, I could figure what had tightened my skin, gripped my head so tightly and pinned me upon a hard, lumpy mat. My desire to leap up and look had the opposite effect. Whatever had me pinned was coiled around me like a swiftly growing net of heavy roots, sucking deeply into the soil to anchor me in the darkness. I lay there, going nowhere.

A stabbing trail of pain carved along the side of my head. No. It was her head. Her anger. Her stern jaw. The old woman had charred me with her gaze. It seemed as if my ashes had been vacuumed into her hold. The harder I struggled to find my own feelings, find Reed, the more scattered and dusty I became. I felt on the verge of disappearing forever. I knew I must surrender to the woman. She had a firm, twisted hold on me, like the thick scar tissue on her head had hold of her. We were knit together with a sinew I couldn't fathom.

I stopped struggling against the idea of being in a different body. The old woman relaxed. Her shoulders lowered into the pillow and she took a rattling, cavernous breath. Reluctantly and with great effort, she pried open her eyes.

A filmy haze flickered. A square shaft of sunlight edged the end of the bed. Something moved nearby. Familiar. A small window thumped in the breeze and a young woman reached out, pulled a dark fabric curtain away from the hinge and wedged the window ajar with a wooden rod. She pressed her face close to the shady dance of pine branches outside. Weathered skin on a young face. Her sun-lightened hair was tied back with twine, eyes worried over the horizon. Daughter. She was the old woman's daughter. She smoothed beads of perspiration from her temples over loose hairs pushed behind her ear. She started when she turned back and found the old woman staring.

For a scented moment, the old woman wished to fly away. Didn't belong here. It was an oily feathered feeling, another world calling to her, or the mourning of angels sending her back to earth. She imagined for just a moment that she hadn't survived. Then a tug at the head and a yellow-haired man with a thick moustache dropped a wad of cloth bandages beside her as her own oily, gray strands of hair drooped onto her shoulders.

The man expelled a satisfied breath at his own accomplishment. "Miss Beigler is fortunate." His voice was like the thick slurp of churning butter. "Cursed savages leave a rare victim half scalped. My soldiers shall hunt that tempersome villain. He'll be drawn and quartered."

"'Tis ample violence, Doctor!" The young woman hissed and pressed a fist into her own stomach. She rested her hand on the front buttons of her high-necked blouse. "How may a doctor trained in healing abide so?" she whispered. "'Tis ceaseless bloodshed. When will it end?"

The old woman curled from the tightness pulling at her muscles and bones. Every noise felt like a fire held against the red metal of her joints. Every breath was an effort. The voices continued to hum.

"When they all be far gone. Wicked of me, 'tis your view?" asked the doctor. "Fathom the butchering I witness. I see the darksome savages' fierce outcome. I see a people empty of all good."

"You shan't speak so generally to me," said the young woman. "I was born in an Indian village, Doctor Connolly. My mother lived her life amongst peaceful folk. In Shamokin, the white men dug spade for spade with the natives."

The doctor scoffed, "To my way of thinking, trusting a few virtuous Indians led her to a den of snakes." He stood back, relaxed the crease between his brows and murmured. "You're educated, Missus Foote. A teacher? Most folks around here are unlettered and ignorant."

"I owe my education to the Moravians," she proclaimed.

"Bethlehem?" the doctor asked.

"'Twas the Lehigh River Valley where the Moravians missioned to the natives," she said. "I was a teacher at the Indian school."

"And Mister Foote?"

"Lettered as well. After marrying, we came west. In Pittsburgh, I've taught only my own children and occasional neighbours who ask help with correspondence."

"Well then, your opinion has merit. Yet, I see blessed few natives taught to behave in a proper manner." He leaned over the older woman and rolled a stained strip of cloth from her forehead. She flinched and aimed to push his hand away, but could force no muscles to move. She would beg for quiet but words refused to come.

He murmured, "You are knowledgeable, Missus Foote, yet you remain here?"

"Our farm is all we have." The young woman peered over the doctor's shoulder, grimacing. "Seen through other perilous times." She added in a near whisper, "Never have I seen her down such as this, like a tree tipped upon broken roots. Seems naught the same woman who once braved the Susquehanna currents in all seasons' weather."

"She'll be down for a season now surely, gaining her strength."

The old woman fixed her weary eyes on the whitewashed log walls, dredging up an inner resolve to be thankful for each log, the roof over her head, for her life that was spared and the care being offered. What surfaced was a desperate yearning to be left alone. She begged the noise to cease. Both people who tended her left a dust of discomfort hanging in the air. There were tiny flakes of memory from the days since the trauma; being delivered to the fort in the back of a wagon cart by several soldiers; seeing her daughter, only a glimpse of Eleanor's pale, drawn face peering past the doctor as he finished the stitching, looking as if she may faint.

Maggie barely recalled her silent days at the fort's infirmary. She had turned away from any who attempted to converse. One morning she spoke briefly to Doctor Connolly, asking him to take her home.

She heard him report later to Eleanor. "She's well enough," he said, "providing you'll be looking in. Make certain she is nourished and keep her wounds dressed."

"'Twas only a day ago," Maggie thought. He delivered her home by buckboard. Though Connolly offered the best skill this side of the mountains to heal her wounds, she hadn't trusted him or his Virginia soldiers, even after many days of care at the infirmary. In the first days, she was confused as to her whereabouts. Now, home in her own bed, she wanted no more of him, no more smirking smile dimpling the edges of his ashen blonde moustache.

Maggie searched her memory for glimpses of a less careworn Eleanor. She most surely walked the several miles into town from the farm where she lived with Edmund and their boys. Playful images of the little boys were pushed away by thoughts of the violent outbreaks in the valley since springtime. Large numbers of settlers were retreating, abandoning their farms, moving back to the eastern provinces. Maggie winced and wished she could forget.

"I have no notion of how she came to such perils," Eleanor said, pulling the doctor to the side of the small room. Maggie stretched her aching neck to look about the simple, familiar quarters. There was just enough room for her spinning wheel, her narrow bed, one cupboard, and a central standing wood stove. The room was clean, surely the work of the weaver's wife. Eleanor could not have had the time or inclination. Milky white log walls surrounded a pine-planked floor. The spinning wheel stood between the stove and window where she could spin while looking out at the side yard and the solitary pine tree that provided cool afternoon shade and scents. Eleanor stood beside the door that opened onto a back porch, beside the rear entrance to the weaver's cabin, where Missus Emory often hung freshly washed laundry.

The Emorys were her keys to independence. When Maggie had agreed to move west from Bethlehem with Eleanor and Edmund, she was determined to make her own way. She had bargained for this room at the rear of Mister Emory's log house in Pittsburgh and was settled in before her young family had even raised the walls of their farmhouse. Emory, the weaver, allowed Maggie to spin flax for him in exchange for the lodgings.

Eleanor picked up her mother's short-legged spinning wheel from in front of the window and moved it into the corner, out of the way.

"Gently," came a gravelly growl from Maggie.

Eleanor turned, saw Maggie continuing to stare blankly, but the doctor's blue eyes sparkled. "Take heed," he smiled. "She'll be up and well, posthaste."

"I trust she'll not be spinning flax so hastily. She must regain her strength before she takes on the weaver's toils."

"What of your own toils?" asked Doctor Connolly. "How is Mister Foote managing the farm in your absence?"

"The boys offer some avail."

"But they're a young lot."

"Strong for six and eight years and eager to please their father."

The doctor nodded. "Less hardy souls have fled for peaceful territory. Have you considered such?"

"My only fears are for my children. We have seen through worse. We arrived in the wake of Pontiac's attacks, during the land rush following the Bushy Run defeat. By then, 'twas a semblance of peace to the valley."

"Could it be ten years?" thought Maggie. When they moved from eastern Pennsylvania, Pittsburgh had been rebuilding for the third time, following the destructive Indian siege of '63. Cheap, abandoned farmland was available, scattered between the rivers, but the town had clustered its forty-some buildings, most of them log cabins, closer to the Monongahela and upstream from the fort.

Eleanor set a bowl of fresh water by Maggie's bedside. "A good many Virginians have surrendered their free land grants and returned."

"Your land was purchased?"

Eleanor nodded. "We bought a fine parcel from George Croghan, the old trader friend of Mother's."

Maggie closed her eyes, holding an image of tiny Eleanor, pleading for stories of Croghan and other characters she had known. She had often been unwilling to dredge up the memories Eleanor begged her to recount. Before Maggie had left the cabin recently and ridden into the hills, Eleanor had brought a newspaper article that mentioned the name of an Indian they had known years before. Maggie told her the man she knew had died and pushed the article away.

But after Eleanor left her alone, Maggie wondered how many Indians were called Logan. She had to quell her curiosity and see if it could be Tahgajut, her Logan, still alive. Tahgajut's father was an early friend of the colonists. As a friendly gesture, he had given his son the English name of William Penn's secretary. How could it be Logan who was provoking the settlers, being cited in the newspaper as a madman? Days later, Maggie slipped out of town, leaving behind a note telling that a friend was driving her up the Beaver Creek to a friendly Indian village. Edmund must have followed her into the hills for a time, she supposed, then sent the soldiers further to find her.

Pittsburghers had been embroiled all summer in riots. The town had watched Pennsylvania Quakers pull their meager militia out of Fort Pitt. Virginia's governor, Lord Dunmore, overtook the fort and inundated the hills with Virginia farmers with free parcels of land. Doctor Connolly was commissioned to oversee the Virginia militia and the newly renamed Fort Dunmore. But with the recent outbreaks of violence, the Virginia farmers were fleeing back over the river. Many who remained called to rename the town to honor Lord Dunmore, a thought that seethed in Maggie's bones.

She was angry at the thought of driving the Indians further west. The Mingo and Shawnee neighbours who often wandered into town seemed friendly, harmlessly laden with baskets or pelts to sell at the market. But Doctor Connolly claimed they sold their pelts to buy guns and tomahawks, devising devilish plans to attack the settlers.

The pine planks creaked as Eleanor and the doctor moved toward Maggie's bed with strips of clean muslin. Eleanor inched around the high post bed to a position in the crowded room where the sparse window light shone on her work. The sound of the cloth ripping held a comfort, Maggie thought, gave a resonant definition to the split feelings she had about survival. She watched her daughter stuff the cloth strips into a muslin bag, and then rub a fold of her skirt nervously between her fingers. Eleanor was succumbing, Maggie supposed, to the handsome doctor's winsome eyes pleading for her assistance. When Maggie saw his hand reach out for her daughter's muslin, she gathered her ire and her strength and slapped it away.

"Mother!" Eleanor whispered harshly, "Let the doctor do his work."

Maggie glared at Eleanor and grunted, "Leave me be!" She slapped at the doctor's hand again.

Doctor Connolly pressed his thin lips together, making them disappear between the puckered hairs of his moustache and beard. "Missus Beigler, I'll be showing your daughter so she can do the bandaging henceforth." He persisted and Maggie let him peel away a final, greasy layer of cloth. She saw him cast a warning glance at Eleanor. "Remove the bandaging on occasion," he said, "to clean and give ease from the itch."

Eleanor took a deep breath and nodded. Maggie glared as the doctor unwound cloth strips oozing with brownish salve and let more strands of hair fall beside her face.

"These head wounds are of a concern yet," the doctor said, peering at the slash of a scar, still dimpled and pink.

Eleanor set a small black pot of warm water and lye soap near the doctor. She said, "She's healing directly, would you agree?"

He dipped a clean cloth and nodded, "The wound is not so grievous as a fortnight past. She'll be stiff and lame as the gunshot grazing heals." He patted Maggie's hair and scalp with the soapy water, then showed Eleanor a clay pot. "A vessel of the hickory-nut salve, most soothing," he whispered. "'Twill assist the bare patches to grow more plentiful." Maggie pretended to doze. "Less bandage should do for now," he said. He rubbed the brown, sticky nut butter into Maggie's scalp and covered it with muslin strips fastened with a small knot.

The doctor packed his belongings while Maggie watched every move. He set the salve by the bandages and walked quietly to the door. "I shall look in on her in time," he winked at Eleanor, "but should there be infection, inform me directly."

Eleanor hurried out the door behind him.

Maggie sighed, "Peace, quiet." But outside her door, she heard Eleanor's lament. "Doctor, are you certain she is fit to be home? I'll not be able to stay here, leaving my family all the day and night."

The doctor assured her, "Miss Beigler will best improve where she's most comfortable." He started down the path.

Maggie imagined Eleanor grabbing his arm to stop him. "Did she talk to you?" Her voice was anxious. "Tell you what took place on that mountain?"

The doctor paused. "'Tis nary a doubt, the attack upon your mother left her near speechless. But as she heals, 'tis certain to change. She'll speak when she has a mind to."

Eleanor sighed, "As a rule, when she has a mind to do anything, she hastens to it. I cannot fathom, Doctor. My mother has lived among the Indians most all her life. Her letter said she was going to a friendly village. How did it come to this?" Her breathy voice rose with the strain of her questions. "Are we destined to another violent outbreak? I might want my children at the fort, before..."

Stopping her in mid-sentence, the doctor said, "Missus Foote, we've spent all our worries, but don't surmise the worst. Your mother put herself in a dangerous area. She trusted the Indians. For this reason, this unfortunate mistake, she suffers. She simply left all caution aside."

Eleanor said, "How could she stir things so? All these years, she has known my fear of another Indian war. We've told none of our neighbours that Edmund is part Indian for fear that another uprising will find us all run out of town," she paused, "or worse!"

"Your husband seems a fine man," said the doctor. "'Tis a fitful time, but if you choose to remain, I wish you well."

Maggie closed her eyes and relaxed into her pillow as she heard his steps move farther down the path. Then he called out to Eleanor from the front of the weaver's house. "Forgive me. I left her belongings on the wagon."

Moments later, Eleanor pulled open the heavy door and entered, carrying a worn leather bag. Maggie had sunk lower in the bed, her back to the door, but when Eleanor loosened the lace curtain to let the fabric fall over the window, Maggie grunted.

"You prefer it open?"

A moan confirmed Maggie's wish, and Eleanor re-tied the curtain stay. She stooped to pile extra firewood near the stove, put a fresh candle and a basket of biscuits by the bedside. Then she lifted the tattered bag onto the foot of the bed. "My, my, Mother," she mumbled. "I believe this bag is older than myself. Have you had it all your life?"

"Ummm hmmm," Maggie said.

Eleanor opened the bag and removed two muslin dresses, both clean, and hung one high on a peg beside Maggie's bed.

"I see an unfamiliar frock." She held a patchwork brown dress against herself, smoothed it, and then hung it on a peg beside the first. Maggie recognized the dress as the one she had been wearing, patched in the place ripped open by the musket ball and dyed to cover the blood stains. It was not Eleanor's handiwork.

"I pray you'll come to the farm and stay. Edmund and the boys would get to see more of you," Eleanor said.

Maggie grunted. "Quiet is all I need now."

"I'll help you up to relieve yourself before I take my leave."

"The chamber pot is nearby," Maggie said.

"You'll call to the Emorys if in need? Have you drunk the bitters today?"

Maggie nodded. Eleanor reached again into the bag and brought out a round piece of dark rock carved into a small turtle design, hanging on a slim leather thong. "You have this little turtle yet?" She held it up to observe the carved lines, the four stubby legs poking from the sides. "What more have you carried about these many years, Mother?"

Maggie turned over, seeing the necklace swinging to and fro. Dizzily, she groaned and swatted at the air. "Put it away," grumbled Maggie, breathing heavily.

Eleanor watched the turtle swing. Maggie had been a girl of twelve when old Swataney made it; the first time she had ever met an Indian. Swataney said it would protect her as she traveled in the backwoods. Eleanor slowly lowered her hand with the cord twisted on her knuckles. "You were wearing this, Mother." She stared at the rock. "Were you? You had a thought that it would protect?"

Maggie snapped at Eleanor, "Put it away and go! Give me peace."

Eleanor's hands fell into her lap. "See what violence has come to you! That doctor had it figured." Eleanor dropped the turtle into the bag and pushed it under the bed rails with her foot. She stood for a moment scowling at Maggie's bandaged form curled on the bed.

Maggie appeared to lie still, but her head was whirling with lights and sharp pains. "Go, I beg you," she cried. She turned away before Eleanor could see tears spilling from her eyes. When she heard the door latch, she felt sobs rise from deep in her belly and crash like waves, convulsing her aching body.

ζ

I woke myself with a yelp as I gasped for air. My eyes were dry, but I felt the whole-bodied exhaustion of a sorrowful sobbing spell. That was no dream, I thought, looking over at Quinn's slumbering face. Her sleeping bag was pulled snugly around her shoulders. The first morning light was scattering through tree branches outside. I lifted my pillow slowly and gazed at the stone turtle lying underneath. I didn't want to touch it. I didn't believe that such vivid images could pass through time or be broadcast like they had been. It had seemed like watching a movie, except that I was behind the screen or inside the projector.

The part that bothered me the most was that I had enjoyed it. At least from the perspective of being back in my own body. After feeling the crippling pain of the old woman, my fear of her had settled to a deep curiosity, a need to go back. It felt like a craving. I had to know more.

According to old Joe, it was no accident that I had found the token. I don't know if I believed that, but there was definitely something about the rock. I slipped it into the pocket of my sweats and shuffled into the kitchen to find the pancake mix. Quinn had left the package of powder in the refrigerator, next to the milk and sausages.

The kitchen window was drafty. I pushed the curtains open to look out on the swift creek, flowing only sixty feet beyond the fire pit. The leaves had fallen from the shoreline bushes and I could see fish jumping on the dark surface water. I was mixing pancake flour and cracking an egg when Quinn walked in behind me and stretched with a roaring yawn. I flinched and dropped a shell particle into the bowl.

"Oops. Sorry," said Quinn.

"Not a problem. Fixed! Got it." I held up my pointer finger with an egg flake on the end. "I'm a little jumpy this morning."

"Yeah. You were way jumpy last night."

"Oh, God. That was nothing. The whole night was wild." As I finished stirring, I said, "I have to tell you some bizarre stuff, Quinn. I think this whole state is haunted or something. Maybe it's me, but I've never had anything like this happen before."

"Slow down, I'm just waking up here." Quinn rubbed her eyes.

"Did you know this used to be Virginia?" I pointed out the window. "Right here where we are now. Did you know that?"

Quinn stared sleepily at the skillet with sausage sputtering. "Good morning, Reed. Did you know I wake up slowly?"

"You have to wake up so I can tell you this before I explode." The griddle was hot and I spooned batter from the bowl into saucer-sized puddles. "Where should I start? I know I should have told you yesterday, when I came back up to the schoolyard, but I knew you'd be upset."

Quinn's eyes lit up, fully awake. "The schoolyard? What?"

"Okay. When I went down into the woods, I met this crazy old black guy. Joe was his name. First, I stopped on the ledge and dug this thing out of the dirt." I pulled the token out of my pocket, but it seemed dull and misshapen, like a lump of coal. I was embarrassed to set it in Quinn's outstretched hand.

"Very nice," she said, turning it over in mock scrutiny.

"I know. Seems like nothing. That's what I thought. But then all these strange things started happening. Joe was just the first. Then I saw that woman on the street in Pittsburgh. And last night..."

"Whoa. Do you mean the old woman with bad hair?"

I nodded exuberantly. "So last night I had this really real dream or something. It was like I was her. And she was in a bed, hurt from an attack. The room was so real looking, with a wood burning stove and a spinning wheel. I could feel her thoughts and everything."

"Wait a minute. Who was this?"

"I don't know. She's Maggie. She's an old woman who spins flax for the weaver."

"Spins flax?" said Quinn, incredulously. "What? Flax seed?"

"I tell you, I'm not making this up."

"When was this supposed to be?"

"Okay, I know this. It felt like summertime. They had been in Pittsburgh for ten years. It was right before the Revolution."

"Pittsburgh?" Quinn's mouth dropped open.

"Yeah. Things were really messed up and Virginia soldiers had taken over the fort."

"Reed!" Quinn was squinting with her mouth hanging barely open. She looked like she was going to ask a 'W' question but couldn't decide which. Who? What? Why?

I went on. "This is the thing. She had the token. It was in her bag and it had something to do with her getting hurt. Her daughter got angry and then I woke up. But it was there. A turtle. It had legs and lines on the shell and it hung on a leather cord like a necklace."

Quinn held the rock up and touched the protrusions on its edges.

"And Joe, the guy I met in the school's woods, told me I was supposed to find it. Or he said he let me."

"Like destiny?"

"I didn't think I believed in destiny." I flipped the pancakes and rolled the sausages to brown.

"Reed, you're describing some kind of time travel. It's not possible."

"I'm serious. This was the most believable dream I've ever... I even smelled the scents. Pine trees."

"That could be here."

"Hickory nut salve. It stunk. The doctor used it on Maggie's wounds."

"The scars on her head," Quinn said.

I nodded. "Like she had to show me what happened."

"So what did happen?"

"I'm not really sure. The doctor thinks she was attacked by Indians, but I don't think Maggie believes that. I don't think she remembers."

"Reed, you've never had a knack for making up wild stories." Quinn set the rock on the table. "You're saying that this thing morphed you back a couple of hundred years into a past life?"

"Well, it's somebody's past life! I don't know that it has anything to do with me, except that I stumbled over it."

"Do you think you can get rid of it?" Quinn asked. She looked more serious than I had ever seen her before.

"Well, I tried to give the rock back to Joe. He refused. He said my journey here is solemn."

Quinn stood up and slowly, deliberately removed plates from the cupboard. She stabbed a couple of sausage links with a fork and dropped them onto a plate, handing it to me. "Here. Let's eat. We'll figure out what to do."

We piled pancakes on our plates and squirted them with cold syrup. I thought it best to let Quinn eat in peace, without pushing the issue further. Before she spoke again, she had mopped up the last of the syrup and started filling the sink with soapy water.

"So how are you feeling, Reed?" She asked as we cleared the plates from the table. She looked skeptical and concerned, like she thought I might throw up at any minute or my head might start spinning around.

I thought about it and tried to recognize what I was feeling. "I admit that I'm still scared, Quinn, but it's different. I don't feel as scared as when I thought I was seeing things. It felt real. I felt what it was like to be in the old woman's body and I felt my own body when I came back."

Quinn sat across from me, shaking her head.

"You think it's schizo?"

"Definitely bizarre."

"I know. But I'm so curious about Maggie. I have a feeling that she witnessed something and never got to tell about it."

Quinn looked at the rock lying on the table. "And you think there's something locked up in the token?"

"I want to know how she got hurt." I sunk my hands into the dishwater and cleaned plates while Quinn scraped the sausage pan.

"How do you know how this works, Reed? What if it could hurt you?"

"I feel okay. I feel better than okay. Kind of tingly and alive."

"But you're talking about hundreds of years. People don't have dreams that carry them through time."

"Maybe we just think we don't. Maybe it happens all the time and we don't notice. I'm paying attention, Quinn."

"Reed! This is weird."

"Ha! You just can't handle me being the one who's off the center track," I said. I dried the plates and put them back in the cupboard. "I think you like being the peculiar one."

"There's nothing peculiar about me." Quinn looked pouty.

I laughed. "Quinn, you love being seen. You have the whole twisted gender thing going. You're the lesbian. The woman in sports. You have lots of girlfriends."

"Twisted Gender. Isn't that a band?"

"That was Twisted Sister."

She pulled a kitchen chair away from the table and sat rapping her finger tips on the formica top. "How did you get the impression that I have lots of girlfriends?" she asked.

I swept the token from the table and dropped it back into the pocket of my sweatpants. "You used to talk about Amy. You always smiled when you spoke of her. I thought you were falling in love. Then suddenly it was Judith. Why can't you settle down?"

One corner of her mouth twitched, not a smile. "I'm only in my thirties. I don't think I'm ready."

"You're thirty-five, like me."

"Well, you haven't settled down," she said.

"Yes, I have. I own a condo."

"I mean settled *with* anybody." Quinn rubbed a finger between her brow, pondering. "It's different. When you're straight, everyone expects you to get married, have kids. I don't think I've ever been interested in that traditional route."

"I remember this discussion. We both decided that we didn't have biological clocks," I said.

"Or maternal instincts."

"That doesn't mean you have to run around forever," I said.

"I know," said Quinn. "I really thought I would settle down with Amy. I thought I could commit myself and mean it. We had a pretty great thing going. Then Melissa Etheridge appeared on the cover of Rolling Stone with her lover and her children. Amy admitted that having kids is really important to her. I mean, I think that's great. She should." Quinn was stuttering and her eyes flitted from one corner of the room to another.

"But you don't want them," I said.

"I just don't think I'd be good at raising kids. I'm not interested in that scene. She wanted the whole ceremony and picket fence deal. I'm okay with same sex couples having kids, adopting, whatever, but it's not for everybody. As soon as I told her that, things cooled off."

"Ha," I laughed. "You sound like some guys I know who like to have fun but won't take any responsibility."

"Hey, heteros can get pregnant by just winking at each other, from the looks of it. But for two women, it's tough. And expensive. I'm just saying out loud that it isn't my thing." She sighed, exasperated.

"Relax! I don't want to have your baby."

"You! Reed? Hey, are you telling me you're available?"

"I didn't mean that. I just meant..." I stuttered as I dropped the towel I was twirling. "I guess I still get nervous, you know, wondering if you'd ever come on to me, or if I'd even know! I'm so dense sometimes, Quinn." I picked up the towel and turned my back to her. "Is that why you wanted me to come on this trip?"

"To get cozy with you? In our sleeping bags and five layers of clothes?"

I shrugged my shoulders and faced her. "I don't even know what it would look like."

Quinn grinned and turned a light shade of pink. "Ooohhh," she squealed. "I'm going to show you what it would look like! Let's just get the big 'come on' out of the way!" She puckered up with fish lips and waved her long arms around in circles. "Here I come, Reed."

I snapped the towel and backed away from her flailing limbs. I stumbled into the main room of the cabin, chuckling. "You goof, get away."

"I know you want me!"

"I deserve this." I fell backwards onto my bed and closed my eyes, laughing so hard I nearly peed.

Quinn jumped beside me on the bed, but sat on her knees, quietly. She seemed a little hurt.

"My good friend," I said. "Did I hurt your feelings?"

"I *am* your friend, Reed. We're a long ways from home and we have some serious stuff happening. I'm concerned about you and this dream or vision or whatever."

"I didn't mean to muck things up."

"Well, we have my basketball games to think about. We have to figure out where we're going today. What do you feel like?"

"I wonder if we can find an Indian or someone who can tell us what this token is all about."

"I don't think there are many Indians in Pennsylvania anymore," Quinn said.

"But you're willing to look? You're okay with exploring this token thing?" I asked.

"I'm with you, Reed." Quinn's voice dragged as if she were miserable.

"We didn't eat our sandwiches last night," I said, hoping to perk her up. "We can put them in the cooler and have them for lunch."

She snickered and grinned just a little. "You don't have to tempt me with food. I said I'm with you."

2

Quinn drove the Beetle around the curve of the exit and pointed to a grassy field below. She said, "There's the old site of Fort Pitt."

"Is it just a park now?" I asked.

"There's some old stuff. A museum, I think."

She turned onto the Boulevard of the Allies toward the middle of downtown Pittsburgh. I rode with eyes squinted, trying to envision the place with no skyscrapers, no city at all. My stomach fluttered at the idea of parking in a garage that could have been standing on the site of Maggie's house. Quinn stuffed our sandwiches into a backpack and took a bottle of water from the cooler. We walked to the pleasant park that had remnants of the fort's bastions trenched through the lawn. Posters indicated current city festivals and concerts were held there, but only a few people were present, walking or jogging. Passing under the highway bridge, we saw the tiny museum. One side looked like an original wall of the fort. Across from the entrance stood a small stone guardhouse and a plaque honoring all of the forts that had been built on the prominent location. The museum doors were locked. A small sign posted the winter hours, mostly weekends. We gathered a few brochures from a small wooden case and sat on a bench overlooking the water.

"Okay, so where exactly does the Ohio River begin?" I asked.

Quinn leaned over and picked up a rock. She tossed it out past the point of land at the end of the park. "Right there," she said.

I nodded. "And from there, everybody went west."

We sat and watched a few boats cruising the rivers. The weather was still mild for the end of October. Quinn offered a sandwich. It was almost better than I remembered from the previous day.

"So, Reed. What was that really about this morning?" Quinn asked.

I straightened up on the bench and swallowed. "You mean, my outburst?

My thinking you would come on to me?" She nodded and waited. I said, "I've always had lots of questions, Quinn, but for one reason or another, I got in the habit of pushing them down. Now all my curiosity has surfaced. I want to know about everything! Everybody. I've wondered about your life before. Wondered what it's like to be attracted to women. And even if you'd ever thought of me that way. I guess I was scared to ask."

"Yeah. Scary," said Quinn.

"I don't mean I'm afraid of you. I just mean...I didn't know how to talk about it."

"Why do you think it surfaced?" she asked. "The curiosity."

"I told you I felt alive when I woke up, like when I came back to my own body, right? Well, I mean...I really feel," I said. I closed my eyes and thought for a moment. "You know when you roll pie dough onto a board, it spreads out real thin? That's how I feel. Like I have more surface or I'm taking up more space. I can feel my skin all over my body. It's like a satellite dish, picking up all kinds of information. I'm just not very good at sorting through it all, yet."

"You said you got in the habit of pushing your questions down," Quinn said.

"When my mother was alive, she'd answer everything. But my dad was less patient. He'd snap at me or tell me he wasn't a library. If I asked Miss North, the housekeeper, she'd go off on a long tangent. It usually wasn't what I was looking for at all. One time I was confused about how menstruation worked and she started telling me about a tribe in Alaska that hikes across the tundra every summer to collect an herb that soothes cramps."

"But she didn't have any handy, right?" said Quinn.

I shook my head. "With a dad that didn't talk much and a nutty woman who twisted up our conversations, it just got easier to bury my questions. I've avoided talking about your life. But not because of you, Quinn. You know you're my oldest friend."

"Well, that 'twisted gender' comment kind of hurt." She turned around and swung a leg over, straddling the bench. "Shall I tell you about the Alaskan guy I know?"

I flipped the back of my hand toward her shoulder, punching lightly.

She pulled her cell phone out of her backpack. "Seriously. I'm calling my friend Larry. He's not really from Alaska. He's Canadian...Native American." She punched a number on her call list and waited. "Machine," she whispered. "Hey, Larry. It's Quinn. If you get this message, give me a call on my cell.

I'm in Pennsylvania and have an important question. See you soon. Bye."

She put the phone away. "Shoot. At our last meeting he said he was going to Canada to spend some time with his nephews. I'll bet he's already gone."

"You know a Native American guy named Larry? I never heard you talk about him before."

"He goes by Larry," Quinn said. "He told me his Lakota name but I'm not good at remembering it. I even have a hard time with English sometimes. He's part of a healing group that I go to in Chicago. A support group...gays, lesbians, bisexual, transgendered...Who did I miss?"

I shrugged. She went on. "One night last summer, a young guy at our meeting was struggling...feeling misunderstood. Then he choked up and admitted that he didn't even understand himself. He didn't feel like he fit in the world. Didn't want to be here."

"He didn't want to be alive?"

She nodded. "Larry started telling about a Lakota word, 'winkte.' He said the word referred to "men become women" but he used it for people who have the spirit of both genders."

"That helped the young guy?"

Quinn nodded. "Larry tells it better. He's like sixty something. Has this real mellow voice that sounds as wise as that water. Said since the 'two-spirits' embody both male and female, they don't have the usual need to find a mate of the opposite sex. Some might feel complete living alone. A lot of us hook up with someone of the same sex, another 'two-spirit.' The kid sat there listening to Larry and brightened up like a flower. You should have seen him. Said it was the only name he'd ever heard that didn't feel derogatory or medical."

I nodded. "But finding a partner to feel complete? Do you think all 'straight' people do that?"

"I know it sounds sappy," said Quinn. "But listen to songs and movies. When I saw *Jerry Maguire*, I almost choked when Tom Cruise told Renee Zellweiger, 'You complete me.' It's corny *but* it's how some people view romance."

I thought of the acupuncturist at my office. I usually avoid him but I like the yin/yang poster on his door. "'Two spirits' sounds like yin and yang," I said.

"Exactly," Quinn said, punching her fist in the air. "Eastern philosophies also respect balance—and the unique individual. People have both yin and yang characteristics, even though female behavior tends toward yin and male behavior tends toward yang."

"So 'two-spirits' balance both?"

Quinn seemed delighted. "That's the idea," she said. "Larry told us about some of the old native villages that embraced the 'two-spirits' living among them. These people were often very intuitive, the seers and medicine people. They were the go-betweens, bringing mediation between male and female, between disputing groups or even between night and day."

"Night and day?" I asked.

"Darkness and light. It was very much about spirit," Quinn said, "until that whole concept of sexuality was repressed by missionaries."

"Are there straight people with two spirits?" I asked.

She shrugged. "Switching gender roles is not uncommon. Men who nurture kids instead of a business? I suppose there could be many paths leading to two-spirit land. Larry said his family calls him 'the mediator.' He's always intervening in the family squabbles."

"That would have been you."

"I'd have been a scout, probably. Always looking over the next hill to see what goodies lay ahead." She stood up and stretched.

"So," I said, "you understand why I feel compelled to check out this rock and delve into the story that seems attached?"

Quinn walked a few steps to the fence between me and the river. She leaned against it, facing me. "Delve in. You're sure you want to go that route?" she asked. "It seems like there could be dangers with a journey like that. You're venturing into the land of 'two spirits.' The seers."

"I guess that's why I feel all right. I have a good scout. You don't think I'm crazy, do you?"

"Crazy," she said. "That's just an excuse to disregard your vision."

"You think I had a vision?"

"Okay. You're right. Maybe you're having a breakdown."

"Thanks," I said.

"No, seriously, Reed. It seems like a cry for you to look at something. Whatever...I told you I'm with you." She held up her hand, like a salute to the faraway. "I'm glad you told me about your wild rock," she said.

"There's no way I could have kept it to myself," I said.

"Whatever that little turtle holds," Quinn said, "we'll figure it out."

I felt anxious as we drove around downtown Pittsburgh. Being in the car again, I rambled nervously, not caring whether Quinn was listening or not. She was looking at street signs to figure out where we were going. "I want to find the meaning of the turtle totem," I said, "but I like to have multiple options."

"I thought we decided to start at a library," Quinn said.

"I could also find a good therapist when we get home and examine the turtle's presence in my creative psyche."

"Right. Or just keep dreaming. I think you have to be asleep to travel to Maggie." I looked at her quickly. She continued, "We could go for a hike or do something strenuous to exhaust you and put you to sleep."

"Travel?" I almost choked on the word. "I don't know what to call whatever happened. I'm not sure it will ever happen again. I thought you were going to worry about me and make me be cautious," I said.

"That was before you decided to keep the stone. If you're going to do this, you have to commit to your game. You have to move up the court. Get into position." She slapped the steering wheel with her hand.

"Well, I'm not thrilled about a hike unless we go back to the woods behind your old school and look for Joe."

"No. No. That's not what I meant. I'll do just about anything but that." Quinn's defiance made me realize how I enjoyed seeing the rare, cowardly side of her. Ever since we had met, it had been Quinn who prodded the rest of the group to try the fastest roller coaster, eat the spiciest food, climb to the highest peak of the mountain and get there first. I was fascinated, though guilt-ridden, that I'd found a little path down a long lost trail of Quinn's childhood that she refused to revisit.

"And I don't want to miss my basketball games," she said. "Remember? That's what we came for."

I found a public library building on our Pittsburgh map. There were several recollections from my dream about Maggie that I wanted to investigate. Maggie's daughter had mentioned the Moravian mission and school for Indians near Bethlehem. According to Quinn's map, Bethlehem was on the eastern side of the state, north of Philadelphia.

Downtown Pittsburgh during afternoon traffic was busier than it had been on Sunday, but the people seemed orderly and swift moving, focused on their business. Quinn wound through the streets and found the library, and once inside, we quickly located an information kiosk. After an elevator ride to a higher floor and a lengthy computer search, we found a book on Moravian architecture that told about their history in the U.S.

"Look at this. They settled Bethlehem in 1741. Their European craftsmen built some incredible buildings." Quinn pointed to a photo of a large, four-story stone building with rows of narrow windows and a steeply pitched roof. "Check out the beautiful stone work."

"Where is Moravia?" I asked.

"No idea. Somewhere in Europe, I suppose."

"They had to be a religious group," I said. "Christian. They named their town Bethlehem."

"Here it is," Quinn said, pointing to her book. "Moravia was a Czech province, like Bohemia. Looks like there were divisions within the province, Protestants against Catholics, German-speaking against Czech-speaking, lots of economic strife."

"Sounds like most of Europe," I said, "especially, back then." We looked through more pages and pictures, learning about the group's history. They first arrived in America in Georgia, then traveled north and acquired the property on the Lehigh River where Bethlehem was established as a communal village. The men lived in one building, the women in another.

"Cool," said Quinn, pointing to a drawing of several women in black dresses. "They had one of the first schools for girls in the country. That was early 'equal opportunity,' before anyone else thought that educating women was worthwhile."

"Quinn, this book says they were run out of Georgia for trying to educate slaves and Indians," I added. "Pennsylvania was more tolerant, so they came here and started schools. Did I tell you Maggie's daughter is married to an Indian? He's part Indian but they don't tell the other townspeople."

"God, I thought things were bad now. At least people can get educated." Quinn saw the reference librarian return to his desk and waved to him. "Show him the rock," she said as he walked toward us.

I pulled the stone from my pocket and said, "We think it's an Indian carving. We were visiting her childhood home and found it nearby on a hillside."

"Hmmm," he moved his glasses up and down as he turned the rock around. "I don't know much about these things, though I've seen this type of stone before. It certainly looks worn."

"Do you know of anyone who could tell us more about it?" Quinn asked.

"Here in town? Well, you could try the Carnegie Museum of Natural History, but they're closed on Mondays in the fall. There might be someone at the Fort Pitt Museum, but they have seasonal hours this time of year, too."

"We already tried them," said Quinn. "No one's home."

"Are you here for long?" he asked.

"No. We're headed toward Reading," Quinn said.

"If you pass through Harrisburg, there's a state library. The Native American curator may be able to identify the period or the carving style."

"Great idea. We could go there tomorrow," Quinn said.

"Large building in the center of town. You can't miss it." The librarian smiled and wished us luck.

We weren't Pittsburghers so we couldn't borrow anything from the local library. We made copies of photos of the communal buildings still standing in Bethlehem; drawings of the first municipal waterworks, an early grist mill and tannery beside the mill race.

Walking out the library's glass doorway, we stepped into air as wet as rain. The moisture hung close to us like our breath. Evening clouds collected into a misty fog that shrouded the street in front of us. We raised our jacket hoods and hurried to the parking lot.

Quinn was not intimidated by the fog. She followed directions toward the turnpike east of town. When we got beyond the river, the fog lifted, but by then it was dusk. Quinn grabbed my arm and pointed to an old stone roadhouse near the highway junction. "The old stone buildings are even more eerie and beautiful in the dark. That one seems hundreds of years old." She pulled into the gravel lot beside the narrow, three-story inn, built with rough gray chunks of limestone and lit by candle lamps in all the main floor windows. "Aren't you hungry?" she asked. "Let's see what they have for dinner."

We enjoyed a true Yankee feast of pot roast and potatoes. The building turned out to be barely over a hundred years old, but it had replaced an older one that burned after the Civil War. Quinn stopped at the bar on her way back from the restroom and appeared to have struck up a friendship with the innkeeper, who had offered to give her a brief tour. I settled into an ample, high-backed chair next to the crackling fire and enjoyed the comfort of apple pie warming my stomach. As my eyes drooped, the light of the flames seemed to flicker right through my eyelids. I wanted to move my chair further away, but my muscles seemed paralyzed. My body flinched from a repetitive thump deep within.

ζ

Maggie had been resting soundly until the annoying window began banging in the breeze. She expected some reluctance to waking. It had been happening lately. She'd been feeling heavy as an old canvas sandbag. It worsened by dreaming of large meals and apple pie. Pain cramped her hip and she stirred. She kept thinking there was someone there with her, someone who could leap up easily and quiet the window. But she realized she was alone. Her thoughts were muddled. She took a labored breath as if underwater, breathing through a reed. Reaching out to steady herself, she struggled to a dizzy sitting position. She pushed the candlestand out of the way, then paused and looked at her spotted, wrinkled hand. She needed a sturdy hand to brace herself against the night table. She moaned and pulled her body straight up.

"Umphh, come, old bones, see if there's a coal alight." She lifted the candle and walked a few steps, feeling the air before the stove door; it felt cool, no chance of burning herself. Upon opening the creaky iron door and stirring the ashes with a poker, she found a red, glowing coal. She held the candle wick close and blew gently until a flame leaped.

She shuffled closer to the window, peeking past the thumping casement. No stars in the sky, she noted. A summer storm had blown over the mountain range and the early morning sky was cast with low clouds. Fog spiraled off the river and up the street, bringing with it a deep silence. She wedged a wood shim into the window hinge to keep it from thumping in the slight breeze. The town lay muted and nearly invisible, but Maggie's mind chattered. She had loved her walks into town to hear the local news, often going on long tirades on subjects of political and social interest with old man Henderson at the ferry or Campbell, who tended the general store. It had been some time since she had gone into town.

But sitting all alone, the fog invited visions of her family. Once again, she had sent Eleanor away. Guilt swelled up like a rain-fed gully. Maggie fumbled with the wood, trying to revive the fire when she heard a light tapping at the door between her room and the weaver's cabin.

"Missus Beigler, are you well? I heard stirring."

"Come, Mister Emory." The bald-headed weaver poked his round red face in the doorway as she waved him in and sat back on the bed, breathing heavily.

"Allow me to give you a scoop of hot coals." He opened the stove door and aimed his half-full shovel, then fastened the iron latch as the fire caught. "Forgive me. I was up and about already in the dark parlor with my own Missus feeling poorly; the catarrh has filled her lungs once more. Your head is healing? We've been most troubled."

"Ummm," said Maggie, lifting a weak hand to hide the side of her face. "I am fortunate, I hear, to have the doctor's miserable stitching."

"'Twill heal in time. The spinning no doubt will wait for you to receive your rest." He wore a heavy robe that drooped to the floor and wrapped about his middle, tied at the widest part of his round body. He glanced around the small room. "Miss Eleanor took her leave? We expected her to stay on."

"Sent her home. I am melancholy, I fear. A joyless laggard."

"Nonsense. You deserve your healing spell. Miss Eleanor must be pleased to see you strong and whole."

Maggie leaned back against the pillow and peered through one eye at Emory. Why, she wondered, did associations feel so precarious, as if bound by the thinnest of strings? She could explain to Emory for the remainder of her days and he would never understand her earlier travails as a young widow, a woman suddenly alone with a child cleaving to her skirts. At the very time Maggie had wished to appear competent, the early years of her widowhood, her young child had been a constant reminder of all of her fears. She said to Emory, "Our paths separated when her father died and never met in the twain. I suppose a soft lap and an attentive mother was her simplest desire."

"There's time aplenty, Missus Beigler. And your fine grandsons are treasures." His eyes twinkled as he turned for the door. "Care for porridge?"

She shook her head. She had been wishing she had someone she could communicate with, someone to whom she could disclose her tangled thoughts. Like hacking through an overgrown woods, perhaps it would clear the way for her ongoing journey. "Mister Emory, I've a notion stirring about. Could I write of matters I recall, my way may be cleared to the forgotten portions."

"I know little of the script work, but we've a stack of ledger paper if the notion abounds. And plentiful candles. I suspect this cloud cover may keep the daylight low for hours."

Maggie nodded as he waved and closed the door. Kind man, Mister Emory, but he would never understand. She had much more than a few hours of turmoil to undo. She leaned back, eyes closed, and allowed her maternal guilt to pool an image of Eleanor's long walk home in yesterday's afternoon heat. She entertained a vision of Edmund meeting her with the horse and cart before she went far past the last log houses where yards spread out into farmland. Their farm was several more miles out of town, near the narrow road toward Bushy Run on the long lane winding past Braddock's Field and Turtle Creek.

She pictured Edmund standing up on the buckboard and waving, holding the reins of Coal, the large black plow horse. The boys, Whitney, who was eight, and Morton, six years old, sat on either side of their father, holding onto his legs playfully. Edmund pulled the horse's reins to stop before Eleanor and offered a hand up onto the bench seat.

Maggie thought the two boys were vastly different, though anyone could cull them from a crowd as brothers. Both had their father's dark hair and round, Frenchman's eyes. Whitney, the oldest, was a serious fellow who carefully observed the world around him with all his senses. Morton, however, was sweet and playful. His greatest joy was to tag along behind his brother, though he depended on Whitney to choose the coming and going. Maggie imagined their disappointment upon learning they must postpone their visit and her reverie came to a swift halt.

"Yes, yes, I know," she said to herself. "'Tis time to stop inventing and be fair with my memories. What a nagging conscience has arisen of a sudden." Maggie reached into the drawer at her bedside for her quill pen and ink pot. A few pages of paper remained in her supply. Pittsburgh had no paper makers. Few could read and fewer could write; it was an occasion to have a newspaper in town.

Maggie rubbed her temples for a moment then ran a finger down the aching scar along her weathered skin, etched more legibly than any words to be scrawled upon paper. In the glow of the candlelight, she began, with unshaken handwriting.

Dear Eleanor,

I can scarce explain my state of being, but let me attempt to tell as I understand. Though I lie like a lump upon the bed, I seem to feel aware of my past as if I could leap from my old body and become young once again. I am exhausted throughout, though at times when all is quiet, I do come alert for several hours. Other times, I feel as if I am at the back of a dark cave, hearing muddled voices in the distance. They give no answers, though I do seem to want to follow them to my release.

I am painfully aware of your anger. I had to beg your departure when I felt it slicing through me like a sharp knife. You can surmise how I cannot abide such a feeling at this time.

Forgive me, daughter. I feel quite lost. I want very much to find my way home and be with you and the boys. I have caused alarm and inconvenience. You must leave me and trust my journey from this cave. There must be a lesson for me. I can assure you that the pain has eased greatly. All this will surely pass, though I don't know quite why I am alive. I know you disbelieve, but I have it in my mind that it is related to the turtle totem. I recall so little of my terrible attack, but this turtle has been strong medicine, as Swataney would have said.

Somehow, I seemed to come back to life on the day long ago early on my journey in America when the totem was given to me. A nightmare of loneliness had ensued before leaving Britain and even prior to my mother's death. It greatly increased when my father trusted me into the care of the Moravians' School for Girls and then sailed back to England. He promised a swift return, which, as you know, never came.

The Moravians took me on a visit to a farm in the Cocalico valley where I first met Swataney. 'Twas the home of the Indian interpreter, Conrad Weiser, whom you recall as our friend and guide through many a year.

When the totem was placed in my hand, I looked into the lively eyes of old Swataney. You recall the old Oneida chief who held some order of peace for many years at the forks of the Susquehanna River. We lived there near the Delaware and Shawnee tribes who had been displaced from their homelands. All the Indian paths in Pennsylvania were like spokes in a wheel with the village, Shamokin, as the hub. Visitors came from all directions, some with a terrible chaotic noise and some with civility. This is the village where you were born, Eleanor, at the center of the wheel, the womb of the world as I knew it.

For the time, 'tis enough for you to know that I believe my life has dangled on this leather string. I desire no one to think ill of it. I trust I will learn more of its story as my mind clears. Roads and rivers guide some on their journeys. Others follow whispers and songs with drum beats that vibrate. Do not fret over me, Eleanor. The meaning of the name of Shamokin has been unclear. The area was known as Otzinachson and refers to 'the Demon's Den,' a hidden cave upriver from the forks of the Susquehanna where spirits were known to carouse. By this we explained the chaos attending the village, year upon year. I know I will be delivered from my own cave, my pain and memories. I trust this as I trusted the turtle to keep me alive.

For now, give my love to the boys and my apologies to Edmund, who must be utterly besought with chores.

Your mother.

As she finished the letter, Maggie had a fluttering of excitement beneath her skin. At the same time, she was exhausted enough to lay her head on the pillow and, with a few deep breaths, come close to sleep. She opened her eyes once to glance at the stove, thinking the door had come ajar when she heard the fire crackling. Finding it secured, she closed her eyes again.

ζ

Quinn was staring at me when my eyes fluttered open. The fire was down to glowing embers, with only a few flames crackling. The restaurant was empty, except for several employees in the bar area. Quinn's eyes widened in anticipation, then she blurted, "Well, did it happen? I convinced the manager to let us stay for awhile. I was hoping you were there, you know, with Maggie." She whispered with a giggle, "He thinks you're sick or something. It got us a cheap room rate."

"We're staying here?" I sat up and brushed strands of brown hair from my face.

"Why not? We're here. The place is great. Our rooms are tiny, but it's only for the night."

"Rooms?"

"It's all they had. Two rooms, each just big enough for a twin bed and a desk. There's a bathroom in the middle. Very quaint. I took a peek," she grinned, obviously proud of herself.

"What time is it? How long have we been here?"

"It's a little after ten. You dozed for over an hour." She looked closely at my face. "So?"

"So, they roll this place up early," I gazed past her as Quinn's eyebrows knit together in a frown. Then I said, "Yes! It happened again."

"See?" said Quinn. "It helps to be exhausted."

"This time it was incredible," I said.

"Tell me! Or should we take you upstairs and get you back to sleep?"

"I'm not sure I even need to be asleep. But right now I want to write something down. Maggie wrote a letter to her daughter and I could feel every word of it. I want to get it copied while it's fresh in my mind."

Quinn stammered, "You, you go on up. Use the inn's stationery. I'll get our things from the car." She handed me the room keys—yes, there's a hotel that still uses metal keys—and I wandered up several flights of stairs, following small calligraphied signs and arrows. The stairs were covered with a slightly worn burgundy Oriental carpet and the walls had varieties of golden floral wallpapers. I opened the door to one of the smallest hotel rooms I'd ever seen in the States, but clean, blending European charm and folksy comfort. The bathroom was about three feet wide, with a toilet and a small shower. Doors into our rooms were on either side. Each room had a personal sink next to the desk.

I sat with a couple of sheets of paper and recounted every word, every feeling that Maggie had written to Eleanor. Quinn came in before I finished, but retreated into the other room, leaving me in the stillness. I called out through the bathroom doors when I was done and she popped through the shortcut. Reading the whole letter was difficult; I had to keep blotting my eyes. Holding it in my hand, I felt as if Eleanor was my own daughter and the sentiments had come from my own mind and heart. Trembling as I finished, I looked up at Quinn whose hand was clamped over her mouth.

For a moment I thought she was speechless, which never happens. Then she reassured me with a torrent of questions. "How did you do that? What does it feel like? Can you smell things?" We talked for an hour as I tried to understand it all myself.

"Writing the letter wasn't done from memory," I said. At least, not any form of memory I'd ever experienced. "It was as if Maggie were there with me, writing it all over again."

"I think you're helping her write," Quinn said.

"Or remember things. I think she has some sense of me," I said. "Like tuning into the same frequency, through time, to access each other's data."

She laughed, "You mean like how you can sometimes pick up on another person's portable phone conversation?"

"Maybe!" When I sat at the desk earlier and took the pen in my hand, I had sensed an inner relief. As if my spirit, or Maggie's, had been trying to convince me that we had a means to cross our worlds' boundaries. We could pass notes through the astral hallways of time. It still seemed so impossible that I couldn't even say it out loud to Quinn. I felt that I was some kind of captive. But I wanted to be held. I was willing to submit, but it seemed I had to allow my will to be replaced, at least temporarily, by Maggie's.

To Quinn, I said, "It seems that we've both agreed to it now. Maggie is eager, against all odds, to find energy and paper and to delve into her memories that had been quite guarded before. As she lets go of her resistance, my own doubts tend to fade. Though not quite all of my fear," I admitted.

"Yeah. It's strange," nodded Quinn. "In a way, I envy you. But I don't think I could do what you're doing." She shivered, as if the cool energy of a ghost had walked through her. She asked, "What do you think you get from it, Reed?"

I pushed the pen away and looked down at the desk. I knew the writing had eased some of the trepidation I had about sleeping, but not about the whole project, if one could call it that. I said, "I want to know what it all means. I still don't know what it has to do with me. I just hope it will be easier to rest now."

"Amen." We said good night as Quinn dashed for the first turn in the bathroom.

After our toiletry rituals, I heard the click of Quinn's light and a few creaks from the bed springs, then all was quiet. I pulled back the floral chintz bed cover to find a puffy comforter and climbed up onto the high mattress. I heard a few cars and trucks pass by on the state road in front of the inn, and then relaxed into a deep sleep.

ζ

Maggie was curled beneath the coverlet, dozing lightly, when she heard the door creaking. Her senses descended like a flock of birds alighting, squawking on a pond. In her mind, she quieted the birds, "Shhhh, now. It must be Eleanor. No need to go on squawking. She takes a comfort in feeling pity for her old mother. And 'tis favored over her anger." She pulled the coverlet up around her shoulders, cradling her aching jaw and her gums that felt fiery hot. She heard Eleanor's pause, then a deep breath.

Eleanor said, "Thank you, Mother, for the letter."

Maggie stirred and grunted, feigning sleep. She didn't feel like talking about the letter, sent by the weaver's kind delivery to Eleanor's and Edmund's farm the day before.

Eleanor sighed and said, "At first I fretted, all the talk of demons and drums and...and hearing voices." She paced the room, straightening the drapery, and then stopped at the foot of the bed. "I had no desire to show it to the doctor. I feared 'twould lead to more worrisome news. 'We can cope with this ourselves,' I told Edmund. But he found your words profound."

Maggie raised her head to look at her daughter. Was she hearing correctly? Was this truly her daughter? "Who are you?" Maggie asked. "Don't answer! I know who you are. But how can my own daughter subject me to more torture?"

Eleanor seemed nervous, flustered. She loosened the bow on her bonnet and pushed it back onto her shoulders. Looking away from Maggie's fiery gaze, she said, "Edmund has ridden to the fort to fetch the doctor for his further opinion."

Maggie moaned and dropped her head back onto the pillow as they heard a wagon clatter outside, turning from the direction of Water Street. The only welcome sound was the squeal of the little boys when the wagon stopped outside, but Eleanor sped outside to detain the boys. Maggie turned her face to the wall as noisy rustling sounds indicated two men entering her room; Edmund must have followed the doctor.

She heard the thump of the doctor's leather bag drop alongside her bed, but it was Edmund who peered over her and laid his familiar hand on her shoulder. He patted and rocked her lightly, thinking she was asleep. "Mother Beigler, 'tis the Doctor for a visit. Will you wake?"

"No...no, leave me," she mumbled.

"Now, Missus. Show your eyes," said Doctor Connolly's voice from behind Edmund. "Open them, or must I open them for you?"

She turned slightly and peered over her shoulder through dark slits.

"Open your eyes widely," he repeated. As her eyebrows arched, he leaned past Edmund and held her lower lids to look closely at her pupils. "Quite fine." He took hold of her hands and said, "I shall pull you. Swing your legs over and sit. You must move about today."

"No!" she complained loudly, but he continued to pull and Edmund reached down to help lift her legs over the side of the bed. She sat with her shoulders hunched and her head spinning dizzily while the doctor checked the back of her head bandages. "Let me be," Maggie moaned as Edmund slipped her leather moccasins on her feet.

"You must rise and move about each day," said the doctor. "Your hip will stiffen, otherwise. When your daughter visits, you must allow her to help." Maggie groaned as the doctor pulled her to her feet. How she wished she could unleash the bile in her belly. He deserved to be soaked in it, she thought. He let her stand still for a moment, and then tugged her hands to pull her slowly toward him as he watched her feet. She limped and shuffled, but was able to put her weight on both legs.

While the doctor led her around the small room, Edmund went to the door and waved. The boys ran inside before Eleanor caught up to them on the porch. They stopped and stared, eyes and mouths opened wide. She turned when she heard them and held out her hands. Joy swept over her, erasing all the pain.

"Granmama, you're not sleeping!" said little Morton. The boys tiptoed tentatively, and then hugged her waist. She patted them on their heads and offered a weak smile.

"Come boys," Eleanor said flatly from the doorway. "You can visit Granmama soon." They waved goodbye and ran under Eleanor's arm through the open door. Eleanor stirred the broth that sat on the stove while Edmund stoked the fire. The doctor put an examining tool back in his bag, motioned to Edmund and walked stiffly toward the door. He and Eleanor began murmuring with their heads lowered as Edmund helped Maggie back into the bed. He knelt alongside her and carefully tucked the blanket around her waist. Edmund smiled patiently, deep crags punctuating his high cheekbones, eyes with a dark stone glimmer. His black hair was cropped close to his sun-reddened ears. He seldom wore a hat.

Edmund picked up the turtle totem and dangled it before her. He whispered, "Mother Beigler, you sense the totem rightly. Turtle clan is the oldest clan, very strong." He placed it in her hand then pleaded with her to come to the farm with them until she finally turned her head away and closed her eyes. "Then let Eleanor help. She needs to help," he said. He placed his large hands over both of hers on her lap. "Tell us your story when you are able." Edmund walked quietly to the door, where the doctor and Eleanor still talked in low voices.

"Might she read?" the doctor asked.

"What would we bring that she won't bewail?" said Eleanor. "The Bible fails to calm her, and the news is printed with suspicion of every action taken by Parliament. They rile her with their speculation on the new taxes."

"'Tis true." Edmund shrugged. "The town and fort are awash with military news and border squabbles. Are we part of Virginia or part of Pennsylvania?"

"She is scornful of all," Eleanor said. "Her mood is dour without adding further reason."

"She is a different sort, though," said the doctor. "The Indian uprisings had hundreds fleeing eastward. She went the other direction." He shook his head. "How could she reason that the feuding Indians might parley with her?"

Eleanor and Edmund were silent. Maggie waited politely, expecting them to offer some kind of defense. She felt the heavy weight of their judgment in the lack of words.

Doctor Connolly fastened his jacket. "In any regard, she must eat more to gain strength. And move about each day, more so as time goes."

"And her letter?" asked Eleanor. "She says she is awake at night. Must one of us stay with her?"

"She has folks nearby if needed. As to offering your company, follow her desires."

Maggie heard the doctor tap his hat, finishing their conversation and pulling open the door as Eleanor slipped back into the room.

Doctor Connolly squeezed Edmund's hand and leaned close, but his deep voice carried inside. He said, "Eleanor mentioned that you have some Injun blood; said most around here don't know. Best to keep it quiet, eh? Don't want mischief."

"What mischief do you mean?" asked Edmund.

The doctor said, "I intend to say nothing. There are folks who have no faith in an upright redskin."

"Upright?"

The doctor cleared his throat loudly, "As you know, Pennsylvania's governor planned to abandon the fort...leave this frontier to the mercies of the wild."

Edmund replied, "I know Virginia's governor signed your militia commission."

He nodded. "I expect to hear you touting Virginia's promises to your fellow ploughboys." Doctor Connolly slapped Edmund on the shoulder. Maggie heard him thumping down the steps.

Eleanor poured broth for Maggie and said, "I beg you to eat, then I shall depart." Surprise registered on her face as Maggie sat up. Eleanor sat on the edge of the bed and helped Maggie hold the wooden spoon to her mouth. Maggie sucked in as much air as broth. "Shall I cut some fruit? Will you eat?" Maggie nodded and Eleanor lowered her tense shoulders as well as her voice. "I beg your forgiveness for my anger, Mother. I am rageful, watching you suffer so."

Maggie slurped the broth. "Time is what is needed," she said. "I've earned a rest." She considered apologizing, but felt a thin shred of acceptance from Eleanor and considered it to be enough. Eleanor nodded and picked up her shawl. She draped it over her shoulders and went out the door, calling to the boys.

Maggie huddled lower in the bed. All was quiet. She closed her eyes and thought she felt herself rising from her blankets, from her body. She wanted to disappear into a time without injuries and painful memories, a time without children and parents and disappointment and death. She began to rock slowly.

Her early days in Pennsylvania became alive and present. Her knotted limbs felt young and pliant, her breath was easy and the air was full of the scent of the woods.

ζ

I used to wake from my dreams and feel them evaporating, then and there. I'd have a vague sense of cast or setting, but all the other facts would jumble or disappear completely. The voyages with Maggie were different. Her pungent visions stayed with me, like something I couldn't scrape from my shoe, like someone living in a parallel world that roomed next door and played the stereo too loud.

I woke, knowing I was in my little room; there was enough of a glow from the street light coming through the sheer drapery to get my bearings. I stumbled from my tall mattress and turned on the desk lamp without chasing away the smoky, wild story coming from Maggie. It taunted me to chase it over the pages.

Dear Daughter and Family,

The night quiets, but for the pain in my hip from the doctor's torture. I know I must behave and be more active, so I have walked about on two occasions since you departed. Your pleasure with the letter inspires me and Mister Emory kindly offered ledger paper to continue writing.

I miss you little boys and I ponder the thought of holding you on my lap and telling you these tales one day. Your mother will be taken aback to hear such coming from my pen, since I have not been wont to tell of the past, only march onward to the day thereafter. Yet I have beheld wondrous places and known a few lively folks that deserve to be shared with you.

You boys may ask how your old Gran, when not so very old, might have arrived at that Tulpehocken farm? We must go back even further. 'Twas the town of Philadelphia where I first set foot on American soil with my father in the spring of 1742, barely less than a year since my mother had passed. We were expecting to tour and explore the countryside of Pennsylvania. Father had a foundry business in Yorkshire, England though as economics suffered, he was contemplating establishment in America. In Philadelphia, we promptly met Count Nikolaus Ludwig von Zinzendorf of the Moravian community, who then introduced my father to persons north of Bethlehem in the foundry business. He was greatly excited about an acquisition they recommended. He made haste to return to Yorkshire and sell his ironworks, whether to my uncle or another party, and peddle or transport all our belongings. Aiming to spare me the difficulty of additional ocean voyages, which indeed caused me dire illness, he entrusted me to the Bethlehem Moravians and their newly founded School for Young Women.

'Twas Zinzendorf's idea for a summer excursion to the Indian villages that found me accompanying him and his daughter, Benigna. She was older than myself and very much a young woman, with plain, well-tailored clothing and a fair use of English. She had arrived in Bethlehem shortly before us and was swift to befriend me.

The woods were rather ungentlemanly and no place at all for young girls. The trip itself was frightful, even had I not of recent been abandoned by my father. Many a night have I lain awake with the mystery of a man who could leave his daughter, yet shy of thirteen years and grieving my dead mother, in the care of people barely known. But that he did and sailed back across the ocean to England.

Would he have been so hasty to leave had he known my first educational outing was to accompany Zinzendorf on a visit to the woods? The journey was remote, departing the bad roads for no roads at all but only faint paths over rocks, fallen trees and Indian trails cut through dense forests. Would my father have departed knowing Zinzendorf's passion for following God's call, a mysterious voice that only he could hear? With no warning, Zinzendorf had halted the party of a half-dozen on horseback, alerted by his perception, and aimed our group westward through brambled ravines and scrub oak forests, scarce going a mile without steep ascents or descents. No argument arose from his devoted followers. I was bewildered already by my father's departure and clung to the rear of Benigna's broad-backed mare, helplessly going wherever I was taken.

The primitive path, barely visible, led across the Schuylkill River to the Tulpehocken road where Zinzendorf sought guidance to Conrad Weiser's home. Benigna, five years my senior, sat before me, reassuring me that her father could be trusted and that my own father would return with godspeed. On occasion, I buried my tear stained face in the hollows of her shoulders and the comfort of fine spun fabric. I questioned her about a notion I thought I had surely misunderstood, having heard one of the Bethlehem ladies refer to Zinzendorf as a nobleman from Germany.

Benigna whispered over her shoulder that her father begs for similarity among all, including themselves. She said. "Even as a count, he wants no treatment above another. Years ago, he invited a group of wandering people who escaped religious persecution in Moravia to settle a small town on our estate in Germany." Benigna's voice was low and melodious and her German accent quite faded from my hearing.

Asked if she was truly a countess, she shrugged. "Father says not to think such. In America we are all townspeople." We laughed and talked with ease. It seemed odd to think of her as royalty as I considered her most ordinary habits. Yet I marveled at how she could eat a leg of rabbit without a smudgeon of grease upon her cheek. Her clothes seemed never soiled, though she did a share of work and never acted overly prim.

'Twas late summer of 1742. A slight breeze kept us from choking in the heat and dust kicked up by the line of horses. My legs straddled the broad

end of the saddle, skirt hiked up about my knees. Having been not long on the American shores from England, I had no sense of distance or landmarks. Mountains and trees towered about. My senses of smell and direction were baffled as well. The horses made a steady progression and, as I surmised, we were several days in some direction from Bethlehem in the province of Pennsylvania. Benigna hooked one leg around the saddle's horn and kept her horse in line amidst a train of a half-dozen others.

Tulpehocken was one of many farming communities further inland. Settlers from the German Palatine region flocked to William Penn's colony and pushed their farm acreage as far west as the Susquehanna River. I quizzed Benigna about Bethlehem, founded by the Moravian group two years prior on a tract of land north of Philadelphia on the upper branch of the Delaware River. They had previously abandoned their Georgia colony and moved to Pennsylvania where tradesmen laid out a carefully planned town.

Benigna told me the Moravians had zeal for extending good works. "Unity," she said. "Moravians make missions to Indians, to Negroe plantation slaves, to poor farmers. Critics accuse Father of sending missionaries where he dares not go, hence, he defies them. We come to Pennsylvania."

Zinzendorf arrived in Bethlehem in 1741, grandly believing that as he had unified the Moravian refugees into a Brotherhood, he could unify the many branches of Christian believers flocking to America into one cooperative spiritual movement. I suppose Zinzendorf was not a bad man. But in his efforts, both words and deeds seemed to tangle, missing his aim in some causes.

Our directions beyond the cluster of log buildings called Tulpehocken took us to a well-worn trail through cornfields. A sturdily built, small stone house appeared like a miniature fortress overlooking fields of grass and corn. Benigna pointed alongside the house to several huts of woven tree branches covered with long bark strips. She said, "Conrad Weiser interprets for local Indian tribes. Lived among the Mohawk in his youth."

My voice was caught deep in my throat. I had heard tales of the native people, but no amount of imagination could have painted such an image. We entered the midst of a makeshift Indian camp, set up in the yard of Weiser's farm. As our horses strode into full view, many bronze-coloured people crawled from the huts. They stood on blankets in the cool shade of the oaks, twenty-some watching our party. From a distance, they appeared brown and bare. I thought to turn away in embarrassment, but curiosity fastened my gaze. Chiefly 'twere men, wearing at the least, some small scrap of cloth or leather strung about their waist to cover their most private areas. Even the few women and children showed ample skin, dark as the richest earth. Most of the females wore simple buckskin dresses with scant, colourful decoration.

As we drew near, a thin white woman in indigo muslin approached us from within the midst of the Indians, waving, "Halloo." I thought correctly that she was the interpreter's wife. The yard filled, everyone mingling closer as they conversed among themselves and pointed at our caravan.

This was a simple moment in which a world of divided feelings tumbled over me. Fearful, I wanted a refuge, a hiding place where I could crawl back to my narrow view of the world, proper and reasonable. In Yorkshire, I had ridden the woods of the River Swale, yet 'twas springy grass beneath my feet, not brambles. There are empty moors and lonely miles, yet none so utterly dark as Penn's Woods. The farms there are edged with stone walls and until the lead carts dwindled, all seemed abundant. Even our household servants dressed in fine clothing. Everyone in our small village knew my father. 'Twas my private tutor who began whispering that the business was suffering. Soon after, Father announced our plan for an excursion, leaving Uncle George in charge of the foundry.

So just as we had boldly set sail on a two-masted, square-rigged ship bound for Pennsylvania, I held a sudden yearning to leave my old world behind and learn all possible about the new: the natives' language, their customs, how they came to decorate their clothing, skin and hair with pictures and baubles. Perhaps knowing the strangers would set aside my fear. I searched the grounds for the interpreter named Weiser who could give some assistance. Zinzendorf waved his large brimmed hat. His dark hair, flecked with silver, streamed past his shoulders. Among so many gentlemen wearing powder wigs, Zinzendorf's hair was his most distinguishing characteristic.

My boldness faded and I was seized by sudden trembling. I gasped when one of the dark skinned men shrieked and whooped, then ran toward us at a great gallop. I clamped my arms hard afast Benigna's waist, watching the wild man with only a dark, feather-wrapped strand of hair dangling about one side of his face. Behind him, a small naked boy of four or five years scrambled to catch up. Zinzendorf trotted ahead and dismounted. I breathed with relief when their meeting resulted in an embrace and the two men shook hands warmly. Zinzendorf leaned over as the little boy caught up and pulled him off his feet with an embrace. The boy squinted, clutched Zinzendorf's hand and dragged him toward the house.

Thus were we casually introduced. Zinzendorf motioned for us to follow him into the yard. Brother Mack tied the horses while an older man with a thick, grey-streaked beard stepped out onto the porch. He called to us in loud German.

I stuck to the horse's rump, though Benigna pointed to Conrad Weiser and said he offered refreshment. Noticing my ashen face, she added, "Naught to fear. The people are most friendly."

The difficulty of the trip had left me as confused as the tangled web of trails we had followed, oft in circles. I yearned to know where I had arrived. How would I return? How would my father know to find me?

I kept a shy distance to observe the bronzed people from my hiding places behind bushes or tree trunks. Benigna urged me closer, telling me they were donning their brightly trimmed clothing for a welcoming ceremony and I risked offending them by staying away. They wanted to celebrate our party's rescue, she said, from the forbidding thorny underbrush. I could not argue that. She interpreted Weiser's German as he spoke of the "edge of the woods," the place of safety where we had arrived. She said the natives offered to brush the briars from our clothes and clear our ears and eyes of fatigue.

I stayed near Benigna's side, hazarding a close enough view of the natives' vestments bedecked with small shells, colourful feathers and silver beads. Intricate patterns were sewn into the hides with quills. In addition to the hair wrapped with feathers and strips of leather thongs, some wore leather or silver bands on their arms. I shivered at the sight of several men with dark drawings etched on their skin. I became squeamish at that and at the silver rings piercing their ears or noses, but took note that there was no bright paint as in stories I had heard of the wild Americans. I told Benigna I felt astonished that anyone could differ so remarkably.

"They are beautiful, I believe," she said.

Native women stacked wood by a fire pit and prepared to feed the growing crowd. Their faces had prominent foreheads and sharp cheekbones, deepset, dark eyes. The unfamiliar cast a fluttering disturbance through my throat and belly.

The story is far from finished, though my supply of paper has dwindled. I shall beg more from the weaver on the morrow, for I believe I have found the path from my cave. This trail of words serves to bring relief, so I shall find a means to continue.

Signed, Your stubborn Mother

ζ

I set down my pen and noticed that there were no more pages of stationery from the inn. "Did Maggie really run out," I wondered, "or did she sense that my own supply had dwindled?" I had noticed the bleed-through feelings from Maggie and could usually tell if something was coming from her or was my own present feeling. I wondered how she was adjusting to me and my presence or what she might be noticing. Our worlds are so different.

Reviewing some of the pages I had written, it occurred to me that Maggie had truly come to a new world. Her daughter and others wanted her to look back, but she had had to leave her world behind and come to a strange country. Her focus was on the present, on staying alive.

I had to put down the papers when my eyes started to ache. I closed them and saw dancing triangles of colored lights, radiating around the periphery of my vision. My head aimed for the pillow and I sprawled, face down on the bed. The shapes danced like geometric snakes until I felt a shudder of breath, then bright white lights opening up old, unwelcome thoughts.

ς

Maggie listened to the storm raging through the night. The weaver's cabin was solid and simple. Neighbors' shutters were banging and their fresh split shingles tearing off in the wind. She wrapped a shawl around her shoulders and pulled herself out of bed to sit in the rocking chair where she could watch the bright streaks of light flash across the sky.

Tulpehocken was fresh in mind and she drifted straightaway to that trip, its summer thunderstorms, her first in Pennsylvania. They were remarkably different from the constant dribbling sort of storms she recalled on Yorkshire's highlands.

In Pennsylvania, storm clouds stacked up at a distance for days and churned with the smell of dank dust. The group of weary Moravian travelers escaped swarms of insects and retired early, their fire burned down to red coals that glowed through the canvas walls of the large tent. Maggie huddled with the women, separated by a canvas curtain from the men at the other end. Wind flapped the tent sides and whistled through tree boughs that bent in the night sky. Thunder grew louder and flashes of lightning cast fearsome silhouettes thrashing over the thin screen of cloth.

Maggie recalled numerous roiling bouts with storms at sea, but the mountain storm bore a pressure upon her ears and head that left her cowering. The others had fallen asleep. When the storm unleashed its downpour, Maggie's tears began. Her grief at being left in America by her father was shaken loose by the shuddering wind and the muffled snores of unfamiliar men.

The image of her father was always tall, astride his chestnut horse, trotting handsomely along a forest path until the tranquil scene was interrupted by his transaction with Zinzendorf. The Moravians' leader had arranged for her father's tour of local foundries. On the road a half day's ride north of Bethlehem, they met Zinzendorf and Maggie's father thanked him for his kindness in introducing the country. "Once my dealings in Yorkshire are settled," he had said, "I shall return to make my permanent home in these woods." He waved his map from the land merchant he had met at the last foundry visited. After negotiating for an escort to Philadelphia, Maggie's father pulled an envelope from his pocket and walked his horse closer to Zinzendorf, handing over the brown package. "Twill account for Margaret's education and boarding for a full two years. I plan to be back in your presence in half that time. Assure me once again that I can entrust her to your care."

Zinzendorf nodded. "As our own treasured child."

Maggie heard the voices from the tunnel of her memory. She felt her own heart shout, "A year! Father! Please...you must not leave me." Her refusal to kiss him goodbye felt like a sharp stick in her chest.

He spoke curtly to her. "These are good people with a fine school. You were deathly ill the entire ocean crossing! You know you dread a return voyage to England. You shall be well cared for in my absence." He turned his back, glancing briefly, and then galloped away. She sat on the back of Benigna's mare.

Maggie recalled their ship sailing from England's shores. Father and daughter had watched the land disappear on the horizon. But when the crossing became rough, Maggie was forced below decks among the dank, spoiled fish air that hovered throughout the belly of the ship. She heaved into a pot next to her narrow bunk as her father repeatedly shuffled down the gangway with a fresh chamber pot. He wiped Maggie's face and stayed by her side, though Maggie knew the noise of her cough reminded him of the ailing wife he had buried only months earlier.

Coming into sight of colonial shores on a calm day, her father had carried her above deck to witness the scenic green horizon mixed with a floral scent, blossoming roses. With her first breath, she told her father that she never wanted to return across the ocean.

Maggie felt a crack of thunder reach her own fiery core and seal some inner fissure. She felt connected to the raging earth like the trees that swayed over the mountain path. The storm howled as Maggie let her fears be washed along with the plants, trees, and soil.

In the morning sprinkle of light rain, the travelers conversed about the previous downpour. Maggie saw calm trees, solid as wooden masts, that had been stretched sideways in the wind hours earlier, thrashing their tiny leaves against the brutal sky. Even so, a tree's roots grow deeper, trunk sturdier and leaves suck heartily at the sap of life in a proper storm. Maggie had weathered a new breed of storm and anchored herself on fresh roots.

Whenever storms approached, Maggie still relished the tingling vibrancy, the promise of thunderous upheaval that would rinse clean and change everything. The Pennsylvania soil became her home, a landscape of hickories and sycamores. She breathed the forest air and craved fruits and vegetables that tasted of the electrified, storm-tossed earth.

ζ

Waking full of energy, I dressed and walked downstairs and across the street to purchase film for the camera and a thick notebook. I strolled the neighborhood and decided that the inn sat beyond the road to Eleanor and Edmund's farm, but wasn't old enough to have been there then. It was the only ancient building on the street. It had been a roadhouse at a time when only a rutted one-lane highway was there, no sprawling, smoggy layer of ramshackle shops, apartments, schools or factories. I tried to envision broad furrowed fields, dirt roads and Indian paths.

I knocked on Quinn's door from the hallway, sure to confuse her. She answered, looking puzzled, then opened it wide. I heard a television reporter's crackly voice, interviewing a military commander via satellite. Quinn walked back into the room, leaving me in the hall. Over her shoulder she said, "They just showed one of the packages of relief food the cargo planes are dropping near Afghan villages."

I walked in as they broadcast more pictures of the pouches. "They seem hard to open."

"Right," she said. "Packets of Pop Tarts and peanut butter. The reporter said the Afghan people are suspicious, so a lot of it is wasted or fed to their animals."

"Well, their animals need to survive the winter, too," I said. "Will peanut butter hurt them?"

"Looks like they prefer the crackers," said Quinn, stepping toward the television to turn it off.

"Hey, why did you get the room with the TV?" I asked, looking around to see what other amenities I might have missed.

"You picked your room," Quinn said.

"I didn't even notice. No big deal. I probably wouldn't have turned it on and then we'd walk around all day without craving peanut butter." I dropped Sunday's edition of the Post Gazette next to her duffel bag. The paper had been laying in the lobby, open to an article about the commandeered flight that had crashed last month in a field east of Pittsburgh, not far beyond where we stopped. I had read the account of the ordinary lives of the people on board, some who had changed their reservations that morning to get on the nearly empty flight. I thought about driving off the turnpike to view the crash site, but they say it's just a hole in the ground.

One of Quinn's basketball games was in a town east of Harrisburg on Wednesday night so we planned to head that direction. Quinn elected me to the first shift of driving because I was the hungriest. She thought that would prevent side trips, dawdling or getting lost. After the short night's sleep and an early lunch, I had to return the driving duties back to Quinn. As we cruised onto the turnpike through the rolling hills of the Chestnut Ridge, I started writing my memories from the previous night in my new, fat notebook. Within a few minutes, the hypnotic lull of the traffic pulled my head against the soft headrest.

ζ

Maggie dozed in the stream of sunshine pouring through her window and continued to kindle the static crackle of energy from the previous storm as if it had been breathed into her body to uproot memories and snap branches of her family tree. When she sensed a colossal tumble and Eleanor's outstretched hand slipping from her grasp, she struggled to find her voice.

"Eleanor!" finally slipped from the tight grip of her throat. The noise of her own gasp woke her in her chair. Maggie heard shouting voices and a scuffle of commotion in the street, drawing her up to peer from behind the window frame. Her heart raced and her sore gums throbbed when she heard a gunshot ring out down the hill. It was an early hour to see a bearded man dressed in buckskins and bare feet, shouting curses at the boatmen who dragged him by the arms, back toward the river. The rabble startled Maggie, though there had been disturbances here and there in town, all the summer months with the shipping crews and merchants embroiled amongst each other.

She had taken a short stroll through the side yard only moments before, and all had been serene. But the added pressures of increased taxation from England, she thought, were causing people to act in fanatical ways. The weaver had said that without an official boundary, the feuds between the Penns and Virginians often turned to fist fights, usually kept to the river quarters or the edges of the fort. At times, the misunderstandings made their way up the street from the direction of Semple's Tavern, where they were inflamed by the hot breath of the local rye whiskey.

Maggie saw a blur of soft blue and squinted to see Eleanor avoid the swirl of activity and dart into the weaver's yard. Maggie felt her heart settle as Eleanor passed under the window, waving her fingers from beneath her awkward basket. She pushed aside the open door with a cheery greeting. "Mother? You look well. Full of color." Maggie dropped wearily into the chair beside the window. Eleanor set her load on the table and removed her wrap, hanging it on a wall hook. "The door was ajar. Have you ventured out?"

"I had a mind to feel the sun's warmth, prior to the commotion. You nearly marched into the midst of those ruffians. Adverse news from the east?" she nodded toward the window, where the noise had ceased.

"Take no heed, Mother. Those fellows would fight over a one-legged rabbit pelt, just to have their way." Eleanor unwrapped a cloth full of wildflower blossoms, and set them in a pewter mug. "From your grandsons who care more for you than their early morning fishing."

Maggie said, "Dear boys. I spied freckled blisters on Morton's nose. 'Tis possible the sun has burnt him while he works to make up for my folly?" Maggie also noticed Eleanor's roughened hands and the corners of her eyes and mouth pinched like a dry gully wash.

"'Tis not how they perceive."

"I will beg their forgiveness. I intend to be well soon and our lives will resume a normal course. What of the thundershowers? Does it mean misfortune for the farm?" asked Maggie. "You've been away."

"We worked long days to salvage the drenched wheat crop; some fields were swamped and Edmund fears them lost. He's hard at work at present to spare the remainder."

"You should be there."

"Hauling must be done and Edmund has taken on the help of some neighbors."

"What neighbors?" Maggie asked.

"Fellows from Suke's Run, closer to the river. They're having a corn husking at week's end and came by to offer their help with the wheat in exchange for ours at the husking."

Maggie stopped rocking in her chair and peered at Eleanor. She had never heard Eleanor mention knowing anyone from Suke's Run. "Who do you know there?" she asked.

"Folks came by to offer a helping hand. Edmund was reluctant, but I convinced him that a day's labor was worth getting the wheat in before the next storm. I left them with a pot of stew for their dinner."

What have you in that bundle?" Maggie craned her neck at Eleanor's basket on the table.

Eleanor removed a pan of corn pudding and placed a large melon in Maggie's lap, beneath shaking, entwined fingers. "Look here. Missus Henderson sent it along. She begged me to wish you well."

"Musk melon?" asked Maggie.

"Ummm. Taste?"

"No, no," Maggie mumbled. With a slow effort her fingers bent around the melon, petting the rough rind while her eyes remained fastened on the street. Eleanor unrolled a clean dress from her shoulder pouch and hung it on a wall peg alongside Maggie's woolen jacket. She unpacked apricots and pears and cut slices of salt pork to leave with biscuits for Maggie's supper.

"'Tis cooling on occasion in the evenings," said Eleanor, pushing the window nearly closed. A light breeze carried smells of fresh cut hay fields and the smoke of burning leaves. She removed her final offerings from the bag, two fresh dipped candles and the last of the paper she had carried from Bethlehem. "I brought more paper for your journals," said Eleanor.

"Ahhh, bless you. I borrowed more from the weaver last eve for the Tulpehocken story. 'Tis there on the table."

Eleanor leaned over Maggie's shoulder and said, "We best change that bandage." She paused, then added, "No argument?"

"Hmmph," Maggie grunted. "An argument will fetch that dreaded doctor to march me about until I'm mortal ill."

"Don't speak of mortal ill," Eleanor scolded. "You are vast improved. 'Tis common to need new bandaging." She retrieved the salve and the muslin bag of cloth strips from the table and loosened the stay on Maggie's bandages.

"Ahhh, a putrid salve," Maggie winced and turned her face away.

"Helps a considerable amount. 'Tis what the doctor said."

"Quack remedy," Maggie mumbled. "Don't care for him."

"Doc Connolly? He's easily liked. Charming," said Eleanor. "A handsome man, as well," she blushed and laughed, breathily. "He devoted fine care even whilst the local politics were upheaved and Indian battles busied his men." Eleanor unwound the strips, slowly, carefully.

Maggie frowned, "Makes no sense. Those Indians were peaceful for years. When they fought, they did so on the side of the English." She paused, still frowning. "What has become of the fight?"

Eleanor paused and rested her hands on Maggie's shoulders. "The fighting? We heard naught from the Pennsylvania men patrolling the rivers, though they say hundreds of farm folks have fled eastward. They say the God-fearing have abandoned Dunmore, as our Virginia soldiers now call the town."

"Were there some here who were God-fearing?" said Maggie dryly.

"Mother. You'll be interested to hear the trading Indians are staying away."

"Wise fellows."

"All the town awaits news from the Continental Congress," Eleanor said. "Virginia soldiers claim they continue to meet hostile tribes."

"Claim indeed," grumbled Maggie. "That ambitious lot has an aim to run them all westward."

"I don't suppose they would start another war, risk all our lives," said Eleanor. She changed the topic as she dropped the bandaging into a wooden bowl on the floor. "Last eve, Edmund read a portion of your letter to the boys. I'm astonished, Mother, that you can be so clear-minded during the night. Write all those pages." She mixed lye soap with water in a small clay dish and dabbed with a soft cloth along the pink scars and unhealed places. "You wrote a great deal, but the boys had many a question once Edmund finished reading. I truly wished you were sitting by, so they could question you directly." She ran her fingers gently through the matted strands of oily hair. "One day soon, Mother, I pray you'll be well to come for a visit."

"They asked about the Indians?"

"No." Eleanor paused. "Your father is the one who came to mind. They knew naught of your being alone from your youth." Maggie felt her tongue clamp behind her teeth as her mouth stretched a taut line. Eleanor continued, "I told them he had failed to return, lost at sea." Her voice softened, "Naturally, they later wanted to hear about your mother. We had not spoken of her until then."

"You told them?" Maggie's voice cracked.

"What could I tell them? You've told me so little." Eleanor's voice was gentle as she moved around to the end of the bed, facing Maggie's chair. "I know she died when you were a young girl, when you were yet in England."

Maggie's mouth twitched with emotion. "Seems the thoughts I desire to keep buried are tangled with the ones that yearn to surface. All seem to come up in a mass. I thought I could keep all of that old life away, across the sea." Maggie felt the tangles unraveling and pushing their way up, against her tongue. She had a growing feeling that the stories had their own will to emerge and that she had only to let herself move out of the way of their emergence. She began to talk. "I was a mite older than your boys when my mother passed on. I recall little more than her lying upon her bed endlessly, much as I have been wont to do as of late. 'Tis why I have refused to stay with you. Shan't have them remember their Gran stricken as I am."

"But you'll not die from this!" Eleanor exclaimed. "She had the consumption, did she?"

"As I understood. Father spent many an hour, before and after she died, talking to me about her illness."

"Did it go on long years?" Eleanor asked, turning to find a clean cloth.

"Seems so. In later years, she had only moments of alertness and few conversations. I bear the shame of not abiding by her bed at the end. I was so disturbed by her labored breathing and by then, her cough had a clang and an echo, seeming to declare the emptiness. I knew, even from my distance, 'twas over, that her spirit slipped free with a final violent, rasping purge."

"Mother," Eleanor said, "however did you get on?"

"I hesitate to admit to a certain relief when we were finished with all the long days and nights of nursing and fretting. There was no time that I recall her being well, and by the time of her passing, we knew it must be so. We could willingly let her go." Maggie's eyes had a tremor; she struggled to locate a place to focus, to calm her thoughts.

Softly, Eleanor asked, "You missed her?"

"Missed having a mother, even whilst she lived," Maggie nodded, closing her eyes as Eleanor wound fresh cloth strips around her head. "'Tis only today that I have allowed myself to wonder more deeply how might it have been to have a healthy mother. How would she have taken to this land? I knew only her broken shell. Until this day, I believed that broken shell was all she offered. Finally, I understand, 'twas the portion she was shedding."

Eleanor finished wrapping and tucked the end of the strip under the bandage. She had sliced some of the melon and placed a bowl nearby. When Maggie tasted a piece, she moaned as the cool juice slid over her sore gums.

"I must thank you, Eleanor, for pushing me closer to these thoughts and to the wisdom of the old turtle. On the very same day that I received the turtle totem, early in the morning so long ago at Weiser's farm, I had wandered into a garden behind the house where there was a grave site. Maria, Weiser's daughter who was my age, came outside. We struggled with German and finger signs, until I understood 'twas the grave of Maria's oldest sister, Magdalina, and that her mother and youngest brother had been very sick in the spring as well.

"I recall staring at the mound of earth, in mind of Mother's garden grave at home in England. She had died only months before Maria's sister, but time had taken on a distance with the ocean crossing, more than I knew to measure. I conveyed to her that my mother had also died. Maria sighed, nodding at the mound. I was sad then that Mother had died without meeting the Americans or even sharing in our plans."

"Would that she had improved her health and come along," said Eleanor.

"She could dance to the wild drumming and the native songs. Father claimed she had been a grand dancer," Maggie said. She looked at Eleanor and felt a crust fallen away from her own heart. She wondered if it was perhaps possible to shed her own broken shell while yet alive and allow the two of them to improve their caring for each other. There had been too many years, she thought, of burying her heart along with all thoughts of mother and father.

A quiet moment, ever brief, was interrupted by Eleanor's nervous chatter, nearly tripping over herself as she scurried. "What shall I do first? Would you have me sweep this floor?"

In spite of a faint, unformed image of sitting quietly and holding Eleanor's hands, Maggie heard herself snapping at her daughter. "No. Best to get on your way. Fetch the news from town, I beg you, before another visit."

Eleanor leaned the broom beside the door. "What is there to fetch?"

"Perhaps someone has collected a news pamphlet or some tale of the Congress."

"Mother, let the politicians do their jobs. Your task is to mend," said Eleanor, gathering her wrap.

Maggie tapped the chair arm with her flat palm, "If His Majesty is at risk, my own well-being is threatened as well. His parliament stirs a fight to be fought here among the colonies!"

"'Tis no threat equal to getting yourself riled." Eleanor paused at the door.

Maggie brushed a futile wave toward her. "Go, then. Go," she scoffed. "The Congress will have us in a war and you'll not surmise until the point of a bayonet puts a new crease in your buttocks." Eleanor spun around and flung the door open, marching out onto the porch and slamming the door. Maggie heard a choke of smothered laughter from the other side. A pause felt like escaping air, hissing and rising to a dark surface that was too far distant to see.

ς

The loud noise made me jump, pop open my eyes and race to get my bearings. I'd been sound asleep and Quinn had pulled beside a gas pump at a small market as a black SUV pulled away.

Quinn apologized as she got out of the car. "Sorry, sorry. I was pulling in here, trying to figure out how to do this without waking you, when that guy slammed his door." She nodded at the car driving away. "We're out of gas, though. Had to stop."

I sat up. "It's okay. I need to stretch." I felt heavy, as if I were covered with a thick net. I brushed my jacket when I stood up, then left Quinn at the pump and strolled into the station. I looked around the tiny market for a restroom sign, noticed a small, black man stepping around the corner into the garage. When I peeked inside, the mechanic's shop was dark, empty.

A cashier called out from behind me in the other room. "Can I help you?"

"Uhhh. Looking for a restroom." I spun around. "Was there another guy just here with you?"

"You casing the place or somethin'?" he said, chuckling.

"I thought I saw someone."

He shrugged. "Well, you're headed the right way to the can. If someone else is there, the door'll be locked."

I headed back around the corner where I saw a smudged, white door with the international symbolic stick people side by side, a unisex bathroom. As I reached for the door, something glimmered across the dark shop. A man in blue work overalls bent quietly over a cabinet with his back to me. As I stared at the thin, white curls on the back of his head, he turned.

His dark face shone with sweaty streaks. I said, "Joe! What are you doing here?" I knew it was a stupid question, but nothing made any sense. I was still reeling from the dream of Maggie and Eleanor. I felt dizzy and unprepared for Joe.

He shook his head. "Ah'm jus' here."

"Tell me what's happening," I pleaded as my eyes began to puddle. I wiped at them impatiently. "Tell me, Joe! Am I going crazy?"

He waved his hand, pointing around the garage. "You folks love all a' your machines. You sayin' you don't like my time piece?"

"Time piece?"

Joe's wide grin was unsettling because I felt like I was inside a puzzle and he knew more than he was admitting. "Look close," Joe tapped at a map on the wall. It was a large map of Harrisburg, the state capital. We had apparently stopped in a western suburb. "Over here." His crooked finger stretched slowly across the map from one end to another, crossed though downtown Harrisburg and southeast, near the Susquehanna River. Joe whispered, "Here's your fella. He knows." I peered at the map, looking for a street name or a landmark. Then I heard Quinn's voice in the doorway behind me.

"What are you doing in here?" she said.

I looked over at Joe, but he was gone. My mouth fell open.

"You found a map, huh?" she said. "Don't worry. I picked one up to take with us. Come on. Let's get a snack." She waited by the door and when I didn't move, she called again. "Reed?"

I looked behind me once more, and then walked to the doorway.

Quinn was convinced that we'd find someone at the State Museum and Library who knew about the totem and its meaning. She found the large building easily in the center of town. I barely got inside the doors before restlessness nearly tore my notebook from my pack. On a bench near the second floor lobby, I sat and wrote while Quinn wandered off to find a curator.

Maggie's letter had been writing itself in my head, bursting from my pen with an energy that it seemed she was also feeling:

Dear Eleanor,

Once more, I've been a blunderous boor and given offense. But truly I am appreciative of your care and most especially for this gift of fine paper. I hasten to its use as the tale of meeting the Indians at Tulpehocken repeats itself in my mind, so fresh does it seem. 'Tis nearly boiling from my pen, faster than I can dip the ink.

As the Indians' children ran freely about, I saw three blond haired youngsters at the small stone springhouse, squatting alongside a rock-lined pool. They gathered a pottery crock with a snug hide covering, several melons and a basket of wet greens. I followed them into the kitchen bustling with supper preparations. Missus Weiser, gaunt and dark-eyed, called out orders over a massive table mounded with corn cakes.

I called out a greeting in German to one of the blonde boys. He turned and replied haughtily that he knew English. He was ten years of age, weathered and straight as a corn stalk with a tassel of blond hair poking up from his head. He offered a dry, grubby hand, "Name's Sammy." He pointed out his sister Maria, a girl my age, and his little brother, Freddy.

Sammy and I walked to the outdoor cook fire where several men skinned a deer carcass and hoisted it onto a spit. I tried to be bold and not turn away. They stirred coals to raise a fresh fire as with one arm, Mister Weiser hoisted the deer skin over his head. A tall Indian said something in a catching, clicking language, chants rose and the drumming quickened.

I shivered and thought I must have come to the middle of America, feeling the foreign drum rhythms pulling me with the current of the strange landscape. Alongside Sammy, I found the courage to get closer, saw two white-haired elders passing a long pipe and filling the air with pungent smoke. By dusk, a full feast was at the ready.

The Moravian group stood overlooking as the chief named Canasatego put on a fancy headdress of deer antlers and spoke a trail of words in his native language. Zinzendorf nodded and gave thanks for the meal.

I was at first fearful to taste the venison, having seen the hide and carcass. Others dipped chunks in the oily soup, so I allowed a small taste. 'Twas woodsy and delicious. The cool melons were passed around in runny, red chunks. No one could eat them without a smile. As night fell, the Indians used blankets to fan smoke from the fires to chase away mosquitoes and passed a leather pouch of smelly grease—bear fat, I learned. Shirtless men spread the dark mixture over their chest and arm muscles and smeared it upon their faces. The women liked a runny red sauce that deepened their skin's reddish hue. I understood it to be protection from the insects, but the odour was painful to endure.

When Zinzendorf signaled and complained loudly about the stench, Weiser pulled him aside. I asked Sammy what his father's counsel must be and he mentioned the meetings to be held the following day with all the chiefs. A favourable meeting, Sammy said, would depend on a friendly evening and tolerance of each others' odd customs. Even so, though the mosquitoes were biting, I stayed away from the pouches of rancid fat.

The deer carcass was stripped of its meat, bones carefully taken apart and saved in a leather wrapping. A crowd collected at the larger fire pit when someone coaxed an older man from his blanket. "Swataney," whispered Sammy. "His Oneider name. English say Shickellamy."

The old man had well-defined muscles, though bent-legged and wrinkled. A hide vest over one shoulder was stitched with clumps of beads and shells. His fringed leggings ended at his knees, like an apron. He stood up and sang in a loud, shaky voice. I could fathom no meaning from his words, but I was enchanted by the movements and sounds.

Sammy leaned and said, "He's telling a story of Turtle Island, name of this land, he says." I inched closer to Sammy, appreciating his help. The old man, wrapped in a long, leather cape, hummed and walked in a slow circle as others drummed and shook gourd rattles. Faces glowed with orange firelight, all eyes on the storyteller.

Swataney's low voice vibrated with a chant. Sammy whispered, "He says Turtle is oldest creature...travels earth 'n sea...keeping watch. Every tribe has turtle clan."

"Sky people lived in the air. Sun was unborn, but light shone like flowers on a tall tree," Sammy said as Swataney waved his arm and motioned to the stars, voice hushed, drumming softened. Swataney thumped his chest.

Sammy said, "One day, a woman spoke of mothering children. Her jealous husband uprooted the tree." A young man and woman joined the dance, imitating the uprooting. "Sky woman looked through the hole left by the uprooting. Then he pushed her." I gasped as the youth shoved the woman dramatically.

Sammy nodded. More Indians stood and held the young woman's arms. Sammy said, "Sky woman was falling but people became ducks...helped cushion the fall. Some changed to muskrats and scooped mud on turtle's back." Swataney stooped and picked up a handful of clay in a ball, singing, walking in a wide circle. I don't know how that old man made a lump of soil look so important, but something about his song, his demeanor made the clump seem like a precious gem. "Big sea turtle," Sammy said, grinning. "They brought sky woman to turtle's back where she walked around and around until the tiny earth grew to the size of today."

Swataney placed the ball of soil on the ground and danced around it with a turtle shell rattle. He spread the dirt with his bare feet. Benigna, in front, gathered her skirt and held it from the scattering soil. Weiser stood to explain the dance to the startled Moravians as it ended with a rousing burst of drumming. They smiled nervously and nodded polite praise. Zinzendorf promptly stood up, stretched, and went around the circle shaking hands, saying good night.

I thanked Sammy for his helpful interpretation. He smiled shyly and ran off. I followed the Moravians' quiet row to the tent pitched on a grassy field below the Weisers' house. On the trail, Zinzendorf muttered to the Brothers that ministering to the natives must come before all else. "God-forsaken" and "lost in sin" were phrases I gleaned from their German. The natives' chants went long into the night and I felt the drums filter into my dreams where I danced in circles.

Early the following day, the meeting preparations had begun. By midday, the men moved toward a circle of blankets under a shady sycamore in the yard. The native men wore dignified matchcoats given by the English governor they had met weeks prior, shirtless underneath. One wore leggings instead of a usual loincloth. Small tufts of hair on the sides or tops of their heads were freshly tied with leather thongs or silver clips. Silver bracelets were wrapped around their muscular upper arms.

I stood back, but close enough to witness the event. Missus Weiser was inside her house, the Moravian Sister Nitschman had disappeared and Benigna had departed with Maria Weiser for a walk. As the council got under way, several native women entered the circle, seemingly expected and received with gratitude by their men.

I was feeling less shocked and I enjoyed the natives' drumming. I hoped to hear more stories or songs in rhythm with my beating heart. Of the two native leaders, Canasatego, sixty years, was younger than Swataney though he bore no ordinary signs of aging. A tall and imposing figure, he seemed a most gentle man. They bore a polite organisation in their manner of sitting down to a serious discussion. It held a potency unlike the style of my father's friends' meetings on town policies. The English had a practice of drowning each other's voices with their own howled opinions; rarely did one of them listen to another.

My heart pounded as Weiser stood to interpret. I heard him speak the name of William Penn, apparently raising old bonds of friendship established by the past colonial leader. Brother Zander raised questions about the other colonies' tales of rampages, Indian against settler. Before Weiser could finish translating to the Indians, Zinzendorf interrupted. His German was swift for my understanding at the time, but later, upon asking Sammy, I learned that he had made a request for the Moravian Brethren to be allowed to journey into Indian country to bring the Indian people messages from the Great Spirit. He insisted that Weiser tell them he spoke regularly with the Great Spirit.

After listening politely, the chiefs withdrew and walked to the creek alone. Zinzendorf began to raise his voice but Weiser stopped him, explaining the native customs. He said they live in a world apart from ours and 'tis good manners to go away and spend time with deciding. 'Tis sign of serious consideration, he told the brooding Zinzendorf.

Brother Zander made a comment about rum, fearing the meeting would go nowhere. Zinzendorf then took up this argument. Weiser agreed and said Swataney did, as well, begging for the rum traders to depart the woods.

Zinzendorf and the Moravian men sunk into a prayerful mumble. Weiser retired to his house as the native women gathered pots and trinkets. An old woman among them held a wood splint in the shape of a bow, strung with several fibers secured across the end like warp threads of a loom. She had a bowl of shell beads in her lap and a long needle in her hand. She placed seven beads through the needle and strung them along the width of the beltlike string, running her thread at right angles to the long fibers. A design of purple and white was taking shape.

Suddenly the old woman paused and slumped to the ground, scattering the shells across her lap. I yelped in fright and climbed from behind my bush, stepping tentatively forward. Yards away, the Moravians continued their mournful prayers. I was unsure of whether they had failed to note the collapsed woman or perhaps we were forbidden to step to her aid. The native women rushed to her and patted the old woman's hands and whispered into her ear.

One of the women saw me standing by the bush, watching. My conscience needed no more prompting. I motioned to the nearby springhouse and helped lift the limp, old woman. We carried her to the cool, stone building and set her feet in the stream of water seeping from the overflow trough. She opened her eyes wide and breathed deeply as the other women made exclamations of pleasure and nodded happily.

Missus Weiser's kettles sat in the springhouse pool. With a cup, I poured the punch steeped of tea leaves, a native blend of herbs sticky sweet with maple sugar, and handed it to the old woman. She smiled a wide grin, showing off little stumps of brown teeth. Her earthy colour returned. We sat in silence while the younger women brought her items of comfort or nourishment. I guessed that she was the wife of their old chief.

When the Weisers returned and saw how the heat had affected the old woman, they fetched more cups and pitchers of water. I twirled my skirt and pushed the bonnet off my head to cool myself. We served everyone a cool drink and corn biscuits while the Moravians opened their cache of dried fruit. While everyone was refreshed, I went to the old woman's blanket and helped two young women gather the strewn beads into a clay bowl.

The chiefs returned to the council circle as I hid and prayed Zinzendorf would not force my departure. The women handed me a bowl of shells and indicated that the white beads should be separated into a separate bag.

Canasatego gave the natives' formal reply after their private meeting. It was a complicated series of translations, from Canasatego's language to

Mohawk, which Weiser interpreted into German. Sammy explained to me that Canasatego had commended the Moravian's journey from beyond the sea. He thought their meeting each other at Weiser's home was a sign of the Great Spirit's favor and he welcomed the Moravians into their lands.

Canasatego offered wampum, a belt of beads, with small shells strung in the pattern of connected trees. He handed it to Zinzendorf, who graciously accepted it. Wampum was more than decoration or valuable trade goods, more than a primitive form of writing. The language of wampum was one I have yet to fully understand, though I know 'tis a statement of union. 'Twas some combination of a story and a prayer. They believe the Great Spirit spoke to their ancestors with wampum strings so they continued to pass messages with the beads, whether to friends or enemies, or to their departed spirits. Giving and receiving wampum was a prayerful honour, mending social ills and formalising conversations.

Zinzendorf had been granted an open door to the wilderness. Through the earlier ceremony of the 'Woods' Edge, 'they had cleared our group's eyes and minds of any fatigue or fear of the unfamiliar territory. But through the gift of wampum to Zinzendorf, they had welcomed him on a tour of their world, amongst the deeper woods. Even Weiser seemed impressed and begged to accompany Zinzendorf as his guide. The men passed a pipe and began to feast again. The children came running as I slipped away to watch the trickling creek. I wanted to disappear from an irritated Zinzendorf who might have seen my help as interference.

I sat down between clumps of tall grasses, where the sun rays yet reached. Closing my eyes, I breathed the freshness of the corn fields that stretched out below the hill. When a large shadow passed by, I jumped to see Canasatego standing over me. Then old Swataney stepped alongside him. In the gaze of the old story dancer I remained poised, even though my heart pounded. Swataney held out his hand, dangling the carved turtle totem on a circlet of leather. The carving, decorated with coloured paint, had four short legs poking out.

"Made this for my woman...turtle clan," said Swataney, placing the carving in my hand. "She give to you. No wampum lost, broken." He smiled with a slight curl at the corners of his mouth. Nodding at the turtle, he said, "Promise of safe passage in woods. Turtle clan give aid." Swataney spoke fitting English after years of dealing with white traders. I learned later that tradition required his formal native language at the councils. I admired the carving as tears moistened my eyes. There stood two men, their dark skin *nearly naked, one old and one as tall and large a man as I had witnessed. 'Twas the time in life when I felt most alone and they offered to assure my safety within their native world. I caressed the treasure, examined it closely. The men politely began to back away.*

"Sirs," I said, from habit. They turned back. "I know not how to give thanks but to wear it proudly," I said, slipping it over my head.

"Good," Swataney said, smiling gently. Canasatego nodded and they walked back toward the gathering.

I walked down the grassy banks by the creek, stood in a patch of shade under an apple tree and listened, looked up and down the creek for the turtles. There were none. I felt an urgent desire to show the necklace to my father. I felt like he was missing a rare experience. How would he ever understand America?

Through the distant bushes, two women approached, Missus Weiser and the Moravian Sister Nitschman, who asked if I was lost. When I shook my head, she swaggered closer and locked eyes on the turtle totem.

"What have you?" she asked.

"Swataney gave me a token, a turtle," I said. 'Tis for safe passage in the woods. I helped his...family."

The woman's chuckle rattled and she picked the cord from off my chest, holding it for a moment, and then dropping it with a grimace. "Careful to accept gifts from Indians. They have differing ideas. Younger girls have been dragged off to the woods for wives."

I was shocked at her misunderstanding. Though unsure of her meaning, I trusted she was mistaken. Shaking my head, I said, "No." I held the totem in my hand and claimed, " 'Tis an honour for helping."

She continued, "Brother Mack will tell you about worshiping idols." I held my tongue in anger, having been taught to respect elders, but I narrowed my eyes and peered through her haughty manner.

Sister Nitschman continued, "I suspect the 'honour' is meant to deliver you from misfortune as you act apart from our custom." She tilted her head down to look from the tops of her eyes. "When Brother Ludwig gets you apart from their watchful gaze, the honour will cease."

The dark-frocked woman turned sharply and marched up the hill. I held the turtle protectively. Missus Weiser, who had watched in silence, took the turtle from my clutch. "My English no goot," she said, with a solemn face. "But thees honour. No worry. Turtle ees goot."

When I learned more about the Iroquois, I found that their women were indeed highly honoured within their tribal custom. Children are born into their mother's clan, not their father's. Some women are noted elders who decide which men will sit in the council meetings. I decided then that I would always consider the turtle totem a very fine honour to spite the Sister's unpleasantness. My turtle is 'goot.'

3

The tires rumbled over a patch of rough road. I pulled my head up from my notebook as a small sign with a green arrow pointing toward the Pennsylvania Turnpike caught my eye. I snapped at Quinn. "Where are you going?"

She flinched. We'd been driving in silence for nearly a half hour after leaving the state library. "This goes to 76," she said, "the Turnpike."

"The sign said to go left." I pointed over my shoulder to the phantom sign.

"Must have been for the other direction. This is the right way for eastbound." Quinn shifted gears and accelerated.

"Doesn't look like a freeway entrance," I said doubtfully, seeing a maze of cross streets and few directional signs.

"Hang on," Quinn sounded impatient. Maybe worried. I tried to sit back in the seat and trust her to find the way, but my eyes darted back and forth, noticing a forlorn strip of warehouses and a large empty lot with dried weeds standing waist high around a tall 'for sale' sign. Among the weeds, rows of beat-up cars lined the road, as if they were for sale also, if anyone could ever be convinced to pay money for such rust heaps.

After a few minutes I said, "You made a mistake, Quinn. We should turn around." I knew I sounded pushy.

She squirmed in her seat and exhaled a long sigh. "No," her voice lifted, as if it were a question. "It's going to be dark. We're really lost if I start turning around."

"We shouldn't have stayed at that museum so long," I grumbled.

"What?" her head flipped around. "We went there for clues about your turtle thing. You're the one who glued yourself to a bench and started writing a damn novel."

"I wasn't glued. I would have left any time, but you were chatting it up with some fat, old guy who's probably never even met a live Indian."

"He was quite knowledgeable," Quinn said, defensively.

"He didn't think the turtle had been buried," I said. "Know what? I dug the thing out of the ground. What do you call that?" My voice became increasingly louder and high pitched.

"He meant buried, as in, placed in a grave," Quinn spoke slowly like she would to a child or someone with a hearing impairment.

"God," I breathed. "How would he know that?" A shiver that started in my arms vibrated through my whole spinal cord, top to bottom. I huddled lower in my seat.

"Now what?" It was less of a question than a scoff.

"Something, eghhh." I crossed my arms to squeeze away the shiver. "When I found that turtle, I noticed ashes all over my hands. I was grossed out then, thinking it was industrial junk. What if it was, you know...a body?"

"Damn it." Quinn slapped the top of the steering wheel with her hand. "We're lost. There's no way this goes to the Turnpike." Her nostrils flared, her mouth turned down at the corners. They were slight indicators, but she was definitely irritated. I put all my creepy thoughts on hold, tried to focus on the moment, which appeared to include only a blank stretch of road. Quinn mumbled, "Looks like a shopping area up here. I'll ask."

We drove in silence until we found a place to turn in and ask directions. I was nervous pulling into a rundown neighborhood in a shiny, new car, and at the same time, embarrassed that I felt so nervous. Quinn practically slammed the car door and sauntered into a convenience store, bent casually over the counter and checked a map with the clerk. After a few minutes, she bought a pack of gum, gave him a handshake and strolled back outside. We sat wordlessly while she unwrapped the gum.

"What happened? Why are we fighting?" she asked.

"We're both tired," I said.

She turned around in her seat to face me. "We've known each other for a long time. We've never talked so nasty to each other. I never get mad at you and I'm really mad right now. I know I'm tired. I know I feel the burden of doing most of the driving and getting us around because you're sort of in another zone, but we chose this. We decided to take this crazy trip." She stopped and let her words sink in. "So we have to quit picking on each other. I've seen great teams crumble in the final minutes because, not only are they exhausted, but they start playing against each other, instead of as a team. You get mad at someone on your own team and you defeat yourself. It's that simple."

I hadn't realized I was angry. It was typical of Quinn to find a basketball anecdote to dribble some sense into me. I said, "I admit, I've been depending on you to find our way."

"Yeah," said Quinn. "Except you don't believe I can do it."

I gazed out the window, didn't say anything. I wasn't sure either of us could find our way through the strange mix of dream time and musing. Or was it all a mirage?

"Did you get good directions?" I nodded at the brightly lit storefront.

She started the car and leaned her head back, sighing. "We took a roundabout route, but we were actually going the right direction. The guy admitted the signage is lousy. It's a crappy part of town. I know that's partially why you freaked."

"Sorry."

Quinn grabbed the gear shift and started to depress the clutch when we both noticed a man standing beside the car, bent slightly to peer inside. He waved with pink fingertips that poked through cut slits in his brown cloth gloves. He stretched out a pointer finger and tapped Quinn's window. She promptly pushed the electric window button and lowered her glass.

"Ladies? Got a dollar for coffee?"

Quinn reached into her change cup and dropped four quarters into his outstretched hand. He pushed a 'Pirates' hat back off his melon-shaped forehead and scratched at the skin pressed pink from the band. He smiled politely, gave a pause then let his lips roll back slowly from his slightly discolored Chiclet sized teeth. He nodded, "I thought there was something about this pretty little car, pretty ladies sitting here." Quinn looked over at me, rolled her eyes and reached again for the gear shift. Then the old man said, "Just like a shiny, black turtle, she is..."

Quinn stepped on the brake. My mouth fell open. I leaned around Quinn to get a better look at the man. He was around fifty, short gray strawlike hair poking from the bottom of the cap. His frayed jacket was too thin for these evenings after the sun's warmth had vanished, though he didn't seem chilled. He wore dark brown slacks that a UPS delivery man might have cast off years before. He could be indigent, but certainly didn't seem a dangerous character.

I said, "A turtle?"

He nodded, ""Meant in the best way. I like turtles."

"Me, too."

"Something special," he repeated, grinning at the car. "See the colors, too. Lots of blue, some green. Real pretty." He waved his hand from one end of the car to the other.

"Where are we, Quinn?" I whispered.

"What do you mean? Harrisburg? We're a ways southeast of town."

"Near the river?"

She nodded. "Not too far."

"We're supposed to talk to this guy. This is the one."

"Which one?" she asked.

I reached over and tooted the horn as the man started to walk toward the store. He turned around and I told her to ask if we could buy him dinner. "We can just pull over there." I nodded toward a small cafe a few doors down the street, its windows glowing with a blue neon coffee cup.

He insisted on the spaghetti special, though we offered him anything on the menu. "No, no, dears. They have fine noodles. All I need." He patted his belly, giving no sign of concern for future meals, no glimpse of fear on his face for the fact that only four quarters separated him from being penniless. With his jacket off, his shoulders seemed narrow, but somehow not slight. He looked strong like a woven wire cable; you could see the wires in his neck, his jaw.

Quinn had been quiet, possibly dazed, since we parked the Beetle out front under the blue neon. She was a good sport, followed my lead with few questions. I think she's mystified when I usurp her role as the adventurous one. She watched me just as I watched him; Gibbs, he told us, was his name. We didn't ask if it was first, last or nickname.

Gibbs fairly devoured his dinner without small talk or even an occasional glance at Quinn and me. I can't say he was rude or even sloppy, though it seemed a good guess that he went most days without a full meal, especially one with garlic toast and the green salad I insisted on ordering. He was focused on cleaning his plate of every noodle, every leaf and crumb. Once finished, he relaxed back in the booth to sip his coffee.

"So Gibbs," I said, setting my fork beside my half-eaten grilled chicken. "Do you work? Have a job?"

His eyes twinkled shyly and he shook his head slowly back and forth. "Don't you get all pitiful," he said. "I have my own style of liberty. People here know me. I take care of things for them and they treat me fine." He nodded down the row of booths toward the kitchen. "May get hungry at times, but I won't starve."

"Do you live around here?" Quinn asked.

He nodded again. "Got a warm bed, that is, mostly warm. Not too far." He tipped his head toward the door of the cafe. Then he nodded toward the Beetle outside the window. "Look there," he said. "Car still has the blue light, even though you brought the big one inside."

"What do you mean, the big one?" I asked.

"The big blue," Gibbs dragged the word 'blue' and glanced over our heads. "You got it here with you. Real nice, too. I like that one."

Quinn and I shared a nervous glance, then I thought again of Joe and his words to me back at the garage. Joe had tapped on the map near the river. I remember his words: "Here's your fella. He knows."

Knows what? I decided to take a chance. Pulling the turtle totem from my pocket, I set it on the table in front of him. "You like turtles, don't you, Gibbs?"

He reached out slowly with both hands. "Oh, goodness," he nearly whispered. "What have you done?"

We both watched him pick it up, as if it was a piece of precious treasure, a polished gem. His big chapped fingers held it tenderly, caressed the edges as if they were his lover's lips. His wide eyes moistened, and a soft smile made his face seem years younger. After a moment, he placed it back in my palm, cradled in the warm, crackly embrace of his hands.

"What a feeling, hmmm?" He breathed deeply, as if standing atop a mountain peak, taking in the fresh air. "They say turtles are some of the oldest creatures still alive. That one there feels alive."

Beyond Gibbs' skin, outside his dry edges, I did sense a vibration, an energy that I can only explain in terms like 'aura' that I usually try to avoid. There are several 'New Age' energy healers at the clinic who take care of that department. I tend to stay focused on the muscles and bones. I knew the unusual things that had happened since I had obtained the turtle, but even so, I was startled by his reaction. It was as if he had just popped out of a toaster, with heat waves rippling the air around him.

I said, "We're trying to find out more about it, Gibbs. We're not quite certain what we have here."

He whispered again, leaning close over the table. "What you have is a window. Clear as that."

"A window," said Quinn, flatly.

"Everybody, I mean ev-er-y-body," Gibbs said, "settles inside their box, big walls all around. See it ev-er-y-where. Closed up boxes." He rolled his eyes dramatically and tipped his head side to side. "A few people might go banging on the walls, but nobody tries to get out, unless they go from one box to the other or even the one box that gets put in the ground. Most pay no attention. No, I say most don't know they're in a box."

We stared. I suspected dementia. He reminded me of a bag lady that stood outside my Evanston grocery store, reciting poetry for handouts. The words flowed in an eloquent stream from her mouth, but didn't connect in any way that I could comprehend. Quinn fidgeted beside me. Gibbs sipped his coffee and held his cup up to signal the waitress. As she approached, his voice lowered again. "She gets up every day and does what she did the day before. That's all."

The waitress filled all of our cups. As she walked away, Gibbs said, "Man thinks he knows his job, his house, family. He don't know he's in a box."

Quinn decided to play along. "Sounds like a trap. Is that what you mean by a box, Gibbs? A trap?"

Gibbs shook his head slowly. "Even a dumb animal knows he's in a trap."

Quinn squinted at Gibbs and pursed her lips. "What about drugs? Do drugs fit into this box?" She raised her eyebrows when I glanced at her nervously.

"Oh, yeah," he nodded. "Drugs, alcohol, sex, food, all the obsessions. Fill up the box. Makes us real fat or happy or 'who cares,' huh?"

I still wasn't following, but I wanted to give him another chance to explain while I figured how to apologize to Quinn for our wasted time. The old guy was a nut. "We got distracted," I said. "You started by saying the turtle was a window."

Gibbs became very quiet and serious. I thought he was going to cry. He said, "I tell you that little turtle gives you a chance to see your way out." He shook his head back and forth, slower and slower. "I don't know why everyone goes along. They're lured with any kind of feeling good. Just go to sleep, wake up tomorrow. Might be pouring coffee, might be selling stocks, might be shooting heroin. Don't matter. Money and souls. All the same." Gibbs pushed up the frayed sleeves of his baggy cotton shirt.

I was feeling seriously depressed. But Quinn leaned forward, suddenly interested and asked, "It's all about money, right, Gibbs?"

"No, baby." His dark eyes pooled with moisture. "All about feeling safe. Safe." He hissed the word and tapped on the table next to the turtle. "You don't give your soul away unless you feel safe without it. You got a Subaru? You feel okay. You got a college education? You feel okay. You got a needle full?" He shrugged.

"And the turtle?" I asked skeptically.

"Turtle indeed keeps you safe. You can go out of the box, because the native people who made it, they knew the world without walls. No time, no need to control anything, pin anybody with walls. They believed there was plenty of everything for everybody." He shrugged again. "They once believed."

Quinn asked, "How are you sure the Indians made it?"

"My people came from a fishing village in the north of Ireland. They knew the world without walls. I feel it," said Gibbs.

"La puerta al vaci'o," I said, though it felt like Gramama Inez's voice spilling from my mouth. Quinn and the old man both stared. "Something my grandmother used to say. It means the door to the void."

"You see?" said Gibbs. "Mexican?" I nodded and he said, "Had to have some Indian blood. She knew the mystery."

"Enigma," I said. "She always spoke of 'la enigma.'"

"La enigma," whispered Gibbs. "All over the world, they've tried to put 'la enigma' in a box. Bury it. Silence it. My people were poor. I thought I had to work hard to get ahead. Boss said, "Come on son, come inside these walls. We'll take care of you." Bang, slap on the chains. Inside a box."

Quinn and I were silent. A sadness vibrated around me like the mournful fugue of a loved one. Mmmm. Mama. Sometimes I feel her near me. My Mama, who left this world through a wall. Head first, through car window, then stone. Can I hope that there was a passage? A doorway? Am I allowed to wish that there had been less pain than I have always imagined? Can 'la enigma' restore her in my memories?

The moment of peace was interrupted by Gibbs' loose, rolling laugh, a deep-bellied yank back to our table, our cups and empty bread basket. His body language said, "Come back here and pay attention to what I'm telling you." Out loud, he said, "Black people were not the only slaves." He rolled his head from side to side, like a boat on a slowly churning sea. Other than Gibbs' chuckle, the restaurant was eerily quiet, no glasses clinking or voices humming. Gibbs watched me, so closely that I knew he could sense my desire to turn myself inside out and disappear. I wanted to throw something into the middle of the quiet and shatter it.

I wanted to scream at Gramama to get herself back here and tell me what she had meant, banging pots around in our disorganized kitchen, muttering angrily about the lost grandeur of the ancient people. "Los que el tiempo pesa," she had said, over and over. Those that time oppresses.

Instead of screaming, I stirred my coffee and watched the surface swirl like a snake of blue light, reflected from the neon. "Todos cambia," another of Gramama's wise sayings spun with the light. Everything changes.

ζ

Clop, clop, clop. What awful noise. Maggie peeked through one aching eye, feeling the clock's ticking like nails scraping inside her head. Louder yet, more noise. Once more she heard the clop, clop, clop, coming from out front; that was the noise that awakened her. A large horse was coming up the street. And murmuring voices. The horse stopped nearby and Maggie flinched at the banging of Mister Emory's wooden plank door as he walked outside to greet his guest. She pulled her dark scarf over her eyes and rolled over. Then she recognized the boys' squeals and her headache dove deep into her belly, as if she had swallowed fire.

She sat up and leaned toward the window, then lurched back dizzily, startled at the sight of the wagon loaded high with goods, crates, even a few chickens. Eleanor scurried up the side yard and burst through the door apologetically.

"Whatever happened?" asked Maggie, grimacing. "Tell me softly lest I shatter. All night, I've suffered a throbbing head."

"'Twas dreadful," Eleanor whispered, adding more suspense to her story. "When I returned home last eve, my own three met me with ashen faces, sitting all hushed in the darkened cabin. The men who surmised to assist with the wheat threshing had absconded with nearly all the crop once the threshing was completed. They threatened with guns and promised to return with more mischief if Edmund resisted." She brushed her hair back with trembling fingers. "I'm appalled with myself for encouraging the barter with those strangers."

"You've abandoned the farm?" asked Maggie.

"We slept naught all the night. I was absent at the time of the misdeed, and yet, fear has settled utterly in my bones." She cradled her face in her hands and whimpered, "All is spoiled."

"Now, now," said Maggie. "I beg to fathom. These were the Suke's Run fellows?"

"So they said. They indicated to Edmund an association with the Virginia rabblers. Worse yet, they portend to know us, perhaps observed our dealings."

"Why believe such?"

"They spoke of Croghan by name," Eleanor said. "Told Edmund the Virginia soldiers at the fort would dispute our legal title; said to be restoring the rightful grain to the fort. We would thank them later, they said, for keeping favor with the soldiers who will now be obliged to consider our keeping the farm, as it becomes Virginia territory."

Maggie asked, "They had muskets drawn before the boys?"

Eleanor nodded. "Vile and desperate men they were, to invent such a scheme. They toiled near all the day before making off with the wheat."

"Did you ride out to Suke's Run? Are they known amongst any there?"

"'Twas all a ruse," said Eleanor. "Edmund spoke to each farmer we passed this morn in hopes of uncloaking the thieves and indeed forewarning the neighbors." She paced back and forth across the small room, twirling her muslin skirt with each nervous turn. "One man reported his cows stolen from the field before him, by a different fellow in the light of day. The whole countryside is a-clamor."

The boys ran by the window outside, where the older one suddenly turned around and pushed his brother to the ground. In a gruff voice, he said, "Yuh don't threaten Virginia men, mister." Eleanor looked horrified as she watched him spit an arching globule to the grass by the fence. She bolted through the door and demanded to know what the boys were doing.

"Nothing, Mama," they both looked up with innocent eyes. When asked where their father was, they indicated the back of the house. Eleanor told them to stop acting like ruffians and marched off in the direction they pointed.

Maggie, alone in her room, glanced outside as Edmund walked around from the front of the cabin alongside the weaver. The older man was pointing down the street and jutting his jaw angrily as he talked. She cracked open the window to overhear their words.

"You can't deal with Connolly or his soldiers, Edmund. They're a hindrance." Mister Emory pulled at his suspenders nervously. "Last eve a group of roustabouts bothered the Smiths' place on Ferry Street. Yonder. I heard shouting down the road, then breaking glass." As Edmund craned his neck, Emory continued. "I hastened out to check on the commotion. Witnessed four, perhaps five men hurling stones through the windows with all their might."

"Where be the Smiths?" asked Edmund.

"Over to Staunton. Short visit is what I heard. I ducked out of sight for fear of being followed, or receiving the same hostility." Emory motioned to the back of the cabin. "Then I saw the thieves in uniform! They walked out with trunks full of the Smiths' belongings. The Smiths have not abandoned the place. They aim to return!"

Edmund's face bore deep lines of concern. He said, "Virginia soldiers? We can trust none of them?"

"Not a muckle," said Emory. "Nor Connolly. Tell not a one you've quit your farm."

Maggie heard a woman's voice call from the front of the cabin and the men walked toward the porch. Maggie had a few minutes to fret about how the story would affect her son-in-law's decision to move into town. Perhaps the turmoil had reached a point where no one was safe in town or out. She wetted the cloth on her forehead and leaned back against her pillow, then heard shuffling and voices outside her door in the weaver's hallway.

It was Eleanor's voice. "'Tis not a good day for her," she was saying. "She's having the headache...had it for days, she says."

Edmund asked, "She's wakeful? Headaches aside, she must be told." He asked her to send the boys to hunt for scraps of wood to stack on the Emorys' porch. Then he knocked lightly and pushed the door.

"Pity you're feeling badly," Edmund said as Maggie rolled over in the bed, squinting through her least pained eye. "Eleanor told you of our misfortune at the farm," he said, settling into the rocking chair. "The boys are frightened...truth be known, we're all frightened."

"Eleanor told you we aim to move into town." He shifted nervously in the chair. "After the morrow, we aim to move into the Emorys' cabin. Missus Emory has taken a slight ill, enough so they'll depart to Lancaster for winter."

Maggie sat up when she heard the news, catching the rag as it slid from her forehead.

Edmund continued. "Appears to be peril everywhere about the town. 'Tis time we're all together," he said, decisively. Eleanor walked in from the hallway, followed by Mister Emory. "The Emorys want no one taking note of their absence," said Edmund, looking back at the older man.

Emory nodded at the two women. "I cannot risk my looms being stolen nor pillaged. "'Twould be a great benefit to us, truly, if you moved your family into our cabin. We'll mention our leave to no one. With distractions aplenty, an old couple should go unnoticed."

"What of those who visit your shop for the woven goods?" asked Maggie.

"I have a surplus to bide some time. Those bringing their own woolens must leave an order," Emory rubbed the top of his hairless head, squinting. "Once we're to Lancaster, I shall send you an apprentice. He can work by day in the shop and bed down there at night. 'Twill leave you folks the run of the main cabin."

Maggie reached out for Mister Emory's arm. "Will the Missus fare well on a long journey?"

He moved closer still and confided, "She refuses to see any doctor west of Harris' Ferry. Leaves little choice. She suffers so from the catarrh; it pains her as well."

Edmund stood up, seeming tall next to the tiny old weaver. "Lancaster will suit her," he said. "And we're fortunate to have a refuge near Maggie." He rubbed the sides of his chin and watched Eleanor's face soften. "I'll ride out to the farm by day and finish chores. Come spring, we'll settle an account of the land with the Virginians."

"I beg you to use caution, Edmund," said Emory. "I intended to take my complaints to Connolly this very morn; found him in that odorous room up the stairs at Semple's Tavern. Several fancy businessmen were there, puffing their pipes, leaning over a table barely large enough for the map spread across."

"What map? Did you see?" asked Edmund.

"Didn't have a need. Connolly dragged a farmer by the arm before the businessmen. Said to his investors, 'any number of ploughboys like this'n be yearning to abandon his little farm parcel and move to better land. Kaintuckee country is fertile, to be sure.' That's what he told them. Told them Colonel Washington himself had been in that very chair, expressing interest."

Maggie scowled. "Kaintuckee, is it? The Virginians are offering parcels of land further west. And after the Quakers have squeezed their pockets, why wouldn't an offer of free land make a man take up arms against the Penns?" She had been worried about a pending fight since hearing that the British Parliament had censured the colonies for barring the import of tea and sugar.

"'Tis worse yet," said Emory. "In Massachusetts, they rebelled against taxation. The Crown has taken away the elected assembly and independent town meetings."

"'Tis too severe," Maggie shook her head.

"'Tis the very repression the citizens argue. They'll not allow it," said Eleanor.

"'Tis already forsook," Emory said, nearly whispering. "I want the Missus to fret naught, but 'tis true; thousands of people, armed and unarmed, prevented the judges from entering the court."

"Emory! You're saying the local people cast out the British governors?" asked Edmund.

"'Tis done. County after county," nodded Emory.

Maggie's heart pounded and she struggled to take a deep breath. Her fingers clenched the muslin neck of her dress as she choked back fear. She caught the flicker of a worried glance pass between Edmund and Emory. Edmund said, "We have more than a border skirmish to await."

Casting her eyes downward, Maggie saw the sun speckles dance across the floor, changing color and shape while the breeze whipped the tree branches sideways. She told everyone to leave her room. She needed rest. Eleanor squeezed her hand and they filed through the door into the main cabin. Maggie's head fell back against the pillow as she stared at the floor beside her bed. It seemed that the lights were lining up, sending a colored ribbon over the pine planks.

ζ

"Oh, God." I pressed my forehead with two fingers. My coffee cup sat on the table in front of me. The old guy, Gibbs, was smiling, his light gray whiskers sprouting like fuzzy specks on his cheeks.

He said, "What is it? You look surprised."

I was unable to speak. I just stared at his dark, swimming pool eyes.

He nodded, "You've been through the window, huh? I've seen that look before."

Quinn leaned forward beside me. "Did you, Reed? Right here?"

I reached out and pinched her fleece sweater in my fingertips. I asked Gibbs, "It can just happen like that? Was I sitting here for an hour like a zombie?"

He chuckled. "Honey, I don't suppose your coffee's even cooled. Maybe a minute or two, I'm thinking you're quiet. But that's it. See? Time has less rules than we think." He puffed his cheeks and blew a mouthful of air. "I need to be thanking you ladies for your kindness. I'll say good night," he said, reaching abruptly for his jacket.

"Now?" I felt my heart quicken. "What am I supposed to do, Gibbs? What if I need to come back and talk?"

"We're all done," he shook his head. "Told you all I know."

"You're just going to leave?" I couldn't believe he had his coat on so quickly and was scooting out of the booth. "What is it? This scares you?"

He stopped at the edge of his seat, looked back at me. "Baby," he said, "You're looking at the one who's not scared. You're have to get on with it and do as you're gonna do." He pulled his cap down firmly, bowed slightly and laid his hand on Quinn's shoulder. "I'm truly delighted. Enjoy yourselves." Then he was out the door and gone.

Quinn glanced over at me uneasily as she gathered her jacket and the check. "We have to get going, too, Reed."

"I know," I mumbled. "Hey, we're a team, right? Let me drive?"

"I'll look at the map. We need to find a place to stop for the night. The closer we get to Reading, the less we have to drive tomorrow to my game."

We got a late start the next morning after a wonderfully relaxing, dreamless sleep. Quinn stopped in the lobby of our little roadside inn to ask about breakfast places. Beside the lobby counter was a wooden stand with area brochures and maps. My eyes landed immediately on a title, 'Conrad Weiser's Homestead.' "Oh my God. Conrad Weiser," I said.

The cashier didn't even look up from her paperwork. She said, in a droll voice, "Our local historical celebrity, except if you didn't take Pennsylvania history in school, you may never have heard of him."

Quinn said, "I took Pennsylvania history, but I didn't recall his name. We were just acquainted a few days ago." The cashier looked up.

I asked, "How far is this homestead from here?" We had hours before Quinn had to show up at the Sycamore Catholic High School gym.

"Right off the highway. Probably a fifteen-, twenty-minute drive."

"Quinn," I begged. "Can we go? We don't have to stay long."

"Of course we have to go," she agreed. We ate a quick, delicious breakfast at the local pancake house. Their coffee was great, but I didn't need any additional stimulant. I was hyper and chatty all morning, filling Quinn in on the chaotic times in Pittsburgh. I told about Edmund moving the family into town as if they were our friends or relatives or at least soap opera characters that we discussed regularly. She nodded and asked a few questions when the signs for Weiser's place started to appear.

"My God. This is incredible!" Weiser's Cocalico Valley followed a gentle rolling curve with colorful tree-covered hills, one after another, displaying diminishing shades of orange and green in the distance.

"Imagine how remote this must have been a few hundred years ago?" Quinn said. When she turned into the long drive I asked her to go slowly. I squinted my eyes to block out the view of telephone lines and manicured lawns. It seemed amazingly familiar. Quinn pulled up beside a large white barn and parked the car. I hopped out and walked toward the stone house, painstakingly maintained as an historical landmark. On the front lawn I stopped and pointed down the hill from the house. "There's the springhouse," I told Quinn. "But it used to have more of a stream flowing out below. That's where Maggie splashed the old Indian woman with water...Swataney's wife." I pointed, "The sycamore meeting tree would have been over there."

My knees buckled and I sat on the grass in front of the rock terrace wall. I stared at the neat stonework, the freshly painted door and white window shutters.

"It's really here," said Quinn.

"It is," I nodded. "It's different. Cleaner or neater or something."

"Pretty amazing, when you think it's been here over two hundred years."

There was no one around to give us a tour or open the museum. Again, we were off-season during the week. But I liked walking around, peeking in windows, traipsing through the gardens. We saw a flagpole marker with an inscription for Weiser...born on November 2nd, also my dad's birthday. It occurred to me that my dad also knows several languages.

Quinn pointed across the lawn. "Look over there. It's a statue." We walked through the garden and over to a large boulder where a bronze Indian reached to the sky.

"He was a hunk," exclaimed Quinn.

"I think that's his glamour shot," I chuckled. "Of course, Swataney was an old guy before Maggie met him." The muscled Indian statue honored the meetings between Shickellamy, the English name for Swataney, and Conrad Weiser with their aim of establishing peaceful relations in the area between the natives and the colonial settlers.

I held the turtle totem up in the same pose as the Indian's outstretched arm. "So we're safe with this, are we, Swataney? But where are we supposed to go?" The only answer was the rustle of a slight breeze in the treetops and the chattering of a few birds.

Quinn squatted on the ground and sighed, "I sure do feel safe here. It's the most tranquil place I think I've been in ages."

I put the turtle back in my pocket. Through the thinning tree branches, I could see cars passing on the highway beyond. "I suppose we should head back out. I don't want you to worry about your game."

"Too late," said Quinn. "I'm already worried. No, this is where I'd like to stay." I spun around as she settled back against the rock. "Seriously," she said, "I don't want to leave."

I sat down next to her. She was staring down the hill, where Turtle Creek flowed into the valley. "What's up, Quinn?" I asked.

"Nerves, I guess," she shrugged.

"That's a new one! You?" I had always thought my friend had nerves of steel.

"It's an old one. I have anxiety attacks, too. OK, maybe not like yours. But I do. I just don't talk about it."

"Prove it. When's the last time you had one?"

"The idea of flying here gave me some trouble," Quinn said.

"No, that doesn't count. That's everybody."

"OK. Well, two months ago someone invited me to go to the beach and while we were in the water, I felt something brush against my leg."

"You're kidding me," I said. "Tell me what I'm missing. I thought you were excited to watch the basketball game."

She fidgeted back and forth against the rock and had a genuinely nervous manner. "You know, when the game's over, I'll talk to the girl's coach, probably her parents, too. They're going to ask me tons of questions."

"So? You have an answer for everything." She was silent. A furrowed line pinched deeper between her eyebrows. I probed. "So what's the question? What is it that you think you can't answer?"

She sighed and began pulling at blades of grass. "People who send girls off to college, especially to be involved in sports, want to know things. Like, will the coaches pay attention? Are they watching out for their innocent daughter? Are there gay girls on the team? Are there staff who are lesbians?"

"Wait a minute. Wait a minute. Where is this coming from?" I asked. She looked exasperated, like I was supposed to know already. I said, "Are you afraid they're going to ask you if you're gay?"

"Point blank. What would I do? I hate lying." She bit her lower lip and convinced me that she was near tears.

I felt terrible for her. I thought she had always seemed self-assured and confident. I hadn't realized the burden she carried. "Quinn, I feel like a dope. I had no idea you had these worries. I always thought you were happy being a lesbian."

She turned her head away, but not before I saw her eyes fill. "It makes me so mad," her voice trembled. "I *am* happy. But at work, my life's a complete secret. You know, always off to meet 'a friend,' having a date with 'someone,' that sort of thing."

"I know it's a Catholic college, but I thought you all were everywhere. There are lots of gay Catholics. Isn't there anyone else on the staff?"

"There's one woman I suspect, but she nearly runs from me. Which, of course, is why I suspect. I haven't gotten to know her or anyone else very well. I thought I was okay with it, but it's been eating at me lately."

"What about when they hired you? What's their general feeling about gays?"

"Most places I've worked just look the other way. Nobody asks. I never talk about it, at least not before I know people pretty well."

"Don't ask. Don't tell."

"Right. Keeps everybody happy."

"We haven't come very far," I said, looking across the gardens at the stone house from an age before highways or cars. I thought about the interpreter, Weiser, and his career of negotiations between people of different backgrounds.

"Why do you think the parents are going to ask?"

"They'll ask because my parents did," she said. "Whenever they talked to a scout or coach. The first time, I almost died. I'm sure I turned every shade of red, probably with a big scarlet 'L' glowing on my forehead."

"You knew back then?" I asked. "In high school?"

"I was starting to wonder, but I hadn't talked to anyone about it. When my parents asked those questions, I wanted to curl up and disappear." Quinn poked at the ground with a stick.

"Your parents knew before you did?"

Quinn smiled. "After I told my mom, she said she had wondered since I was a little kid. I reminded her about the college questions. She didn't remember it the same at all. She says they were looking at coed colleges and were asking about housing. She didn't recall being concerned about my teammates or coaches." Quinn laughed and said, "Before long, they were busy bailing my little brother out of jail. They forgot their worries about me."

"Quinn," I said quietly and waited until she looked up, "I think you're taking this too personally. I think it would help for today, if you just backed off personally and became the school's representative. Just let yourself answer any questions from the school's point of view."

"Oh oh," she said. "That might scare me worse."

"Seriously," I said. "I'm the parents now. I say to you, 'Uh, we're concerned about our daughter being influenced by lesbians on the team or staff.'"

Quinn laughed. "That makes me feel stupid."

"Come on, you're a player. Play with me."

She paused, took a breath, then said, "Okay. Let's see. We like the role of an extended family. We expect all of our staff and students to act responsibly and we also try to create an atmosphere of support. If your daughter is met with any uncomfortable situation, I feel confident that she'll find the guidance she needs."

"Well," I said. "Nicely non-committal. Was that so bad?"

She shook her head. "But what if they ask about me?"

"Okay. What would you say, not from you personally, but from the school?"

She sighed. "I guess I'd say that none of the staff discusses their personal lives and that's one of the ways we keep the focus on the girls."

"That's true," I said.

"It's such bullshit. What do they think is going to happen? No straight girl is going to want to become a lesbian just because she has a gay teammate or coach. And if they have a gay kid, that kind of repression can lead to really unhealthy choices. It can twist your mind to always need to hide or pretend."

"So listen to yourself," I said. "Maybe you need to look at how much you've been hiding."

"Damn it, Reed. It's not a comfortable place to be broadcasting that I'm gay."

"Why don't you work someplace where you don't have to hide? That's all I'm saying."

"Well let me have that turtle and I'll fly through time another few decades. Maybe it won't be an issue then in women's basketball!"

Her anger hit me like a stick. I realized how much she had been impacted by her own hiding. I said, "I don't blame you for being angry, Quinn. I've never thought much about the social consequences. But I understand that it isn't fair."

"Right."

"The world might be too big for you to change all by yourself. But some of this seems to be about you holding yourself back. Maybe you can do something about that." I squeezed her hand. "I'm with you. Remember?"

"Thanks, Reed," she said. "Just help me get through this day, okay?"

We walked out past the phantom cornfields that had become rolling lawns and rose gardens. We crossed circles of ground where Indians had danced and where Maria had shown Maggie her sister's grave; where Maggie remembered her mother who died before she came to America. We took one last sweeping glance at the narrow creek meandering down the hill where Swataney had bestowed the turtle totem upon young Maggie. Missus Weiser had assured, "Turtle is goot."

According to Quinn's statistics, Sycamore High School had one of its lowest scoring games that afternoon. But her girl was a star defender and the other team wound up even lower. The game was wild with strong defense, lots of rebounding and fouls with terrible free throw shooting. Quinn watched the square jawed Pennsylvania girl run up and down the court. I sat beside Quinn in the stands and looked over her shoulder as she jotted notes. The girl was definitely a star, her shaggy brown hair flipping in all directions as she kept track of the whole court.

"We need good rebounding," said Quinn. "She's everywhere. Look at those long arms."

"She doesn't seem fearful of anything," I noted. Neither were her parents. Quinn's fears were wasted on the plump, pale couple that eagerly chatted after the game. They had some concerns about Chicago and city life, but from the pride they beamed toward their daughter as she jogged out of the locker room, we decided they had invented unconditional love. The coach wanted to make sure the girl went where she'd get to play right away.

"She's looking at schools that are serious about their women's programs," he said. "I don't buy into any 'man's game' stuff. I know my history. Women were in the game within a month of its inception."

"Good for you," smiled Quinn, her relief obvious only to me. "That's what we aim for. We keep the bench strong by giving them lots of attention, both practice and playing time. I'm not the one who makes decisions," she said to the girl's parents, "but your daughter looks very strong." Quinn glanced at the player who was nodding and smiling assuredly.

Quinn sat for awhile answering their questions while I walked out to the concession stand and got a bottle of water. The crowd had nearly departed and players were beginning to string from the locker room past the gymnasium. One of the security guards got out of his comfortable padded armchair and waved to me.

"I gotta check the doors," he said. "May as well be comfy if you're waiting." I thanked him and sunk into the seat, the kind that tips back and swivels with your weight. I heard a squeal from the concession girl as she waved at some smoke pouring from the popcorn machine. Her laughter assured me that it was nothing serious and I leaned back and closed my eyes, wrinkling my nose as the smoke odor wafted past.

The smell reminded me of a few failed attempts to cook dinner when I was a youngster...Saturday nights, when Miss North was out of the house and my dad was not home from work. I baked a casserole once. Another time I tried to fry a chicken and heated the oil too hot. I was distracted by a pot of water boiling over, making a mess. I didn't see the smoke pouring out under the frying pan lid. Dad walked in the back door and yelped, covering his nose with his handkerchief. His eyes were full of panic and pain. I turned off the heat and we opened the back door, waving at the smoke with a kitchen towel.

ζ

Someone else was there in the kitchen. It couldn't be Mama. I strained my eyes, stinging from the smoke, saw the flames flickering beneath the pot. Ahhh. It's Maggie. She was stirring a pungent mixture in a kettle. Must be the Emorys' part of the cabin. It had larger rooms, a big fireplace. Maggie was concerned that the couple had departed so hurriedly. They rode out of town in the dark of the morning with an oilcloth strapped over two trunks on their buckboard. Edmund, Eleanor and the boys had ridden with them out to the farm.

Edmund had wanted the farm to appear occupied. There had been discussions of stringing a laundry line of old work clothing next to the cabin where it faced the road and leaving stacks of firewood visible to anyone who rode near. A few chickens left to roam about the yard would add activity. They would leave extra straw and feed in the coop. They were going to bring the other chickens and the equipment they would need for grooming and feeding the horse. There was more winter squash than they could take on one unremarkable wagon load meant to attract no attention. The squash would remain stored in barrels in the stable where it had already been passed over once by thieves. They would bring a trunk of clothing and blankets and several bins of flour, maple sugar and cornmeal.

Maggie left her kettle to simmer over the coals and sat down to rock, pulling the blanket snug around her shoulders. She closed her eyes and hummed, thought of the Emorys who had opened up their back room when she arrived in Pittsburgh years before and made it feel like home. They never treated her like an old woman. She was but several years their senior. They understood that she needed some parcel of independence, needed to make a contribution, even one as simple as spinning threads. She would miss them, she thought, as she removed some of the ledger paper they had left her from the box on the table. She filled her pen with the last drops of ink in the bottle and began to write.

She woke hours later to the clatter of Eleanor coming in the cabin's rear door, complaining of the odor as she entered the parlor and peeked into the kettle.

"'Tis crushed nutshells," said Maggie. "I'm in need of fresh ink. 'Tis yet light brown, but another day will darken it, surely."

"Gran!" squealed Morton, running inside. "'Tis a foul odor!"

"Less foul than some. I've smelled the bitter powder the Shawnees rubbed into their skin paintings. Those fellows boil putrid herbs."

Edmund and Whitney were settling the animals in the weaver's shed. As they came in the door, Eleanor stopped them and brushed hay from their jackets before hanging them on pegs. "The Emorys trusted their home to our care," she said, "and I aim to keep it tidy."

Maggie watched Whitney stoke the small fire in the fireplace that opened wide along the wall in the middle of the house. He made no comment on the smells coming from her kettle. Behind the fireplace wall was a large bedroom sharing the chimney for its smaller fireplace. Edmund brought a candlestand from the bedroom and handed it to Morton, asking him to follow him to the weaver's shop facing the street. With two candles in the windows, any marauders prowling about the town looking for abandoned cabins might move on.

Maggie pulled her ink kettle from the fireplace as Eleanor lowered another pot over the flames, filled with water and pieces of chopped orange squash. While the pot boiled, Edmund lit a fire in the bedroom fireplace. The boys had a loft room over the parlor with no stove or fireplace, but as the parlor warmed, the chill faded. Their straw mattress was raised off the floor in a box frame and when he stood upon it, Whitney bragged to his grandmother, he could see out the tiny window over the angled roof to a portion of the street. Houses nearby had lights in the windows and trails of smoke lifted from their chimneys.

Fire had burned the clay lining of the fireplace and showed outlines of chimney rocks. A low bake-oven door opened in the corner, level with the hearth where black iron tools were propped. A large kettle hung on a trammel, an iron lift that could be moved to varying heights. Skillets and a waffle iron hung from hooks. The kettle Maggie used for her ink sat on its own tripod stand in the corner and was mostly used for dying and leaching.

"Boys! Supper!" called Eleanor. She was mashing squash and spooning it onto crockery plates. Cold biscuits and salt pork lay on a platter in the middle of the table. They sat and bowed their heads as Edmund murmured a quick blessing. As they ate, Whitney asked Maggie to tell them a story.

Maggie finished her biscuit and sat back in her chair. She said, "As I prepared to make ink, I recalled some of the native boys from my first visit to Weiser's farm who were unsettled by the written words. Do you remember when Sammy Weiser interpreted the story of Turtle Island for me?"

The boys nodded. She continued, "He and I later sat by the creek with two young Indian boys and Sammy asked what became of Sky Woman after the earth grew on the turtle's back.

"They told about Sky Woman's children, one named Sapling who was gentle and one named Flint, who had a hard mind, like stone. Wherever Sapling ran, fresh soil and trees sprung up in his footsteps, birds and animals followed and rivers flowed in two directions, coming and going. Then came Flint with his hard mind. The rivers changed to one direction with many falls and rocks. Sapling created fish then Flint put tiny bones in them to make them difficult to eat." Maggie leaned forward, widening her eyes. "Then Sapling made humans out of the earth."

"Gran, they said such?"

She nodded. "Sapling put his own mind in each and reminded them that as children of Sky Woman, they have power to create. But Flint gave them part of his cruel, hard mind also," Maggie whispered. "Then Flint and Sapling disappeared leaving a divided pathway of light in the sky. Sky Woman fell on the fire and flew up on the smoke, crying, 'You cannot follow me. Send your thoughts on the smoke from fires.'"

"This is what the pipes are for," Edmund added. "Sending prayers."

"What has this to do with the written words?" asked Whitney.

"While Sammy interpreted the boys' story, I was writing down the words," Maggie said. "When I repeated some of the story, the oldest boy was startled. He said, 'Make words speak again.'

"I read his words about the smoke and the boy stopped me. He said, 'With a quill from a goose held in your fingers, you can tell my words to stay on this birch bark?' He was unsettled because his eyes were as good as ours, but he saw only scratched lines, no words. 'How can little marks make sound?' he asked. 'Is your memory keener than ours?'"

"The boys were insulted and marched away, but Sammy followed them and told them they remember all their stories for many generations and that their eyes were as good as ours. He told them that some day they may choose to see words in the scratched lines."

Maggie noticed her grandsons' faraway eyes and wondered if they could imagine not being able to read or write. She also wondered if they could imagine a story that came to life each time it was recited. She was pleased that they liked to hear her stories and thought of talking to Edmund later to encourage him to tell them his own stories as well.

"Grandmother, when you went to school, was it only for girls?" asked Whitney.

"Indeed. My classes were for girls, but the boys took classes as well at the Gemein'haus, a busy building then, yet under construction." She told them about her friend Benigna, the count's daughter, who returned to Bethlehem from Weisers' farm, put on fine dresses and became the schoolmistress of the Moravians' School.

"What about Sammy?" asked Morton.

"Sammy stayed at Tulpehocken, but some weeks later, in the fall, Conrad Weiser arrived at the school with his daughter, Maria, whom I had awaited anxiously. Weiser explained their tardy arrival with a tale of riding into the woods to rescue Count Zinzendorf's mission party from a Shawnee village on the Susquehanna where he had found the count stripped of his silver buttons and buckles and begging for his life."

"What happened?" begged both little boys in unison.

"Weiser said the count had insulted the guides, told them they smelled rotten, and camped far from the village, by chance atop the Indians' secret silver mine. The Shawnees thought they were there to rob them. Zinzendorf gave up his silver trinkets, intending a peaceful gift, but they misunderstood and thought he wanted to gather more treasure from their secret mine."

"Weiser tried to acquaint the count with the strange customs of the Indians, but in an arranged meeting, the chief declined the proposal of a missionary in their village. He said he liked the Indian way of life and had no desire to learn to pray with words."

The boys were quiet as Maggie let that idea sift through their thoughts. Then they asked, "Did the count go back to Europe then?"

"Oh, no," said Maggie. "There were more mission trips for himself and the group. That only set them afire to save the Shawnees from 'Satan's grasp,' as he described. Zinzendorf complained upon their odors, their indigestible corn and their aversion to wearing breeches. He nominated a large group of missionaries to carry on their work amongst the natives."

"And you were nomimated?" Morton stumbled over the word.

Maggie shook her head. "I was yet a schoolgirl. Maria and I had our lessons. Her English improved, as did my German, and we were fine friends. We bunked next to each other at night and during the day, aside from studying, we explored the town. The villagers rumored that Zinzendorf's effort to unify the Christians had been met by a counter effort from the Lutherans. Unity was fraught with disagreement."

"Did he stay or go?" asked Eleanor.

"By the following winter, he and Benigna retreated to Germany, leaving me without the guardians my father had assigned. I had heard nary a word since Father's departure."

The quiet pause was interrupted by Whitney's soft voice, "When did you hear, Granmama?"

Maggie thought she could feel a soft layer of snow falling on Bethlehem. She felt the merriness of a winter festival, though as if in a room next door, separated by a thick wall from the musicians' boisterous tunes and dancing feet. In her own room, it had felt dark and somber. She recalled Maria packing bags when her mother became ill again, and the stinging sadness of another friend's goodbye. A few short weeks later, her new teacher, Sister Agatha, brought her to the hallway where Brother Anton waited.

Maggie remembered the winter storm. Brother Anton had wet patches on his shoulders from his journey to convey the news. Her Father's ship had sailed from England and had not been received or observed by any port as yet. To her family she said, "I held out hope for many months, but finally received a letter in the spring." She sent Whitney to reach under the bed for her bag and find a small leather pouch. When he returned, she took a fragile fold of paper from the pouch and held it up for the boys. "'Tis one of the items I've saved all these years," she said. "From the ship company, dated the fourteenth day of May, 1743. It reads:

> *"Dear Miss Hadlan,*
>   *We have confirmed the unfortunate demise of our ship, Atlantica, her crew and passengers. A passing ship bound for England reported coming upon her mid-sea and fully afire, prior to sinking. They plucked one man from the sea, who survived only hours, claiming that pirates shot most on board, including your father, Daniel Hadlan. The ship was sunk in high seas, therefore unsalvageable.*
>   *Our deepest regrets for this personal misfortune."*

Maggie turned the letter over in her hand, absently holding it up to smell the oily ink. The still pungent odor carried memories of a biting springtime wind and torrents of rain making gullies in the dirt paths of the village.

"The additional misfortune," she said, "learned months later, was that my uncle George, my only other relation, was on board the ship as well. I threw quite a fitting tantrum upon the sister who bore that news, earning myself a reputation of hot vapors that I never outgrew among the Moravian brethren."

As Maggie's hand with the letter rested on her lap, Whitney reached over to run his finger along the edge. He asked, "'Tis the sum of your possessions from Grandfather?"

Maggie nodded. "Ummm, that and the old bag. There was no salvage from the ship and nothing left behind unsold in England. I had another trunk and a few finer linen skirts and dresses, by then outgrown, and was obliged to pass them along to the younger girls."

"Was the ship not insured?" asked Eleanor.

"The company said 'twas a private charter, beyond their responsibility." Maggie placed the letter back in the pouch and gave it to Whitney who carefully carried it back to Maggie's room.

"I had another year of schooling due, but the choices beyond that were to stay in Bethlehem and take a position among the brethren, travel to a Philadelphia home for orphans, which surely posed hard work and no rewards, or leave and make my own way. I decided to cast my lot with the people who had been kind to me."

Maggie thought it best not to mention the schemes she had plotted as a youngster to escape Bethlehem or her letters to Weiser asking his help to place her in a nursemaid job like Maria's. When Maggie gave thought to the day she actually disguised herself and ran off from the Moravian town, she became melancholy. She excused herself, stood from the table, patted each boy's head and blew a kiss. She shuffled slowly toward her door, begging her feet to deliver her to her private refuge. Each step felt like she dragged her whole body, until she pushed open the door and collapsed on her bed.

ζ

A phone was ringing. I reached sleepily for the muffled musical vibration of Quinn's cell phone. I can't say why it was in my pocket. She'd carried it since leaving home and used it occasionally to check office messages. Hesitant to answer her business call, I examined the lighted caller ID viewer and recognized my father's home number. I pushed the button and answered.

"Reed, my girl, is that you?" His voice was grainy and tired.

"Dad?" I hate my squeaky voice when I'm surprised. "What are you doing?"

"I had a message to call you at this number. Where are you, baby?"

"Did Quinn call you? This is her cell phone. But we're in Pennsylvania.

She's scouting basketball players and I'm sitting outside the gym waiting for her." I immediately wished I hadn't described myself as such a flunky.

"Why are you with Quinn?" his voice always flattened when he said her name. He had disliked Quinn since we'd started running around together.

"Pop, you know Quinn's working for Loyola. I needed a break from work so I drove over here with her to see some basketball games." I'm thirty-five years old and explaining to my father like I need a permission note.

"Well, I didn't like hearing her voice on my machine," he grumbled. "Tell her it worried me. Sounded like you were in some trouble."

"No trouble, Pop. We were talking about you today. We came across a historical guy with a birthday the same day as yours." I'm good at switching gears. He usually enjoys being the focal point.

"Historical, huh? Is that ancient history?"

"Touchy, are you? What's happening for your birthday? It's only a few days away."

"I'm inviting a few dozen of my closest friends to join me on a Caribbean cruise." He poured on the sarcasm.

"Really, Dad. Any plans?"

"Nope."

"Are things getting back to normal there, I mean, after 9/11?" I had called him the week of the terrorist attacks and he said his practice had gone flat; people were skipping their appointments. Finally, we had something in common.

"A-Okay," he quipped, cheerily. "Listen, hon. If you're well, I'll carry on. Came home to oversee yard chores. We had a beaut of an afternoon."

"Oh," I said. "Fine. We can talk later."

"Reed, I wish you weren't mixed up with Quinn. I always thought she was queer."

I felt my face flush. Heat? Anger? A long history of impatience with his bigotry? "Dad, don't say that. You sound mean."

"I'll get mean if she tries anything funny."

"Excuse me. Did you notice that I'm thirty-five? I don't need my dad's protection anymore. Besides, you're being ignorant." I couldn't believe how quickly I wanted to get off the phone with him. I was on the verge of saying something horrible. "I gotta go."

"Be good, sweets."

I blew a puff of frustration. "Reed, Dad. Call me Reed, will you?"

We ended our conversation as Quinn exited the gym door and bounced down the hallway. When she saw her phone in my hand and my face full of fury, she slowed her steps and grimaced.

"How could you?" was all I said.

4

"It's been such a strange few days," Quinn said. "I thought you needed to talk to someone. I didn't know who else to call." She was driving down the dark highway. The night sky was overcast so it darkened the winding highway. There was no starlight or moonlight, only the Beetle's headlights guiding us toward our little inn.

"Not him."

"I know he has his faults. But he's your family. Your only family, Reed."

"Not really," I said. "But he's the only one you know. Why are you so worried? What do you think I'm going to do?"

"I'm not sure. This whole thing has me a little crazy. I guess I've felt jittery ever since we met Gibbs," Quinn said.

"I know. I didn't like how he got up and left just as we were starting to connect."

"You mentioned your grandmother. What other family is there?"

"Not much. My family is the typical American melting pot, but our pot has sort of boiled dry. My dad's siblings died young. He has some distant relatives down south, in Georgia and Arkansas. I've never met them. I'm not sure he has. They're from the German and Irish side of the family that used to be here in Pennsylvania."

"And your mother's side? I know your grandmother outlived your mom," said Quinn, "but I never met her."

I nodded. "You would have liked my Gramama Inez. She died about a year before you moved to Metropolis. She actually died at our house. I was holding her hand when she breathed her last breath."

"Wow," Quinn said. "When you talk about her, I feel like I knew her."

"She still helps me be brave, even though she's gone," I said. "She faced tough things in her life. Once I asked her where she got her strength, expecting to hear some Catholic wisdom. She was very devout. But I think her answer went beyond her Catholic faith, maybe to the Mayan mystics. She told me that everything in life possessed a bit of tender madness."

"God," Quinn said. "Tender madness."

"Locura tierna," I nodded. "I wish I knew the Mayan words."

"It explains everything," Quinn said, smiling slightly.

I nodded. "It's chaos and order. The duality of life. For every storm, there's a river; for every hunger, there's a fruit."

"Yin and yang," Quinn said, nodding. "You calling me a fruit?"

"You calling me hungry?" I laughed. Then I shook my head, flooded with more serious thought. "God, my dad called you queer tonight. I was so pissed."

"I'm not shocked," Quinn said, wrinkling her nose. "Or surprised. He's a guy who's always been upfront with his dislikes."

"I don't like hearing it. He's done too much damage already. That word and worse," I said.

"What damage?" She was pulling in to the parking lot of our roadside inn so I agreed to tell her the story of my cousin, Tomas, when we got inside. We dropped our jackets on our beds in the small, plain room and while we got ready for bed, I told her about Tomas traveling by bus all the way from Puerto Vallarta, Mexico, a few years after my mother died. His mother and mine were sisters, but my Aunt Vera, fascinated with her partial Mexican heritage, had gone to Puerto Vallarta with some friends in the 50s, after Elizabeth Taylor and Richard Burton's love nest there was splashed through the news. Americans thought it was a very cool place then.

"Her friends hung out for a year, but my aunt wound up marrying a local guy and staying, having little Tomas and a daughter, Martina. They sent a lovely letter on every birthday with a piece of silver jewelry and a box of avocados from their orchard in the hill country about ten miles from town."

"Let me guess," said Quinn. "Little Tomas was no farmer."

"Before long, Tomas found his way to town and into trouble with his father, who began beating him regularly. Trying to make a man out of him, you know?" Quinn sat on the edge of the bed as I continued. "But Tomas liked boys and music and dancing. So Aunt Vera, trying to save him from his father, sent him to us on the bus. I was almost fourteen. I didn't really know how my father felt about gays. Until then."

"He didn't beat him like his father, did he?"

I shook my head. "He used words. 'Queer' was one of the milder ones. Tomas lasted a few months with us. I felt so sorry for him. He was a little guy, you know? Really slim. Good looking, though."

"Where did he go?" Quinn asked.

"I wish I knew. I didn't have much time to gain his trust. He left in the middle of the night after coming home late and having a big fight with my dad. He had made a couple of friends at the high school. He was only a year away from graduating. But no one knew where he went."

"Was your grandmother still alive then?"

Painful memories began erupting. I choked back tears. "She had a sense that things were bad," I said.

"Of course," Quinn said quietly.

"A few days after the final blowout, when I was still expecting Tomas to walk back in the door at any moment, Gramama Inez walked in. Dad was behind her, grumpily carrying her bags. She had called from the airport. He hated that about her. She'd always just show up that way."

"I like her more and more," Quinn said.

"She was heartbroken when he confirmed that Tomas had run away. She fell into bed, had a fever but refused to go to the hospital."

"My god," said Quinn.

I rubbed my temples, thinking of those days I sat by Gramama's bed, bathing her with a cool cloth, listening to her mumble. Dad would thump around in the hall outside her door, swearing under his breath. He was so angry.

"I remember writing things down that she said in her delirious fits. I kept a notebook by my side to write down unfamiliar words. I hadn't spoken much Spanish since my mom died. I knew 'de luz,' was 'the light,' but I had to look up 'escanciados.' Flowing, it meant. Flowing with light. For days she moaned over and over about 'las sombras,' the shadows."

"Tomas was her shadow," said Quinn.

"Now he's lost in the shadow world. Where would a seventeen-year-old have gone?" I asked.

"Young? Cute? Gay? Hmmm, let me think," said Quinn, stepping into the bathroom.

"I try not to think of him as a male prostitute," I said. I hated to imagine the difficult life we may have driven him into. I supposed he could have survived in any big city, even after his visa expired. "Wonderful, supportive family, huh?"

"It's a sadly familiar story," said Quinn. She poked her head around the door, her mouth foaming with toothpaste. "Happens to kids from every walk of life."

I crawled under my blankets and waited for her to finish and come back into the room. "So what about yours?"

"My family? They didn't quit talking to me, didn't send me to a shrink or make up stories for their friends. They took it in stride. My mom says she wouldn't have planned it. She thinks life is difficult enough, but she loves me. They've had so much trouble with my brother and drugs, though, that I seem pretty tame," she said.

"Your straight little brother," I said, with a hint of sarcasm.

"Right. He's only straight in terms of sexual orientation. He's cleaned up a little, though, lately."

"They want one of you to produce some grandkids," I said.

"True. I'm sure they wish I'd have kids, but I don't think I'd want to bring a child into the world even if I was straight or married." I noticed Quinn's eyes tearing up as she turned down her blankets.

"What is it?" I asked. "Why the tears?"

She shrugged. "I know I'm one of the lucky ones. I've heard so many tales of families torn apart, kids disowned, thrown out, beaten. I can't imagine giving birth to a child, raising him for years, then turning against him for something he didn't choose or can't control."

"See? You'd be a good parent. You'd accept your kid no matter what."

She sighed and climbed into her bed. "Do people want the old days of hiding in closets? When nobody talked?" she asked.

"Most people are doing better, don't you think? Getting a bit more educated?" In my head I was counting how many years it had been since I last saw Tomas. More than twenty. I wondered where he might have gone. If he was still alive. I heard Quinn mumbling about people and the secrets they keep, the lives destroyed by child abuse, molestation. She slapped at her covers and began reliving the basketball game to distract herself after getting worked up.

Somewhere in a dark corner of my mind, a faucet turned on. Water was running. As if an irrigation stream poured into my baked fields, I felt flooded and revived all at once. There was an image there that always lurked in the dark hallways of my mind. It was the image of a door barely ajar, and the shadow of someone passing by on the other side. My stomach tightened and I felt my whole body perspiring, though the room wasn't warm and I'm young for a hot flash. I pulled the covers up around my neck, gripping so tightly that my knuckles whitened. Quinn asked if it was okay to turn out the light. She rolled over and saw me, pale and shivering.

"What's wrong?" she asked.

I dropped my jaw but no words came out. Closing my eyes, I felt myself slipping out of my body, as if I were the water, spilling soundlessly over the edge of a full tub. I watched from a distance. My body became young, prepubescent. The faucet was running and the bathroom door was ajar. "Oh, no," I whispered. I saw flashes of a face in my memory; jowly cheeks and a pinched mouth that seemed to smile, no matter what emotion was gushing. She always gushed. It was the housekeeper, Miss North.

After a few minutes, I could breathe enough to tell Quinn what I was picturing. I felt the bathroom door, barely ajar, between me and the fleshy cheeks.

"Were you inside the bathroom?" she asked.

I nodded. "I was getting into the bath. She would watch me."

"You knew?"

"Sometimes. She never let me see her. But I could hear her in the hall."

"Why didn't you close the door?"

"At first I always closed the door, of course. It all started with my bedroom door. At night I'd go to bed with my door closed. Dad and I had a ritual. He'd come home, knock on my door, poke his head in and say, "Sorry I'm so late, hon. Good night." Then he'd pull the door closed. But in the morning I'd always find it ajar."

"Sorry I'm so late? That was your ritual?"

"Yeah. After a few mornings of noticing the door ajar, I would get up after he came in and check to make sure it was closed. Still I'd find it open in the morning."

Quinn sighed and asked, "Did you ever say anything to your dad?"

"Once. He just shrugged. I'm not sure he understood how much it bothered me."

"He didn't want you to bother *him*," Quinn said.

"The worst was that I was entering puberty, you know. Sometimes touching. Masturbating. I'd stop because I'd think I heard footsteps outside my door."

"Ewww. It was the housekeeper? That woman was creepy."

"She never touched me," I said.

"Doesn't matter. She invaded you. Go back to the bathtub part. What were you going to say?"

"Well, I figured out that if I shut the door, she'd get hot-tempered, vicious. She'd tell me strange things about my mother, even though I don't think she really ever met her. She told me she'd heard my mother was sick for years and then tapped on her head, like she was crazy. Sometimes she'd tell me she had found something of my mother's. Something that would look very pretty on me when I got older. If I was good, she said, she'd show me. She would bribe me with this for days, getting me to do things for her. Then she would just drop it. I'd beg and she would act like I had made the whole thing up. 'You're obsessed with your dead mother,' she'd tell me. Or she would hurriedly show me some dumb thing like an apron, something that was probably not even my mother's."

"Ughh," said Quinn. "I want to choke her."

"But if I left the door ajar, if I'd just get in the tub and ignore her, she'd be the sweetest thing."

"You could ignore someone peeking at you in the bathtub?"

I sighed. "I must have really tuned out. And I took very quick baths. But there were times when I had a definite sense of her in the hallway." Even with Quinn, it was very painful to admit the shame. I felt stupid.

"Reed, how long did this go on?" Quinn asked.

"She lived with us for several years."

"Years!" said Quinn. "God. Whatever happened to her?"

"Don't know," I said. "Or don't remember. I just came home one day and her room was empty."

"And your dad said...?"

"That I was old enough to stay by myself in the evenings. He'd get a maid to do occasional cleaning and cooking."

"You know, Reed, you're very sensitive," Quinn said. "I think you knew at some level that the woman wasn't healthy. It was like a psychic attack."

"It affected my sleep," I said. "It affected a lot of things."

Quinn nodded. "To you she was a housekeeper. But to her, you were her obsession. Sexuality had gotten all twisted up for her, just like her conversations and mind games. I hate to think of the next kid she took care of."

I groaned. "I should have told someone." A tear ran down my cheek.

"People scare kids into keeping secrets," Quinn said with disgust. "Who knows all the awful things she said to you." Her face was sorrowful. We both knew I had opened a memory that would take more than a night to heal. More than a week away from the work where I had become so adept at focusing on others—avoiding myself.

I was still clinging to the blankets when she asked if I'd be all right with her sitting closer, holding me. When I nodded, she climbed over me, on top of the blanket, and settled beside me with her arm holding me. "You know I'd never hurt you, right?" she asked.

"Of course, Quinn." She put her arm around my shoulder and I let go of the blanket to grab her hand, my life preserver. "So many thoughts," I said. "It's all beginning to make sense. I've always been so cautious in relationships, even gym classes when I had to get undressed. I never wanted anyone to touch me or look at me."

Quinn petted my back and arm. "I'm sorry for anything I said. For any time I teased you."

I started to sob and rolled over with my head against her t-shirt. Quinn put both her arms around me and held tight while I let the old demons rinse out of my skin. She tried to soothe me. But it felt like something was ripping from my gut, tangled with many years of roots and barbed tendrils. The tears came, whether I was willing or not. The flow had been turned on and there was no stopping. Finally, I felt a breath reach all the way into the bottom of my lungs, loosening tight knots in my chest. The tears slowed. I felt a bit lighter.

"Quinn," I whispered. "There's been something bothering me since we talked to Gibbs."

"What is it?" She brushed a hair from my mouth.

"He talked about breaking down the walls, getting out of the box."

"Right."

"After Miss North left, I shut all my doors. Tight. I've worked really hard to get that box closed and locked. So no one will bother me again," I said. I caught a breath and quivered.

"I understand, Reed." Quinn reached to the nightstand for a tissue and let me wipe my eyes and nose. She ran her strong hand down the length of my arm, squeezing every few inches.

"That first night Gramama arrived after Mama died, she sat beside me and rubbed my back until I went to sleep. It was a comfort just like this," I said.

"I'm glad."

"Gramama lived with chronic pain in her body and probably in her soul. I'd ask her about painful things in her past and she would shake her head. "Don't do as I do," she would tell me. She would point to her arthritic joints and call them "muy mal."

"Very bad," said Quinn.

"She would say, 'la memoria acuesta en silencio.'"

"Silencio," said Quinn. "Silence."

I said, "The memory lies in silence."

"Right. In your muscles, your bones, your organs," said Quinn.

"Is it the same thing Gibbs meant?" I asked. "The memory goes into a box?"

Quinn nodded. "And we have to choose to open it?"

"I wonder," I said, "is that what this is all about? Why I met Maggie?"

"Isn't Maggie trying to remember some piece of pain in her past? I think you're helping each other."

I sighed. "Tender madness." I felt Quinn nod in agreement, but I was exhausted and don't recall any more. I fell asleep with her petting my head. I breathed deeply and relaxed with Quinn's arm around me all night. No matter what demons were stirred within my bones, I felt safe, felt all would work out somehow. The madness would be gentle with me.

ζ

The warmth of the fireplace was comforting to her tired, old bones. She pulled the shawl closer around her shoulders and stretched against the back of the rocker, aware of whispering nearby. Looking up, Maggie saw Edmund's head bobbing near Eleanor's as he laid a small portion of dried venison on the table before her. "'Tis time for another hunt," Maggie heard him say. "Here lies the last portion of venison brought from the farm."

"Hunting deer?" Maggie called from the parlor.

Whitney jumped up from the parlor rug and ran to the kitchen, grabbing a biscuit from the table as he passed. "Papa, let me go with you," he pleaded. He had never been hunting with his father.

"'Twas discussing with your mother, son. The town is disorderly and I fear leaving the womenfolk for any length of time." Whitney's shoulders and eyes drooped toward the floor. Then Edmund continued, "I've a notion for all of us to ride up the northern bluffs. Seen deer there one month ago when..."

Both boys bounced at Edmund's side, hugging his waist and covering the dropped sentence. But Maggie had a sense that when Edmund saw the deer, he had been looking for her and was unprepared to hunt. The family busily proceeded to gather all that was needed for their departure in the early light of morning.

"You found a feather?" Maggie asked quietly, eying the long black and white plume clutched in Morton's hand as the buckboard lurched ahead over the craggy road through the lowlands along Hogg's Pond.

He brushed it along the bumps of her knuckles without looking up. "Out back. Whit says 'tis from a hawk's tail."

"Save that. Stick it in your hat. See this old hat of mine?" She patted the floppy brim of a bedraggled buckskin hat. "Pulled it from my old bag. Had it since I was a young boy."

Morton looked up, grinning. "You were ne'er a boy." He set the plume in her outstretched palm.

Maggie held it at the base and brushed upward. "Brush in this direction. 'Twill stay nice for a good long time." She tickled his nose and handed it back. "No, ne'er even told your mother about running off from Bethlehem and taking up like a boy."

Eleanor leaned back from the buckboard bench seat. "What are you telling these boys?" she asked.

"Granmama ran away," said Morton. His mother jerked her head to look at Maggie in disbelief.

Edmund spoke up. "You best relate the tale from the start, Mother Beigler." He clicked and the wagon lurched as Coal headed up the steep, jutted road.

Maggie adjusted herself to face toward the front of the wagon and settled the boys, one on each side. "I worked in the Bethlehem laundry for over a year," Maggie said, "bent over steaming lye kettles for long hours and then sitting up late with my studies. One afternoon, I looked up to see Weiser dressed all in buckskin, strolling down the aisle of the laundry. I was certain he had come to deliver me from my Bethlehem drudgery.

"He bellowed a greeting that echoed in the rafters. When he spoke of a treaty conference in Lancaster, I begged to go along and he laughed. 'A treaty meeting in the woods is no place for a girl,'" Maggie mimicked Weiser's gruff voice. "He inquired upon my health, repeated condolences for my father and as swift as he had appeared, gave me a strong embrace and departed. Said he was there to organize a train of Moravian wagons to supply the conference, then he'd be riding north to gather the Onandagas."

"They were the Indians going to the meeting?" asked Whitney.

"One group. There would be hundreds come to the Lancaster treaty," said Maggie. "I was sorely disappointed. When Weiser walked out, I dropped my laundry paddle and fell to my knees in tears. In that moment, I hatched a plan to leave Bethlehem."

Whitney dropped his jaw wide. "You did dress like a boy!"

"'Twas no place for a girl, Weiser had said." Maggie shrugged, "The laundry made simple work of collecting items of clothing, even this old hat. I made one brief stop at the women's choir to collect belongings, my turtle, the old leather bag. Borrowed a razor and sheared my hair in the darkness of the outbuilding; blonde locks they were then, dropped in the privy pit aside my skirt. To any observers, 'twas no fragile female, but a thin, young boy who emerged and climbed upon the rearward wagon in the train."

Edmund looked back at Maggie, his boys huddled beside her. He asked, "Was this the well-known treaty meeting of Lancaster?"

Maggie nodded, "'Twas the month of June in '44."

"Were you discovered?" asked Eleanor.

"I was convincing as a boy for days, riding with my cap tugged low, traveling to Lancaster with a young German man, Helmut, on a wagon loaded with bags of flour, salt and the like. I recall his story well. He'd been raised in an English orphan home and sold to a miller in Germantown for sea passage and seven years labor. He was scarce commencing his freedom. Told me some servants were indentured, practically slaves, but he had been released fairly upon turning eighteen."

"At nightfall we pulled off the pike, circled the wagons and slept on the ground beneath. By the following day at dusk, we began to pass more farmhouses. We rode into Lancaster after dark on King Street, past inns and taverns toward the lamplit town square where King met Queen Street. A handsome red brick courthouse towered over the square where curious townfolk pressed faces to the glass window panes or gathered in darkened doorways."

"Were the Indians there, Gran?" asked Whitney.

Maggie glanced over the edge of the tipping buckboard as they went higher up the bluffs. The road had nearly disappeared and the wagon rocked from side to side. "By the sounds we heard and the smoky scents, I knew my yearning had been satisfied to return to the woods and the native people. Drums and chanting voices led to a trail of hundreds of brown Indians streaming from the north woods to a giant bonfire in the midst of a field."

"Bright colors and feathers waved like little flags from scant, festive clothing. Silver bands sparkled from their arms or hair. Women and children came on horseback, with little boys waving small bows and arrows. The men walked, orderly, proudly strolling in time with the beating drum, chanting a harmonious, friendly greeting."

"They joined the early arrivals who had set up huts of poles, boards and bark in the field near the fire. We circled the wagons behind the courthouse and unloaded carts of provender into supply tents well into the night: packs full of bacon, casks of butter and cheese, loads of kettles, utensils and barrels said to contain maple sugar." Maggie paused. Both boys looked up as she slowly shook her head, then continued. "There were gifts and supplies for the conference: clothing, hats, blankets, kettles and tobacco pipes, tools such as hoes and fish hooks, sewing supplies, powder and shot."

"The barrels, Gran," said Whitney. "What was in them?"

"Saw with my own eyes several nights hence. Old Swataney spoke angrily with Weiser about the rum and said the meetings could not continue. Weiser took the chief to our supply tent, picked up an axe and began to smash the oak barrels, sending several of them toppling over and gushing their potent smelling liquor. Swataney stood calmly at the side until satisfied, then he returned to his hut."

"What of being discovered by Weiser?" asked Morton.

"I was often hiding, though I also took comfort in his presence," said Maggie. To herself, she remembered that first night standing beside the giant oak when the music and drumming stopped abruptly and Weiser approached the field on horseback. The interpreter called out over the crowd in the Mohawk language and they responded by growing respectfully quiet.

"'Twas Weiser's meeting from the first. Some of the colonial dignitaries were greatly offended by his ideas of following the Indians' traditions. They wanted to show off their fire power and warn the Indians not to cross them. 'Twas the Pennsylvania governor who defended Weiser. He told the group, as I recall, that a war with the Six Nations would be disastrous to the English and a very costly blunder. Crushing them would destroy the best barriers against the French.

"Weiser explained that the Indians wouldn't meet unless their ways be honored. Their meetings were ordered with a purpose for everything and included the whole company. He begged everyone to make no jests upon the natives' dress or behavior. When someone murmured that they were savages who didn't understand the white men's talk, Weiser whirled around and bellowed, told them many Indians speak English and many more can fathom. Tradition dictates that they speak their own tongue in treaty talks.

"We heard drumming resume in the distance as the revelry began. For the next days we were to feed the guests well, make certain of their comfort and rest, and give them gifts. On Monday the treaty meetings would commence."

"You saw the meetings, Gran?" asked Whitney.

Maggie nodded, "I climbed up on a window sill, next to another servant boy. Everyone was dressed in finery; the colonial men in dark suits of clothing and wigs of powdered, white wool. Native leaders came in colored matchcoats decorated with quill patterns and woven shell chestplates. Their short tufts of hair were braided with feathers and they cradled their pipes in their arms. Others wore new shirts from the supply of gifts and crowded the floors and hallways, the stairs of the judges' bench."

"The big man, Canasatego, settled an early dispute about who would speak first by saying it was nothing to the Six Nations who was the oldest colony. A man from Maryland had given a brief speech so Canasatego repeated their claim that they had possession of the Province of Maryland for over one hundred years. He said, "What is one hundred years compared to the length of time since our claim began? Long before one hundred years, our ancestors came out of this very ground." He pointed to the colonial men and said they had come out of the ground in a land beyond the sea; there they may have a just claim. But here the Indians were the elder brothers. They lived on the lands before the colonists knew anything of them.

"He had their attention, that he did. He spoke of the suffering that had occurred from past 'pen and ink work,' referring to the clerks who wrote the treaty notes. He mentioned the deed giving their Susquehanna lands to the New York Governor to hold for them in trust, only to learn that 'he carried the land to England on such paper and then sold it.'"

"They quibbled over various deeds and complained that every colony had differing policies and communication with the natives. Life would be easier, Canasatego said, if the colonies could form a union. I saw the commissioners wriggle in their chairs as he spoke of the Six Nations, all independent nations that conferred on important issues for united decisions. Canasatego held a handful of sticks in his square fist. He snapped a longer stick in two pieces as the whole room hushed. Conrad Weiser told the English governors that Canasatego spoke of Deganawidah, the Peacemaker, who visited his people long ago and told them they were like the stick; weak, fragile, easy to break. Alone, they could not hold back the force of the wind or a strong enemy.

"But if united with their neighboring nations," Weiser said while Canasatego picked up the other sticks, bundling them together in his sinewy hand, "together they would resist and conquer the enemy." The chief puffed out his chest and strained at the bundled sticks, trying unsuccessfully to break them. Weiser said the chief wanted them to be like the bundled sticks. "Whatever befalls you," he told them, "do not fall out with one another."

Edmund turned and spoke to the boys over his shoulder. "They took his advice to form the Continental Congress to discuss issues affecting all the colonies, such as the meetings now about taxation." The boys nodded, but pleaded with Maggie to learn how she had been discovered.

Maggie shook her head. "'Twasn't so very long, I fear. After the meetings each night they cooked a steer to feed the throng. The natives smeared white paint or dark bear grease on their bodies and colored their faces, playing music and dancing or singing into the night. I helped haul firewood to the cook fires and stirred the bubbling pots of mush and corn. After the food was gone and fires burned to embers, we tumbled the pots on their sides to wipe them, then rolled them back to the supply tent.

"There I heard Weiser's voice boom over the sound of the drums. He hollered and waved us toward his tent. I pulled my hat low and ran behind Helmut to find Weiser tugging a huge canvas bag through the tent flap. He wanted us to take it to Canasatego. Helmut bent to pick up the hundredweight bag of tobacco as I rushed to the rear and lifted. We balanced the large bundle on Helmut's shoulder and my head as I ducked out of Weiser's sight.

"We had seen Canasatego by the main fire so we made a wide circle to go around the celebration. But one of the spinning dancers careened toward Helmut and pitched him forward under the weight of the bag. I stumbled into the path of the dancer and his large arm and fist slammed into my head, knocking me sidelong off my feet.

"There was hollering as someone pulled me from the fire. I had yet to realize I had fallen among the embers. Canasatego barked an order and one of the black-painted dancers picked me up and carried me toward the main huts. The last image I recall was Canasatego nodding approval of the tobacco and filling his pipe."

"The last image? No, Gran, what happened then?" asked Whitney.

"Best keep this brief. We're nearing the bluffs. I will tell you that I woke the next morning in the tent of Madame Montour, a French woman who lived among the Indians on the upper Susquehanna for many a year. She had an Indian husband, but he had long since died. She was older with grey hair pulled back in a braid laced with feathers and trinkets."

"Were you badly hurt?" asked Whitney.

"I took a bad enough bump on the head to lose my senses, and had a burned hand. The worst injury was waking to find that I was discovered. Madame Montour and her Shawnee helper whispered to Weiser. They had felt the turtle totem and when they opened my shirt, discovered my small but unmistakably girlish breasts."

"Gran!" said Morton. Whitney jabbed him with his elbow and told him to hush.

They pushed at each other while Maggie, paying no attention, wrinkled her nose. "I smelled of field onion salve, painted on my blistered hand. Weiser leaned over my swollen face but I pretended sleep. He breathed a heavy sigh and departed the tent without a word."

"You were in a quandary," Whitney frowned.

"What did Weiser do?" asked Eleanor, who had turned around to listen.

"I heard Madame Montour slip out behind him and ask why I would flee Bethlehem. Weiser told her that I had written him and asked to return to Tulpehocken, but he refused, believing I was best overseen by the Moravians.

"Madame Montour told Weiser that a spirited young woman is ill-suited to a proper life anywhere. She told him most white men like their women pale and weak, with no book learning. Though my hand would heal, she said, there was no herbal salve for a wounded spirit. I recall her words to him: "Some of us need ample leeway to let the storms blow through. Shan't be shackled in a scant room in a small village." I thought she spoke of herself, as well. Weiser though, had determined to take me to Philadelphia for doctoring at the same time he delivered the treaty notes for publication. He told her he would use that time to ponder further plans for me."

Whitney leaned his head against Maggie, then asked, "What became of the meetings?"

"By their close," Maggie said, "the Indians had promised to forbid the French to pass through their territories to hurt the English colonies. In exchange for lands west of Virginia, the Iroquois had heightened their influence. The English acknowledged their dependence and loyalty to the Iroquois, admitting to themselves, at least, that they could not hold off the French advancement without the Indians' aid."

Maggie winced and Eleanor asked if her head still ached.

"Will it ever cease?" Maggie complained.

Morton spoke up. "Perhaps telling the story made you recall that old knock on the head." He said, "Gran, did you know the Indian who hurt you?"

"'Twas accidental. He was dancing and stumbled into me."

"I mean the one that hurt you here." He pointed at the scar beside her face.

She lowered her eyes and Eleanor began to scold Morton. Maggie stopped her. "Let him be," she said, holding her stomach. "He's curious, 'tis all." Edmund glanced back as Maggie took a deep breath, "I have scant recollections, Morton, but many say 'twas a savage that hurt me." She licked her dry lips. "This I know. I went in search of an Indian friend, someone I very much admire." She patted both boys on their backs. "If I made a mistake," she said sullenly, "I lived to regret."

Edmund reined the horse to a halt and they all sat in silence for a moment on a hillside overlooking the Allegheny River winding like a sparkling silver snake along the carved valley below. Edmund whistled several sharp notes, like a bird call. There was no reply. He looked along the bluff and down into the river valley, studying the shoreline. Then he said, "'Tis along those shores I've come upon the old fisherman, Joseph. You remember him, boys?" Both boys nodded, following his gaze along the riverbanks.

"Certain he lives on this bluff, though he's likely to be out on the river on a day such as this. You boys stay here and help your mother harvest these field onions." He pointed at the side of the hill covered with pungent blossoms. "We'll not be making a salve, Mother Beigler, but a mightily fine soup. I'll take Coal into that ravine where there'll likely be deer." Whitney stood nearby as his father unhitched the horse from the wagon. Edmund said, "You boys stay nearby. I may be several hours in my return."

As Edmund rode over the hill, Eleanor reached under the buckboard seat and pulled forth a stack of canvas bags. She handed one to each of the boys and Maggie, but said, "Mother, find a spot of shade and rest yourself."

Maggie shaded her throbbing eyes and wandered toward an embankment of stones that left a narrow band of shade beneath. She lowered herself slowly and settled back against the cool embankment, resting her capped head. Despite chaos broiling in the valley below, she closed her eyes and felt the peaceful afternoon breeze. There were no threatening marauders or heavy handed blue-coats on this hillside, nothing to fear. Her headache eased, her shoulders drooped and her fingers uncurled.

Before long she heard the boys struggling to hoist their plump bags of onions onto the buckboard. They ran over to her side with Eleanor following close behind. As Morton squeezed himself into the shady place beside her, he asked, "Gran, did Mister Weiser take you to Philadelphia?"

Maggie smiled. "Indeed. 'Twas there we delivered the treaty notes to the shop of Benjamin Franklin to be printed."

Whitney squinted doubtfully. "You met Benjamin Franklin?"

"Such an impression I made with my bandaged hand and my locks rough shorn with a razor! Ha!" chuckled Maggie. She pulled her bonnet closer and gazed into the distance. In a quiet voice, she recalled, "Helmut drove us to a busy cobblestone street, High Street, before a row of shops. He pulled to a stop in front of a painted sign reading, 'Benj. Franklin, Printer.' Weiser carried his leather satchel containing the treaty papers while a young man emerged from the shop and offered me assistance, helping me to a seat inside a front parlor of the printing office. He then departed with Helmut to fetch the doctor. The pungent ink smell was heavy. The shop was cluttered with tall wooden presses blocking my view of the character called Franklin—but for his round head, dark hair thinning, leaning closely over Weiser's treaty documents.

"Weiser spoke with excitement about the Iroquois alliance with the English as Franklin perused the papers. He told him the Indians were weary of the patchwork of agreements and had asked the colonies to unite in their handling of treaty affairs.

"Franklin called it a sensible request, I recall. He told Weiser he had parties on both sides of the sea who were eager for the notes. As they shook hands, they moved to the front office where I sat. Franklin rubbed his prosperous belly, his dark printer's apron loosely tied. Helmut arrived with the doctor who examined my head and wrist. He assured that there were no broken bones and no infection of the burned tissue, then covered my hand with ointment and cloth bandages.

"Preparing to leave, Weiser mentioned the exchanges made at the meeting to assure good feelings. Franklin frowned and said that giving up claim to the lands west of Virginia seemed to be a grand piece of cooperation." Maggie nodded. "I now understand his meaning. Mister Franklin grinned at me over his spectacles and said he should like to hear the wild tale that fetched my injuries, though I never had a chance to tell him."

Morton tugged at Maggie's sleeve. "What did Mister Franklin mean, Granmama?"

"Perhaps the Indians meant to give permission for the white settlers to come live peacefully upon those lands. But the settlers meant to own them, to send the Indians further west."

"And us?" asked Whitney. "Will we go west?"

Eleanor interrupted. "We're going back to the farm once the chaos in town settles. 'Twill be a short time, surely." She looked sternly at Maggie, who realized she had frightened the boys.

"Surely," she agreed. "Shall we give our legs a stretch, boys? Gran is feeling rigid, hard as a rock upon the ground." Whitney helped Maggie to her feet while Morton bounced ahead of them along the embankment. As Eleanor was about to call out to him, Morton skidded to a stop and turned back to them, wide eyed.

He scooted back to Eleanor's side and whispered, "Mama, I heard something." He pointed over the rocky hill.

"Silence," said Eleanor. "Perhaps your father has returned." As they all sat quietly, they heard an unmistakable low moan, though it was unclear whether it was man or animal. They sat where they were, huddled against the wall as the guttural sound was repeated. Maggie looked down the hill to the twisting river in the distance, then glanced to her side where the same river curved around in the other direction. Startled, she felt a dizziness tugging at her head and she pulled the boys closer to her sides. Eleanor was whispering, but the words disappeared in the air between them.

ζ

"Oh no. Oh no," I moaned. "What have I done?"

Quinn stirred beside me and sat up. She scooted away slightly, both of us startled upon waking in an embrace. Then she asked, "Dreaming? Are you all right?"

"I know where they are, Quinn. Maggie and Eleanor. They're right up on the bluffs, where you used to live. Remember how we saw the river winding from two different directions? Maggie saw it, just the same way and I must have been so shocked, I leaped right out."

"Oh," said Quinn, puzzled and rubbing her eyes. "Well, isn't that kind of exciting? To know where they are? And right where I grew up?"

"But there was some kind of noise nearby. They may be in danger," I said.

Quinn got up and peeked through a crack in the draperies. It was still dark, barely dawn. "Can you go back? Will you be in danger, too?"

"I don't know." I pondered the idea for a moment, and then said, "Maybe I can check it out. You know, get close enough to sense the problem and then warn them."

"Wow," said Quinn. "I don't really like this."

"Apparently, I can leap out if things get hairy. I think I have to try."

Quinn scowled slightly, short hair poking comically in all directions. She said, "I feel helpless. What can I do?"

I winced as I moved my neck. Grabbing at my knotted spine, I told her, "Last night was amazing. I fell asleep so relaxed. You really helped, Quinn. But I think 'el silencio' has settled in my neck here. Do you think you could squeeze it, work the knot out?"

"If that will help. Sure."

I turned on my stomach and she began gently kneading the tense tissue above my shoulder. She said, "Last night you mentioned that you'd been afraid to say anything to your dad." I fidgeted and winced when she pinched a tender spot. She said, "I have a nagging suspicion. I'm just going to say it. What if he found out? I think he fired the woman, Reed."

I closed my eyes and let myself feel the pain that was shooting through my neck. "Ouch. I've been angry for so long because he hadn't paid attention. Why wouldn't he tell me?"

"He might have caught her at something unrelated to you. Maybe he was embarrassed to tell you. Or thought he was protecting you."

I felt like holding my breath, but I remembered one of my tennis-playing clients who always holds his breath during his serve. The knot inside his shoulder just kept growing until I got him to breathe. I let air escape while the fire in my neck kept burning. I hadn't realized how angry I'd been. I thought my dad was disappointed with me. But I was the one disappointed in him. I'd been the one holding onto that energy in our family.

I said out loud, "I've blamed myself for what happened to Mama, for not helping her. It made sense to me that he was angry with me, too. He was always disappointed. I just accepted it." More tears came and I reached for a tissue.

Quinn eased up on my neck muscles. She said, "Being frightened of the person who is supposed to be taking care of you; that's one of the worst things that can happen to a child. That woman forced you into a world of fear."

I said, "I can't even imagine what pain people must feel who are actually abused."

"Believe me, an invasion is an invasion," she said. "And you had just lost your mother."

Between my shoulders, I felt a fiery blade twist the muscles that hold my head onto my body. I breathed through the pain as it seeped into my chest, right through my heart. A tear slid down the side of my nose. "I can see what a confused kid I was. It wasn't my job to save her."

"No, it wasn't," Quinn whispered.

"But my dad's a doctor. You'd think he would have talked to me."

"Yeah. But you already know he wasn't perfect."

"I guess he was grieving, too," I said. I supposed I was closer to understanding, forgiving. My neck and shoulder relaxed and I felt like dozing. But someone was there, close to me, barely breathing, struggling to stay alive. My eyes were closed, but I could see a slice of light, a face lying at the base of the light. It was Joe, old Joe. I knelt down by his side and put my hand on his shoulder. I felt love for the old guy. I didn't want to see him die.

The compassion in my heart rose up and called out to Maggie, "Come quickly, Maggie. Don't be afraid."

ς

Long shadows were creeping over the valley, darkening the hills to silhouettes against the deep blue sky of dusk. The last rays of the sun sliced the hillside before them. Maggie's legs ached as she squatted beside Eleanor and the boys. They were all motionless and tense. Maggie felt her mind clear as if she had drifted away and then returned. She was slightly surprised to find herself in the same predicament, huddled, listening for the noises that had frightened them into their silent perch. She felt suddenly brave, as if scouts had returned with their report. No danger ahead. Proceed.

"Eleanor, the ruckus has ceased. I've a mind to peer over that hill," said Maggie, pulling herself up to stand by the rock embankment. Before Eleanor could stop her, she took a few steps up the hill. "My Lord," she exclaimed.

"What do you see?" whispered Eleanor.

"'Tis some sort of rock chimney upon the ground," said Maggie. "A dwelling of sorts."

"Maybe Joe lives here. Papa knew 'twas nearby," said Whitney.

Maggie nodded, certain that Whitney was correct. She called out in a tentative voice, "Oh, Joe? Mister Joseph, you here?" She took a few more steps to the top of the hill and looked down upon a log facade patched into the side of an earthen wall, part hut and part cave. There was a path down and around the backside of the hill, leading to a timber-lined doorway beneath the short rock chimney.

"Mister Joseph," Maggie called again as she stepped down the path. "'Tis friends. Come calling." She looked back at Whitney and Morton stepping timidly over the hilltop, watching her every move. Eleanor's face behind them tightened in a worried grimace.

Maggie called another soft greeting as she peered around the corner of the thick timber, wincing at the dank air. She ducked her head through the low entrance, and pushed at the narrow door. "Mercy," her voice echoed in the dark hole.

Two posts stood before her in the middle of the room, bracing a plank and earthen roof. Stones, stacked and molded together with clay, formed a fireplace streaked with black soot. The rock walls were chiseled into the shape of benches, one short one beside the fireplace and a longer one against the back wall, covered with a lumpy canvas sack. Fish nets and animal traps hung on spikes in the walls above. Clutter and debris were scattered across the dirt floor and a single wood plank aligned in front of her feet in the entryway. There was no motion in the cave, but as the boys poked their heads around the door, it occurred to Maggie that the canvas cloth covered a human body. She turned to stop the boys' entry, but was too late.

Whitney bounded across the plank to the back of the cave. "Joe, wake up!"

Maggie reached for his shirt to pull him back, but he had tugged the cloth away from Joe's face. The faint light from the doorway showed a small, curled form with dusty grey skin. Whitney shook the bony man's shoulder until his black eyes opened wide and the old man stretched his silent cracked lips, mouthing surprise. He struggled to sit as Whitney put both hands beneath his shoulder to ease him upright.

"I fear we startled you, Mister Joseph," apologized Maggie. "Are you well?"

Morton walked in beside his brother and stared at the old man. Joseph nodded at the boys and Eleanor who had pushed the door open further and looked inside. "Where's your papa?" he breathed.

"Huntin' a deer," piped up Morton, cheerily. Then, noticing a long, dry scrape on Joseph's leg, he asked, "You hurt, Joe?"

Joseph nodded and looked at the fireplace. "Must slept all the day. Poke in here, boy and see if some coals's hot." He pointed toward a long stick beside the fireplace and Whitney dropped to his knees. Maggie sent Morton outside to the woodpile then seated herself beside Joseph to inspect his leg. Eleanor sparked a strike plate to light a wax lamp, casting eerie shadows over the uneven cave walls.

Fatigued from sitting up, Joseph leaned back on the stone bench.

"Have you eaten?" Maggie asked.

Joseph's bottom lip protruded and he shrugged. "Don' recall," he said, as he combed shaky, thin fingers through the white curls behind one ear.

As Whitney gathered a flame from the wax lamp to light his pile of coals and sticks in the fireplace, Morton scurried through the door, dropping an armload of wood on the floor. "Papa's coming!" he exclaimed and ran back out. Whitney grabbed more sticks and fanned the flame so that in a moment, when Edmund and Morton poked their heads through the door, the fire was crackling.

Edmund entered silently and knelt by Joseph's bench. He pulled the shredded pant leg away from the wound and looked closely. "When were you hurt, Joseph?" he asked.

"Day ago. 'Twas soldiers, give me a solid kick. Twis' m' leg and bust it up." The old man's eyes were bulging wide. "You shoot a deer?" he asked.

"I got a deer, Joseph, but tell me about the soldiers," Edmund said.

"Organ meat can spoil in a hurry. Bes' fill the stew pot, eh?" Joseph's eyes watered and his hand reached shakily for Edmund's arm. He moistened his cracked lips with his tongue. Edmund glanced at Maggie sitting beside the old man. She nodded.

Later, Eleanor brought in several blankets from the buckboard, after it had been decided that they would stay the night in Joseph's cave. Maggie saw her jump back, startled, as she laid the blankets on the bench beside the old man. Joseph had reached over to the short plank where Maggie sliced raw deer liver. The dark red slices lay side by side. He leaned back on his slab bench, vigorously gumming a piece, with bubbles of blood collected in the corners of his lips, his eyes glazed and appreciative.

Eleanor stepped further back, ducking her head under the various nets and ropes hanging about. She glanced nervously at Edmund.

"'Tis bad off, Joseph is," Edmund nodded. "Good you discovered him here." Edmund laid a hand on the old man's shoulder, poured water into the kettle and hung it on a chain over the fire. He tossed in several wild onions and found a tin cup with more than enough salt. "Perhaps he'll tell us what the soldiers did."

Joseph's head started to bob. He leaned on the bench while everyone jostled past each other in the tiny cave, preparing the meal. "Ah stay away from town fer a reason," Joseph shook his head. "'Twas up the river, fishing, when some trappers come across from the west with their Shawnee guides. Got across, and there sat soldiers waiting with a wagon, forced all the Injuns on the buckboard, ransacked their goods and tossed blankets over the folks."

"Trappers come nigh, said they's peaceful folks, but the soldiers took 'em. Could scarce believe my eyes. Ah jumped on one a the horses and rode with 'em to the fort entrance, all the while arguing with the soldiers. There at the stockade gate, we had a skirmish and the soldiers give me a drubbing." He patted his leg. "Told 'em, them Shawnees ain't about botherin' this town!"

Eleanor spoke up, "Why arrest peaceful folk?"

Edmund looked at her. "Seems they're spoiling for another Indian war."

Joe shook his head. "Mingos be the only warrin' bands in these hills."

"There's a bad smell to the 'Kaintuckee' business," said Maggie.

Edmund cleared his throat and agreed. "They want the natives to move further west, open up Kentucky to the farmers. They figure to rile the Indians and cause the whole settlement to take up arms and chase them beyond the Kentucky lands."

They sipped venison soup from cups. The boys fell asleep in their laps so Edmund piled leaves on the rock slabs and helped Eleanor and Maggie wrap themselves with blankets. Edmund and Eleanor sat up discussing the Penn governors' abandonment of the area. Old Croghan, Joe had heard, had taken it upon himself to raise a band of rovers to keep peace on the rivers.

Maggie turned over with her back to their conversation, though it was some time before she was able to sleep. Her thoughts retreated into the days of her youth, when she lived among peaceful Indians, the Delaware and Shawnee, in the village of Shamokin at the forks of the Susquehanna River. The memories flowed into dreams, but dreams with wild scents and strong rhythms that made sleep impossible. When Maggie woke, the cave's darkness was tempered only by a faint red glow in the bowl of the fireplace.

She sat up, found the wax lamp and lit it from the coals. She pulled her old bag close, gathering papers and pen and ink. Looking around the cave at all the still bodies, she noted Edmund's absence; he was outside, she assumed, guarding their hill. But her thoughts were unguarded, and while they were fresh with scents of the forest and the deep drumming of rawhide covered kettles, she wanted to capture them with the scratched lines on paper. She wrote:

Dear Family,

As I lie awake with thoughts and prayers that the peaceful Shawnee people captured by Dunmore's soldiers will be returned safely to their homes and left undisturbed, I shudder to think how unlikely are my hopes. But we shall not give up. Someday our hopes may lie heavier in the balance.

Awash with thoughts of my first introduction to Shamokin town, I must tell you how I came to be there. From Philadelphia, Weiser had taken me to the Ephrata cloister, or to a farm down the road from the cloister where I cared for the elderly father of one of the Ephrata monks in his dying days. I knew the old man for less than one year, but caring for him helped me lay my own father to rest as well. By the time he was buried beside his wife on the farm they had settled and loved dearly, I was sixteen years old and ready to rejoin the world. I had seen Weiser regularly. His Tulpehocken farm was not far away. He was the one who informed me that the Moravians had chosen me in their lottery to marry a German fellow named Carl Beigler, who would assist the Shamokin blacksmith with repairs of guns and farm tools. I had a choice, of course, but the opportunity to live in the woods held a powerful lure.

I recollect sitting behind Conrad Weiser on his horse as we rode into Shamokin. I was still an unmarried girl, though I had arrived in Shamokin to meet my intended husband. We entered town on a steep, heavily forested hill, past a cluster of round, bark huts at the edge of wide, unkempt fields. The air was scented with tobacco and smoke-cured deerskins. The Lenapes' huts were built of layered, black bark strips for both walls and roof. A nearby cluster of longer wood lodges were the homes of the Shawnees. The village amounted to fifty homes with nigh three hundred villagers, though some lived upon the island in the river.

Swataney was there, the Oneida overseer of the international village. He and his family were set apart by living downstream. Weiser and his men had built Swataney a most impressive fifty-foot-long lodge standing on poles, with a wood floor and a stone chimney rising through the roof. Nearby were the log buildings of the Moravians, one a sturdy English-style house of the sort built for Swataney, and the other a rough-hewn hut with a lean-to smithy's shop out back.

The native people crawled from their huts with furs about their shoulders and pictures painted on their skin and clothes. I recall vast steaming pots with clumps of boiled grass hanging beside them on sticks.

The Macks and a blacksmith had returned to Shamokin, with the Indians' permission to run the smith shop. Swataney had refused the offer of a mission years ago, but was thankful for the Moravian 'axemakers.' He praised their willingness to work in the fields and their restraint from 'making the Indians into white people.'

I knew nothing more than your Granpapa's name upon leaving the cloister with Weiser. Even as we rode through the birch and sycamore trees to a clearing near Swataney's cabin, I knew not whom to expect. Weiser escorted me into the dark lodge, lined with deer and wolf skins to keep the winter drafts away. We sat upon bear hides while all about our heads hung ceremonial robes and dry strands of corn and squash. Behind us lay another fireplace and walls lined with bunks built of long poles and leather lashings.

My eyes adjusted slowly to the darkness. I first saw Swataney's firelit face, his peaceful nod as several men crowded through the narrow doorway across from Weiser. Weiser moved aside so Carl Beigler could sit at my side. I held out my hand nervously to the smooth-shaven man of ordinary features, older than I expected...past thirty years by then. He took my hand and said simply, 'Pleased.' I was relieved to find that he spoke English, though he was never a man of many words. He had lived among the English Moravian colony in Nazareth.

Weiser told us to sit in silence and wait for the chief's blessing. Swataney's head rocked as his words flowed. Weiser interpreted the song about a young brave who was adopted when he showed the people a new hunting ground. Swataney said his people had lived long with no guns for hunting and he was pleased with the new tools, sharp hatchets and knives.

Then Swataney turned to me and said, 'Welcome, Mag-way.' 'Tis what he called me. I touched the turtle totem and asked Weiser to tell the chief of my pleasure and honour.

Swataney spoke English to Carl, 'We trust our adopted daughter to take pain from your heart. Make you new wife...new child.' 'Tis how I learned that Carl's former wife had died in childbirth some months prior. He had arrived afterward in Shamokin and had only known Swataney a short time. When I asked about his mourning, Carl said simply that his family had gone with grace into the Lord's care. Nothing more. Ever.

We had a mere fortnight to prepare for the wedding. I wore a doeskin wedding dress, made by my first native friend, Swataney's daughter. Missus Mack could pronounce her Cayuga name, but the others of us embarrassed ourselves. She had come to be called 'White Hawk' because of the bundle of six white feathers intertwined in her waist-long, black hair. Her eyes were nearly as dark, fluid pools like the chief's. She and the others all called me Mag-weh, because Swataney was the village authority and 'tis what he called me. The Ephrata monk had given me a pale tanned doeskin, from which White Hawk made the dress, adding flowing, colorful quill work. She was indeed like a hawk, both strong and soft, swift and watchful. We were fast friends, though she was older by perhaps ten years and spoke Cayuga, her mother's language. We found ways to communicate and often sensed each others' thoughts.

Then there was Mister Carl Beigler, who strode about with one of two looks upon his face: either a hard-working stern look, or the same with a faint softening at the corners of his lips, a smile of sorts. People seem to have their soul's messages rising through the lively pools of their eyes, but not Carl, not to my sight in any way.

A visiting minister performed a rightful joining. The Moravians invited the natives, though few but Swataney's family attended. Imagine your young Gran, tiny bosom bound with quilled rows of feathers, shells and fringe lacings, clutching my turtle and a bunch of wild blue flowers. I felt as if I were a packaged gift to my new husband. He gazed with the same politeness as the day we met, ice blue eyes steady, as if 'twere commonplace for a maiden of sixteen to appear in soft doeskin and offer herself for betrothal. He fixed his gaze upon the minister's Bible, held open before us until the words ended. The Moravians' lively songs and Brother Mack's brass horn were all that lifted my doubtful, heavy anchor. We shared a love feast with Swataney's family, who provided celebration music and drumming.

Marrying a stranger was a difficult thing, especially with Carl seeming less than pleased with the notion. But his manner improved as years went along. As I sit in this cave considering the disturbing times upon us, seems near all my days in this land have been so unsettled.

Shamokin's name refers to a cave also. A den of mischievous spirits is said to lie upriver from the village. The town was known as a gathering place, the hub of many Indian trails and the fork of two great rivers. Where the water merged into one wide flowing stream, people had gathered for generations, merging their thoughts and voices. But the mischievous spirits floated like clouds over the valley, keeping it unsettled. Differing cultures disapproved of each other's habits. Varied languages kept people further apart.

I learned posthaste that one never knew what the day may bring. All tribes knew their way to Shamokin. Warring parties from the north would stop only to excite the village and drink their fill of rum. Delaware and Shawnee families trickled through, oft stopping for several seasons before continuing to the Ohio country. Some stayed for years, many stayed only days. At times, amidst the chaos, it seemed a different language flowed from every mouth.

The Moravian huts were closer to Swataney's lodge than to the main village. We considered ourselves set apart from the noise and activity, though the Delawares and Shawnees regarded our shop and huts as set apart from their world. We were considered unfriendly by some of the villagers, farming inside our fences and rarely venturing closer. Missus Mack had described months when she and Brother Mack huddled afraid at night because a visiting tribe had been so dreadfully wild, howling and shooting firearms near all the night. She thought peace had surely come to Shamokin since they had gone across the river and taken with them their barrels of whiskey and loud celebrations.

I was content to settle into the blacksmith's tiny back room with a man and a marriage I knew nothing of. I was hungry for the woods, yes, even the dirt floor and the hard work of providing our own goods.

The blacksmith shop was constantly aclatter as the smithy, Hagen, shoed horses or repaired tools or guns. Hammers and tools hung from pegs and several hatchets leaned next to a grinding wheel, ready to be sharpened. Indians visited all through the day, but Hagen had no patience. He sent them away at the end of the day, of course refusing their offers of rum.

English fur traders came from the north and the south, from the trading posts of the Susquehanna. They always took an offered bowl of stew from the villagers, then procured a cup of rum and became loudly insulting to the Moravians whose garden filled their bowl.

"Them missionaries are here t' make slaves of yuh," one told the Indians as he spit his tobacco juice. "Put no mark on their paper. 'Twill lose yer land t' save yer soul."

Gaining the Indians' trust was a struggle after those visits. We mended their clothes and sewed new shirts, dug weeds from their fields and opened our stores of flour and maple sugar. We dared not risk putting them off with our prayers. We sang hymns only at the Saturday service. We near likened ourselves to slaves on their behalf. Our long hours of labor resulted in occasional visits from the friendly villagers or a rare Indian voice joining in our songs.

I would come to learn about the village by following Anna Mack from hut to hut. She did more than any other Moravian to bridge the cultures because of her knowledge of Mohawk, having lived near the tribe as a youngster. She knew the Lenapes' language as well, more than most of the whites. Whenever a villager was ailing, she would go promptly to bleed him or offer a tonic. 'Twas not unusual for the Shawnee medicine woman to call on her assistance.

She was a small woman with a serene smile and powdered cheeks. An excellent gardener, she was kindhearted to the natives and unshaken by their primitive ways. Mister Mack was quiet and serious, though kindly. Both seemed unlikely persons to be living among Indians in the woods, but they taught me that giving an ear to the Indians' stories was always met by their willingness to listen to ours. I was comforted to live among them in Shamokin.

'Twas wintertime when I approached White Hawk to show me how the Indians tanned their hides. She removed them from a scalding pot with a long stick and draped several skins over a branch to drip. We stretched another over a sturdy log frame beside the fire. She leaned over the deerskin with her sharp bone tool and began scraping the wet hair from the hide.

We talked, with hand signs and a few words, of our husbands. She said she had admired Cajadis and had sent her mother to speak to his mother, arranging their union. I liked that better than the Moravians' lottery system, which I struggled to explain.

The Delaware women gathered for sewing, cooking or other domestic duties with the children afoot. Missus Mack was known to walk amongst them since she could speak their language. They often made community meals in large kettles. She took goods to add to their stews, though our participation was rarely invited. Hagen had insulted them mightily with comments about their manner of eating vile parts of beasts. The Moravians preferred to keep to their own kettles.

Carl, unlike Hagen, ate all flavours of stew without a pause or an inquiry on the contents. Carl gave few compliments, but I must say he also gave few complaints. In short weeks I understood his preference for quiet and learned to be less needful of his company. I refrained from embracing, merely placing a hand on his shoulder upon his arrival. As his tension eased, he became less reserved.

In the winter months, the Indians' tradition was to send out hunting parties on long ventures. In springtime, the men helped clear land, but tending the plants was the work of the women. The Moravians, though, working alongside the Indian style of farming, planted their own separate neat rows surrounded with split rail fencing.

The Indians' corn, beans and squash intermingled and thrived. They explained that the plants were sisters, eager to grow together. The three crops supported each other by the life they gave back to the soil. Much of the community land was planted with corn, their most dependable and versatile crop.

On days when work was finished in the gardens or during high winds or rain, the women sat together and wove baskets from old corn husks, straw reeds or elm strips. They used larger strips than the ones in your mother's fine baskets and brooms. The men built canoes with sapling pole frames, bent and wrapped with heavy bark strips laced together and sealed with a staining dark pitch. A thin wood edge curved forward in a point, where the canoe sliced through the water.

Though white people were a constant presence in the area, our crossing into the Delaware or Shawnee domain would raise a stir of voices and send children scurrying into huts. Eager to offend them naught, we stayed at a respectful distance. My closest experience of the Delawares' acceptance was when they proceeded to unearth a cache, removing a bark mat protecting the deep pit full of last season's corn. Either they felt they could trust Missus Mack and myself with their hiding place or they intended to relocate it before the next season's use.

Carl and Hagen had busy seasons in the blacksmith shop. In addition to their guns, the Indians brought tools and knives to sharpen or repair. Carl often took tools into the fields to show the women how to ease their backbreaking labor. With interest, the Indians watched the white men plow, but never wanted to learn to use the implement and kept it out of their own fields.

We came upon difficult times in midsummer, when a sudden fierce illness overcame the young child of Tagnehdorus, Swataney's oldest son. One morning I observed the young father carrying his small child into the river, rinsing her fever. His younger brother, Tahgajut, waded to his side. You've heard me refer to Tahgajut by his English name, Logan. I knew his walk from a distance because he limped from an old injury. I set my basket down and watched from the shore. Tagnadorus held his listless child whose tiny eyes were puffed closed. Her mouth fell open, dry and cracked.

"Has she awakened?" I asked, knowing both men had a fine understanding of English. Tagnehdorus shook his head, with no explanation and no words of hope. The little girl shivered as Tagnehdorus pulled her close, his massive arms cradling her tiny brown body. Later that night, the plaintive wailing began, sending a clear message of grieving: Swataney had lost a grandchild.

While the villagers wailed and Swataney's lodge prepared for a condolence ceremony, a messenger from Bethlehem arrived at the blacksmith shop, looking for Brother Hagen. He carried the news that Hagen's wife and child would not be joining him. They too had died of a fever.

The wailing took up from all corners of the village, Hagen and the Moravians on the edge of the forest and Tagnehdorus at the river, bellowing cries over the water. The Shawnees and Delawares joined in the wailing when they learned how close to them death had visited. 'Twas Tahgajut, or Logan who suggested a joint condolence ceremony, offering Hagen a grieving robe and a string of wampum. The small carved shells strung in patterned rows were said to carry messages directly to and from the Great Spirit. A fire was built at the edge of the woods where Swataney's lodge gathered, wailing and singing. Grief was the language spoken, known by its deep spasm of despair in any tongue.

ς

The door opened and I put down my pen, wiping tears from my cheeks. Quinn had packed all of our things and while I wrote, had finished loading the car. She sat on the end of the bed, looking at my notebook.

"How are they?" she smiled.

"They make my life feel so simple. I feel ashamed for thinking I've ever had a problem," I said.

Quinn squeezed my neck, playfully. "Remember the messages your body sends you. Fear is fear. Tension is tension."

"This was quite a letter from Maggie," I said, closing the notebook. "I'll read it to you in the car."

Quinn picked up her jacket and a backpack and sauntered toward the door. "Thanks to your pre-dawn awakening, it's still early. We're close enough that we could have lunch in Philadelphia. I guess we should see it, right? Later we can drive up to Bethlehem," she said casually.

"I thought it had become a nasty steel industry town," I said.

She turned around as she held the door open. "I asked at the desk. They said the old historical Moravian buildings are still there, built like stone forts, you know."

I was still saturated with the grief of Maggie's recollections from Shamokin village. I struggled to mix those feelings with the exhilarating thought of finding a whole and preserved town of old Bethlehem, shielded from the industrial revolution it helped conceive. I thought about calling my father. I wanted to grab hold of Maggie's hand. And Quinn's. I felt like singing in the sanctuary of forgotten time that I was inexplicably remembering every day. I wanted to cry and dig through the past to see my mother's face, just one more time.

5

The entry into Philadelphia was less of a visual shock for me than driving into Pittsburgh. The skyscrapers eased onto the horizon as we emerged from the rolling Schuylkill River valley. We had joined Highway 76 before Norristown and wound along the river through the thinning orange and yellow canopy of the forest-covered hills. Massive stone arch bridges carried increasing car and train traffic across the river as we neared the city.

Signs of the urban contrasts became frequent: 18th century stone buttresses beside cement, graffiti-covered walls; graceful bridges topped with the steel-post and wire jungle carrying electric current for the commuter trains. Abandoned industrial carcasses had rusty or collapsing roofs and broken windows entangled with ivy vines. After passing through, or over, some of the decrepit areas, I felt relieved when Quinn pulled onto the broad expanse of Ben Franklin Boulevard, headed directly toward City Hall. Atop its tower, William Penn's statue is no longer the tallest site, but he's still at the center of the city, extending his brotherly hand.

On the drive, Quinn had been less talkative than usual. From Reading to Norristown, I had recounted Maggie's letter, telling about Shamokin, Maggie's marriage and life among the strange village in the woods. "Imagine," Quinn nearly whispered, "being in such a different world."

We passed through the busy financial district and meandered through an older neighborhood of narrow, weather-etched brick facades that seemed to call out to me to come closer and feel them. Stone curbs and cobblestones lined an old alleyway barely wide enough for the horse drawn carts that had once delivered ice or food. We pulled into a parking lot beneath a hand-painted wall mural. We'd been encouraged by the hotel clerk in Reading to go for a walk through historic Olde City.

There were numerous directional signs to aid pedestrian tourists. Washington Park was nearby so we took a diagonal path through one of William Penn's original town squares. A woman stood in the walkway,

photographing a small memorial wall. The park had once been a burial ground
for Revolutionary War soldiers and prisoners and we stood among thousands
of unmarked graves. The grief I felt in Pittsburgh returned, tugging like a
needy child at my hands and arms.

I felt a knot close up the airway in my throat. I said, "Quinn, I don't know
if I can do this."

"Maybe it was a bad idea to come here," Quinn said. She saw a sign to
Penn's Landing and glanced at our map. There appeared to be a waterfront
park where the early docks once stood.

"That would have been where Maggie first set foot on American soil," I
said. "I think we need to see that. I'll be okay."

Quinn pointed to the next block. "We're passing by Independence Hall,"
she said. Grassy park land extended toward the red brick colonial State House
and the tower that once held the Liberty Bell. I agreed to walk closer, though
I felt my breath shorten as the tourist crowds increased. As we approached
the small pavilion that housed the famous cracked bell, we noticed numerous
construction barriers. Posters announced the new Visitor Center that would
open across the street within weeks. Hordes of people stood in queues behind
waist-high concrete barriers lining the edge of Market Street.

"Oh, my God," said Quinn. "Imagine the security they must have here
now."

We passed the makeshift building set up by the Park Service to search
bags and secure the crowds visiting America's birthplace. I looked across
the construction site to the front of the old State House, where crowds had
risked death hundreds of years ago to gather on the square and listen to the
revolutionaries read the Declaration of Independence out loud. I watched the
crowd of a hundred people standing in line and wondered if they thought of
themselves as patriots. Maybe by the end of the tour, I thought.

Quinn was talking to one of them who showed her his ticket for a visit of
the bell pavilion and Independence Hall. "He said they're free, but you have
to get tickets for timed tours," she said, walking back.

"I have to tell you, Quinn. I can't do it today. Just standing near this
crowd feels like holding matches to my skin," I said.

"Ouch," she said. "I believe you're the one who said not to let the terrorists
get to me."

"It's not that. I'll come back and see it someday. So much national history
happened here. But these buildings seem so formal; the marble, the columns,
the sprawling gardens."

"Yeah," said Quinn. "And you want to peel back the layers to get to the first dirt street, or some crooked little cobblestone path winding down to the boat landing."

"Hey. Sounds like you're picking up on Maggie's bleed-through thoughts now. I thought I was the only one."

Quinn shrugged. "It's the letters, I guess. I think about her, too, you know."

I shook my head. "You're not thinking. You're seeing."

"Don't pull me into your dreamality. I'm just a regular gal. I don't remember the last time I saw a ghost."

"Ah ha! Now I know why you're being such a good sport. You believe in ghosts."

"Well. Don't you?" said Quinn. "Now that you're having daily chats with one?"

"Whatever," I said. "Anyway, use your intuition and tell me which way to that crooked little cobblestone path."

She pointed at an angle, through another parkway. We walked past several more noteworthy sites and stopped to read their small historical markers; the Carpenter's Hall, host of the first meetings of the Continental Congress and the reconstructed City Tavern where the Founding Fathers had "unofficial" meetings. Shortly past the quaint tavern, Quinn stopped walking and stared ahead. A cobblestone street spread out before us. I glanced at a signpost by the intersection and read, "Dock Street." I smiled. "Wow. You're good."

Something about the pleased look on Quinn's face made me certain that I had a steadfast partner to the end of our journey. She was no longer tagging along on my vision quest. The cobblestones curved around a Korean War memorial and led to an overpass for the Interstate alongside the Delaware River. Dock Street ended, not at the old docks but at a towering Hyatt Hotel and a small park.

We walked behind the hotel to the brick and concrete riverfront. Only a few boats cruised the area where the city's main docks had stood. A sign for the RiverLink Ferry pointed to the New Jersey State Aquarium and several other attractions across the Delaware in Camden, New Jersey. The shipping industry appeared to concentrate there and further downstream.

A few tourists and kids roamed the riverfront which stretched for several city blocks. A line of old fashioned lampposts was the only reminder that the same area had once been crowded with the young town's first immigrants. Not only Maggie's ship, but my dad's German ancestors and Quinn's had sailed to this site. A small seaport museum and a posted sign declaring Penn's Landing honored the multitude of sea crossings.

A terraced plaza was built up the hillside, dotted with trees and flagpoles. The amphitheatre that likely hosted small outdoor concerts was occupied by a few African American young men hopping up and down deserted steps. A rap cadence carried on the breeze, but words were unintelligible from our distance. Clapping and a little shoving accompanied their pulsing rhythm.

We saw signs for a pedestrian walkway that would take us back over the Interstate. As we headed past the group of young men, I noticed that they changed directions to watch us. Quinn noticed it, too. She seemed to have caught the eye of one of the youths. He jabbed an index finger toward us as if he was addressing the two of us, but still, I heard nothing but a hum. I was nervous and wanted her to walk faster, then I saw the piercing stab of her eyes and knew she had heard something she didn't like. Then I heard it, too. I was pretty sure. Something about "dykes."

My thought was to leave. Quickly. But Quinn stood firm, as if daring the young man to come closer. "Oh, god," I said as my stomach lurched. I thought to myself, "You can't fight this, Quinn. Not now." Aloud, I asked, "Quinn, what are you doing?"

Her eyes remained steeled upon the young man who was becoming even more loudmouthed, as if her challenge invigorated him. She said, "This punk thinks he's so tough."

"Come on. Let's walk."

"I'm not going to be chased away."

"We were leaving anyway. Come on," I said, pleading.

The guy saw us talking and slapped the shoulder of one of his friends. All five of them started walking toward us. I should say they strutted. I looked nervously up and down the riverwalk. The few people that had been around were too far away to hear even if I could get a sound to come out of my throat.

Quinn shook her head and pointed a foot casually, jutting a hip toward them. As they came closer, I noticed they were younger than I had thought, barely old enough to drive. Facial hair sprouted from a few chins. Quinn held up one finger as if wanting to make an important point. Two who followed the young man laughed and elbowed each other, like they knew a dirty little secret. Then the guy stopped abruptly and stood glaring at Quinn.

I wanted to grab her arm and drag her away as the others fanned around us, watching with amused smirks on their faces. Quinn had enough boldness for both of us, but I struggled to keep my face as steely and unshaken as hers.

She tipped her head and calmly asked him, "What do you think it was like?"

He squinted and smiled. "You mean makin' it with a woman? I know what it's like." The boys all laughed and slugged each other's arms.

"No. You saw New York," she said, staring him down. "Imagine all the ash. Like the world was ending."

"Damn." He screwed up his face and spun around. "Come on. Dyke's crazy, man. She's sick," he whined to his friends. The group scurried along the plaza toward the riverwalk, a few looking back at us, jabbing each other.

I was nearly as shocked as they were, though very relieved to see them go. It was as if Quinn had thrown a stone at a flock of birds, but a stone no one could see.

"What did you just do?" I asked.

She was watching them all the way down the riverwalk. She turned and went in the opposite direction. "You remember Gibbs? The old guy from the restaurant?" she asked. "Something he said popped into my head. Something about how everybody does the same thing today that they did yesterday. You know, creatures of habit." I nodded, urging her on. "Well, that boy was setting me up for a fight. He used his words, his body, pushed all the buttons to get to me. He thought he knew just what was coming."

"Me, too," I admitted.

"He's so full of anger." She headed up the steps that led to the pedestrian walkway. "Something in his eyes. I'm not sure. I just felt he was really afraid. Deep down…traumatized."

"Not New York."

"No. No. Long before that. But I knew that would remind him. My God. When those buildings came down, all anyone could feel was bone-chilling fear. I don't care how angry they were, before or after."

The walkway, lined with planters of dried flowers and grasses, had tall brick walls that blocked the noise of the highway below. I might have relaxed as if walking through a quiet garden, but I continued to glance behind, in case we were being followed.

"Back to what Gibbs said. Anger's a habit?" I asked.

Quinn nodded. "Habits are tough. I've seen players who can't shake a bad habit no matter how much trouble it causes them. Can't learn a new move because they keep reverting back to one that's comfortable."

"So that kid knows how to pick fights and relies on the 'play?'"

"Gibbs wanted me to toss him something he wasn't expecting," she said.

"You defused him. But I get flustered by angry people," I said. "You know how to keep your cool."

"I have to tell you," Quinn said. "At first, I wanted to rip that boy's tongue out. I hate being harassed because of my gender or sexual orientation. Then I sensed Gibbs. 'Do it differently.'" She imitated Gibbs' throaty voice. "The old guy warned me about being hooked by the anger. I didn't take the anger bait. That's a new one for me."

"You think that boy lives with anger?"

"Totally. He studies it." Quinn shrugged. "He's built a wall of anger. Anger is his box!"

"Wow. I don't know. I think a lot of people—those young men—feel they have plenty to be angry about. Look. Isn't this a school day? They're not there. What chance is there for college? What do they look forward to? What about people who've had their families ripped apart. I'd be angry, too."

Quinn said, "That's just it. The kid grows up hearing he's not good enough, not smart enough. There are so many ways to make a person feel bad. Feel left out."

"How does acknowledging fear make him feel better?" I asked. I tried to remember what Gibbs said about building walls to feel safe, in control. I made a mental list, my idea of someone in control; job, education, money, clothes, power. Those kids were being left out.

"The world without walls," said Quinn. "Ugh." She jerked like she'd been physically hit and slapped a hand to her chest. "Oh, Reed," she moaned.

"Oh, god," I said, feeling my chest collapse with a crumbling pain.

"We can't control the world," Quinn said. "None of us wants to face that fear."

"Our sense of security collapsed," I said.

"We're all made of the same stuff, you know? Flesh and blood," said Quinn.

"But the other images are so strong. All the people helping," I said. "Through all the dust and chaos—people just reached out wherever help was needed."

"That's it."

"What is?"

"If we could do that every day, without the trauma," Quinn said, shaking her head. "Just help each other. When it comes down to it, we talk about the heroes, but in the back of my mind, I'm afraid I might have choked. I might have crawled under a desk and sobbed."

"Not you, Quinn. I don't think so." I hadn't seen her turn around once to check for those kids. She must have sensed they were no longer a problem.

"Courage. Where does it come from?" I asked. "If I had only a moment to tell someone how much they'd meant to me, I don't know if I could even make the phone call."

"But you're answering Maggie's call," Quinn said. I stared at her. "All this time," she said, "I've thought you were courageous. I don't think I could do it. I'd keep hanging up if Maggie was calling me."

We had walked a few blocks and headed toward town on Chestnut Street. Most of the district fronting the river was not clean and quaint like other parts of Olde City. Standing in front of a dilapidated building, we stopped and looked around. Fences blocked off deconstructed sites and piles of rubble. It was a street of aged three- and four-story buildings, some with the old business names or numbers etched in the stone facade.

Maybe it's my small-town upbringing, but even though I'm accustomed to Chicago's rich cultural diversity, I was surprised at the number of ethnic restaurants in Philadelphia. We had passed a typical Italian pizza joint and a Chinese restaurant on Front Street closer to the river. This short stretch housed representative eateries from Thailand, Brazil, Mexico, India, Cuba, and we were passing the second one from Afghanistan.

Quinn also noticed and stopped to read the menu on the window. She said, "How weird is it that there are two Afghanistan restaurants in one block?"

"Across from Independence Mall," I said.

"I'm curious to try this after watching those people on television struggle with our packages of peanut butter. I should know what Afghanistan's food is like."

"Looks similar to Indian. I like that." Once my nerves had settled I realized I was hungry. I agreed that we should try their lunch. We opened the door to scents and melodies, we assumed, of Afghanistan. Soft colors were accentuated by bright textiles and garments decorating the walls of the narrow room. The front window had a platform seating area for traditional Afghanistan-style dining on Oriental rugs and cushions. There were people seated already at several front tables.

Spicy hot tea and a Sambosa appetizer, chick peas and potatoes in pastry, preceded our entrees. My salmon kababs were delicious and moist. But I realized I felt completely ignorant of Afghan culture. Knowing only that it was a landlocked, mountainous country, I asked the waiter if they actually had salmon there.

"Oh, yes," he said. "In the north. But closer to Kabul they have mostly trout."

"Rainbow trout?" I asked. I tried to imagine brooks full of trout in the mountains of Afghanistan. I wondered what sort of bait or style the fishermen used. I pictured our southern Illinois county fairs and the paper dishes with a trout on top of mounded French Fries. Then I imagined the native people from the Delaware River valley who taught the early colonists to fertilize their crops with fish from the river. I could walk outside and crumble a handful of soil from the lot next door and it could be the same soil where a young German farmer had planted his first crop.

I said, "I wonder if Gibbs took our walls down. My thoughts seem all mixed up; different times and places."

Quinn nodded and asked, "Maggie?"

"Not really. I was thinking about the Indians who taught the colonists to use fish for fertilizer."

She scowled. "Oh, thanks. At least one of us is finished." She was eating a variety of Chalow, a mixture of vegetables, chicken and lentils on Basmati rice. "Since we saw Gibbs, I'm feeling things more intensely, too. These vegetables are very fresh." She set down her fork and rubbed her chest beneath the collarbone. "Are you feeling okay?" she asked.

"I'm better. If I can't calm down in this place, I'm in trouble," I said with a hushed voice. Soft melodic tunes had filled the restaurant during our lunch. Quinn signaled the waiter for our check as I watched passersby out the window. "I think I'm ready to head out of Philadelphia," I said. "I feel antsy."

She agreed. But as we exited the restaurant, I glanced down the street and spotted a faded blue awning with yellow printing that read, 'Pow wow.' We walked closer to see the front of the building, a meeting place or museum for the Delaware Valley Indians. The door to the storefront office was locked, a poster covered the glass and several small newspapers lay in a pile. I stepped up on a pipe to see through the high and dusty front window. There were empty glass display cases inside, a rack of cards, some Powwow posters on the walls and small American flags on tiny wooden sticks, stuck in a cup on top of the cases.

"Well, it's not exactly empty," I said. "But maybe they're moving."

"Maybe they don't have much money," said Quinn. "At least to spend on offices. But they're here. We'll see if we can find a phone number or a website."

"Why do we keep coming up empty with these museum places?" I asked.

"Get a clue, Reed. This is not something anyone else can help with. You're not going to find the answers in a book or a display case."

A hefty man came out of the sandwich joint next door and announced the best Philly cheesesteak sandwiches in town. I groaned. "Sorry, we just ate," I said.

"What did you eat? There's always room for Philly cheesesteak. How long are you in town?"

We waved at the guy and walked up the block to Market Street. We'd decided to ride the bus as far as 10th Street so we could find our car and get on our way. The driver of the first bus that stopped told us the next one would go near Washington Park. When it came, we eased into seats on the sunny side of the aisle. Afternoon rush-hour traffic had begun, slowing everyone. The bus crawled into its lane. I gazed out the window as we passed a beautifully restored colonial red brick building with prim yellow shutters along the row of tiny storefront windows. One sign announced a Post Office Museum and another read 'Benj. Franklin, Printer.'

I smiled and closed my eyes. I tipped my head sleepily against the bus window, listening to the slow hum of traffic and the clip-clop of a horse-drawn carriage beside us on Market Street.

ζ

Maggie stepped outside the cave door, expecting to find Edmund standing watch on the hillside. The skinned deer hung in the morning light, hoisted by its roped hind legs to a high branch of a lone sycamore tree to protect the carcass from scavenger animals. The fresh hide had been flung over a nearby leaning log.

She looked over the embankment to the road below that wound along the river to the edge of town, marked by a group of flickering orange fires. Maggie craned her neck to watch the movement in the shadows below as Edmund stepped into the sunshine, holding the reins of Coal walking behind. Coal's coat glistened with moisture, as if he had been ridden hard. They crisscrossed the hillside. Edmund looked up as they came near the rock embankment that hid the cave. He motioned to her, and then glanced behind him as if expecting to be followed.

"Mother Beigler," he said when he crossed the embankment. "'Tis early, yet."

"You returned to town?" she asked.

He nodded and tied Coal to a shaded stump. Peering around the rocks, he pointed to the group of fires. "I came out in the night. Sky was lit all along the river through town. Must have been hundreds of fires. Soldiers, they are."

"You saw them?"

"Men in the streets in the early hours," he barely whispered. "I chased a lone soldier who was tearing planks off the sides of Emory's shed. On Market Street, soldiers camped in clusters as far as Watson's Tavern, fully six streets from the fort."

"What befalls us?" Maggie asked.

"A tavern keeper said Lord Dunmore himself came from Virginia. With upwards of a thousand men, heading down the Ohio," Edmund said, scowling.

Maggie gazed down the rocky hillside. "Could have but one goal there. Indians live solely in those parts."

Edmund nodded. "Heard Daniel Boone was sent into Kentucky to warn the land surveyors of an Indian war."

A noise down the hill made both jump. Old Joe hobbled from the bushes leaning on a walking stick, a pail of water in hand. Edmund leaped up and took the pail, helping the frail man over the rock wall.

"Thank ya," Joe said, holding Edmund's arm. "A glory t' see the sunlight. Saved m' old hide, you did. Ahhh." He took a deep breath and stood up straight. "Saw no sign of you, Edmund. Nor the horse."

"I rode into town during the night hours." Edmund told Joseph about the soldiers headed for the Indian villages on the Ohio. "They aim to take two divisions, one by land and one by water. I have a mind to float your fishing raft downriver, sound a warning at the villages."

"No, no, no!" Joseph shook his head adamantly. "You'll not take m' raft!" The old man said, "Ah'll be the one takes t' th' river. Soldiers seen me time and again. Pay no mind." He poked at Edmund's chest, "You got a fam'ly t' heed."

"You're weak, yet, Joseph. Your leg..."

"Much improved. Ah jus' float n' steer." He gave Edmund a friendly slap on the back. "Mah raft. Ah go."

Maggie went into the cave to tell the others while they gathered provisions, paddles and a blanket from the hut. Edmund and the boys hiked down the hill where they launched the raft and aimed Joseph to the far side of the river. Maggie and Eleanor watched from the hillside as the old man's raft floated to the shady shore and on toward Pittsburgh.

Eleanor sat in the speckled light beneath the sycamore to read Maggie's pages while the older woman continued writing.

A grievous autumn continued, following the deaths in Tagnehdorus's and

Hagan's families. The only redemption was within my growing belly, as I was expecting our baby, our Eleanor. Having been ignorant of the growing of babies, I thought to ask White Hawk about my dizziness and the monthly blood gone awry. She whispered that Swataney had told her I would bear a daughter. "He is never wrong," she told me. "The child's image comes in a dream and cries at the edge of the forest until the chief brings it into the village." Carl, a quiet man as a rule, spoke proudly and often of our expected daughter.

Cold weather arrived earlier than usual and with it, a harsh sting. The Moravians were called to Swataney's lodge as Conrad Weiser and several Mohawk men smoked a pipe with the chief and spoke about rumours passed to the north about a secret alliance between Shamokin village and the French. The Delawares' aging chief, Allumapees, was dying. For twenty years, there had been rancor between the Delaware leader and Swataney, since the forks' area authority had passed to the Iroquois. Allumapees' nephews had recently departed the village, spitting bitter threats.

Weiser warned of the suffering French fur trade and the coming winter months, sure to bring hunger. He had sent a messenger to Bethlehem to request that the mission build a store so that they appeared more as a trading post. To the Moravians, Weiser said, "Swataney knows you have not cheated or tricked. No one asked them to depart to another country to be out of your way. You have become brothers."

The men spoke of the French forts being built in the western woods. Brother Mack told of the Shawnees that had departed angrily for the Ohio country, feeling encroached upon by the growing number of Delawares. With strained tones, he told of old Allumapees' nephews and their bitter claim of the rights to the Shamokin area. There had been confusion among the Iroquois and the colonists about the old Delaware chief's living relatives. The Iroquois had given the area leadership to Swataney and 'twas too late to repair ill feelings. Allumapees' nephews were gone and rumours of the Moravian and French alliance were spreading.

The rumours caused a meeting with the Iroquois to be set downriver near Harris' Ferry. Weiser escorted Swataney on horseback, and then returned with a deer to feed the hungry villagers. Supplies from Bethlehem had yet to arrive. The sparse, surviving crops grew slowly in the cool weather.

Carl became concerned that we had not been visited by the Indians from the west branch of the river in many weeks. He took several natives to visit the Montours' old village. I argued naught, for I admired his concern. I bade them well as they forded the river at a broad spot, holding high their guns and bags. Carl returned days later with patchy beard stubble and his usual stoic frame drooped with weariness. Most importantly, he had lost the vigor for hiding behind his mask of stony strength.

I stopped short when I saw him and waited for the inevitable barriers to be raised. I saw naught but fear. Carl was fretful as he described the sickness that had claimed many lives in the villages north and west along the river. The men brought the feverish survivors to the river island across from the village.

Carl said, "They are exhausted from caring for the sickened...and burying them. Surely, Swataney will agree to share some of our remaining food until more supplies from Bethlehem arrive." In private, he confided to me that 'twas the pox, the disease from our distant side of the sea. "They have no resistance and no medicines," he said, telling little more about his witness, but no longer appearing untouched.

Weeks passed with the food supply steadily dwindling. Failed hunting parties returned with stories of abandoned villages or warning flags of sickness. On occasions of success, the hunters' meat was divided and one of the men carried provisions to the island villagers yet recovering.

The difficulties mounted. Frequent storms threatened the harvest. Men, women and children brought in the surviving vegetables and prepared them for storage. One of the Macks' children took sick of a sudden and Missus Mack became dark eyed. As the Macks' child grew stronger, his mother failed and fever glistened brightly in her eyes. Brother Mack sat at Anna's side as she passed away. We huddled by our fire and cried without shame.

I had counted on having Anna Mack for my teacher for untold years, but there was no time to be spent kneeling for her. The mourning was curtailed by the appearance of a stern Brother Mack with his children loaded upon pack horses. They marched off toward Gnadenhutten where he sought assistance. For several years, he returned to our village frequently, sharing time between Bethlehem and the mission towns.

All corners of the village took sick. Carl shuffled between the fields and the shop while the harvest tool repairs were critical. One afternoon, he found Hagen crumpled on the ground. Sweat dripped from his forehead and his bony white fingers wrapped around the handle of an iron pincers.

Carl dragged him to the Macks' vacated house, saving our cabin and our unborn child from the fever. I continued to fetch supplies, remaining separate from the sickly quarters. Together with Tagnehdorus and the Shawnee medicine woman, Carl bathed the feverish smith with cool rags, but Hagen died on the third morning. Carl built a simple wood coffin and we quietly buried our blacksmith in the village burial ground.

We noted the Indians' ongoing preparations for the harvest ceremony in spite of the sickness. The natives believed in celebrating every gift they received or the Great Spirit would cease to provide. White Hawk's husband, Cajadis, the village's best hunter, returned from the hunt, tired and feverish. He and many in Swataney's lodge became gravely ill, including White Hawk.

I was fatigued, being with child, and could not sit with my friend. I prepared a kettle of turnip stew and Carl carried it to the stricken lodge. Tagnehdorus wept upon receiving our gift and gave a summary of the dim conditions inside the lodge: his own wife and infant were ill, as was the chief, Swataney's wife and three of his sons. White Hawk and her husband lay ill together, along with several of the grandchildren. We gave Tagnehdorus assurance that traders had been sent to Tulpehocken with a message about the epidemic.

Early the next morning the wailing began. The crowd outside Swataney's lodge mourned his little grandchild, the infant child of Logan, the middle brother. The mourners sang from a ledge overlooking the river. Small villages had sprung up across the river and on the island, dependent on Shamokin's strength and prosperity, but by the woeful songs, they knew Shamokin had joined them in burial of their dead.

White Hawk's husband, Cajadis, succumbed to the fever while she lay in a delirium. The wife of Tagnehdorus, the oldest son, also perished. Thankfully, Conrad Weiser rode into Shamokin with vials of medicine from a Philadelphia doctor. Anyone showing signs of the fever and willing to try the white man's medicine was given a dosage. But before the epidemic was finished, Swataney's dead outnumbered his living family.

A train of pack horses brought sacks of flour and corn from Bethlehem. The trading post was stocked with blankets, kettles, hoes, fish hooks and scissors, needles and thread. Carl received a shipment of smithy goods and word that a new blacksmith would arrive. Weiser promised to return to Bethlehem and deliver word of the illness that had devastated the village, especially the lodge of Swataney. Our relations with the other natives were further hindered by the fact that the heaviest casualties came to the lodge located nearest to the white men.

Before the pack horses were unloaded, the chief appeared at his doorway, eager to thank the Moravian horsemen. He hobbled about, making his way to every hut, assuring all that he was finally well.

In the midst of the harvest preparations, the Delawares' elderly chief, Allumapees died. Shamokin was seriously weakened by the sickness and caught in the dilemma of needing the white mission's food and assistance to survive.

The Delawares were weary of accusations that they drank too much and cheated the traders. We begged them to set aside their hostilities, fearing that Allumapees death and the meagre harvest might unleash their wrath. Some blamed the whites for the misfortunes that befell the village. We reminded them of our own losses and handed over all the remaining stores of the Macks' goods.

In truth, Shamokin village was deeply in need of help to survive the winter ahead. The natives depended on Moravian charity. Their first step came with accepting our shared harvest of beans and vegetables. They allowed us to be hospitable as Shamokin villagers had been to us and all visitors in their abundant past.

The harvest ceremony preparations went on inside the huts because of heavy rains. Drums announced the return of a small hunting party. The hunters brought one lone deer hanging on poles to the relocated fire on high ground. The villagers wandered out of wet huts with kettles of rinsed cranberries, split squash and shucked corn.

The villagers in ceremonial dress danced with loud drumming. At Swataney's lodge, I found White Hawk, finally recovered from the fever. She smiled with sunken eyes and pointed to a pair of moccasins hanging on the wall, made for me. I glanced at the worn shreds of leather tied to my feet then stepped into the moccasins. Dropping to my knees where she sat, we embraced.

The deer roasted on a flaming spit while kettles boiled. Dancing, storytelling, wild drumming and chants filled the evening air to a raucous pitch. During the commotion, Conrad Weiser returned and Swataney shuffled from his lodge in a robe of fur and feathers to meet him. Rum began flowing heavily and Carl and I retreated to our darkened cabin to wait for the celebration to pass. We fell asleep to the rhythmic beat of the drums.

In the morning, Weiser's urgent voice near the recently finished trading post announced the coming arrival of the new smith and trader, hopefully settling the talk among the province. He said, "Even gentle Quakers are unsettled by Moravian missions, with no understanding for how right-minded people can live in the woods with savages."

When I suggested the savages were those people who would run the Indians off their own lands, he said there are more arriving, shipload after shipload, expecting vast and plentiful land. He told us to keep close ties with our neighbor mission town of Gnadenhutten and keep the whiskey and rum away as much as possible.

Weiser spoke of colonists in the eastern cities who would get the Indians drunk to provoke a turbulence, and then shoot them. I gasped and he said, "It happens...and worse. No justice served."

Weiser planned to write to Ben Franklin, the new postmaster, to tell him how the Indians had taken to our presence and suggest a visit.

"What can the postmaster do?" asked Carl.

"Educate. Franklin has influence. He calls for a volunteer militia. If Pennsylvanians raise troops for defense, you need them to be for you, not against." Weiser added, cautioning, "Send for me if suspicious."

I was, of late, in the habit of dwelling solely on our misfortunes, so I hid my worried face. Should the pacifist Quakers be raising troops, surely, a battle was drawing nigh. When I considered the toll of the terrible illness and our daily struggle to keep mouths fed, I could not fathom the possibility of the colonists mistaking our efforts.

ζ

'Mistaking our efforts.' I put down my pen. When Quinn realized I was in and out of dreaming, she had pulled over at a roadside restaurant in Bucks County so I could finish writing. I was agitated when we arrived. All I recall is the sign at the entrance showing an Amish buggy lit up in neon. While she was drinking coffee and watching me write, Quinn's cell phone had rung. She left the table to walk up front and answer the call. I could see her by the plate glass window, waving her hands and talking.

I looked back at the pages I had written to tally Shamokin village's casualties. I was shaking. A piece of apple pie sat in front of me, untouched. I picked at the edge of the crust with my fork until Quinn came back to the table.

"What's wrong," she said. "You look like somebody died."

"It's a pretty grim outlook in Shamokin," I said. "Your phone rang. You have a girlfriend at home who's tired of waiting for you?" I asked, prying.

She looked more sullen than I felt. Saying nothing, she sank into the booth across from me and picked up her coffee cup. She made a face when she found it had cooled.

"Now you're always going to have to tell me if you don't want me to pry," I said. "What's up?"

One cheek twisted into a half smile. Quinn said, "Dang. I'm afraid of screwing up royally. I've got trouble."

"So I figured. Work?"

She nodded, followed by a long sigh. She seemed nervous, playing with her napkin, signaling the waitperson. "I'm so embarrassed to tell you this," she muttered.

I leaned back against the back of the booth, as casual and nonthreatening as I could look while her cup was refilled. "It's just me, Quinn," I said.

"Okay, here it is," she said. "That call was from the girl we watched play yesterday. I made a mistake and mentioned that I'd be in Pennsylvania for another couple of days, had another player to visit. She got my cell phone number from her coach and she's trying to find out if...you know, if I had made a decision."

"So? She's excited, anxious, a bit aggressive." I shrugged.

"I tried to explain to her that I don't make the decision. That we'd look at them both as individuals and someone would call her next week to tell her the next step."

"Right. So what's the problem?" I asked.

Quinn bit her lip. "She's gay." She stretched her arms and squeezed the back of her neck. "I don't know. I just got a vibe, you know? Gay-dar. She wasn't exactly coming on to me, but she seemed to be begging, like, 'Please take me away from this little town.'"

"Could that be all it is? Just eager to get to the big city?"

"The big city where she can meet some lesbians...bat those big, brown eyes, spread her buff arms and fly."

"Quinn?"

"I'm okay," she said. "Who knows if she even has a clue yet, but she quickly figured me out. She had her own gay-dar turned on, I'm telling you. She was checking me out and was pretty delighted, thinking she'd found an advocate."

"Has she? I mean, does it affect the way you see her skills?" I asked.

"I want to do what's appropriate, but I want to be careful, both with her and with my bosses. I don't want to give her the green light unless I'm a thousand percent sure she's right for us."

"Really?" I asked.

"I don't want it to look like I'm only interested in recruiting baby dykes."

I snorted. "So really, she has a disadvantage."

Quinn's eyes narrowed to slits. "I'm not sure I like this new Reed that says what she feels." Then she smiled. "So you think I need to find some balance?"

"You know how to balance. You were so good with that boy on the riverfront. Why do you put so much pressure on yourself?" I asked. "What's your real responsibility here?"

"Just a recommendation, based on our program's needs. Yes, we pursue. No, we don't."

"Someone else decides, ultimately," I said.

"Exactly."

I shrugged. "I saw her, too. She's good."

Quinn said, "So I give her the green light and she winds up on the team next year..."

"You'll be her hero," I said.

Quinn leaned forward, palming her head like a basketball. "I told you I wanted to get more involved, feel more of a part of the program," she said. "This is just closer than I wanted. I feel vulnerable."

"Yes? Why? Because you have to behave yourself?" I asked.

"Of course."

"Do you doubt that you can?"

"No. No, I haven't any reason for that. I just feel like I have to do this perfectly or I'm back to clerical work," she said.

"You're going to do a great job," I said. "And it doesn't have to be perfect."

"I don't know. I'm suddenly exhausted just thinking about it."

"Good," I said. "Then you'll let me drive."

We got into the Beetle and found our way to the highway onramp. Quinn said, "Weather report was maybe fog or rain. We don't have far to go, though." She closed her eyes. I let her nap. I could wait to tell her about Maggie's travails. Eight busy lanes of traffic flowed over the gentle hills, but everywhere I looked, I sensed creaky wooden wagons, narrow horse trails.

"You have to wait, too, Maggie," I said. "I have to drive." So much had happened in the last few days. I wondered again about Gibbs taking down our walls and my remembering Miss North. "It happened on the same night," I said out loud. "Of course it was because of him."

I believed I wanted a life outside the box, relieved of my fears, but as I thought about it, one thing was certain: I was alone inside that box. Quinn thinks it's a marvel that I can connect with Maggie, but I say Quinn is the marvel, connecting with everyone else in the world. I don't know if she'll be able to teach me. I've just assumed anyone I connected with would leave or die. Why hook up at all? Quinn's the exception. And Maggie.

We drove into Bethlehem after dark. Quinn woke up a little, enough to help me with directions. We found our way to a small hotel up the hill from the historic part of town, near the Moravian college. Quinn was so exhausted that I carried most of our belongings and watched her stumble into bed. Before closing her eyes, she said, "You were thinking while you drove. What did you figure out?"

"Nothing. That's just how I stayed awake."

"You liar," she mumbled.

"Okay. If my walls are down, I'm thinking that leaves you and Maggie sifting through my dusty self, seeing if there's anything left."

"Oh, there's a lot left, girl," said Quinn. "Don't doubt it. And tomorrow we're going to sift through Miss Maggie's life, too."

I was more exhausted than I realized and fell into bed soon after Quinn. The temperature had dropped and we had to turn up the heat to take the chill off the room. My head ached but the hum of the heater was somewhat soothing. If I had the energy to get up and hold my head under a cold faucet, I would feel fine. I lay on the pillow and imagined the shady bank of a river, the soft, gray current drifting past my eyes.

ζ

Before Joe had left for the river, Eleanor heated stew to send with him. Everyone had their fill before gathering belongings and riding back to town. It was dusk by the time Edmund drove the wagon along the edge of the swampy land at the town's edge. Everyone huddled silently until reaching the safe haven of the cabin. An eerie quiet hung about the town, the soldiers apparently having moved on.

The trip home had been long, stopping to chop and dig every decent sized stump or bundle of roots, whatever could be found on the sparse, brushy hillside. Bits of firewood were stuffed beneath the oilcloth along with the deer carcass.

The next morning, Maggie limped up the back steps, feeling every muscle of her lame leg, aggravated by her fitful night on an unmerciful slab of rock. She had been outside inspecting the pine tree that grew beside her rear window. Several of the lower branches appeared to be broken, but the tree withstood any major damage. Coming back in, she heard Edmund's uninterrupted snores rattling from the bedroom. Eleanor had sent the boys outside to assure Edmund a few hours of undisturbed sleep. He had kept watch all night from the front shop window, flintlock across his lap.

Eleanor stirred a kettle of barley porridge that hung over the kindling. Maggie entered and watched her lower it over the glowing embers. Eleanor asked if she fancied some hot porridge.

Maggie took the bowl and eased into the rocking chair, pointing to the window. "Mind your boys. I believe they are communing with our pine tree. They have Lenape blood, Eleanor. Need to listen to trees now and again." She finished her porridge, and then said, "I believe I've had a pine tree in sight of my window since I arrived on these shores. By account, they seem to watch over me." Eleanor simply nodded.

The boys, bundled for the cool air in their patched woolen jackets, gathered dried, woody weed stalks from along the former fence line. Most of the fence wood had already been pilfered and the remainder was stacked beside the fireplace. Not a stick of wood lay about and no logs floated downriver to the mill because of the troops' efforts. More than one townsman had been seen dismantling their own outbuildings, fences or shingled roofs for needed firewood.

The door creaked again and the boys' heads appeared. "Mama? We're hungry," said Whitney.

Eleanor rose to fill bowls. The boys tiptoed to Maggie's side and stood, waiting for their grandmother to look up. Finally, Maggie said, "That tree sent a message?"

"Says dry branches underneath would offer up a fire," said Whitney.

"That so?"

He nodded. "Fathoms hard times."

"That it does." Maggie said, slipping her legs under a comforter. "Old Mister Emory told of finding the dry scrap of a twig in this field of weeds upon arriving in Pittsburgh...before he was so old," Maggie said, winking. "Built the cabin alongside it and fed that tree until it began to grow green."

"Now it reaches high as the roof," said Morton, smiling.

"'Tis a bird's nest high up," said Whitney.

"Saw the fledglings fly last spring," Maggie said, as Eleanor handed bowls to the boys.

Eleanor said, "Inform your tree to hold fast to its branches. More than a few sticks of firewood are needed and we'll not be ravaging that fine tree."

When Edmund rose, he set off for Market Street to inquire about the soldiers, but returned with no news. He seemed restless and watchful. Days passed as he paced back and forth to the shed, stripping the deer meat and hanging portions over a smoke fire to dry. The boys stayed underfoot, cleaning the shed, combing Coal, running inside to tell Eleanor whenever the hens produced a few eggs.

After several days of Edmund's treks to Market Street, Maggie witnessed his hasty return from one of his inquiries. Beside him walked the Hendersons, the old couple that oversaw the Monongahela ferry. They had often inquired about Maggie and sent gifts of melons and cakes whenever Eleanor or Edmund passed the ferry launch on Water Street.

Maggie pulled her wrap over her shoulders and walked out to the front porch. Red-cheeked Mister Henderson waved his straw hat and limped up the embankment. Maggie waved back, head held high, wind blowing through her hair.

Henderson panted and exclaimed, "Good Lard, woman! That butcher nigh took yar face."

Maggie had a bonnet tied around her neck but it flapped in the breeze, laying off her shoulders. She stepped back, startled, as Eleanor rushed out the door to her side, speaking quickly. "'Tis an improvement over nigh killed, Mister Henderson. She fares better each day." Maggie grabbed at her bonnet and covered her head.

A plump-faced Missus Henderson spoke up, "Come! Let me see you." She paused, as Maggie approached. "Gawd, a mighty. 'Tis a blessin' you're alive!"

Edmund quickly said, "The Hendersons have news of the soldiers' retreat."

"Aye," said Mister Henderson. "Had to hire fellers, run the ferry near full time. S'many soldiers crossing back to Virginia. The farmers continue to leave as well; the ones come for the free land, that is. Knew when we laid eyes on 'em, they'd ne'er remain."

Missus Henderson looked at her husband nervously. "We mustn't linger. Best to return." Maggie felt a chill as the woman patted her hand and shoulder and they scurried down the hill.

"I'm regretful, Mother Beigler," Edmund said. "I knew naught of their coarse manners."

Maggie glared past Edmund at Eleanor, shaking a finger. "You tell me I appear fine. Those people were horrified."

"They know naught," said Eleanor. "They are simple!"

"This scar brings people to their worst," Maggie said, tightening her bonnet. "Even now, one look at my face stirs old hatred of the Indians to boiling. There's nary a ridicule for the soldiers taunting the peaceful tribes."

His forehead creased with concern, Edmund said, "Tavern keeper says peace has been imposed on the Ohio Indians after they put up a bloody fight with the soldiers. Another division marched on them downriver." Edmund ran a hand through his hair, a habit of distress. "Dunmore brought back an agreement from the Indians to abandon all of Kentucky to the whites."

"'Tis done," said Maggie.

Eleanor said, "As you surmised, Edmund, 'twas about Kentucky land."

"And selling it to farmers who'll not tolerate Indian neighbors," he said. "That doctor touting 'Kaintuckee' parcels."

Maggie went quietly inside and sat before the fire. With the news that most of the soldiers had gone back to Virginia, Edmund set off for the farm to gather the remaining firewood they had stockpiled. He returned shortly after nightfall with more disturbing news.

"The stacks from the fallen tree by the creek are gone," he said. "But a pair of wolves has settled in to the shed, surely chasing anyone who approached. 'Tis confounded, they let me close enough to retrieve the few piles of wood near the house."

Morton whispered, "Did you shoot at them, Papa?"

"No need," said Edmund. "Appears they're protecting the place for now."

"What about the chickens?" asked Eleanor.

"Small price for such able guards," Edmund said.

Maggie slipped into the dark shop at the front of the cabin while Eleanor finished preparing a venison stew. Edmund followed Maggie and asked, "What troubles you?"

"When you're older, Edmund," she said, "there are plentiful memories. Some are deemed best to disregard. This injury has caused them all to tumble forth, with no proper aim."

"Perhaps the aim should be to give them regard."

Maggie smelled wild onions sizzling in the hot fat. She said, "I stood by our tree this morning and whispered a prayer, not whispered as such, but carried on the wind."

Edmund smiled, "You raise a memory of my grandmother."

"Indeed. I asked the wind to search out the ancients, the ones who might help us yet." Maggie wiped damp palms on her apron. "Some in Shamokin gave up praying to the ancients after so many deaths."

"I recall the words of the disheartened elders," Edmund said. "They thought the sickness proved that the spirits of the wind and trees had abandoned them. Many decided to say the white man's prayers to cure the white man's fever. But to no avail."

Maggie said, "When White Hawk's mother failed her second bout with the fever, I found my friend in the woods, her dress shredded, covered with ashes and wailing. I surmised that she had added the mourning of her husband and child who had died the year prior during her own delirious fever." Maggie tapped against one of the wood loom supports with her gnarled fist. "White Hawk fell to the earth, wailing. I held her and assured her that the ancient ones heard. And I whispered into the wind myself, asking deliverance."

"You rejected the white man's prayers?" asked Edmund.

Maggie shook her head. "I could not. As we sat there, my child stirred and kicked. White Hawk felt it. I prayed for that child, for her to survive."

"And she did," said Edmund, as Eleanor stepped through the door beside him.

"Born days later," said Maggie.

Edmund leaned and kissed Eleanor's cheek. Morton poked his head around his mother's skirt and pleaded. "Please, Granmama, tell us."

Maggie ambled back into the parlor, to the rocking chair in front of the fire. The boys sat at her feet. "Your mother was born in the spring, amidst newly planted corn and green maple buds. An old Delaware woman was sewing up the freshly stuffed deer hide ball in anticipation of the first ball game of the spring; the women's team against the men and boys. The games began with a prayer of thanks for surviving the winter, profoundly true that year. Folks were collecting the maple water to boil sap into sugar. Those sweet scents were on the wind when the birth pains began.

"White Hawk ran to fetch Carl and we all three walked to the riverside birthing hut. Carl built a fire then disappeared, jumping on a horse to ride to McKee's trading post and send a message to the Weisers that the child was coming. I knew Weiser would not arrive in time, but I maintained a hope that Carl would return for the birth."

"He returned?" asked Eleanor.

"That night, though you were more hasty than he."

"Born in a birthing hut!" Whitney shook his head.

"With soft husk mats and blankets," said Maggie. "White Hawk sprinkled water over hot stones to make a warm cloud of steam. She placed a wrap around my shoulders and a root between my teeth; from the plant where the butterflies land in summer, she said. I breathed hot steam and felt my womb contract. My mother wiped perspiration from my cheeks."

"Your mother?" said Eleanor.

"'I felt her put her hand aside my cheek, as she did when I was young.

White Hawk said she brought good medicine. I was pulled to a kneeling position and as White Hawk pulled, the baby emerged. Your mama kicked and cried, pink and wrinkled and very alive. White Hawk placed her in my arms, wrapped and calmed. I gazed at her wee face, enchanted."

"Mama!" whispered Morton. Everyone smiled at his wonder.

"You boys born at the farm came forth in elegance, as I compare," said Eleanor.

"How long did you remain in the hut?" asked Whitney.

"White Hawk tied the cord with a small sinewy lace. Cleaned and wrapped in a soft tanned blanket from the Montours, the baby was tucked at my side as White Hawk coaxed her to suckle. We fell asleep, but when Carl returned that night, your mama's tiny belly was round and full and her skin had calmed from its bright pink color. At our cabin, Logan came to chastise Carl for not calling on him to run the trader's message. Carl barely took notice, staring as he was at your mama. I had scarce seen him look so lovingly upon another face," Maggie said, adding in a whisper, "including my own."

"Mother," said Eleanor.

"He adored his little daughter and named her Eleanor Rose after our two mothers."

"I wish I had more recollections of him," said Eleanor.

"His spirit seemed to soar with your arrival," Maggie said. "His manner became warmer." Maggie sighed and continued, "The villagers showered attention upon us, relieved for a new arrival after the loss of many souls from sickness. They called her Rose since 'Eleanor' became a tangle in their throats."

"In the heat of summer when her skin darkened, her golden blonde curls were all that set her apart from the native children. White Hawk was a great help and like an aunt to Eleanor. I denied some habits of my own people to explore White Hawk's advice. She told me the native women bathed their children in the cool river water for strength. Hence, in the mornings, with no others about, your mama had her river baths."

"For this, we can thank Gran for the cold baths we must endure," complained Whitney.

"Not on this night," said Edmund. "To bed, straightaway." He swatted at the boys as they ran past. They stopped to kiss their grandmother on the cheek. Maggie sat silently in the light of the glowing coals.

"'Tis a beautiful story, Mother." Eleanor paused and then said, "When did those feelings about me change? Was it solely Papa's death?"

Maggie turned her face away. With a rasping monotone, she said, "Perhaps I may explain the difficult story with my pen." Days later, Maggie passed along the pages she could not speak aloud.

My dear family,

As I consider all my days, 'twas Eleanor's arrival that convinced me I was not alone. I recognise now that I bore a fear of telling her such. I had always felt alone. Those I loved would depart. I failed to say it lest saying it out loud would invoke her disappearance or cause her to be taken from me. Becoming a mother gave me a greater sense of being alive as well as a great sense of fear for the possibility of losing my child. As I learned, the sense of foreboding was not about losing Eleanor, but I knew naught at the time.

Because so many had died during the months prior to her arrival, Swataney's lodge especially seemed to adopt her and delight in her presence. She was the community's child. She went to the fields with me in a cradleboard. White Hawk constructed it of willow bark lacings and a sturdy board lined with soft deerskin. The older children would sit in the shade and watch over her. Her only plaything, a corn husk doll made by White Hawk, went everywhere with her.

As fall commenced, I cut up pumpkins and strung slices on a rope to dry by the fireplace. They were tough and not as tasty as those we grow in the garden now. Your papa has been known to bury a cache of corn like we did. We stored supplies of turnips as well and kept bundles of flour and other provisions from the Moravians stored in a stone cellar for the winter.

A less eventful year passed. Swataney's hunters shared their meat, though hunting trips became longer as hunters had to venture further away. Logstown on the Ohio River became a common meeting place. It angered Swataney that the colonies' interests had shifted to the westward tribes. He felt Shamokin slip from the center of Pennsylvania backwoods power. The trading post, though beautifully built, sat quiet on many days.

One day we heard Weiser arguing with a forlorn Andrew Montour. Weiser said, "The Iroquois claim to be neutral between conflicts of French and English, but if they cede more land to the English, beware of wandering Delawares." Weiser turned to us, pale and shaken. "As frigid weather arrives," he warned, "hungry tribes come."

"Be prepared," Montour agreed. "Hunting is poor." He excused himself soon after and disappeared in a canoe on the river.

The moment of our world's unraveling came sometime in the following weeks, though 'tis all atangle, to be sure. Swataney was the adhesive that held us together; surely he held me together.

In the midst of the autumn chores and feast preparations, Swataney had been consumed with questions for the Moravian Bishop. He was insistent that he must be taken to Bethlehem for a visit. We were shocked that anything would interrupt the feast. The idea of the chief making a long trip during the cold months seemed ill-advised but Brother Mack yielded and they departed on horseback.

As predicted, cold weather arrived early and with it came a group of Lenapes, distant relatives of the Munsee Delawares who came to the forks area twenty years prior. Shamokin had fared better than some areas where entire villages were devastated by sickness or poor crops. The village at the forks was an established stop on the Susquehanna, a place where strangers traded pelts for supplies, perhaps gun repairs or powder and shot. Strangers were treated to a bowl of stew from the community pot before going back on the river or path. The Munsees set up shabby leaning huts on the edge of the village. Staying together in their group, they offered scant help with the hasty harvest chores.

The celebration went forth even though the chief was absent and many in his family were still grieving. Full kettles and heaping baskets of corn cakes concealed signs that the stores were low. When the hunters returned with a deer, the dancing and music began. 'Twas soon apparent that much more rum than usual had slipped into the village. Loud howling went late into the night, with shots from the guns the Moravians had recently repaired.

Near dawn, 'twas discovered that the newly settled Munsees had stolen away, taking many bags of corn and grain. Carl was among a group that pursued them across the river but came back wet and empty-handed. Henry Fry woke all the Moravians to discuss the threat of the neighbouring colonists turning on us for arming the visiting group.

"We have offended our own Shamokins, I fear," said Carl. "We armed those who stole from them. How can they avoid feeling betrayed?"

Brother Fry decided we should go as a group to Tagnehdorus and Logan and assure them that we were saddened by the thievery. We wanted not to risk their turning against us. Tagnehdorus gave us a warm greeting but had decided that hospitality would no longer be shared with all who passed through Shamokin.

As I mentioned, I had a feeling of unraveling. It went far beyond the personal. The Montours had long held the philosophy that the forks Indians were on the brink of war. The Delawares had been demeaned for over a dozen years when the Iroquois named them 'women' before the Lancaster treaty meetings. Native tribes understand women as peacemakers, but the Europeans and English held women in lower esteem, thus weakening the Delawares in the colonists' minds. The treaties went in the favour of the Iroquois. The Delaware tribes were forced to live under their direction and Montour surmised they were near the end of their patience.

Weeks later, Carl joined Montour on a good-will hunting expedition with several of the native men. The weather turned bitter. Swataney returned from his journey to Bethlehem, though White Hawk sent a message that he was gravely ill. I rushed to her lodge, taking Eleanor along. She toddled eagerly to a blanket beside the fire, chattering to White Hawk's nieces in a blend of several languages. The children seemed to understand her well enough, while I yet struggled.

Swataney was lying on a stack of husk mats by the fire, covered with bearskins. His demeanor was tranquil but for his rattling breath. I reached for White Hawk's hand. Her face showed fatigue, but her dark eyes glistened. She had been at his side since Brother Zeisberger, the missionary who traveled often between the mission towns, had brought him on horseback from Bethlehem.

"He will not live long," she said, her English much improved. "The others make prayers and songs. We will sit and listen. He may have more whispering." White Hawk gazed at Swataney's face.

"He was warned against a hard journey," I told her.

White Hawk dangled a carved manitou on a cord. "Brother Zeisberger told me that my father removed this and now wears the cross of the Moravians. He too, has given leave to the ancient ones."

The dark lodge was circled by a delicate orange firelight. The little girls' voices chirped in the corner and White Hawk hummed, leaning over a collection of clay bowls. She lifted one full of reddish grease and motioned me to Swataney's side. Pulling down Swataney's bearskin cover, she began rubbing the grease slowly under his shoulders and neck. She handed me some grease and I mimicked her movements.

White Hawk spoke softly about Swataney's favourite story. She said he told it so often that she could hear his bones and skin singing of Deganawidah, the Man from the North. White Hawk began telling of the mother and daughter who lived alone then she lowered her grieving face.

I knew the story. "'Tis my favourite, as well," I said. I recounted the *daughter's dream when she was with child that the Master of Life was sending a messenger to teach a New Peace and a New Mind.*

I said, "The woman's son was Deganawidah. He was honest, smart and handsome, but when he spoke to his tribe about peace, they called him foolish. His tribe was well known for their warring acts against the Mohawks. Other young boys practiced war skills while Deganawidah grew up talking of a world based on peace."

We spread grease over the old man's arms and sinewy hands. I said, "Deganawidah knew he must leave home. He told his mother that his business was to stop the bloodshed among human beings. His name meant 'The Master of Things,' but when his grandmother saw his canoe carved from stone, she laughed and called him crazy."

"But Deganawidah said, "By this impossible act, you will know my words are true, and that I will bring peace to the nations." He pushed the canoe into the water and paddled away."

I felt a ripple flow through my fingers and heart, felt blessed in the presence of Swataney and his daughter in his last hours. I said, "Deganawidah reached the lake's far shore where men ran, pointing at his stone canoe. They had been hiding in the woods because there was danger everywhere: intertribal warfare, starvation, the slaughter of innocent women and children. Deganawidah told them the Creator had sent him to teach them how to live without killing each other."

We rubbed the taut muscles in Swataney's legs and thighs as I continued, telling how Deganawidah stopped at a lone Erie woman's lodge. Located on a neutral place on the path, she had been feeding all the warriors. She was shocked to hear his plan. He told her about the longhouse meetings, his vision of peace, where each tribe had its own place but was united, engaging in peaceful trade instead of warfare.

We moved down Swataney's legs, greasing his feet. Covering him gently, White Hawk whispered a prayer. She gently pulled me toward the bearskin rug close to the fire and sighed, "His spirit has gone to find another camp. It will return soon and take his body." I was honoured to witness Swataney's final hours, but humbled also. I regretted having nothing to offer to convey my gratitude. I simply bid him farewell.

We sat in the warmth of the fire. The palms of my hands were stained orange from the grease. White Hawk cut several dried apples from a cord hanging from the ceiling. Calling to the children, she held apple slices for the two little girls who ran with their hands outstretched. They padded quietly to their dolls and to little Eleanor, who bit into a shared slice.

"My thanks." I held the apple to my lips. White Hawk walked to the far wall and lowered a tied bundle of deer antler pieces. Holding pieces of broken horns no longer than my hand, she took a long stick and began to push the jelly middle into the clay pot that held the reddish grease we had used on Swataney.

" 'Tis the liniment?" I asked, trying not to sound aghast.

"With rabbit grease," she said. As she poked a horn and slid the jelly into the pot, she urged me to continue.

"The woman warned Deganawidah of a dangerous wild man who lived in the forest. He proceeded to his house. Finding him gone, he climbed to the roof and waited next to the warm smoke hole. The wild man returned and boiled a kettle of water to cook his gruesome kill. Deganawidah shifted his weight to see into the kettle and the wild man saw Deganawidah's reflection. Believing he saw his own wise and good face, the wild man reconsidered his life.

White Hawk said, "The man had witnessed and committed every evil to dishonour the enemy. He had stopped caring about all life. When he met kind Deganawidah, he sat across the fire and spoke of his changed life, but he was anguished over his past deeds. He needed to make amends."

Swataney shuddered and exhaled. White Hawk said, "The man had been a great orator, name of Hienwatah, who had lived near a terrible sorcerer. When Hienwatah's wife and daughters became victims, their deaths motivated him to outdo the sorcerer's evil."

"Outdo him. 'Tis the way of all men. Revenge," I shook my head.

White Hawk said, "Deganawidah, who spoke with a stutter, told Hienwatah that he needed his voice. Instead of being banished, Hienwatah spent the rest of his life as a healer and Deganawidah's trusted friend."

I nodded. "Swataney went to Bethlehem to learn about atonement. 'Tis the same idea...making one's life over for goodness."

Swataney's family had gathered outside, chanting. As the flickering firelight reflected on the chief's face, we heard the wailing increase. The door opened and a man covered with a bearskin and a broad-brimmed hat peered in. Brother Zeisberger entered and sat beside his old friend to witness his last breaths. He asked if the chief's sons had been sent for. White Hawk nodded then collapsed upon the rug where I held her, both of us crying.

Brother Zeisberger slowly removed his rag gloves, hat and bearskin. In his melodious, deep voice, he said, "I walked in his woods this morning, breathing the pine air he can no longer smell, watching the flight of hawks he can no longer see. My senses are filled with his leaving." He sat by

Swataney's side, quietly singing. The old chief opened his eyes, smiled and closed them again. Zeisberger stopped his song and said, "The chief's name means 'one who causes it to be light for us.' I fear that a great light has gone out." A relative let out a piercing howl and the sobbing in the lodge became great. Swataney had gone on his journey.

We wept for several days before Swataney's sons returned for the Condolence Ceremony. White Hawk, determined to help build a coffin, collected pieces of wood and dragged them to Henry Fry, who cut and nailed the large box. Inside it, she placed things Swataney would need on his journey to the Spirit Land: a loaf of bread, a tobacco pipe, some tobacco and a flint.

Swataney's family gathered at the burial ground near the river before Carl and Montour returned. A few words were offered. With no shooting or dancing, the burial party wandered back to their lodges. Quiet hung in the snow-laden branches over the village. Shawnees and Delawares who had watched the burial from their distant huts, dispersed out to the trails. Lines of people walked off in many directions, the spokes of a wheel. The village nearly emptied, evidence of the low stores of provisions. Swataney was the great light holding the fragile peace among the varied tribes in his own village and throughout Pennsylvania. I sensed an ominous shift in the earth and air.

Carl and Montour had left the hunting party before word had arrived about Swataney's death. Messengers departed to Montour's village to find them. Montour showed up in Shamokin, begging my forgiveness for letting Carl travel back to the village alone. He told me Carl had left weeks earlier. He took several men to search the trail between our villages.

By the time Weiser arrived to deliver condolences for Swataney from the governor, I was most downhearted. Weiser appeared at the trading post to ask if Carl had returned. Aiming to cheer me, he said he was recommending Swataney's eldest son, Tagnehdorus, to the Onandago to follow in the chief's place.

I replied glumly, "No one knows the affairs of these woods as Swataney did." The old chief had held together our village trust. With Carl missing, I was truly fearful for the future. Weiser admitted that he knew naught how to get on without Swataney's advice.

He fumbled inside his fringed jacket and removed an envelope. "Ben Franklin and James Parker, a printer in New York, aim to convince the Indians to trade solely with English. They take particular interest in a voluntary uniting of colonies." He held the letter and read. "Franklin says here,

"Strange if six Nations of ignorant savages should form such a union, executed with strength for ages, and yet ten or a dozen English Colonies, who need the advantage more, cannot form an equal understanding of interests."

"Ignorant savages?" I said.

"He makes a challenge to colonists, surely. Franklin speaks of people living among Indians like your blacksmiths. He writes as if he had been to Shamokin for a visit."

Weiser left us with some few springtime hopes. Eleanor grew strong and playful, even on meagre rations. She toddled around the cabin asking for Papa, over and over, until I became annoyed and impatient. Though Montour said Carl's tracks had disappeared in the snow, I began to make up stories for Eleanor. I wonder if you recall, daughter, how I told you Papa had gone to Bethlehem with a message for the Bishop. Perhaps I was convincing myself as to what business must be keeping him away so long.

But there was a far greater disturbance on the wind. Just as we can feel it now in Pittsburgh, we heard it then in the whisperings of the trees. Our hopeful nature may have veiled the message. When you truly settle yourself upon the land, you must become aware of all that is happening in your soil, your surroundings, and your community. The warnings were there, in the shadows of Shamokin following Swataney's death, yet we remained hopeful in the fields of the mission.

6

I felt like I'd been awake all night. I had slept well for hours, but I woke in the early morning with a strained need to be watchful. I knew well enough to pull out my notebook and begin Maggie's letter. But as she recalled massaging the old chief's dying body, I thought my own hands would melt like wax. Even my pen became hot to hold.

The pages were written by the light of a small bedside reading lamp while it was still dark out. Quinn, fortunately, is a very sound sleeper. She appeared to be in the same position as when she climbed into bed, though the blanket had scooted lower on her back and left her shoulders bare. My dim reading lamp cast a soft, gray shadow across her delicate skin. She was as relaxed as a pale flower that had been plucked hours ago and lain across the soft sheets to greet me.

When I scooted to the edge of my bed, I felt a twinge in my crotch, noticeably wet. I jumped up, embarrassed, as if I'd been caught staring at Quinn. I pulled some clean clothes from my bag and went into the bathroom to shower. The water was hot instantly, an advantage for early risers. The awkward tub stall had a short, angled ceiling, prompting a low shower head and a flexible hand-held nozzle. I appreciated it though, for the ease of washing my hair.

As water and shampoo continued to wash over my very awake and swollen vulva, I dropped the washcloth at my feet and slid my fingers over the sleek warmth. I peeked through the plastic curtain to check the door. Closed. Playing with the flexible warm trickle of water, I tried different angles and proximities. The throbbing between my legs seemed like the extra heartbeat of some precious friend who had been missing for a long time. I played like a frolicking child until my adult butt leaned against the cool tile wall and I had a swift awareness of purpose.

Leg muscles sent surges of energy in every direction, some holding me upright, some seeming to turn me inside out. My silky, hard clitoris ruthlessly fired alerts down to my toes and into my vagina, insistent, searing like an engraved promise to claim and be remembered.

I had to turn on the cool water and lean against the tile wall again, dizzy, all my skin tingling. I turned off the shower and sat on the edge of the tub, still feeling embarrassed, certain that I'd been observed. Pleasure turned to quick outrage and a recognition of the damage done by Miss North. After all my efforts to seal up my solitary space, she continued to be in it. I was letting her in.

Once dressed, I felt heavy with sadness. I decided to go for a walk. Our hotel was a few blocks from the historic downtown Bethlehem. Quinn slept soundly as I penned a quick note, grabbed my jacket and tiptoed out the door. It was barely sunrise and the weather pattern had shifted from mild to cooler. Even so, several groups of students and a few joggers were already on the street. I crossed the edge of the wooded campus and walked past God's Acre, the old Bethlehem burial site for the early Moravian settlers. Some of the trees looked like original dwellers and might well have been. They had piled their leaves among the tight rows of tipped headstones with eroded engravings and faded dates. I perused a few stones to see if there were names I'd recognize: Mack, Fry, Ziesberger. I swept the thought of finding Maggie's grave quickly from my thoughts.

Further down Church Street, I passed the oldest buildings that are still standing in town. The Brothers' House was built of thick gray chunks of limestone, perfectly cut and fitted in the solid European tradition. I wanted to touch the stones and feel hard evidence of Maggie's town. Like in Philadelphia, I wanted to peel away layers of time.

I leaned against the stone wall and looked down the hill toward the winding creek. "Maggie," I whispered. "I want to see your town, just a few stone and log buildings, probably a cornfield right there." I looked toward the park beside the Radisson Hotel. "I want a clear view of the creek." There was a fairly steep incline down to the creeping black water before it reached the bridge. Branches overhung, nearly touching the water's surface.

"You might have escaped a classroom on a hot day and gone to that very spot," I thought out loud. There were steps down the hill if I stayed on the street. As soon as I crossed, I had to take my chances with a loose gravel path. The dark water called; there was something about it that felt more alive, more apt to be one of Gibbs' windows than the cold, stone buildings. I wanted to look through a window.

The stream had a scent I can't name, though as I got closer, it seemed to rise from deep in the earth, too rich to take fully into my lungs. I walked down the hill and hiked a dirt path by the water, foregoing the bridge and modern paved pathways. The water hummed with a slow vibration and seemed thicker than ordinary liquid. I tried to disregard the ghostly enigma of former buildings: the tannery, the laundry building nearby that Maggie would have known. I had invited her to show me her town, so I didn't feel I could be too bossy about what I would be shown.

I inhaled the rich scents and watched the morning mist twirl in the air nearly a foot above the water. The creek gurgled slowly, as if I might not understand its language. I recalled my sensory morning and my engraved connection to my body. Determined to claim my rightful pleasure, I carefully climbed over a pit along the bank, found a dry patch of soft sand, and sat.

The Old York Road was upstream at the edge of the colonial industrial area. I had noticed how some places in Pennsylvania treat the rivers like a junky backyard, a place to throw their dilapidated cars, old tires and such. Ahead, the ancient wood frame buildings along the riverfront sat beside an appalling mess of a dumping area. Maybe I'm accustomed to Lake Michigan's north shore, where expensive waterfront property is lined with sprawling estates, parkways and campuses. I cringed at a floating pile of jammed logs, heaped with trash in the stream.

I stared at the junky log pile as it floated close. Then I saw a movement in the middle of the debris and a shiny, black face, twinkling eyes.

"Joe?" My knees would have collapsed if I hadn't been sitting. I slid down the bank where the old guy scrambled to the edge of his log raft and held out a rope. He tossed it to me and I hauled backward to bring the raft up on a grassy knob. Joe hopped off, bent slightly in the middle, and took the rope. I sat back again, shocked at the sight of him.

He took my outstretched hand and with a deep-wrinkled grin, eased down to one knee and gave me a hug. He smelled of fish and many days of campfire smoke and the back of his shirt was moist from perspiration even in the cool morning.

I shook my head in wonder. With one hand I held onto him and with the other I wiped a tear from my eye. "Joe, you must stay long enough to answer some questions." He nodded. "You know that Maggie and I write letters, don't you?"

"Don't know the script work," he said. "But I know Miss Maggie is able to reach you with such."

"She's telling me her story. And she told me about you, Joe. Your trip down the river."

"Ah wish it coulda been a better day."

"It was the right thing to do, Joe. You couldn't just watch while the soldiers marched off to burn the villages."

"No. Couldn' let that young fella go n' leave his family." Solemnly, Joe lowered his head and said, "Ah'm a man got nobody. Got jus' m'self. Young Edmund had folks depend on him."

"You don't have family, Joe?" It was hard to talk as if he were dead, not while I held onto his warm hand.

"Had no one since a child. As a young man, Ah run from a plantation. Survived 'cause nobody had a mind to come after me." He rubbed his throat. "Place in Virginia. Grew tobacca," Joe said. "Come west, aimed for Ohio, but got s'far as that fine river."

"How did you find the cave?" I wanted to know.

A faraway smile crossed Joe's face. "Ah fished and lurked around Pittsburgh fer a time. No one paid me a nevermind. Had some bad luck and was sorely hungry. Came a Mingo fella outta the woods holding a big ol' trout. He stared at my black face then raised the fish and pointed up the hill. Showed me the hut, already fixed up some. Ah slept there that night and, next morn, the Mingo fella was gone."

"So you stayed?" I asked.

"All m' life long. Added a stone fireplace n' a door. Always reckoned that Mingo'd show up someday," Joe said as his voice drifted. "Kept to m'self. Saw a few folks. Edmund. His boys."

"You made it down the river to the village?" I asked, tentatively.

He nodded again. "The Injuns come down to the river that day, lookin' at the ol' black man. They stood there in a line along the bank until I started to whoop and holler. Told 'em the soldiers, hundreds of 'em, comin' with guns loaded. Don't pack up, I yelled. Go. Move out while you can yet move."

Joe waved his finger in the air as if the Indian village was across the Monocacy Creek. He stared at the water while his memories churned with the deep black shadow bottom. "Edmund would a' been faster, stronger," he said.

"Still," I said, "a lot of people lived that would have died."

"Lived to be attacked another day," he whispered. Clearing his throat, he said, "Displaced, starved. Couldn't offer much help there."

"You gave them more time, another chance." I wanted to believe Joe's contribution was significant, that someone had survived, some family continued. Joe understood my hopefulness.

"Did more than I e'er believed," he said. "Finished the mos' important task. Took some pride in m'self." A thin hand rested on his chest beneath his collarbone. I felt a warm wave, the honor of knowing this little man that I had discovered in an amazing shaft of sunlight on an obscure hill outside of Pittsburgh.

He pulled himself to his feet and stretched. Pushing at the logs on the grass with his foot, he said, "My message is always the same: Move while you can yet move." He looked up and down the creek and glanced up the hill at the old town. "This place held answers for some folks. But not for Miss Maggie."

"Joe, wait. There's something I have to know. We met Gibbs. He was helpful, but since we met him, I've been filled with memories, old feelings washing to the surface. It's rough, Joe."

"Darlin'," you got ta move your raft down the river. Throw off all the baggage you don' need. Sometime you got to see what you been haulin' afore you can let go the ropes." As suddenly as he had arrived, Joe pushed the rickety raft away from shore and hopped aboard as he heaved off with a pole into the slow current.

"Joe?" I called. "Wait. Where are we supposed to go?" I stood up and called from the bank as he waved, turned his back and headed downstream, leaning on the pole. I stood there and watched him catch the only current in the middle of the creek to slip under the bridge. When I turned back, I saw Quinn on the hill above, holding two paper coffee cups and staring downstream.

"I don't get it," Quinn said, as she hiked down the hill, handed me a cup and plopped beside me. "That was Joe?"

"You saw him?"

"The little black guy on the junky raft."

"You saw him." I said it flatly, only partly relieved.

"I saw him but only as he was leaving—only a little glimpse. I saw you sitting down here, talking with someone. I figured you came across one of the locals. But it occurred to me, just as he was floating away...that's our guy!"

There, I felt it again. A little twinge of something. Jealousy? If Quinn saw Joe, I felt less crazy, but I also felt less special. Who else sees Joe? Maybe I don't have the only turtle, either. Where does Joe go when he leaves in a hurry? To Quinn, I said, "I don't get it, either."

"Weird," she said, with a long breath. "You've had a few days to get used to the guy popping up, but I just saw him. And just as quickly," she waved her hand over the stream, "he's gone." She looked up and down the creek, then behind us up the hill, the buildings of old Bethlehem. "So? What are we supposed to do?"

"He didn't tell me."

"What were you talking about?" she asked.

"We talked about him. How he came to Pittsburgh as a runaway slave. Had no family. I haven't read you Maggie's latest, but they found out the soldiers were going to raid the Indian villages downstream and Joe set off on his raft to warn them."

"They were at Joe's place, up on the bluff by my old neighborhood."

"Right," I said. "I have to catch you up on some things."

Quinn must have sensed my reservations. She finished her coffee and said, "Reed. I haven't been humoring you. I've believed you, even when I didn't see him. But, seeing him...God! It's cool."

"But, what now?" I said.

"What happened when he went downstream to warn the Indians?"

"I'm not totally sure. But he said they saw him. He told them to get moving." I glanced downstream where Joe had gone under the bridge. "That's it, Quinn. We're just supposed to get going. Stop sitting here. He said his message was always the same: move while you can yet move."

"Yow. I hope we're not about to be attacked. But it's fine with me to get going. My game is tonight in Danville and we have to drive a few more hours. We'll get in the Beetle and point it that direction. Or I'm going to wind up changing jobs and I'm not ready for that, yet."

We walked up the hill next to the Radisson Hotel Bethlehem and crossed Main Street to admire the old Moravian Gemeinhaus, three stories of square cut stone, laid with precise workmanship. A plaque marked the old original log structures from 1741. Some of the stone buildings had inscribed dates within several years of then.

Quinn pointed down the street to the old Moravian bookstore that filled several storefronts and where she had bought our coffee earlier. "A sign said it was the oldest bookstore in America," she said. "Can you believe some of these places have been standing here for two hundred and fifty years?" We passed a stone block building with a tarnished copper plaque by the door that read '1749.' "The fact that's it's all hand craftsmanship is amazing," she said. "They don't build buildings like that anymore."

We gathered our bags, checked out and wound around Bethlehem to Broad Street and the highway. "Did you look at the map?" I asked.

"Yeah," she said. "Danville is back toward the middle of the state. I think we can take the Turnpike to I-80 and cruise all the way. Looks like a pretty small town."

I unfolded the map and found the yellow spot marking Bethlehem, then dragged my finger to I-80 and west to Danville.

"What do you think?" asked Quinn. "Maybe three hours?"

"Oh, god," I said. "It's on the Susquehanna River." I leaned over the map and dragged my finger along the blue line to the tiny blue italics. "Susquehanna. Where would the forks be?" My finger stopped. I let out a squeal and thought Quinn was going to pull the car over. "Sunbury!" I said. That's the town at the forks. It's like an inch away from Danville! What is that? Ten miles? Fifteen?"

"We can go see it," said Quinn. "Walk around Shamokin town."

"We have to. It's practically across the river. When is your game?" I asked.

"I should be at the gymnasium by seven. But, you know, you don't have to go—if you find something more interesting," Quinn said, grinning.

I cleared my throat. It was starting to feel swollen with congestion. "Oh, oh," I said. "This is not a good time to come down with something."

"You just got a chill this morning," said Quinn. "Pull that blanket up and take a nap."

I pulled a blanket from the back seat and wrapped it around my shoulders. Quinn turned on the heater and adjusted it to vent on my cold feet. I leaned my head against the headrest and rubbed the sides of my stiff neck as Quinn loaded a CD and handed me the jacket. Patricia Barber. The Chicago jazz pianist Quinn follows around north side clubs. As the lively music filled the car, I flipped open the jacket, eyes drawn to a passage I read to Quinn. "It says she distills, finds the essence of things in her music. Mmmm. A few small drops of her subtle, undaunted tones..." I lowered my voice with the melody.

"Yeah," said Quinn. "Passion. Moonlight."

The gentle motion of the Beetle on the highway felt like a flowing river. As the rhythm of the music slowed, the current slowed, my eyes closed and my mind went around a lazy bend where the autumn air shimmered.

ζ

The valley temperatures were falling steadily as Edmund's strips of venison hung on racks to dry in the smoke of a hickory sapling fire. While Eleanor dressed a portion of venison for roasting, the boys sat carving on the back porch. They had collected and dried hickory switches and were carving the ends for Eleanor's split-brooms. Morton pressed the strips back while Whitney split the ends with his jackknife, cutting into the brittle heart of the sapling.

Maggie sat in the parlor with a view of the street. The people of Pittsburgh were astir once again. They strolled hastily, many dressed in fine clothes and Sunday neckcloths, though it was midweek. With the family busy with chores, Maggie's curiosity prevailed. Wrapping a shawl around her tattered and smudged dress, she slipped out the front door and followed the crowd down Ferry Street to Semple's Tavern.

She peeked in the door, surprised to see the windowless room lit with bright lamps, the tables and stools pushed aside and a crowd of townsfolk sitting on ordered rows of benches. Maggie slipped through the door and leaned wearily against the back wall of the tavern. Standing beside the bar was a strange man wearing a high buttoned collar and spectacles perched on the end of his thin nose. Wispy, brown hair was parted in the middle and greased over two balding patches that inched back from his forehead.

The stranger began to speak with a loud, high voice, "An inquiry upon your town from the neighboring villages reveals a reputation that would discourage many a minister from venturing here." He strolled along the front row of seats. "There's nary a church built amongst your plentiful taverns and 'tis heard said, there be no God-fearing people found. Of late, thievery and brawling appear to be your highest aim. I am confounded with your interest in myself. Perhaps 'tis news from the east you seek." A murmur rose, with scattered chuckling and people stretching to see the journeyman minister.

"How 'bout gettin' to that news," called an old boatman.

"'Twill surely disappoint," said the minister. "I have not been east myself since early in the month of June. The Congress had yet to convene, and 'tis none but stories heard since."

"Aye, stories," shouted a Virginia Scotsman. "Give us a round of stories."

The crowd applauded. The young minister grew flustered, unbuttoned his collar, then pounded his flat palm on the bar counter beside him. He shouted over the noise, "'Tis a time of serious consequence! Repentance is all that can save your souls!"

Loud guffaws and laughter broke out from several corners. One man shouted, "We came far for our souls to be proper lost." Maggie realized the room was divided in varying support of the minister's words.

"We don't take to strangers calling us sinners!" yelled the Scotsman.

"Let the man be. 'Tis a man of God," came an angry woman's shout.

A gentleman stood up and walked toward the minister. As he faced the crowd everyone recognized Doctor Connolly, but continued to call out their comments.

The minister shouted back, stepping in front of Connolly. "I see 'tis true. This town abounds with tax evaders, fur thieves and grossly insulting ruffians. Even the military captain has spent time in the Hannastown jail."

The crowd's clamor increased until Doctor Connolly waved his hands to quell the noise and turned to the minister. "I am that man," he nearly crowed, "illegally jailed by Pennsylvanians who have no authority in this district."

Someone in the back shouted, "They had 'til your soldiers run 'em off!" More tempers rose at the mention of the troops. Whether they supported Virginia's claim or not, people were hungry and fearful of the lack of supplies and the coming cold weather. The noise increased, and then a crash sounded as splinters of wood slid across the floor, the pieces of a chair broken over the bar. People began pushing and running from the room. Maggie ducked her bonnet toward the door and held her hands up for protection. As she inched along the wall, she looked up to see Edmund glaring at her from the doorway, pushing through the unruly crowd and grabbing one of her flailing arms. He wrapped a hand around her waist, ducked through the fracas and pushed her through the door onto Water Street.

"Are you muddled?" Edmund continued to hasten her away, pulling her by her arm until she slapped his hand. He let go as they turned a corner off Water Street and entered a deserted lane. "Eleanor was distraught with worry."

She stopped and took a deep breath. "I beg you...seemed the whole town was aimed there," she breathed heavily.

"Mother Beigler, 'tis Pittsburgh...Dunmore." He waved his hand down the street. "People come this far west, as one back there said, to escape civil manners."

"And you with your children?"

He leaned closer to her face. "Land was cheap. Though order may be uncertain, we have a home." He began walking up the street, hands combing through his shiny hair. Maggie stared after him. He turned back, waving a finger. "You know about uncertainty, Mother Beigler."

"Uncivil," she hollered at his back. "Nary a common thread to bind! The town will ne'er prosper." She limped up the hill behind Edmund, who marched urgently toward the cabin. "You are Lenape," she called. "A villager." She fell further behind his pace. Edmund stood on the porch and scowled as Maggie dragged herself up the steps behind him. He opened the cabin door, then hedged past Eleanor, mumbling a desire to be alone.

"Edmund!" Eleanor exclaimed.

He turned, "I found your mother. Pulled her from a bar-room brawl."

Breathless, Maggie shook her head. "'Tis an unfair report. A journeyman minister could find no other place..."

Edmund interrupted. "My wrath is upon the entire town." He brushed a wide circle with his arm, then choked on his own emotion. He sat down on the bench, holding his head. "I went to the river early this morn," he said, "to query the boatmen upon the conditions downstream. Upon mentioning Joseph, I was led to his blanket-wrapped body, discovered a day ago near one of the burned villages. I took him to his hillside and dug a grave, buried him near his cave." Edmund stared at his hands, still smeared with dirt. "Appears Joseph was shot while warning the Indian villages of the advancing soldiers." Edmund's shoulders slumped.

Maggie walked quietly to the window, parted the drapery and looked down the street. In a hushed voice, she said, "I beg your forgiveness, Edmund. I meant to cause no additional grief." Eleanor went to Edmund's side, squeezed his arm, and laid her head wearily against him.

Maggie's voice bounced back from the glass as she spoke. "You are my son, Edmund, not merely my daughter's husband. You are a hardworking man and I admire your devotion." She turned, glanced nervously. "But of late, I have learned that accepting the entire journey is of value."

"For this reason you write?" asked Eleanor. "To accept?"

"To prompt the memories," Maggie said. "Times I've wanted to forget my English origins. Forget the family that is gone. But that effort left me fatigued. 'Tis a temptation, Edmund, to deny your Lenape heritage at a time when your native village has scattered. The Lenape-Delaware people have been cast to the wind, and surviving upon your single piece of land must feel like a lonely burden." Maggie continued, "People desire brotherhood, Edmund. Your recent association with Joseph, the boatmen, the Shawnees...I dare say, 'tis your desire for community."

Edmund wiped a moist cheek.

Maggie nodded. "In Shamokin, the whites observed native folks dressed in deerskins and moccasins, but our general manner was to coax them into our tradecloth and breeches. We kept to our ground meal, even though we tried the berries and roots from the woods. We were not curious enough to walk the quiet forest paths and feel one thousand years old. We thought they should want to adopt our modern ways."

Edmund scowled, "Now if one attempts to dress in buckskins and walk the woods, his days shall end there. Someone will put a hole in him."

Maggie nodded, then retreated into her room and closed the door. Days later, she emerged with pages she handed directly to Edmund. She had written:

Dear Edmund,

Times are upon us, my son, when you'll discover that survival goes deeper than merely staying alive. Survival draws us down into our roots, as a tree drawing life from the soil. Our roots have all become enmeshed; our common soil, Turtle Island. Your ancestors have helped me to know Turtle Island. I cannot sit by and watch my son forget. You buried our friend, Joseph, in the soil of the Turtle. I pray you sang in the Lenape language of your youth, Edmund. Forget not your heritage, even as you settle in this valley.

A tale I might choose to forget from many years past came about early in the summer of 1750, when I learned the certain fate of Eleanor's father. The sickness had ceased and as the weather warmed, the villagers from the north began wandering back to their deserted homes. The fever was sweated out of their soil by then and they aimed to plant small community gardens on the charity of Shamokin's seeds. Several men returned shortly, with a large bundle wrapped in a blanket. Perhaps Carl had taken refuge in a storm or become lost. They had found his body in one of the abandoned huts.

I grieved and yet found relief in knowing the end of the search. Eleanor was very young. My intention in sparing her the witness of his burial was to spare her the gruesome sight and scent of a badly decomposed body. Yet perhaps she never believed that he was truly gone. When she saw the riverside gravesite later, her little eyes wandered upstream, as if yet watching for his arrival by canoe. Our relations were never as close after her father's departure, as if she blamed me or disbelieved. But by that time, my concern was our subsistence.

In the warm summer months, several Brethren loaded a pack horse with gifts for our sister village, the Gnadenhutten mission. They returned after a fortnight away with a report of the modern mission: the completed sawmill giving work to their local natives; houses and a chapel rebuilt with the milled wood; and a bell, cast in Bethlehem, awaiting the finished belfry.

When they returned to Shamokin, they dragged a load of milled lumber behind the pack horse, and were accompanied by Brother Zeisberger, who planned to lead an inspection of the river villages upstream. He also reported the attack of a neighboring town and cautioned us once again.

When Zeisberger's group set out upstream, I felt the wallop of grief for the death of Eleanor's father. Watching from the river's edge, I knew Carl would have been among them, taking the smithy's tools upriver to sharpen plows and mend those that broke open the hardened land of several untended seasons. I watched them disappear, then slumped to the ground in anguish.

All tempers swirled through me, from sorrow to joy, as I stood at the forks where skies could open wide upon one river and close with a fog upon the other. One river bore the dark approaching storm of my life as a widow in dismal times. The other river sang of joy for our successful neighboring mission and the reestablishment of the upstream villages. I begged the currents of both forks to sweep away rumours of raids in the back country, tales of militias forming in defense.

One day, I heard the Delaware women shout a greeting to visitors from the north. I recognized the voice that answered: Andrew Montour. Montour's familiar blond scalplock and blousoned shoulders caught my eye as the lead canoe emerged and cut sharply across the river. The canoe behind him carried Weiser between two swiftly paddling men.

Weiser scurried up the bank, asking for the chief. They gathered the Brethren and announced that Canasatego had died. Because the leader had been a friend of the colonists, Weiser feared foul play. With the ominous news, even the Moravians sat and smoked the pipe as the men discussed the political confusion. A treaty meeting in Logstown upset Tagnehdorus and Logan, angry to see Shamokin replaced as a meeting center.

Weiser explained that as Lenapes were forced further west, they aimed to stop further English settlement of the western lands and were making alliances with the French. "If the Iroquois give western land away," warned Weiser, "Lenapes will wage war most certain." He said Pennsylvania looked weak because Quaker pacifists offer no militia and no ammunition for Indians or farmers seeking protection. He left us with a warning to be on alert.

Shamokin village had less sickness than in previous years, but in early autumn, I was besought with a baffling ailment of trembling in my hands and legs. No local prayers, remedies or native dances provided relief. Missus Fry and White Hawk aided greatly with Eleanor's care and helped preserve her shelter.

With Carl gone, I was most concerned with being sent away from

Shamokin, as a burden on the mission. My safety and Eleanor's depended on all the watchful men about the camp, Moravians, Delawares, and Shawnees. But Tagnehdorus, and Logan in particular, provided me a calming sense of protection and care.

I took note and felt less comfort when those two men were away from the village. But they were preparing to travel to a treaty meeting in Carlisle, down the Susquehanna and offered to visit a white doctor there on my behalf. I set aside my sadness and went to the bluff's edge to wish Logan farewell. Looking tall in his dress buckskins, he bowed politely and promised to bring good medicine.

By the time Logan and Tagnehdorus returned, I was eager to accept the bitter liquor, sent in a brown bottle from the doctor. 'Twas revealed to be a mixture of the native remedies of milkweed and skunk cabbage. Logan had searched out the supply of milkweed himself, he bragged.

In the following days, the tremors and aches eased greatly, but the fever returned. White Hawk and Logan visited on days when I felt well enough, a great show of friendship when I consider the fear they might have carried about fever. Logan discussed the Carlisle meeting and though my concentration was lagging, I understood that our friend Montour had humiliated himself with a temper unguarded by rum, prompting a near fistfight and a jealous rift with Weiser.

Weiser, who escorted Ben Franklin and the other commissioners, arrived late to the meetings and, to speed their journey, had left the truck wagons full of gifts behind. Logan said the Indians insisted on waiting for the gifts to arrive, giving Franklin a first-hand look at the protocol of the woods.

After the meetings, it was Weiser's son Sammy, my old friend, who visited Shamokin village on his way back from delivering Franklin to Philadelphia. He told us his father had followed the Mohawks north after the meeting, aware that they were frustrated with the pacifist Pennsylvanians and hoping to uncover their plans.

"My father wants you t' guard yourselves, perhaps take leave t' Bethlehem," Sammy told our group. Later, he approached me with a specific message. "Father wants you to consider returning to a civilised town. With condolences, Miss Maggie, you're alone now. You must go back."

I looked away and said, "When the Frys depart, I'll travel with them." As I said the words, I frantically plotted escape. With a shattered vision of our village life in my frail and feverish mind, I concocted schemes of hiding if the Frys packed their wagon for Bethlehem. I would run off to the woods with Logan and White Hawk, or raise Eleanor in the protection of Montour's farm.

With all the talk of leaving and the reminders of Franklin, I succumbed to a feverishly vivid dream that night of a visit with 'the Electrician,' as Franklin had become known following his experiments with kites and lightning bolts. Franklin peered over the spectacles of his own invention and pointed at Logan, who watched us from a distance. Franklin said, "The Indian cannot protect you from people who do not believe you should be living in the woods."

In my dream, I poured tea, but it spilled onto the floor below. Franklin's eyes became sorrowful, staring at the spilled tea. "Patience is wearing thin," he said. My dream ended when Logan stepped forward holding a tiny porcelain teacup in his massive, brown hand. I know it sounds like foolishness or fever, but I became so heartsick at the image of that fine man undertaking our austere English conventions, it occurred to me that I was more inclined to cross the threshold into his world of nature's woods, rather than see him restrained by the trivial disciplines of the English.

I tell you of my predicament, Edmund, you who have made a fine integration yourself into a dubious middle world, because I cannot fathom finding understanding with my daughter on this point.

I considered forsaking my English world, whether Philadelphia or Bethlehem. I wanted to beg Logan, a good and kind man of steadfast heart, to take my daughter and me with him and disappear into the woods. I wanted to run. The Indians know the shadowy woods. There, the hunt prospers. There are the meeting places for dance, for stories, and for embracing another. 'Tis true, I wanted Logan's embrace.

Edmund, I had sunk my roots into the soil in Shamokin and felt alive. My roots had intertwined in the community of the Frys, White Hawk and Logan. I felt embraced, not alone, when I was ill. I felt in league with the Turtle. I now ask Turtle Island to help my own daughter know that I have always aimed for her best care. I pray she will understand how I could love an Indian man and she will also understand how I could not venture any further into his world.

We will all settle here in Pittsburgh, or Dunmore, whatever we are to call our town. We shall intertwine our roots and be vital among a community. I want not to run further, Edmund. You, Eleanor, we shall be a family, united, after all.

Your mother

Maggie placed her quill pen across her ink pot and bundled the pages in a fold of fabric. She aimed to search for Edmund while also avoiding the laundry efforts on the back porch. Eleanor carried large pots of water from the rain barrel to Whitney, who stirred the massive kettle with a wooden paddle. Anytime, but especially of late, the smell of lye soap sent Maggie's thoughts to her troubled early days in Bethlehem, working long hours and grieving her absent father.

Having declared her intention to settle any old disharmony with Eleanor, Maggie recognized the guilty feelings of avoidance. She brushed it aside by claiming to avoid the laundry, not Eleanor, and tiptoed down the hallway to the weaver's shop and front entrance. She met the heavy scent of Edmund's hickory fire outside the door and scurried alongside the house to the shed. Edmund was nowhere to be seen. Then he backed through the side door with an armload of saplings and dropped them on the floor beside a dwindling stack of axe-cut pieces.

"You were missed, Mother Beigler. You were shut away all the day." He pointed at the wall, hung with dark, dried strips of venison. "We'll not starve presently, eh?"

Maggie smiled. "Everyone has made themselves so useful. My retreat has been worthwhile, I believe." She held out the small, wrapped packet of papers. "I wish for you to see for yourself firstly, Edmund. Perhaps you will advise me prior to proceeding in my efforts of peacemaking with Eleanor."

His dark eyes seemed perplexed as he held out his hand for the packet. "You seldom ask my counsel, Mother Beigler."

She said, "'Tis surely not the last time." Her throat pinched closed as she finished her sentence. Abruptly, she turned and hurried back toward the front of the cabin. Once around the corner, she gasped for breath and lowered herself to the pine plank steps. The shadows of her memory had been in the woods, yet her body was recalling the distinct feeling of the orderly rows of buildings in Bethlehem. Closer than the scent of lye had ever brought her, she felt as if she could reach out her hand and touch the cool stone walls. "I was never one for the bustling town life," she thought. She sat on the soft pine step and inhaled the fresh air, feeling that, despite the current chaos, she was right to have left Bethlehem.

Maggie sat that evening in the cool parlor with a blanket pulled tightly about her neck. She heard rustling noises in the room overhead, probably the boys readying themselves for bed. The back door creaked and she heard the heavy steps of Edmund, removing his jacket and hanging it on a wooden peg in the hallway.

He entered the room quietly, pulled a chair across the hooked rug and sat near Maggie. They nodded at each other, but sat in silence for several minutes. The boys' rustlings ceased and Eleanor's muffled voice could be heard at the top of the stairs.

Edmund turned to Maggie. "You best speak with her. She'll be certain to fathom more than you expect," he said.

"And you? What is your estimation?"

Edmund stretched his legs and pursed his lips. He said, "I know you returned to Bethlehem. I was there when you and Eleanor traveled back with the Frys. It appears, from your letter, you deemed it unfitting for your Oneida fellow to accompany you to town. You wanted to resist the likelihood of changing him into a white man. Have I estimated correctly?"

The edges of Maggie's mouth drooped in sadness. "'Twasn't my decision," she said. "He had no inclination to join me."

Edmund asked, "What is the source of displeasure with Eleanor? You believe she's changed me into a white man?"

"Edmund," Maggie began. They heard Eleanor's steps as she descended the stairs.

Edmund leaned close and whispered, "You must talk with her, but I have other news first." He raised his voice to a normal tone. "I have some news for the both of you. Eleanor, sit here, if you please." He stood from his chair and moved to retrieve another.

"You missed our supper," said Eleanor, as she sat.

"I walked into town," said Edmund, looking first at her and then at Maggie. "People were scurrying toward Semple's Tavern and upon inquiring, I learned that one of the townsmen who had been sent to retrieve news of the Continental Congress in Philadelphia had returned."

"At long last," exclaimed Maggie. "What said the man?"

"'Twas the tanner, Casper Reel. He read from a statement claiming the closing of the port of Boston and the annulment of the charter of Massachusetts. The delegates agreed that the Crown had overstepped their rule. Representatives voted to prepare a colonial militia. They'll not attack the English, but if fired upon, they aim to respond with force."

Maggie nodded her head solemnly. She said, "'Tis some time in coming." Eleanor raised an eyebrow and Maggie said, "Logan spoke of it. Union. Two decades ago a plan of union was proposed in Albany by Franklin. The Indians had been requesting it."

"'Tis true?" asked Eleanor.

"'Twas rejected," Maggie nodded. "Only now have the provinces agreed on a common enemy and chosen to unite. They will say the enemy is the King's taxation, our lack of freedom."

Eleanor said, "I fear we're unprepared to fight against the British army."

"The colonial governors will muster up a fervor," said Edmund, "along with guns and powder. They'll promise free land to militiamen, I suspect, akin to the Virginia soldiers offering up Kentucky."

"What said the townfolk?" Eleanor asked Edmund.

"I heard a good many "God bless the King" remarks from the likes of Missus Semple and other business folks. From Doc Connolly, to be sure. Yet sympathy for the Crown has grown weary since taxation increased. Trader Campbell raised inquiries of the militia, begging to know who would feed them."

Edmund rose and looked out the window. "A flurry of snow has coated the ground," he said.

Eleanor sighed. "The boys asked for a holiday at Christmas."

"We best keep it simple," Maggie said. "Honey cakes? Few others in town will recognize the religious days, most being unchurched."

Edmund said, "I could hunt a fat bird. A turkey or a goose." He walked to Maggie's side and leaned close, whispering, "Tell her."

"Tell me? What secrets abound?" Eleanor quizzed her mother.

Maggie squirmed in her chair and scowled at Edmund. "I revealed something in confidence earlier that my son believes should be shared."

"Indeed," said Eleanor. "Pray tell."

"I must find the words." Maggie rubbed her face. After a short time, she said, "This sprinkling of snow will assist, I beg, to conjure a painful memory. 'Twas the winter of '54, and I was having bouts of fever. The chief's family dressed in rags, once again grieving when White Hawk's oldest son was killed in a skirmish with the Catawbas along with his cousin. Their uncle, White Hawk's youngest brother, was blamed for taking the younger ones into rival territory and inciting a fight, shattering the family's lodge with shame and sorrow. The uncle, himself, had escaped, but remained on the hunting trail to earn back a respected standing by providing food for our poverty-stricken village.

"White Hawk was inconsolable. She lingered in her lodge until taking it upon herself, with several other women, to hike to Weiser's farm to beg for food. Her brothers argued about regaining honor for their family. Tagnehdorus disappeared into the western hills. Logan shredded his clothes and moaned at night, the only man remaining near his family's lodge.

"Our scant holiday cheer came from the Moravians with a pack train bestowing barrels of flour and corn, clothing and fabric from the Sisters, and several tins of chocolate."

Maggie paused and Eleanor said, "'Tis as I recall Shamokin, fraught with chaos and hunger."

Maggie nodded. "'Tis my confession. Brother Fry rode to Bethlehem to replenish our supplies before we became desperate. He suggested that you and I come along and stay the duration of the winter in a proper town...but I refused."

"You desired to stay?" asked Eleanor, raising her voice.

"'Twas in a quandary. I bear shame and sorrow at the added grief and the risk I took. I might blame my senselessness on the fever, but I must confess another source." Maggie held a fist to her mouth, as though tempted to chew.

"Mother, go on, I beg you."

Barely louder than a whisper, Maggie said, "Shamokin was tranquil with so many away, an unusual circumstance. 'Twas serene as if all around, the world moved while we remained still. I had an image of a wheel rolling along a rocky trail, the center moving but slight, compared to the tumbled rim. Our village was the center hub. I could sense that the terrain around us was becoming rough, but I thought to remain, nested safely in the center."

"The eye of the storm," said Edmund.

Maggie nodded. "In the hills above Shamokin, Logan hiked, night upon night. Every sunrise and every sunset was met with his mournful voice like an animal in pain. He cried for his own broken family, but the sorrowful sounds vibrated through my bones. 'Twas then I thought, perhaps the sons of Swataney, one shamed, one disappeared and one mourning loudly, had slipped outside the center of the wheel, the Shamokin center of the world. They were tumbling in the storm we could only sense approaching."

With a deep breath, Maggie continued. "I went to him, Eleanor. One morning, early, while you were yet sleeping and Missus Fry lay nearby in an adjoining room. I left and followed his howling voice up onto the side of the hill. He chanted and moaned, taking no note of my approach. I found him standing between two saplings, with arms stretched from one to the other, wrapping their able trunks. The trees held him, like his missing brothers, the braces to keep from falling from the mountainside. A lock of hair fell over his eyes and grief contorted his face. I witnessed the wheel smashing. For Logan, the village had come undone. The world was coming undone.

"I walked before him and put both my hands on his trembling chest. His eyes opened and filled with more pain upon seeing me. He slumped to his knees, arms still tight around the trees, but his face buried in my chest. I held him as he wept. I cradled his head, caressed his back, wanted him to steal me away into the woods forever."

The room was still for a moment, then Maggie's voice choked, "I asked him then." She gathered her voice and said clearly, "I spoke the words aloud. 'Take me with you. On the day you leave the village, take me with you.'" Maggie looked at Eleanor's tear-streaked face, her hand over her mouth. "Of course, I meant the both of us. I would not have left you. But is this a comfort? I would have, at that moment, dragged you away to deeper woods and a life of untamed complications."

Maggie wiped her eyes and breathed deeply, with a slight crackle in her voice. She looked at Edmund. "But Logan was silent, a silence like death. His wailing ceased, his chest heaved with a barely audible moan. He hung his head as tears dried in the middle of his cheeks.

"Although he rested against my breast, I had no signal that he welcomed my embrace. The arms I wanted to hold me remained entwined with the saplings, as though he clung to the forest. I took a step back. 'Twas no response, though his heart thumped visibly against his chest. I continued backing away, then turned and ran down the hill through the thickets to our cabin.

"We never spoke of it. I cannot say what he surmised of my request. I told Edmund earlier that I could not fathom taking the man to Bethlehem or Philadelphia. I had no desire to see him become civilized in the manners of white men, our clothes and education. 'Twas I who wanted to follow him into his world of woods, smoke fires and venison. 'Twas I who wanted stories danced, not spoken."

Eleanor dabbed at her moist eyes. Edmund fidgeted in the uncomfortable hush, then seemed relieved to think of a question. "Mother Beigler, you survived the starvation after all. By what means?"

"By the grace of Brother Mack traveling through the snow with Brother Fry to bring pack horses laden with barrels of beans and salt pork. Within a fortnight, White Hawk and the other women returned with supplies from Weiser. Weiser himself arrived in spring with a horse load of goods. White Hawk came out of her lodge of despair and Logan, thin and weak from deprivation, hobbled into the village to greet the interpreter.

"Many villagers had hope restored, though Weiser warned Logan he must be of one mind with his brothers. He needed them at the upcoming trip to Albany.

"Logan shuffled away to fetch his brothers. Weiser said no more, though we knew 'twas land affairs of main concern all around Shamokin. Logan and Tagnehdorus prepared for the Albany trip. On their day of departure, some villagers and Moravians hiked across the river with them, as far as a hidden food cache where the trails heading north and east converged. Finding the store of corn and beans, we put on a kettle and set up camp beneath a towering pine tree, where tribes had come for many celebrations and left feathered traces of past ceremonies hanging in the branches. The Indians believed in a Great Tree of Peace with roots spreading in four directions to carry peace to the world.

"A neighboring chief, who would go on to Albany, arrived and smoked a pipe with Tagnehdorus and Logan. Hunters from both parties added game birds to the pots and we feasted beneath the tree. That night, I lay in a canvas tent across the camp and a world away from Logan. 'Twas as close as I came to abandoning myself to the woods. I grasped the turtle around my neck and wished for Swataney's wisdom to help me understand the pine's whispers in the wind, portent of a long journey to peace."

Maggie's voice faded and Eleanor said, sighing, "Indeed. We are yet far from peace. I feel the edge of the wheel tumbling here in Pittsburgh."

"The wheel pulls the wagon of the charging horse," Maggie said. "More and more people."

"People who expect to have a piece of the turtle for themselves," said Edmund.

"Is there a means of reining it in?" asked Eleanor.

Maggie shrugged and turned away. "'Tis perilous to attempt naught." She felt some relief, having told Eleanor of her feelings for Logan. The chasm between old pain and new seemed to grow smaller. But just talking about Logan had stirred a heartsick loneliness. Thoughts about her old friends were lit up like a campfire. She felt herself waiting for the dance, watching for the storyteller. But, she knew, the dance was her own.

ζ

I closed my notebook and looked up through the Beetle's broad windshield. "My God, it's beautiful here." The sunlight glistened from the branches of millions of evergreens, like woven green fabric stretching in every direction, split in half by the narrow gray band of highway.

Quinn nodded. "It's so peaceful. I've been watching the hills dip then rise then dip again. It's so flat in Illinois. I miss hills like these, don't you?"

"Reminds me of home," I said. "The Shawnee Forest in southern Illinois. But these hills are even higher."

Quinn had been driving without the stereo on for as long as I'd been writing, but she tapped the steering wheel, as if she heard music. She glanced at the notebook on my lap. "That's getting kind of full. Should we get you another one?"

"Probably," I said, nodding. "Along with some throat lozenges. I'm still scratchy. There's definitely more to the story. Maggie just admitted to Eleanor that she had a 'thing' for Logan, the Indian guy."

"Whoo-hoo," Quinn grinned. "I wondered how anybody could hang around with those buff guys with no shirts and not be affected. I'm a lesbian, but even I would have to notice those chests all greased up with bear fat."

"It was more than that. I think she really cared," I said. "And even more, there was a draw for Maggie toward the wild...the really deep, wild woods. I think Logan helped her understand the pull that she felt toward nature."

"Oh, baby. I'll bet he did, too," gushed Quinn.

I slapped at her arm. "Cut it out, freak." I flipped through my notebook and found the section I wanted to read. "Here, listen to this." I read the portion where Maggie went up on the hillside while Logan was chanting, where she found him propped by two saplings, contorted with grief. The pain that was sliced open with their touch became clear to me as I read. Logan knew that he was not allowed to feel anything, lust or love, for the white woman who was a family friend. It was as impossible for him to imagine Maggie joining his world as it was for Maggie to imagine him wearing white man's clothing and eating and speaking with English manners.

Quinn sniffed, and said, "Wow." One hand gripped the steering wheel. "Stories danced, not spoken," she said. "I think this is definitely a past life thing." She pulled herself up straight in the seat.

"I'd agree, except that whenever I'm 'there,'" I said, my fingers notching quote marks around the word, "I feel like a visitor. It doesn't feel like my life. It doesn't feel familiar, except as I go along." I didn't know what a past life was supposed to feel like. "It interests me," I said. "Do you know anyone who's explored past lives? I thought it was supposed to feel familiar."

Quinn shrugged. "I suppose it doesn't matter. Like Joe said, it was all about changing his idea of himself. To paraphrase old Joe, 'You'd better get moving!'"

"Where are we, anyway?" I asked as we approached a large bridge.

"About thirty miles from Danville. Can you wait until we get there to eat lunch?"

I leaned to look out the window. "That must be the Susquehanna."

"Right. We're going to exit and go down the highway in the valley. I thought you'd like that," she said.

"Great." I sat back and tried to let go of expectations. I just wanted to enjoy the scenery. "I didn't read to you last night, but Maggie had another major loss—the chief."

"Swataney?" asked Quinn.

"Yeah. She helped White Hawk ease his last hours. They massaged him and told a story that was his favorite. I felt like I was right there. I even felt my hands heat up. One of the Moravian guys came at the end and talked about walking in the chief's woods, breathing the pine air he can no longer smell." I looked out at the rippling river. "Now I have a tiny idea of what he meant."

Quinn said, "These were his woods. When we were in Philadelphia at the riverfront yesterday, you had a sense of the old town...you sort of breathed the air they could no longer smell."

"You saw the cobblestones they could no longer rumble over," I said, grinning. We sat in silence and watched the trees shift from evergreens to thinning yellow birch or aspens; I wasn't sure which, maybe both. But the colors, even though mostly gone, were lively compared to the miles and miles of deep green we had passed through. In a few weeks, the clumps of deciduous trees would be gray-twigged skeletons.

After a while, I told Quinn I thought I knew why Maggie was taking me on this journey. "She's waking me up," I explained. "I think some part of me has been, how do I put it...asleep, perhaps."

"You're helping her, too, Reed. Look how expressive she's becoming," Quinn smiled.

"But she's experienced so much death. All her life. Still, she's willing to wake up and feel. She's dredging her memories. She must know there's something important to remember."

"And pass along," Quinn said, nodding. "I hope we get back early enough tonight for me to read. This notebook is getting fat."

We pulled into the outskirts of Danville, though within a few minutes we were in the middle of town. The downtown area showed evidence of a surviving local economy, with only a few signs of the mammoth corporate chain stores that were devouring small towns and suburbs across the country. The town's architecture was old, some from the 1800s, often neatly painted and preserved. But there were some timeworn buildings sheathed in vinyl siding and cheap replacement windows and a few that were untended, close to collapse. There were mostly two-story buildings with parapets stretching taller, appearing larger than the space they had to fill.

Cars hummed along the streets waving tiny antenna flags or sporting decals and bumper stickers of Old Glory. I felt we had arrived on Main Street, USA. Danville was like Mayberry, Smallville, or my little Metropolis. I felt at home. Quinn picked a restaurant while I was staring up and down the streets. Naturally, she found the friendliest waitress we had met so far in Pennsylvania. Actually, she was the cook, but since the waitress had called in sick, she said she had both jobs, speeding back and forth from the kitchen.

She came to our table with our sandwich plates stacked on her arm and an apology for wearing her soiled apron. "If I took the time to untie the knot in back, your dinner would be cold," she chuckled. There were only two other customers in the place, both men. They had to wait while the cook pampered us. I think she had an eye for Quinn. Every time she walked by our table she had questions. After making sure our orders were all right, she asked where we were from, where we were staying. She gave us a tip on the best cheap hotel. I worried that she was going to abandon the restaurant and go with us to Sunbury. Finally, the cook busied herself with the other customers and left us to sip our coffee.

I leaned over the table and lowered my voice. "I have to tell you something, Quinn." I couldn't keep a small smile from twitching at the edges of my mouth. "You know how I said part of me has been asleep?" Quinn nodded and sipped. "I'm figuring out that I've been really detached from my body," I said.

"That's definitely a good thing...I mean, figuring it out," Quinn tapped on the table top. "And just in time. You're headed into your prime years."

I was still feeling embarrassed about my self-exploration in the shower. I said, stammering, "There's...I think...well, I'll just say it. I'm feeling...attractions. I don't know if it was your story of the basketball girl or you, this morning, looking very lovely in your bed...I guess it's just me."

Quinn leaned over the table as the cook approached with a fresh pot of coffee. Teasing me, she spoke with a voice even lower than mine. "You're trying to say you were turned on?"

I nodded, grinning, as the cook stopped at our table. Quinn leaned back in her chair and watched our cups being filled. Then she got serious. "You know, you're the one who referred to yourself as 'asleep.' When a bear comes out of hibernation, it will eat whatever's in sight," she said with a twisted face. "Tree bark, bugs...I think you have to consider that anything warm could have turned you on. Go slow with this, is what I'm saying."

"I'm not afraid, Quinn. It doesn't scare me."

"Sometimes fear is a good thing. A little caution."

"You've never gone slow," I said.

"We're not talking about me."

"Oh? There's a double standard?" My voice made the squeak I hate.

"You have a lot going on right now," she said. "Just remembering the abuse with the housekeeper. Who knows what more might affect your feelings. You need to finish this thing with Maggie. Like you said, she's got to be sending you a message."

I pouted for a few minutes and picked at my sandwich. "I didn't expect this sort of response," I said.

"I'm not recruiting for the lesbian team, Reed. I want you to be happy. I want you to take your time and figure this out. It's complicated. The whole thing with your mother dying. I've never had anyone really close to me die, but it seems death can cast a very long shadow."

I sat back against my seat. I knew she was right. "I've always thought life was really hard," I said. "I lived waiting for the next tragedy. Really. If I started caring about someone, I'd get images of him in car accidents, hospital rooms, death's door. My imagination would go wild. I guess Maggie has shown me how easy I've really had it. With the exception of my mother..."

"And the wicked Miss North," Quinn added.

"Tragedies kept happening to Maggie and she kept going. Kept living her life. If I had been her, I'd have stayed in England after my mother died and spent my life washing laundry or something while the rest of the world came to America."

"Reed. You're too hard on yourself," Quinn said.

I nodded. "That's another thing I want to change. I noticed this morning that I always feel watched. Judged."

"That makes sense, considering."

"But mostly I judge myself. I'm going to work on being nicer to me."

"Excellent. I'm for it," Quinn said.

"I'm nervous about going, but I'm also really excited to drive over to Sunbury...Shamokin village. Can we?"

We broke the news to our friend, the cook, that we were leaving. She was also the cashier. She handed Quinn her change, winked and said, "We're open for breakfast at 7."

7

Maggie had taken to her bed with a minor bout of catarrh that rumbled with fluid in her lungs. She drank bitters and coughed while Eleanor sat nearby and penned a note to the Emorys. The journeyman tanner, the same man who had brought news from the Congress, would pass through Lancaster within a fortnight and had agreed to deliver a note to the weaver.

"Two letters were sent prior to this," said Eleanor, "though with much less dependable-looking characters. With no news from the Emorys and no sign of the apprentice, I'm fearful that trouble has befallen them."

Maggie cleared her throat with an effort. "The shelves are nigh barren and patrons seldom visit. The town prattlers may have filled ears with tales of the weaver's permanent departure."

"I've no wish to alarm the couple. I aim to muster a cheery note," said Eleanor.

"Pray, give me a listen," said Maggie.

Eleanor put down her quill. "I wished them good health and assured them that we and the cabin are well. I want them to fret naught."

"Read," said Maggie.

Eleanor said, "You thought it unwise to tell them the woven stock was diminished, hence I wrote:

> Some folks have inquired on the woven goods and Mother helps them find something from the shelf stock. She has improved steadily and walks about with nary a limp. We have a concern that your apprentice has yet to arrive and we fear this represents a difficulty for yourselves. Have you succeeded in finding an assistant? We pray Missus Emory's health is improved. Please attempt to send news.
>
> The soldiers completed their aggression upon the Indians, sending them westward. The town is quieter, though besieged

with men eager to take aim with a colonial militia. We await
your response.

> *Sincere regards,*
> *Eleanor Foote and family*

Maggie nodded approval while Eleanor folded and sealed the letter with a dripping of wax. She wrote "Angus Emory, Master Weaver, in care of the Postmaster of Lancaster," on the outer fold. She said, "I chose to make no mention of the fence burned for firewood while the soldiers were teeming about."

"No need to set fear upon their return," agreed Maggie. "Mister Emory witnessed the Smith's cabin run upon by soldiers before they departed. They're aware that times are grievous."

Eleanor leaned closer and lowered her voice, even though the boys had followed their father outdoors. "Prattlers say Colonel Mackay was followed by soldiers a fortnight past. They attempted to arrest him at his home, a scuffle ensued and a soldier swiped Missus Mackay with his cutlass."

"No!" Maggie coughed.

"Her arm's in a sling yet."

Maggie lowered her head and covered her eyes. "A Pennsylvania family," she murmured.

Eleanor nodded. "Another Penn family, the Spears, had their store ransacked. The Hannastown sheriff arrested several men with their stolen property, but his jail was raided by Virginia men who set them free."

"Aye. A further breach of the feuding colonies. Yet this happened prior to the news from the Congress?" asked Maggie.

Eleanor nodded. "Do you fathom the two colonies might settle their feud?" She stirred a kettle of potato broth hanging by the fire and leaned to sniff the herbs.

"'Tis befitting if there's to be union."

Eleanor removed her cape from the wall peg and prepared to take her note to the journeyman for delivery on his way eastward. "Shall I help you lie down?" she asked.

Maggie leaned back in the rocking chair, closed her eyes and said, "I may not be the heartiest among us with a prayer. Yet I shall make my plea to the Great Spirit."

"For your health?" asked Eleanor.

"For us all," Maggie replied. After Eleanor left to walk into town, Maggie dipped the quill pen in ink and began to write.

Eleanor,

My efforts at prayer seem fruitless, though this puts me in mind of a lesson learned from Logan in the final days of Shamokin village when he returned with a report of his Albany journey. While the brethren and villagers returned from the meeting place across the river, Logan and Tagnehdorus had hiked along the Water-That-Flows-Two-Ways, the Hudson River valley.

Weiser convinced the brothers to come to the meeting by telling them that there was no stoppage to the flow of white settlers. He seemed to have conceded that purchasing the land from the Indians was the only way to lessen the tensions and legitimise the settlers' presence. Apparently, he brought the brothers into the bargaining, gaining them enough coins to assure their cooperation.

At Albany, the Mohawks' eighty-year-old statesman, Hendrick, spoke first. Draped in red fabric, he was introduced as grieving for the neglect his people had suffered at the hands of the English.

Weiser defended the colonies and said all land deals would be refused if they failed to include the Ohio country, since it would seem the Indians were contracting it to the French. He cleverly asked Hendrick to be his spokesman to the other chiefs, giving him an opportunity to side with the English.

Hendrick reported the English commissioners' displeasure to the chiefs. Reminding them of old friendships with the Pennsylvanians, he advised them to remove the frowns from the brows of their brothers and grant them the lands. Eager to prove they were not in collusion with France, the Indians agreed.

The next item of business was the colonial union. Franklin and the commissioners studied the organised tribes, each part honoured within the whole. They voted without dissent in support of Colonial union, giving each colony a different number of representatives, based on their population. The plan gave power to the legislature to raise troops and regulate the Indian trade, a settlement long sought by the Iroquois. Everyone departed Albany those two decades ago, believing that a union was underway. 'Twas later halted by the Crown because it gave the colonies too much independence.

At an unofficial gathering the night before that land agreement, Logan was given a wolf mask by the Mohican host. Logan and Tagnehdorus sat at the head fireplace as the native leaders observed the Dance of the False Faces. Logan described a frightful carved mask, bright red with strands of willow limbs sprouting like hair, the face of an evil spirit the people wished to drive away. The dancer spun in circles, stirring the evil, leaping with each drumbeat and shaking rattles in all corners of the lodge.

Despite the frenzy, Logan said that no one shrunk back. They understood that at the conclusion of the dance the evil would be released. As they watched, they prepared to welcome the masked dancer into the village. They reminded him that the mask and the fear were unreal. Evil departed from their midst.

The dance ended of a sudden and Logan said the headmen conversed on the subject at hand. The chief, aiming to avoid being caught in the white men's conflict, set aside differences to join with the Mohawks at the treaty meeting. When the chief gave Logan the wolf mask, he described a vision of white soldiers marching across the hills. He knew that any that stood in their way would perish.

I am uncertain of all the ways the natives communicate. We struggled to teach them writing, yet I cannot write the explanation of an important message reaching the thoughts of a chief at the moment he is to decide.

The two brothers returned to Shamokin in the dismal heat to learn that The Six Nations had sent sixty-five Christian Indians from Gnadenhutten to settle the area across the Susquehanna in an aim to stop the flow of whites into the valley. Tagnehdorus felt his influence for peacekeeping had been overlooked and stormed to his lodge.

ζ

"Well, I hope that was worth all the effort," Quinn said. "They didn't have any more area maps so the clerk took one from the phone book and made a copy. Didn't even charge me." She handed me a plastic bag with a notebook and box of cherry cough drops. "We're all gassed up and ready to go. You wrote some more?"

"I probably shouldn't have been sitting here in the sun," I said, opening the box. "I feel parched already."

"Well, coffee may not be the best thing for a sore throat," she said.

"It might be the turtle, too. It's in my pocket, but I feel it hanging around my neck like an empty canteen. Maggie's guy Logan and his brother just returned from a long journey to New York. That's probably what it's about."

"So open up," said Quinn. She looked down my throat. "Do you have a sore throat or do you *think* you have a sore throat."

"It's Maggie," I said as I snapped my mouth shut. "Maggie was coughing. That's funny. I said I had a sore throat, but you brought me cough drops."

"I refuse to be tangled in this web of yours. I acted purely out of ignorance." Quinn looked at the map and checked her notes for the basketball game. She circled the school and drew a line over to the main street. Then she looked for a route to take us to Sunbury.

As we pulled away from the Mini Market, I said, "So I've been writing and talking about Maggie's story, but I've been thinking about mine. This morning in the car I dreamed about my mother. She's been on my mind a lot, especially since all this stuff about the housekeeper came up. You know, I can't figure out if I'm mad at her, but I have a feeling all those problems never would have happened if she'd been around. She would have known that woman was bad news as soon as she walked into the room."

Quinn nodded, smiling with only one side of her mouth.

"I felt her sitting next to me. I knew it was her as soon as she came close. You know how I said earlier that I've always felt watched? But this was nice. I knew she was looking at me, but she was just loving me, accepting me."

"That must have felt good," Quinn said.

"Sometimes I feel like I just want to disappear. But not then. I wanted her to see me and keep seeing me."

"You've missed her."

"Something about being accepted just as I am, you know? Somehow it helped my molecules spin the way they're supposed to. I felt myself breathe and settle down into my warm body."

"Hmmm. Something you don't do often," said Quinn. "Settle down, I mean."

I shook my head. Even sleep was often fitful, especially with the added journeys with the turtle. Some dreams take a few minutes, but mine could feel like plodding through a desert for days without water. I could wake up feeling exhausted from my long night watch.

"So she accepted you," said Quinn.

I nodded. "She reminded me about our talk of the storm barometer. How I had a feeling something was wrong."

"She knew, too, right?"

"Said she'd been feeling wrong for a long time. She was leaning close to me. There weren't really words. But it was like a searing blade of truth when I heard her. She said, "I was afraid of him.""

"Your dad?" Quinn asked in a half whisper.

She told me my dad always aimed his angry words at others, but she felt that they were meant for her. I saw lots of little scenes, like movies she was showing me: A black man who delivered our groceries was accused of cheating on the bill; Polish immigrants who came to patch our roof were sent away because they couldn't speak enough English to satisfy him; ranting about a gay clerk at his office and accusing him of horrible things."

"She thought he blamed her?" Quinn asked.

"She said he used to call her magical. My magical little Mexican. She was supposed to make everything okay."

"So if anything went wrong..." Quinn said, pausing. "Kind of like you feeling she could have stopped the housekeeper."

"Wow," I whispered, as my skin went cold. "She *was* supposed to make everything okay."

"A tough role, isn't it?" Quinn said, sighing.

I sighed, too. "She said she felt less and less magical. Just a woman. Just a Mexican. Not so pretty. Not so smart. She said she got more and more fearful that she would exhaust his small tolerance of her. And he would leave." As I said it to Quinn, as I said it out loud, I felt her message as if it were pumping through my veins. "She left him."

I repeated it, louder. "She left *him*."

Quinn must have realized what a revelation I was having. She said nothing. She drove the Beetle onto a long bridge that crossed a brown expanse of water. The tires rumbled over the rough road. I looked downstream to the site of a dam and remembered where we were. Glancing at the map in her lap, Quinn took a right turn when we exited the bridge.

"We're here," she said. "This is Sunbury."

I glanced at a street sign. Susquehanna Street. Grabbing Quinn's map as we turned along the river, I said, "According to this, we just passed the site of the old Fort."

"I didn't see a fort," said Quinn. "It's all Victorian and colonial homes. One little sign said 'County Historical Society.' Whatever this county is called."

"Northumberland," I said. I was feeling a bit numb. It still hadn't occurred to me that we had crossed the bridge into Shamokin village. I saw pleasant homes with large, rolling lawns and neatly pruned trees and gardens, scenes that were far removed from my inner vision of the Indian town. As we drove along a business street, we saw American flags in the windows of nearly every store, as they were at home in Evanston since the terrorist attacks. "United We Stand" was lettered on sheets of poster board, slightly faded after a few weeks in the sunny windows. A tree-filled parkway ran down the middle of the street.

Further south of town, a small signpost announced "Shamokin Creek" and I asked Quinn to stop. I hopped out of the car to walk along the loamy creek bank, stacked wildly with flagstone layers. The patches of soft soil sank slightly under my weight. After finding a place to park the Beetle, Quinn jogged behind me. "Wait for me," she called.

I bent down and crumbled a handful of soil. The wild scent tickled my nostrils as I sniffed, trying to conjure visions from the musky fragments. I imagined wolves running up and down the bank, others howling in the distance. I sensed trouble. I smelled wind coming from a direction I didn't know. My old storm barometer was pressing hard on the temples of my inner vision. The wolves lingered, panting and yellow-eyed in the deep woods, and their earthy scent hung in the air.

ζ

Maggie had fidgeted alongside Eleanor's anxiety all the day as they waited for Edmund to return. He had ridden westward to survey the farm and see which neighbors remained. Maggie was relieved when she heard Edmund's horse trotting toward the shed and Eleanor sprang to the window. Maggie said, "Best to take him aside, without disturbing the boys. Let him know the town news."

Eleanor dropped the linen drapery as she heard the boys stirring upstairs. "What will befall us, Mother?" she asked, as she picked up her wrap and headed for the door.

Maggie said, "Edmund will have an answer. I'll attempt to detain the youngsters." Eleanor stepped out the back door as Maggie peered from the parlor window, watching Edmund unsaddle Coal and lead him to the shed. She stepped away from the window as the boys bounded down the steps.

"Whoa!" Maggie hollered. "You boys cannot run a rampage. You near knocked your brother clean over, Whitney." They both apologized and Maggie asked them to step closer to her as she sat in the rocker. Reluctantly, they lined up before her. "I wish to hear about your reading lessons prior to your running out-of-doors."

Morton piped up, "Mama had a pamphlet from Ben Franklin. We read both pages."

Without waiting for her reply, Whitney said, "Gran, we have so few pages to read. Would you consider letting us bind your letters with a buckskin cover and use them as a reader?"

Maggie stilled the rocker and gave them a thoughtful nod. "I can reckon no better use for them. Perhaps I could fashion the cover for your Christmas gift?"

Morton studied the floor as Whitney said, "Er, Papa gave us a piece of deer hide. We fashioned such a cover ourselves."

"Ah," said Maggie, "you anticipated my response."

"Flaps fold over the stack toward the center, then all is wrapped with a cord," said Morton. As Whitney jabbed him with an elbow, he added, "Perhaps new stockings would be nice."

Maggie's amusement was short lived as she glanced out the window to see the fresh snowfall and Doctor Connolly approaching at the end of the lane. Edmund and Eleanor walked from the shed, with no opportunity to ward off a meeting. Maggie felt the blood rush from her face. She turned to the boys and insisted they run upstairs. "I'll call to you when their meeting is finished," she said.

She walked to the back door and pressed her ear to the wood slats at a cracked opening. The doctor bellowed from down the lane, "Where will I find Mister Emory? We have need for winter wool and my soldiers said they received no response."

Edmund said, "Mister Emory has taken ill and cannot produce your wool. You must get it elsewhere."

Maggie heard the doctor pause as they met. With a calmer voice, he inquired on Maggie's health.

Eleanor said, "Her wounds have healed nicely."

"May I be of assistance to the weaver?" asked Connolly.

Edmund scowled and said, "He is well cared for. 'Tis a simple matter of time."

"What sense do I gather of your discontent?" asked the doctor.

Maggie felt her blood boiling. As she reached for the door, she heard Edmund speak clearly. "The Emorys, along with my own family, want nothing more of your rogue medicine."

"'Twas I who saw to your mother's care," Connolly protested.

Edmund stepped closer and lowered his voice, "And then you set about uprooting innocent Indian families, even ordering them killed."

"Ahhh," said the doctor, with a nod. "'Tis a redskin matter. This community has a ruinous history with redskins. Perhaps you need take your leave before there's any further affliction." He spun on the leather heel of his boot and walked stiffly down the lane.

Maggie met them at the back door, Eleanor still trembling. "How dare he threaten!" said Maggie.

Eleanor leaned wearily against Edmund and held the front of his jacket with both hands, tears on her quivering cheeks. She whispered, "Perhaps 'tis time for retreat to the farm. I cannot abide so."

"We'll carry on," Edmund assured, stroking the backs of her hands. "We'll not 'take our leave' at his beckoning. We made a promise to the Emorys to look after their cabin. Leastwhile, in town, there are witnesses to their mischief."

Maggie glanced toward the stairs, and grumbled, "You have your boys to consider, not a stack of logs. You cannot speak so surely when a battle with England may doom us to more chaos."

Edmund tried to assure her, "The cabin's well-being will never come before my family's. For now, though, seems best to stay."

Over the following days, snow quieted the town and everyone's business consisted of surviving the frigid temperatures. Maggie watched Edmund, who was determined to stay close about the cabin. He buzzed like a worker bee from flower to flower, room to room. Beyond their walls, she sensed the town aflutter, the doctor overly occupied and without an opportunity to create personal trouble for them. In February, she heard Fort Dunmore was hosting a Virginia County Court with Doctor Connolly named a justice. He and the other justices arrested several Pennsylvania magistrates. The boundary dispute refused to fade.

The boys' questions surfaced on the quietest days. "Papa, did you meet Mama when Granmama Willow took you to Nazareth?" "Mama, do you recollect the Shamokin trading post?" "Gran, is Ben Franklin a general?"

Edmund settled on the floor before the fire and told his sons about his boyhood memories of the tribal farmland near the Gnadenhutten mission and the pressure from white farmers to abandon it. "The Moravians gave us shelter and let us share in the crops. From there, we went to Nazareth, where crops were bountiful. I went to the school where a pretty girl with wheat colored hair spoke Lenape words like music."

"'Twas Mama!" squealed Morton. "What did she say?"

Eleanor smiled for the first time in days. "I asked him where he found the red clay to make his pots and two years thereafter, he showed me."

Whitney, who had also been sullen for several days, laughed and begged his father to teach them more of the Lenape language. Their mother explained how she came to understand the meaning of the words before her young tongue could shape them. She recalled the Shamokin trading post and its steady stream of Delaware conversation, both from the villagers and their frequent guests.

Maggie reminisced about Ben Franklin, printer and scientist, an unlikely champion of military strength, with thin wisps of white hair, round spectacles and ample belly. "Franklin had a son who commanded Pennsylvania troops," she said, "though he himself was a statesman." She told how Franklin's advice and others' was disregarded by the first English General sent to the Fort Pitt area. "'Twas called Fort Duquesne then, built by the French who were being trained to fight by the Ottawas, using trees in the woods as shields. The English sent General Braddock to march upon the French. He greatly disliked the Indians, an unfortunate mistake, and sent any volunteers away. He marched his men in mass formation, drums and bugles blaring, and the French, hiding in the woods, took aim. Braddock and hundreds of his men were killed, so stubborn and determined was he to march by the old standard."

"Which war was it?" asked Whitney.

"'Twas the opening battle of the war for the domination of this grand continent. Some refer to the French and Indian War, though the Indians were muddled between the French and English. Both nations attempted to sway tribes to their side."

"Papa was a boy?" asked Whitney.

"Nigh the same age as you, too young to fight," Maggie nodded.

Long after the boys' questions ceased and they were asleep upstairs, Maggie lay awake, her memories aroused by emotions. Her candle dripped beads of wax while her pen scratched the pages.

Dear family,

By now, you understand my reluctance to reminisce upon the dark days of the past. Once within the memories, however, I have no choice but to feel my way along their rough, cold walls, searching for light.

The Shamokin trading post was filled with stories of Braddock's troops marching to the mountains, Indians turned away because the General disliked how they looked or smelled. No one could tell us the outcome of the march, but bitterness had begun to foment.

The Albany land deals angered the Delaware and Shawnee Indians. In the autumn, the old bonds of friendship with the English colonies shattered and the Delawares and Shawnees began a warring spree through Virginia and Maryland.

At Shamokin, we gathered in the fall for a village meeting with Weiser. He gave assurances, though several of the young warriors spat upon the ground and declared their murderous intent upon any whites found north of the river. We all were fearful. Tagnehdorus called for his pipe while the Moravians bowed their heads in prayer.

The chief called for patience. They would give the white men one warning by killing only his livestock. Brother Mack protested loudly but Weiser said 'twas a great miracle to hear the chief hold back any measure of anger.

Weiser's grey head and face appeared older. He said, "If the Indians turn against the British, we are finished." His last words felt like a slap. He said he feared we would all die. He begged our return to Bethlehem.

We agreed, but until a fight was upon us, we felt our place was in Shamokin, holding vigil for the people there: The curious Conestogas sat with us in prayer. Toshetaquah was there, the man called Will Sock who later met with a gruesome death at the hands of the Paxton farmers. There were many who behaved with great affection no matter how terrible or wild the village became.

One late evening, bells rang in the distance. We surmised that Braddock's expedition had come to defeat. Villagers shouted and warned of a fire across the river. Brother Fry joined the party that left to investigate. When the village party returned in the morning, Logan ran angrily up the hill. Fry explained that their help had been turned away. One of the settlers held a gun on the Shamokin Indians until they departed. Another called the Moravians 'filthy Injun lovers' and spat upon their clothing.

Brother Mack gathered our group and insisted on a meeting with Tagnehdorus. The rumours were spreading that we were allies of the French and harbourers of rageful Indians. Tagnehdorus and a most angry Logan said plans were underway for the Indians to depart. We agreed that the time had arrived for our retreat to Bethlehem.

The bells we had heard had been alarms, sounded by settlers at Penn's Creek in the new territory west of the river, purchased at the Albany conference. Scant miles from Shamokin, across the river, a massacre had left fourteen dead and eleven others taken captive into the hills. From the Delaware to the Potomac Rivers there ensued violence on farms and settlements, tales of people scalped or carried off and a mass retreat of settlers to the eastern towns.

A young man rushed into the trading post to report a trail of white people fording the river. Fry was first to meet the settlers, forty some together. The Shamokin Indians swiftly abandoned their mourning vigil and retreated to their lodges. The arriving settlers seemed not in a fighting mood. The women especially were frightened and seeking shelter. They had abandoned their farms upon seeing the carnage at Penn's Creek and were begging help and food to journey eastward.

We sent word to Tagnehdorus that we were taking the haggard group to the trading post, but the door was bolted at the chief's lodge. Brother Mack said, "'Tis not possible. His door has been unbolted all the days we have known him."

The village paths were empty. No villagers showed themselves, apparently believing the mob had arrived with intent to take up fighting. We offered the farmers blankets and supplies but, once fed, they swiftly commenced leaving. I was certain they believed a trap was being laid, even as we offered friendly hospitality.

'Twas time for us to depart. My farewells to Logan and White Hawk were brief and painful. I brushed past Logan's outstretched hand and embraced him for an awkward, tearful moment. His sleepless eyes were heavy-lidded, but he stood straight and strong, thumping his fist lightly over his heart. Nodding, barren of words, I rubbed the aching lump in my chest. Logan told me to find White Hawk on the river ledge where we had often grieved or talked together.

From behind, my friend looked soft and pretty as the day we met years before, but those years had worn hard lines upon her face. She pulled me beside her on the log overlooking the river. I gazed out over the sparkling snake that taunted us with its beauty.

White Hawk's hollow-eyed dismay was equal to the forest omens of scattered animals and birds. I said, "I know not how to leave this place. Shamokin has been my womb."

White Hawk took my hands in hers. "I have been inside, as well." She nodded at the river. "We are twin sisters, like the rivers that flow from two directions."

I interrupted. "You could come to Bethlehem..."

She pressed a finger to her lips. "White Hawk circles the sky, feathers float on the wind. You walk the land. One on the earth and one soaring above. Twin sisters."

White Hawk stood and handed me the clump of white feathers that were often tied into her hair. "Remember," she said.

We embraced with sobbing enough to pull stringy roots from the riverbank of my heart, snapping finally, sending me sprawling into its cold current. I could have drowned there, clutching White Hawk's feathers and watching her black hair wave, untethered, as she hurried down the hill.

Brother Fry buried the tools from the smithy while the other men loaded pack horses and distributed goods among the Indians, allowing people to take what they could carry from the trading post. The cool November weather sped our departure as did reports of gunfire along the river path. Trails from Shamokin filled in every direction as various groups headed out upon all the spokes of the wheel.

We had barely taken to the eastern trail when fire broke out behind us in several lodges, flames spreading rapidly. The Indians intended to leave no trace of the town behind. Brother Fry whipped the packhorse to hasten it from the smoke. When we reached the hill overlooking Shamokin, I looked back through stinging eyes. I cried for each familiar person and place, for my dear friend White Hawk and especially for Logan, whose voice howled like a wounded animal above the smoke.

Maggie rested her pen on the rim of the ink pot. In the eerie morning quiet, she pushed the pages away. The boys had run outside, but after their leaping steps from the stairs of the porch, they had run from earshot. A scent from the parlor indicated that a fire was burning, though its slight crackling was the only sound.

The back door banged and two voices chimed, "Mama?" Maggie heard the boys wrestle their jackets and boots, then rattle a lid on a kettle. They were at their parents' door, about to knock, when Maggie walked down the hallway. She rubbed her face and bid them good morning. The bedroom door creaked as Edmund stepped into the parlor to meet the boys.

Whitney, who had peered past his father as the door opened, saw his mother huddled under the comforter. "Is Mama crying?" he asked. When Edmund was silent, Whitney tugged at his brother's sleeve to head back outside. "C'mon, Mort."

Maggie tightened the apron of her dress and said, "If your mother is tearful, I'm accountable. The sad recollections have given her ill rest."

Edmund scratched his head. "Your mother's a-weary. You boys gather some pine cones for the fire. Mother Beigler, she begged to see you." He nodded toward the bedroom.

Maggie cracked the door and peeked into the dark room. Eleanor scooted herself sideways, making a space beside her. "Mother...come sit." She patted the coverlet. "Look at me, Mother," Eleanor urged as Maggie settled herself. "I have ample reason to cry. I am exhausted. I am frightened that we'll not have food or the wood to cook. Outraged that the Indians have been run from their homes yet again. Worried of a war nigh to eruption. None of these reasons have you to blame."

After a moment, Maggie replied, "Your father was this way. Only at the gravest hardship would he reveal his weary feelings. When he could be strong and silent no longer."

Eleanor sunk back into her pillow and sighed. "You've not said I seem akin to him in any way," she said. While Maggie distracted herself, fidgeting with the folds of her skirt, Eleanor probed, "Do you consider me to be other ways similar?"

Maggie smiled. "When you were small, you were vastly gregarious, far more than your father or myself. We pondered where you acquired your sociable traits." Maggie adjusted herself to face Eleanor. "Years of hardship and grief have seemed to melt the spark from your eyes." She rubbed Eleanor's hand for a moment, then said, "I aim to pen my memories of Will and Dovee. You recall them?"

"Oh, yes. And Gardner and the little girls."

When Maggie and little Eleanor had arrived in Bethlehem from Shamokin, it had been bustling with refugees. A stockade gate was being built on the main road, an unusual sight among the peace-loving people. Brother Mack searched for lodgings as Maggie noted the changes in town: newly planted orchards, shops for cabinet makers and potters, the tannery grown to fill three buildings. Everywhere, there were throngs of people. The stench of the shanty town and its refuse was heavy in the air. People hung blanket shelters from the branches of trees and huddled in doorways.

Maggie said, "I recall seeing Will towering above a gathered crowd, begging in English for help. When I heard him mention the mission village of Gnadenhutten, I hurried closer. Their farm had been adjoining the mission and 'twas burned when the mission was attacked and burned to the ground. Twelve mission people died. Will and his family were fortunate to escape, though they had fled all the night and had only their sleeping clothes."

Eleanor nodded. "Miss Dovee lifted me into the wagon with the children. I had grown up among the Indians, but had yet to see skin as dark as theirs."

"Indeed," said Maggie. "There were few Negroes in the region as yet. Will and his wife, Dovee, had been freed by their master after working his fields and kitchen for twenty years, even receiving title to a piece of land. Will said the whites had burnt them out of that farm, and this one, the Indians. Said in five years, he lost more land than most Negroes here have ever owned."

"How did we get to stay in the barn with them?" asked Eleanor.

"The Frys knew a farmer out on the Post Road that had a stone barn. 'Twas a crowd, huddled among the animals, until the Frys went on to Nazareth.

You and I joined them following an offer of a warm room in a house, though 'twas for us alone." Maggie paused. "The two of us. I knew the house so I walked to the owner's door and begged them to include our friends who were in greater need. The woman asked if the friends might be the Negroe family she had seen with me earlier. I said they were indeed, and she replied that they were a hardy breed. Best to bring my fair child indoors. I was stunned and replied only that we were a hardy breed as well."

"In Bethlehem?" Eleanor asked.

"Times were changing. Even Bethlehem needed reminders of the Moravian mission to the downtrodden. Some in Bethlehem had hardened their hearts." Maggie recalled the barn further down the road that sheltered a large group of the Gnadenhutten mission Indians who seldom left their quarters, so uncertain of the welcome they would receive. Bethlehem was the only haven for a flood of terrified families from the outlying districts, many with no love for the Indians, regardless of their friendly nature or Christianized status.

"We are a hardy breed," said Eleanor. "I felt that indeed on this very morning, amidst my tears. Perhaps our early nature dies not...only hides and hibernates until needed. If ever I were to call forth my gregarious, striving nature, 'tis now. Should I awaken her and put her to the tasks ahead..."

"Then we should all be well," laughed Maggie. "In Shamokin, you had the whole village at your tiny command. Especially Logan. That man always bowed to greet you when we met him on the village trails or river paths."

"Sounds as though I was not the one he bowed to greet," she grinned.

Maggie sighed and shook her head. "How our lives changed, of a sudden, upon leaving there."

"We were destitute?" asked Eleanor.

Maggie nodded. "We had naught. We took many meals on the charity of the Moravians."

"The kind-hearted people," said Eleanor.

"My solitary complaint was that the Moravians held meetings for the men alone. My desperate desire was to know what the assembly had ordained. I had to eavesdrop or question the men for news."

"'Tis how you gained your habits!"

Maggie slapped at her playfully. She said, "I had been accustomed to the style of the natives. Their women have a voice in matters. Even the Moravians in Shamokin included the women in town meetings. I was indignant when I learned that after a fortnight of debate, the Quakers refused to be taxed for the support of an army, and naught was done. At that time, hundreds of farmers marched upon Philadelphia from the western farm country, their patience finally exhausted. They angrily shouted down all the Quaker arguments on the steps of the Assembly Hall."

"Such an image," said Eleanor.

"They were forced to call a special night session while the frontiersmen waited outside. The outcome was that everyone else, Lutheran, Presbyterian, Dutch and Reformed, united against the Quaker control of the Pennsylvania Assembly. The irony, I heard told, was a macabre wagon brought silently through the streets to the statehouse steps for the assemblymen to view. 'Twas piled deep with the bodies of the latest victims of Indian massacres, victims most surely of their plodding deliberation."

Eleanor slumped back against her pillows. "It makes me ill," she said.

"All the talk of war with the Indians made me quite ill," said Maggie, "though the bishop implored the Bethlehem citizens to refrain from spreading fear and alarm. He agreed that some of the natives were on a course of savagery, but that decent Indians were among us, counting on us for their own safety."

"I can scarce recall those days, but when you speak or write, they come fresh upon me," said Eleanor.

The boys pushed open the back door, dragging a woven basket filled with pine cones beside the hearth. "Papa told Morton he could climb up and shake the branches," said Whitney.

Eleanor climbed from her bed and wrapped herself in a robe. The boys hovered like hungry fledglings around her until she spread biscuits with honey and insisted they sit on chairs.

She said, "I asked Edmund how he became a fine father with no father to teach him. He said in his tribe, the men were all his teachers. He was especially close to his mother's brother."

Maggie nodded. "'Tis the way of the village. I had several fathers myself. Swataney. Weiser."

"What became of Weiser during the uprisings?" Eleanor asked.

"Weiser became a militia commander," Maggie said. "When Benjamin Franklin visited Bethlehem to explain his plan for a circle of forts, he said one would be placed at the burned-out site of Gnadenhutten, another at our old village, Shamokin. Troops like Weiser's militia patrolled the outlying areas, protecting the farmers and citizens of the interior. We seldom heard news from Fort Augusta, the stockade built where Shamokin had stood."

"I recall seeing Weiser later," said Eleanor, "at the Indian school in Nazareth." Maggie and Eleanor had departed for Nazareth after the Frys sent word of the expanded Indian school. They wanted Maggie's assistance and had jobs for Will and Dovee as well.

"'Twas some years later," said Maggie, nodding, "Weiser passed through Nazareth, involved in treaty talks once again. You took to him as if he'd never been gone, but I commented on his gray pallor. He agreed, saying he had grown too old. He was weary of the convoluted alliances and the problems with the rum. He was headed to Easton for treaty talks with Teedyuscung, the old Delaware chief."

"He reported on his return weeks later that his troops had been met by angry crowds crying out about Indian attacks across the river in New Jersey. It angered them further that the chief arrived in a suit of French clothing and a red-painted face. After the close of the meetings, Weiser confided to Brother Mack and our group that he had feared for all their lives as the Delawares renewed twenty-year-old tensions with the Six Nations' delegates.

"Weiser said they finally agreed to friendly relations when Governor Denny decided to help Teedyuscung find a lasting homeplace for his wandering band. Weiser's troops then escorted some of the Delaware people back to Nazareth for food and rest. I looked for familiar faces and saw none, though there were smiles when I made mention of Shamokin. They told me the people had gone west."

Edmund entered the room from the back porch and heard Maggie's last words. He stopped beside the table. "West?"

Maggie nodded, rubbing her throat. "You understand what prevented another question?"

"You cared naught for the answer," said Edmund. "Had they meant 'west,' toward the Ohio territory? Or had they meant 'West,' the sacred place of the final spirit journey."

"Indeed. I had not wanted to know."

Edmund paced to the shop at the front of the house and back to the parlor, glancing out the windows. Maggie pulled him aside and whispered that he seemed overly anxious.

Edmund said, "Seems a great body of folks heading toward Semple's, considering the early hour of day. I've heard naught of a meeting."

"Perhaps it concerns the river trade, or another area of scant interest for us."

He nodded. "There is indeed more river trafficking. The arrests of

Pennsylvania men have ceased as has activity at Dunmore's ducking stool." Lord Dunmore had ordered offenders of the Virginia rule to be tied to a chair set near the end of the fort's moat then hoisted upon a tower and dropped into the cold water. The severity of the crime would determine the length of time passed before hoisting the offender out by a tether.

Maggie said, "Puts me in mind of earlier years. Governor Denny asked everyone in Pennsylvania to lay down all their differences, whether over liberty or slavery, over independence or being subjects of England. All was at stake, he said, and everyone must act vigorously to maintain life in the colonies."

"Image this town with our differences set aside," said Edmund. "I should hope to be a witness. I believe I'll venture to the shed to give Coal a brushing. The horse seldom judges my mood."

Eleanor sent the boys upstairs to work on their studies as Edmund walked out the back door. She asked Maggie why he seemed to brood.

"He's fretful. We forget that this area has been unsettled for nigh the past decade."

Eleanor nodded. "When massive Fort Pitt was built, the French had already taken their leave. The Indians likely surmised that the guns and cannons were aimed at their villages."

Maggie agreed. "Pontiac's war effort to reclaim the land from the English shed the blood of both peoples. 'Twas barely calmed upon our notion to venture here."

"Turnabout continues," said Eleanor.

"Seems a certainty," said Maggie. "Violence begets violence." She picked up a bottle of honey, thick and dark amber colored. "Look here. Such abundance the bees produce with their cooperative spirit."

Eleanor pushed aside the pair of Whitney's old tow trousers she was patching to hand down to Morton and leaned to open a cabinet door. "In that same spirit, see what it fared? I offered a jar of Edmund's honey to a local merchant and he bestowed alike." She held a bundle of candles, freshly poured, dipped and wrapped in paper.

"A good trade," said Maggie, prying the papers away and inspecting the well-made tapers.

Eleanor rubbed her hands and looked inside the cabinet at baskets of onions and greens that Edmund had brought that morning from the creek banks. "The fire should be revived for our supper kettle," she said. She opened a canvas bag and pulled out several shriveled, dried mushrooms.

"Edmund has done well to keep us supplied with wood," Maggie said, raising herself from her chair. Suddenly, they heard a clatter from upstairs as if something heavy had been dropped. One of the boys squealed and Eleanor was about to run up the stairs when Edmund burst in the back door. "We must go!" he hollered. "Seize some goods, but be hasty. Boys!" he shouted up the stairs. They were already in mid-leap and hustled to his side.

"We heard shouts, Papa," scowled Whitney. "A crowd marches from beyond Market Street."

Edmund lowered his voice and leaned toward the women. "Shouting about 'Injuns,'" he whispered. The look of terror in his eyes froze them in place until the boys scurried behind and jostled them. Eleanor sent them into the bedroom to gather armloads of blankets. Glancing through the parlor glass, Maggie saw a crowd marching their way, filling the street.

"Have mercy," she whispered. She hastened to her room and retrieved her old leather satchel from under the bed, stuffed with several wraps and her collection of letters. Her chest was pounding and she felt her face becoming red with anger.

She huffed down the steps as Edmund pulled the buckboard out of the shed. The boys climbed upon the piles of wood, yet unloaded, and held out hands to hasten Maggie and her load. Eleanor scooted onto the bench beside Edmund. The crowd was at the front of the cabin as Edmund pulled the wagon into the lane and snapped the reins, hurrying north onto the backstreet.

As Coal trotted, they watched behind them and witnessed the mob surrounding the cabin. Sounds of shattering glass merged with the thud of wood being chopped. The top of the pine tree began to waver as Whitney pointed and Maggie cried out. The boys grabbed her arms and skirt to keep her from leaping from the moving wagon.

Eleanor leaned and pulled Maggie back. She held her as Maggie smothered her wailing with her own hands. "My tree! My tree!" She fell against Eleanor's shoulder and sobbed.

Edmund sped on but turned his head and called, "What have the lunatics done?"

"The pine tree," hollered Eleanor. "They're chopping."

He shook his head and cracked the reins. Whitney sat facing the rear, sullen, spitting frequently. Morton looked wide-eyed from person to person and back to the cabin. When the top of the tree disappeared, Whitney turned around and glared at the road ahead. Edmund had made a swift decision to head for the north hills, past Hogg's Pond, certain that they would be easily followed if they turned toward their farm. A few men had run onto the street behind them throwing rocks, but no one followed them on horses. The mob was content to run them out and stone the cabin.

Edmund pulled off the road into the hill country. He took a roundabout route to the bluffs above the Allegheny, and as the evening sky deepened and the temperature dropped, Eleanor pulled blankets around the boys' shoulders.

"'Tis fear causing my tremors," said Maggie, "though we'll soon be at a safe place."

The boys nodded. Whitney said, "Joseph's hut."

As they bounced along the rough terrain and scrubby bushes, they noticed the scarcity of sizable trees, all cut down, even so far from town. They crossed a hill, away from the lights of Dunmore and the river valley beyond. Once over the next hill, they saw the deep carved valley of the Allegheny winding from the northeast. Edmund pointed to a silhouette of tall bushes, pulled the wagon into the stand of scrub, and hopped down.

"The cave is nearby," he announced. "How fares each and all?"

"Fine, Papa," grumbled Whitney.

"Why must we flee?" asked Morton.

"We'll discuss it inside." Edmund handed each boy an armload of blankets. Maggie and Eleanor loaded their arms and followed. The moon had risen with enough light to reveal the short plank wall and doorway cut into the side of the hill. Leaves and branches were scattered from the winter, cluttering the trail and the plank walk on the ground. The wooden door was ajar and Whitney pushed it open then stood back, sniffing and wrinkling his nose.

"Something's living in there," he said.

Edmund came behind him on the narrow planks and set an unlit oil lamp on the ground. As he lit the wick with a flint, Eleanor said, "Edmund, are you certain...?"

"Just some little creatures. They'll not bother us." Edmund said. Maggie handed him the lamp as he reached past the doorway for a shovel lying among Joseph's tools. He came out of the cave carrying the animal nest and scat. "When we build a fire, the musty smell will depart." He kicked aside piles of leaves and gathered sticks, lighting them from the oil lamp and placing them in the small stone fireplace. Maggie ducked her head inside, inspecting from floor to ceiling. She picked up a dry branch and moved gingerly, sweeping cobwebs from the ceiling and walls. The boys poked at insects, chasing them out the door.

Maggie said, "These peculiar lodgings put me in mind of the cliff huts my father and I saw upon first sailing up the Delaware. We looked out at the land of opportunity, only to see people living in caves and utter poverty. Now, here we are..."

"Not long," Edmund interrupted. "'Twill not go on."

"'Tis bearable," said Maggie. "Protected from view. I've endured more than I ever thought possible. We shall give thanks once more for Joseph's haven."

"Joseph would be pleased to know we're here," agreed Edmund. The boys dragged in more sticks to add to the fire.

"Was Joseph fearful?" Whitney frowned. "The place seems far removed."

"He spoke naught of fear," said Edmund, "though he had been a slave, a grievous life. Said he was taken from his parents as a boy. Never claimed to be a runaway." Edmund poked at the fire and looked around the cave. "Surely he had been ill-treated."

"We can all be grateful to him tonight," said Eleanor, "though I myself intend to be tightly wrapped in my blanket." She shuddered as she pulled another web from the corner.

They ate a meal of raw onions and greens, those snatched quickly from the cabinet as they were leaving the cabin. When Morton asked to leave the oil light burning, Edmund said they had to save the fuel. Eleanor produced one of the fresh-dipped candles and said, "'Twill ease all our worrisome thoughts. As I recall, Mother had a disturbance when we were here last. I may be unable to sleep myself, in a cave."

Maggie smiled. "Aside from my longstanding difficulty with such a den," she said, "I feel a measure of comfort in Joseph's shelter."

Edmund nodded and added, "His spirit watches."

The glowing remnants of the fire cast a soft reddish light on the rock walls. The boys lay at either end of the slab benches, shared with Maggie and Eleanor. Edmund lay before the fire, wrapped in a blanket. Morton said, "Papa, you said we'd talk about our leaving. Who were those people?"

"Disgusting thieves," growled Whitney. "People who want no Indians in the town."

"Even part Indians?" asked Morton, quietly. Edmund nodded. Morton gazed through the dark at the scowling eyes of his older brother. He pulled his blanket close. "Would they shoot us for being part Indian?"

"No one is shooting," said Eleanor.

"Most folks have no woes," said Edmund. "They treat people fairly. Only some take it upon themselves to be hot-headed, full of their own furies. They

single out folks who differ; Indians, even those friendly with Indians. You
heard your Gran's stories."

"That's why we don't tell folks we're Indian? 'Cause of those folks?"
asked Whitney. His father nodded. Maggie thought she saw a shadow pass
over the wall, but any ghost who could find the place would have to be
Joseph's. She settled back against the slab and asked the old man to keep
watch.

ζ

I turned toward the Susquehanna River, following the direction of the
spilling stream, a lively runoff that would meet the river a few hundred yards
away. "The main camp would have been that way." I pointed north, the
direction from which we had driven.

"We drove past it?" asked Quinn.

"This town, Sunbury, is so pretty," I said. Even when I saw a large open
space, a playing field or parking lot, my senses were muddled, as Maggie
would say. "I have trouble envisioning it any other way, especially the Indian
camps or the Moravians' cabins." As I spoke, it occurred to me that, if I
focused, I could peel away the distractions of the present dwellings, highways,
schools and shops. I could find the places that time had not been able to
change.

We drove on a winding road to the foothills east of town. "If you can't
envision Maggie, how about White Hawk...or Logan?" asked Quinn. "Can
he help?"

I looked up at the hillside. Orange and yellow leaves blanketed the hills,
fluttering in the breeze. "You're right," I said. "I haven't written it yet, but I
know I already have the story of the last days of Shamokin. It's like it's been
downloaded, but I haven't printed it out. I can picture Logan...and hear him.
He's up on the hill, lamenting over the valley. Maggie and White Hawk had
an overlook up there, too. I'll bet we can find a road."

"It's all fenced down this way," said Quinn. She pointed to the eastern
side of the hill.

"Maybe we could drive around and find a hiking trail," I said.

The road east of town was steep. I thought of the bluffside trail Maggie
had descended on the rear of Weiser's horse, her first view of Shamokin
village. Perhaps it had been this same hill. I turned, but the view of the valley
was blocked by trees. Even in its state of shedding, the forest was dense. The
narrow road offered no place to stop or pull over until we were nearly at the
crest of the hill. We could glimpse parts of the river snaking around below,

slow and silty brownish gray. Quinn pulled to the side of a gravel drive and turned off the engine.

"I don't see any trail signs," she said.

"Let's have a look at the top of that hill. It's not far," I said.

Quinn pulled her jacket from the back of the car and asked if I wanted mine.

"I'm fine. We'll be back in a few." I tightened the laces on my sneakers and stretched as I got out of the Beetle. We started walking toward the top of the hill that rose between us and the main part of town. It quickly became evident that we had to watch every step. Miniature saplings and woven weed vines thatched the floor of the forest. The ground would sink suddenly a foot or two or we'd have to step up over partially decayed logs or tangles of bushes. The trees were larger the farther we got from the road. The birch and beech canopy trapped shadows or let bright slices of random sunlight pass through, hampering my ability to adjust my vision. The incline continued, though we had walked several minutes.

A twig snapped behind us and I grabbed Quinn's arm. I thought I saw a shape moving in the trees.

"Animal or human?" whispered Quinn.

I shrugged. The Beetle was out of sight, so I couldn't tell if another car had pulled into the drive. "Must have been an animal," I said. "I don't see anything."

We turned to continue walking and heard a laugh. "Just a coupla girls, Fletch. C'mon." Out of the shadows came two young men, twenty something, with smudged faces. As they came closer, I saw that the dirt on their faces was amplified by several days of beard stubble. The blondish guy's distended belly stretched a worn tee shirt beneath a corduroy coat with fake shearling lining. I think my dad had one like it twenty years ago. The other guy was skinny and sallow faced. He had sharp, square shoulders and wore a heavy sweatshirt with a front pocket that hid his hands. The big-bellied guy swung a hand from behind his back, revealing a shotgun, which thankfully, he pointed nonchalantly at the ground.

"You ladies lost?" the skinny one said, grinning.

"Not exactly." Quinn spoke up first.

I added, "We were looking for the scenic overlook."

"Well, this ain't public property here," said the skinny guy, hiking his droopy pants. Then he added, "so we figure you're lost."

The big guy said, "Now, Fletch, you sound unfriendly. We could be nice and show the ladies the overlook." He exaggerated the word "overlook" with a sneer.

Fletch began to snicker, showing pronounced gums over lots of large teeth. I said, "I think we've seen enough." I turned around to backtrack down the hill, but when Quinn started to follow, the chubby guy raised the rifle across his chest and blocked her path. With no hesitation, Quinn jerked her knee hard into the guy's groin. He grunted, leaning forward red-faced, then gritted his teeth and slammed the butt of the rifle sideways, hard against her cheekbone. I grabbed my face when I heard hers crack. She stumbled backward, but didn't fall. He had dropped to his knees in pain. He tossed the rifle to Fletch, who swung it around clumsily, aiming at Quinn.

"Hey!" I screamed. "Don't be stupid. Put that thing down. Can't you see she's hurt?" Quinn's cheek had an inch-long cut that was swelling quickly. She reached up and smeared the blood with her fingers. I stepped in front of Fletch and his gun to inspect Quinn's injury more closely. As I took her face in my hands, Fletch poked me in the ribs with the gun barrel.

"Big mistake, girlie," the chubby guy hissed from the ground.

Fletch said, "See? You could have been gone by now. Now you're gonna hafta pay, just like her."

Quinn growled through her teeth, "Already paid with a broken cheek."

The chubby guy was up on one knee, choking on his chuckle. "That's just a deposit. Now you pay." He shoved his hand in his coat pocket and removed a long, twisted strand of rope.

"This has gone far enough," I snapped.

"Shut up!" screamed Fletch, waving the gun in front of my face. "Now, shut your hole. We do the talking."

While the two men whispered, Quinn reached for my arm and pulled me a step closer to her. "My eye hurts like hell or we could run for it," she said.

"Is it too late for me to remind you of the bait?" I asked. She widened her eye and winced. "The anger bait," I said. "You took it."

"I said no talking!" Fletch screamed, waving the rope.

Chubby had reclaimed the gun and was on his feet, though leaning to one side. He limped over, edging past Fletch. He had an odor like he'd slept in a moldy horse stall and then drank beer all day. I stepped back when he leaned close. His words crept in a slow and sputtery drawl. "You wanted to see the overlook. Now you're gonna."

Fletch snickered again, wiping drops of spit with his sleeve.

"We're not going anywhere with you," I said.

Chubby cocked the rifle. "Bertha here says you are."

Quinn said, "Your rifle has a name. How about you?"

"Call me 'Dick.'" His beady eyes got smaller.

"How about if I shorten it to 'Ick,'" Quinn said, looking at me with her mouth twisted with both disgust and impatience.

"Bait," I whispered.

"So how far is it?" asked Quinn. I couldn't believe she would agree to go with them, but I guessed the rifle had convinced her. I trusted that she had a plan.

"Hmmm," thought Fletch. "'Bout two football fields?" He said it as if we might know and reward him for being right.

"Let's go then," said Quinn. I stepped in line behind her with Ick following us; him and 'Bertha.' Fletch led us higher into an area that was increasingly rocky. Rounded stones appeared on the forest floor, then jutted from the steeper hillside. The trees became sparser and more sun reached in and speckled our path. I could see the clearing ahead of us where the rocky ledge dropped away. My stomach felt as if it had pitched over the edge with a thud into the river valley.

The river forks split before us. It was beautiful. It seemed impossible that we could be in such dreaded circumstances and be looking at breathtaking scenery. I was frightened, but as I walked, distracted by the view, I tripped on one of the rocks and stumbled toward Quinn. She quickly grabbed at my flailing arm, holding me to help regain my balance. I squeezed her arm in gratitude.

Behind us, Ick blurted, "What's with all a' your grabbing. You a coupla dykes?"

I glanced at Quinn to see if she would react, but her face was like stone. But with my glance and her silence, Ick burst into loud chortles. "That's it! You brought your girlfriend to the woods to get into her panties, didn't you?" he taunted Quinn, leaning near her face.

The chubby guy stepped onto a flat rock and Quinn raised her boot and stomped on the top of his foot. He doubled over his big belly again. Grabbing the barrel end of his rifle, she heaved her knee into his chin. I heard his teeth smash together. Fletch dove past me like a ram with his head down, tackling her. All three toppled onto the ground in a heap. As the big guy rolled over Quinn, pinning her to the ground, I ran around him to reach for the gun. I nearly had it when Fletch kicked my hand and grabbed it himself.

"I'm sick of this bitch!" screamed Fletch, jumping up and cocking the rifle, pointing it at Quinn. "Let me finish her."

Ick growled, barely audible. "The gun's not loaded, idiot." He sat up, pinning Quinn's arm to the ground with his knee. "Now grab the other one and pull her over to that tree. We'll tie 'em up." To Fletch's disappointed stare, he replied, "I got ammo back at my place. You guard 'em for awhile." He spit blood from his mouth and yanked Quinn to her feet. Holding her arms behind her back, he pushed her toward a tall pine tree that grew out of a rock crevice on the ledge.

I jerked my arm away as Fletch reached for it and whispered, "What do you want? Money? It's in the car. Just take it and go. Leave us alone."

"Shut it!" he said, with clenched teeth and wild bug-eyes. He held his fist up in front of my face and pushed me with the other hand. Quinn had been hit on the same side of her face as before and her eye was swollen shut. Blood was oozing again from the widened cut. The men shoved her down to the ground beside the tree and tied her feet before dangling them over the ledge. They pulled her shoulders against the tree and wrapped her arms around the one-foot diameter trunk, binding her hands behind her on the opposite side. I was pushed down with my back to the tree on the other side from Quinn. My hands were tied around the tree also, passing under her arms to the opposite side.

While they tightened the rope, I heard Fletch spit and whisper, "I'll teach 'em a lesson."

"Save it," Ick hissed. He waved the gun near our faces and said, "Enjoy the pretty sunset. I won't be gone long." The men slugged each other's arms and Ick walked, or limped, down the hill.

"God damn it," whispered Quinn. "I can't believe I'm going to lose my job because of these assholes."

"Quinn," I said, "we have to figure our way out of here." I tugged at the ropes.

"You're just tightening the knots," she muttered. "We had to get stuck with creepy Fletch."

"They're both creepy."

"Yeah, but the other guy won't be hurrying back. He's nearly crippled."

"At least Fletch is too hyper to sit here and point the gun at us." He had hiked further up the hill but we could still see him.

"Hey, shut up down there," he hollered. "No talking. I'll come and make your girlfriend bleed more."

I didn't want to look at him, but I knew he had that sick grin on his face. Quinn said, "Try to squirm around toward me. Does your rope move?" It didn't. I could only get part way and it was on the side of her injured eye. When I saw her over my shoulder with the beautiful river valley behind her, I burst into tears.

"I'm so sorry," I sobbed. "This is my fault. You should never have brought me."

Quinn moaned. "Where's that damn Joe? I thought he comes when we need him." Her voice got louder, "Now would be nice!"

"Joe." I closed my eyes and sobbed harder. "What's happening?"

Quinn sighed and let me whimper. She peered over the edge and reported that it was only about a six foot drop down the rocky face to soft ground. "I picked a great time to leave the cell phone in the car. I figured we wouldn't get a signal here."

"Probably not," I said. I leaned my head against the tree. "Remember...we were just talking about the phone calls people made on 9/11. Maybe, since we don't have the phone...I'd like to think we're not doomed. You know? We can't make our final phone calls."

"Reed, you believe whatever you need. I hope you're right. I'm not ready to cash it in. Especially not at the hands of jerks. C'mon, what are we going to do?" Quinn wriggled against the tree.

I glanced over my shoulder again just as the sun sank below the horizon. The sky was beginning to light up with deep red streaks brushed across the clouds. "God, it's magnificent," I sighed. From our high vantage point, the trees below were like orange pillows, rolling softly along the hillside. From the top of the canopy, there was no sign of tangled undergrowth; there were no twisted limbs or broken spears of wood, no moldy mud holes covered with leaves.

The river had settled into a more natural deep green color, with little red sparkles reflecting the last sky lights. I said, "Maggie told White Hawk goodbye from up on this hill. They said Shamokin had been their womb; they were twin sisters, like the two river branches."

"Right," mumbled Quinn. "Rivers that flow from different directions."

"Quinn. It doesn't matter. You and me, I mean. We could be flowing from any direction and we'd still be friends."

A rock hit the tree trunk above us. Another one shredded the leaves beside us. I heard Fletch yell, "I'm comin' to shut you up."

The noise began like a hum, a vibration. I thought it was Quinn, exasperated and mad. Her hands began tugging at the ropes. "We deserve to live, Reed," she said. "I'm not going to let that jerk lay another hand on either of us."

From behind, the noise hummed again, closer and then all around us. I heard Fletch yelp and thought he had fallen. Quinn whispered, "What's that noise?" We looked in all directions, but saw nothing.

My heart pounded. I could feel it resonate up to my throat and head. Then I whispered, "Quinn, it's Logan." The vibration hummed louder, and then became a song. I felt it deep in my own heart as if Logan moaned from the center of his soul, with a sorrowful heartache, gathering every lost being in his outstretched arms. Injustice, greedy thoughts, prejudice, murderous impulses slid like slivers or knives from the wounded earth. They were drawn into Logan's heaving chest and expelled with his spirit song, ancient as life itself.

"We're at the center of the world," I whispered.

"The turtle, Reed," Quinn said. "It's in your pocket. You have to try to reach for it."

8

Maggie stretched her hip and moved Whitney's heavy head that rested against her as he huddled on the rock slab at her side. As she shifted, she felt the frigid stone jutting through the blanket and a thick layer of straw beneath. The coals had died down to a small red pile, adding color to the shadows cast on the cave's walls by the single candle. Her family had quieted, but her mind had not. Maggie kept her eyes on the candle flame or the glowing coals, figuring those places were free from crawling creatures. She couldn't conceive of lying on the floor like Edmund. Her respect for old Joseph grew whenever she moved and felt the cool shelf below. No matter how unyielding, she was reminded with gratitude that Joseph had labored to create a bed raised from the floor.

Eleanor had been asleep for more than an hour, her face hooded by the blanket and turned toward the faint coals. Suddenly her shoulders shuddered and she began to whimper. Maggie heard Edmund rustle and sit up. He hesitated, as if to lie back down, then he moved closer to Eleanor's side and sat. She moaned slightly and tossed in her blanket cocoon. Resting his hand on her trembling back, Edmund rubbed in slow circles. Maggie understood that the tears had been too long saved. A dream may have come to help empty them. When Eleanor's breathing settled, Edmund pressed his forehead softly against her shoulder, and then he rose, tucked her blanket close again and turned for the door.

Maggie cleared her throat so that he noticed she was awake. He paused, then came to her side and squatted. He said, "I must step outside where I can hear the river. I'm heavy hearted."

"Edmund," Maggie reached out and patted his hand, "we've been through costly times in the past."

His lips held a tight, hard line. "I recall them," whispered Edmund. He ducked through the short doorway and she scooted herself up to a sitting position without waking Whitney. She pulled the candle closer, propped her feet and leaned back against the wall with blankets for cushions. She took a bundle of papers from her bag and began to write.

My dears,

Earlier, I wrote about the tunnel of my own thoughts. I knew my memories were buried and I must journey back to that hollow. 'Tis irony that as I wrestle with my darkest days, we are forced to take refuge in a den such as this.

I am recalling an endless circle of violence over ten years in the past. As I told Edmund, one attack by Indians wrought another by white settlers. Then a militia company killed a peaceful Wichetunk family traveling the Susquehanna. Indian vengeance was set upon a militia captain and his men. At that, the colonial soldiers released their full fury upon the Indians.

The neighbouring people of Nazareth were likewise increasingly bitter against the Indians. As their welfare was threatened, David Zeisberger brought more Indians into our shelter. When an arson attack in Bethlehem burned a flour and oil mill, we forsook all reasoning with the frantic farm neighbours.

As a frequent traveler to the Nain Indian School where Eleanor taught, I recognised most of the Indians who trailed through the stockade doors. I helped where able, finding living quarters and distributing blankets for the cold nights. Zeisberger warned the Philadelphia government that the Indians needed assistance or many would not survive the winter. To our surprise, his request was granted; Philadelphia would take the Indians if they came unarmed. They were reluctant to give up their woodlands, but realised the danger. They agreed to make the journey.

Your grandmother and others were fortunate to be in safe homes, but many had no refuge. Heavy hearted, I watched the Indians hand over their tomahawks and rifles. Reverend Grube and his wife would accompany them to Philadelphia. I asked if he believed they would be safe.

A silent void was immediately filled with all my dread. I spoke on impulse, "I intend to go with you." They were startled, but I continued, "A spare hand to stir the pot...an added voice in their defense."

Reverend Grube said ominously, "We will need more than voices." The wagon train set out with one hundred and twenty seven homeless Delawares hoping for asylum, the women in calico frocks, bonnets worn upon unbraided hair. Wide brimmed hats and long shirts and trousers of the Delaware men matched their Moravian brothers. The wagons approached the Philadelphia barracks where the Indians were to stay, met by soldiers bearing muskets. A multitude of townsmen and women shouted, "Scalp them!" and "Shoot the red devils!"

We were forced to a halt and for five hours we fiercely held off the angry crowds while Reverend Grube tried to reason with the soldiers. Unable to endure, I pushed my way to Brother Grube's side and stood face to face with the musketeers, saying, "The Provincial Commissioners have selected this site to house these people. What right have you to block us?"

"This right, woman," the soldier pressed a musket against my chest. I planted my feet and glared as a timely horseman delivered a message from their commander. We were to proceed to the mouth of the Schuylkill. The Indians would go to Province Island, the pest house, where the indigent and contagious were quarantined or left to die!

Justly fearful of violence, Reverend Grube nearly covered my mouth and assured me that once we had safe shelter, he would raise the issue. We proceeded to turn the wagons while the crowd cheered and waved muskets in victory. We reached the island ferry in the dark. No one was aware of our arrival. After many hours, everyone was safe at Province Island's meagre lodgings: no bunks, dirty rooms barren of all furniture. But there were walls and a roof between us and the cold winds. Huddled in blankets, we sat or sang as Christmas Day passed.

In those merciless days, the Grubes complained about the Indians' dismal conditions and ill treatment. David Zeisberger and Bishop Spangenberg argued with the Commissioners over broken promises. Seeing the barbaric treatment, I told the Bishop I would stay as long as my brothers and sisters are being imprisoned like animals.

Each meeting with the province brought worsened news. Frequent attacks on peaceful Indians fueled acts of vengeance. One day, a trembling Zeisberger arrived. The Grubes led the agonized man into a private room.

"A senseless slaughter," Zeisberger choked. When he could speak, he said a group of militiamen abandoned their posts after witnessing the tortured bodies of settlers in the Wyoming valley. Riding to Paxton, they armed a group and went to the nearby settlement of the Conestoga Indians who had been in Shamokin village and had always lived in peace. Zeisberger shuddered, and then took a deep breath. "Four men and two women were killed," he whispered. "In cold blood...the village set afire." I gasped, then he told us 'twas worse.

"Those Conestogas who escaped were taken to Lancaster and housed in

the work-house. A county legislator asked for help and when the Governor announced a willingness to bring the Indians to Philadelphia, hatred broke loose." He sighed, "Upwards of a hundred armed men, most poor Scottish farmers, rode to the work-house, broke down the door and killed every one. Men, women...babies." Zeisberger shook his head and sobbed. "None came to their aid. A company of Highlanders sat down the road and watched."

I buried my face and cried, wanting to disbelieve. Other attacks were disturbing, but these people lived among us, ate our corn, drank our water. They had stayed and assisted the colonial troops in building Fort Augusta on the site of Shamokin village before they left. Zeisberger held documents in his trembling hand. "This has inflamed the passions of all, pro and con," he said.

I wiped my face and took a pamphlet with a heading by Ben Franklin: "Friends of This Province." I choked on the words, fairly such as these: "If an Indian injures me, does it follow that I may avenge that injury on all Indians? Their only crime was their brown skin and black hair...If one can kill men for such a reason, then, should a freckled face, red haired man kill my wife or child, I may avenge it by killing all freckled, red-haired men, women and children I meet afterwards, anywhere."

Scowling Zeisberger spoke of the disturbance through the whole countryside. The Governor had received threats of a march against Philadelphia to avenge our presence.

"Damnation!" shouted ordinarily quiet Reverend Grube. "The senseless violence repeats endlessly."

Zeisberger said the Governor had offered escorts to transfer our people to New York immediately, while every group floundered in chaos. Reverend Grube admitted concern for his wife's safety. Anyone was free to go, they said. In January, when we received supplies and instructions, our Highlander escort was met by jeering crowds throwing rocks and dirt. The escort made no move to stop them.

I was clad in the same frock and bonnet, wrapped in blankets as the Indians, undistinguishable but for my shade lighter skin. I leaped up when a rock hit a woman nearby. I was pulled by the arm by old Walks with Daylight, who told me to endure the ride. "We will be away soon," he said.

The soldiers became more kind, though we continued to plod across New Jersey. Prohibited from entering New York by a letter from Governor Colden, the Highlanders' orders were to leave us in New Jersey and return to Pennsylvania.

We were temporarily housed in the Amboy barracks until the governors decided the Indians' fate. Then we trudged, days later, back across New Jersey during a blizzard. The armed escorts were to ride back with us to the Philadelphia barracks, but we encountered no crowds, either due to poor weather or questions raised about the riot laws.

Finally returned to Pennsylvania, I helped one exhausted woman lie down in the barracks. I felt her burning forehead. She shivered without complaint while I searched among the group and discovered several others hot with fever. We gathered all with signs of illness into a sick ward set up in one room of the barracks, which expanded frightfully soon to two.

Days passed before Brother Zeisberger brought news that more Moravians would arrive to assist us. The Indians were dying, a dozen in the week since returning and many more treading close. A doctor never arrived. Those who escaped the sickness bore the emotional weight of grieving day and night. The casualties mounted.

Zeisberger informed us that the Quakers' mood had changed. Due to threats that five thousand angry farmers were set to march on the city, the Quakers had called all men to take up muskets in defense. We were stunned. He took us to the rain-splattered windows where we saw curious crowds mingling with the armed Highlanders. An artillery company tugged several cannon to the end of the street. 'Twas Sunday, yet an officer ordered blank charges to test the cannon, rattling windows and sending the Indians scurrying under beds in a panic. I went from room to room, assuring them 'twas protection.

A visitor arrived, a man in a collar who dripped in a puddle where he stood. "Beg pardon...on a Sunday," he said, "but it came up at services that it may be helpful for a party of clergymen to speak to this Paxton mob. We will not ask your company, though if you should like to join us in prayer..."

Zeisberger shook the man's hand and wished him well. I stepped in front of the pastor, carrying my wrap. "I shall ride with you and answer queries," I boldly told him. "The marchers will not threaten a woman." He was surely taken aback, thinking me driven by madness. 'Twas my opportunity, not only to escape the dismal environ, but to witness the happenings. Inside a covered carriage, a young, fair-haired clergy gentleman named Clemens greeted me. We rode to meet several more clergymen in Germantown.

Driving over Chestnut Hill, we found several hundred wet men huddled in a grove of oak trees. The horses were reined before men who stood about wood fires, seeming to steam with hateful glares. Clemens recognised a man talking to the group. He called out and the carriage slowed while our horsemen pulled around to circle behind the hill.

"A large gathering for Germantown, Reverend."

Reverend Brycelius, a local pastor, seemed relieved. "I was acquainting the men with my years in Ireland...some of the best of my life."

"Beautiful country." Pastor Clemens tipped his hat. He offered Brycelius a ride to his church and we pulled away as the rain ended.

A bearded man in front of the mob shouted, "Nobody stands in the way of our march, 'specially not wavin' a Bible."

Another in the crowd said, "We are first to arrive. Thousands more men follow." A cheer went up from all around.

We rode around the bend to meet our group. Reverend Brycelius described being surrounded by the mob and feeling it futile to reason with them. "Their number grows by the hour," he said.

Clemens said, "We can no longer sit and wait for the Crown to ordain a plan. Those men must be stopped." Clemens introduced me as the widow of a Moravian missionary, but I mentioned his blacksmith duties.

"Aye," said Brycelius," and by sharpening their tomahawks, the Moravians gained a bad reputation."

I insisted that Shamokin was a peaceful village and that only when violence struck nearby were we forced to leave. One of the horsemen reported more of the mob coming around the hill. As they marched close, a tall, reddish man with a cloth cap and slivers of serious eyes stepped forward and claimed they meant only to take custody of the Bethlehem Indians," not t' kill th' bastards, mind you...only conduct them t' th' ends a' th' province. We're prepared t' stake a high bond on our fair intentions."

Clemens reminded him that the government had taken the peaceful Indians under their protection. The man roared. " 'Tis th' source of our anger! People in 'n around Philadelphia live a pleasant, protected life and 'ave no feelins fer th' tribulations th' frontier settlers endure, lackin' protection or bare necessities from th' Gov'ment," said the man.

"We aim to see you avoid injury," said Brycelius. "His Majesty's general has appointed a large company of royal soldiers to guard the Indians, for these are people who have lived peacefully among the Moravians for years, never harming a one."

"Same Moravians been supplying guns to the savages who use them on us!" shouted someone in the crowd.

"Speculation!" shouted Clemens, as Brycelius held me down from

standing and denouncing the old rumour. Clemens said, "They teach them the gospel, something we would all do well to look upon this day."

"Gentlemen!" Brycelius held up his hands to calm the tempers. He said, "My fear is this. A Riot Act was passed, making outlaws of all who persist. The inhabitants of Philadelphia have raised up a militia. Even the Quakers have taken up arms."

"How can it be? The pious sheep 'ave a tender conscience durin' th' long Spanish, French 'n Injun War and suddenly, they be willin' to shoot a group o' their own fellows from th' frontier?" cried the reddish man.

"They see you going after the wrong men! Innocent people!" shouted Brycelius. A hush went over the crowd. He went on, "You best gather a small group of your most intelligent men and send them as your unarmed deputies to the Governor."

'Twas murmuring all about, but the men seemed to take note. It was near dark as we made our way back to Philadelphia. As we passed a blacksmith shop, the smith was offering muskets and flintlocks to whoever came to him.

"I fear that some of the mob may have passed ahead," said Clemens. "We shall wait for morning light to deliver you to the barracks." 'Twas best, since by the time we reached Philadelphia, word of the Paxtonites in Germantown had spread. Muskets were distributed along the streets to all who would take them. We drove to Pastor Clemens' church near the town center and witnessed the whole community stirred with tension.

Pastor Clemens begged my forgiveness for being called away to his panicked parishioners. He left me to a quiet evening in the care of an elderly neighbor lady, both of us relieved for the company. I fell asleep on a comfortable padded lounge, exhausted from many days of tension. Kind placement of a blanket settled me undisturbed until morning.

When alarm bells began to ring repeatedly, I jumped up, unkempt yet in my dress, and opened the door. Nearby, windows were being boarded. Shops were barely beginning to open. People ran into the street, looking up and down. Little boys ran alongside an armed Quaker gentleman, shouting about the Quaker musketeer.

Many armed Quakers lined the streets as far as I could see. Shouts traveled along the walks that the Paxtoners had broken the treaty and were marching on the city. Tensions rose as the streets filled with nearly a thousand armed militia. Women and children scattered. I stepped inside the house with my elderly hostess to watch the event.

Sentries were posted on top of some shops. We saw a speeding carriage pass by with Brycelius and several other Germantown gentlemen heading toward the Court House. Other people were walking about the Town Center, so we pulled on wraps and walked to the Court House steps where a crowd had gathered. A spokesman walked out to the crowd, saying matters had been misrepresented. "The Paxtoners were worthy men who were under great distress. Their representatives had come from several counties to complain before the Legislature. They had armed themselves," he said, "for fear of being molested or abused."

"By whom," someone called out, "the peaceable Quakers of Philadelphia?" The crowd broke into laughter. The man walked back into the Court House and the crowd began to disperse. Then we saw the marchers and a hush fell over all. As I strained to see, someone said, "Looks like only twenty or thirty." I was greatly relieved that they had taken Brycelius' advice and sent only spokesmen.

As they neared, I heard what spokesmen they were. They sauntered defiantly down the middle of the road and glared at the armed Quakers. With long blanket coats and moccasins, they looked like the traders and trappers I had known in the back hills. They gripped tomahawks and had pistols in their belts. The advice to come unarmed had not been heeded. One man thumped his chest as he passed a group of white wigged Quakers. "I was there," he sneered. "Lancaster. I took the first scalp."

Immediately sick, I grasped my stomach. Another man nearby, boasted louder, "I am the man...who killed Will Sock," our old Shamokin friend, familiar from the pamphlets decrying the action. Defiantly, he reached for the sky. "This is the arm that stabbed him to the heart!"

I was stunned to silence, as was all the crowd. The Paxtoners were daring the pacifists to take action. We knew a large bounty had been placed on the heads of the Lancaster murderers. Nothing happened. My hands shook as the men walked close. They marched to the Court House and entered the massive doors. Many of the crowd, especially those armed and ready, waited on the steps. When no word emerged, people began to disperse.

We met Pastor Clemens at his home, disheveled and weary about the eyes. "Pray for peace," he said, nodding. "I shall send you, post haste, with my driver to the barracks."

I bade farewell with my thanks. The ride seemed swift. On the road before the barracks we were stopped by the Highlanders until several of them recognised me and waved us through. At the door, David Zeisberger stepped out to greet me and thank my escort.

"They came into the city, Brother Zeisberger," I said, breathlessly as the wagon pulled away. *"I saw them, a small regimen of thirty or so, marching to the Court House, waving tomahawks and proclaiming to be the proud murderers."*

As Reverend Grube joined us, Zeisberger told him about the Paxtoners. *"A small number,"* he said. *"Perhaps they will settle this now."* As we turned, we witnessed two carriages, half a dozen men in each, approach the Highlander horsemen. I gasped, recognising some of the Paxton men whom I had witnessed on the Philadelphia street.

" 'Tis them," I whispered as I clutched Zeisberger's arm.

The carriages pulled through the Highlanders' guard, toward the barracks. Men in top hats stepped out as the Paxton men stayed seated. A legislator introduced himself and the others to Brother Zeisberger. *"We came to an agreement with these men who swear they had a first-hand look at the Indian perpetrators of a bloody massacre. We told them we are not punishing a whole group for the acts of a few, but they could come out and try to identify the ones they saw."* He leaned closer and whispered, *"We know they'll not be among your folks."*

Zeisberger let out a long sigh and scowled. *"What prevents them pointing out one of our fellows?"*

"We made them give a description. Bring your gents and let them see for themselves...they bark at the wrong tree."

I tugged at Zeisberger and suggested he make them enter. He nodded and stood straight. He said, *"If they desire to see our Indians, they must come with us. These people have been mightily inconvenienced and many are sick. I'll not drag them from their cots."*

The legislators took the news back to the wagons, knowing if the Paxton men wanted to see the Indians they would have to comply. The men climbed out, one by one, and slowly walked to the barracks doors.

Inside, I informed the Delawares and attempted to calm them. *"The men will see what you have endured for their hatred."*

Zeisberger escorted the men who immediately drew handkerchiefs to their noses. The sick rooms were in the front so the first Indians they saw were asleep or feverish, moaning softly. The men walked quickly to the back rooms where old men sat at short wooden tables and the women did needlework near a small patch of window light. The Indians' clothes were tattered and they all looked gaunt. They peered up from their work, sadness moistening their dark eyes.

"Witness," sneered a Paxton man, "they dressed them in regular clothes."

"They have worn these clothes for years," I said, "in an aim to live peacefully and thwart the attacks upon them."

"They can fool you folks b' day," said one of the farmers.

I continued, "Yes. This man's name means 'Walks with Daylight.' I met him when I was fifteen years of age and have never heard him raise his voice. He has fooled us well." I placed my hand on a woman's thin shoulder. "Winding River is a master seamstress. She's helped make dresses with the Bethlehem sisters for over twelve years."

The men shuffled uneasily and inched toward the door. I continued. "Over fifty have died this winter of smallpox or dysentery while they were in hiding from the likes of you! Do you care to look at those bodies? They are stacked in another barracks, waiting for the ground to thaw." My eyes flashed. "Perhaps you'll find your murdering savages among them, though most were grandparents, or babies!" I could not hold back my fury. Winding River reached from behind and took my hand.

The men shuffled out. I collapsed at Winding River's knees as my body rocked with sobs. Her hands caressed my back while the old people began to hum. I shuddered as my anger cooled, convinced that, given a chance, I would have taken a murderous hand to any of those Paxton men without a care as to which, indeed, were the actual killers. Around and around goes vengeance. I desired payment for those fifty lives lost in the hardship of a battle with no weapons and no meaning.

The Paxton men left the barracks and soon left Philadelphia without further incident. The ordeal was largely finished. They got less than they wanted. The legislators pledged to demand that Indians return captive settlers. Private meetings with the Indians were chastised, saying it caused the Indians to despise us as weak and disunited.

I beg forgiveness for sinking into the depths of my dismal memories. I mean not to frighten you or sadden you with hopelessness. Now, though we are fearful, we are alive and together. There must surely be hope.

By the time the candle sputtered and extinguished, Maggie had many pages tucked inside her bag. She tiptoed to the door and stepped to the perch overlooking the hillside. Edmund sat stiffly, a blanket wrapped around his shoulders, staring through the predawn haze at the grey river with white ripples feathering the water at each bend.

Maggie smiled. He had responded to the ancient ones. She wondered how long it had been since Edmund had set a small fire out in the open and circled it closely with rocks. He was preparing to build a lean-to steaming shelter. He had gathered long branches and carried Joseph's rusted tin bucket full of water from the stream. Maggie heard his hummed rhythm as he prepared to lift steam from the hot stones. As the sun rose over the river's source in the eastern sky, over Lenapehoking, his native Lenape homeland, Edmund would strip off his shirt and breeches, breathe the cloud of steam and sing words with meanings trapped in the far reaches of his memory.

Maggie ducked inside the cave. Morton was shaking Eleanor's shoulder lightly. "Papa's being Lenape. Listen." They heard Edmund's soft voice harmonize with the morning wind. Whitney began to stretch and rub his eyes. Morton cupped his hand to his ear, pointing outside. "'Tis Papa."

Whitney scowled from his brother to his mother, who was lighting a candle. "What if he's heard?" Whitney whispered.

She shook her head. The older boy noticed the stack of papers in Maggie's bag and leaned forward to inspect. "Gran has written all the night," he said. Eleanor sent the boys outside to relieve themselves, telling them not to bother their father. They ran inside and sat together on the bench, reading by the light of a new candle. Whitney read a portion in quiet voice, then Eleanor continued. Both boys were wide-eyed when she finished. Whitney asked, "Did the Indians leave that barracks?"

"Those who survived," said Maggie. "Little more than half their number. In the spring, the Moravians sent wagons to help the Delawares take the frozen bodies, those who died over the winter, to the Quakers' 'Potters Field.' They had a mass condolence service early one morning while Philadelphia slept. 'Twas the following year, after Pontiac's War ended, that the Indians were able to leave the city."

Morton asked, "Did you go with them?"

"I traveled back and forth regularly from Nazareth," Maggie explained. "I went with the Moravian party that accompanied them on their trek to the Susquehanna," she said. "Some of the missionaries helped them settle villages in the upper eastern plains of the river, near Wyalusing. David Zeisberger requested this of me, though I told him I could no longer serve. My heart was in fragments since the day I heard of the Conestoga murders, when those Paxtoners took the lives of peaceful friends."

Maggie said, "I watched the natives wander into the forest, nearly strangers to the woods, with no home of their own."

"Where did you go, Gran?" Morton asked.

"I took work at The Rose Inn, near Nazareth, in exchange for my room. 'Twas a perfect respite, long hours dusting shelves and unpacking crates from the city or from traders. Bundles of pelts were brought from the Ohio frontier with deer tallow and horns that recalled my old life in Shamokin. The times I sat alone, I would hold the soft fur against my face. I recognised distinct weavers' patterns in baskets, woven by the hands or perhaps the students of old friends. Those I gave prominence on the shelves.

"I asked now and again of travelers at The Rose, but no one knew of White Hawk or her brothers.

"Eleanor was the most constant relation in my life, but she was a busy teacher in both Nazareth and Nain, working with the younger children in each town. She was wont to surprise me, dropping by the store, but one afternoon she appeared in the doorway with a grand surprise. She announced that she was getting married."

"To Papa!" squealed Morton.

Maggie nodded. "We had known your Papa for many years. He tended his Delaware mother, Willow Anna, your other grandmother, until she died that spring. Edmund was raised among the Moravians and seemed eager to adopt the white man's path. 'Twas natural that the two of them, both with native roots, would settle together. I asked Eleanor when the wedding would take place."

Eleanor grinned at the boys. "I told her, 'On the morrow!'"

Maggie smiled. "Traces of the untethered spirit born in a steaming riverside hut."

Eleanor nodded. "We were leaving for Pittsburgh and we wanted your Gran to come along, live with us."

"You agreed?" Whitney asked Maggie.

"With no struggle," she nodded. "People had too often taken their leave, with no choice given. Your mother was all I had and I could never freely let her slip away, not when I had an invitation to join. You would have arrived some years hence and I might never have known you." The boys huddled into Maggie's open arms. Eleanor unwrapped a muslin sack of dried biscuits and passed it around.

Morton asked Maggie why the people in town had chopped down the tree. She guessed, "Perhaps to them it had no value other than kindling."

"'Twas ornery and cruel," said Whitney.

A shadow passed over the door and startled the boys. "Papa?" said Morton, as Edmund ducked through the timbers. His face was smudged with streaks of ashes, darkened by tears. He kneeled in front of them.

"Eleanor, I've said I wanted my sons to have a strong father. I will hide no longer."

"We'll go elsewhere," moaned Eleanor, taking his hands in hers. "Start afresh."

"I cannot run. 'Twould all repeat, perhaps worsen," said Edmund. "I must go into town. Those people are mistaken if they believe they are permitted to torment us."

Eleanor shook her head and began to tremble. Whitney declared, "You need me with you, Papa." Morton also begged to go along.

Maggie reached out for her daughter. She said, "You desired to have this family together." Eleanor stared at Edmund. Maggie clasped his streaked hand as Eleanor grimaced against her immense fear.

Then Maggie bowed her head. She took Edmund's hand with both of hers and forced her words, dry mouthed. "I beg you," she said, slowly. "Your ash streaked face," she said to Edmund, "and the sound of your lament..."

"What has befallen her?" asked Whitney. When Maggie looked up, her eyes were moist and distant. She asked Whitney to bring her old bag. Reaching to the bottom, she brought out a buckskin wrapped bundle and laid it across her lap.

When she began to unwrap the soft but tattered skin, Eleanor exclaimed, "Your wedding garment."

"A fragment. The portion White Hawk worked with her quills." Inside the skin was a bundle of long white feathers, the ones White Hawk had given her when they parted. Maggie sniffed and said, "Her last word to me. Remember."

Eleanor whispered, "She is recalling the attack upon her." She moved closer and opened her arms. "Mother?"

Maggie nodded. "The memory flows like a river," she said, accepting Eleanor's embrace. "I must tell it or drown." Edmund nodded and sat at Maggie's feet. Morton climbed into his lap and Whitney moved closer.

Maggie breathed a long sigh. "'Twas in hills such as these, further north, up the Beaver River. I passed through the sparsely settled birch valley that had borne some of the worst terror of the most recent Indian attacks."

Eleanor said, "Those attacks were blamed upon one man. Was it Logan?"

Maggie nodded. "Blamed upon Logan...Tahgajut, younger brother of Tagnehdorus."

"The man you loved," said Edmund.

Maggie paused and rubbed her forehead. "Our Logan," she said, smiling at Eleanor. "I yearned to know the truth. I had heard Dunmore's soldiers attribute near thirty brutal deaths in the area to one crazed man. The circle of violence is senseless, but it can surely not be blamed upon one man. The sons of Swataney had been friends of the colonists since their childhood."

"You could have come to us," said Edmund.

"The town was in upheaval," Maggie said. "More disturbance ensued while you were at the Hannastown market." She turned to Eleanor and asked, "I penned the letter, telling my intentions. If I had come to you, would you have helped?"

Eleanor shook her head. "I would have attempted to stop you."

Maggie said, "Indeed. I was tormented by the image of Logan in his self-loathing, shouldering blame for the outbreak of violence. There's no explaining how I thought to find my way successfully to Logan. Upon leaving Shamokin years ago, Logan said we were 'undivided friends.' Learning of his present anguish, I slept naught for days. I sensed he blamed himself for the fall of Shamokin, his family's grief, his people's loss. He had been stripped of his influence. He lost face. When a person loses his face in shame, he might pick up whatever mask is given him, believing the worst about himself."

Eleanor said, "It served the military's purpose to blame the attacks on one wicked Indian."

Edmund leaned forward. "The soldiers were involved?"

"The soldiers turned the town's attention away from an attack by Captain Cresap's men. They slaughtered a small peaceful party of old Mingo men and women," said Maggie. "But they were Logan's relatives. He went to the captain to complain. At this, Cresap showed him a letter ordering further violence upon Logan's family, signed by the fort's commander.'"

"Doctor Connolly?" said Eleanor. Her face was wet and contorted. "Who told you this?"

Maggie went on. "He was warned," she said, sighing, "but too late. He returned home to find his wife and young children brutally murdered by soldiers." Eleanor choked and Maggie swallowed to clear her tensed throat. She said, "When his older children had died years ago of the white man's fever in Shamokin, Logan went on. But the hostile bloodletting of his wife and young ones collapsed his spirit. All the strength he once poured into helping his white brethren, he poured into annihilating them, so says local lore. When I sought the image of his face twisted with hatred, I could not. Twisted with pain, indeed, I see it yet.

Eleanor shook her head. "Torment one man, make him out to be crazed and a danger."

Edmund nodded. "I had heard the soldiers' reports of the crazed Indian attacking whites in the area for many months and knew that something was awry."

Eleanor said, "The town was a tumult of prattlers' lore; skirmishes over taxes, borders; the Continental Congress; the king sending his red-coated army to stop all talk of independence."

Maggie said, "When we moved to Fort Pitt, I was already an old woman. If neighboring folk spoke their hard hearts, I quieted myself, held my tongue. But Logan was the son of Swataney, and Swataney was the most peace-loving man I had ever known. The eruption of Logan's violence was evidence that senselessness ruled us all. I could not ignore it, though I was foolish to think 'twas any of mine to change."

Eleanor said, "Though 'twas your thought."

"I am old to be marching about the woods. I know," said Maggie. "I thought of Logan and the knots in my bones became ever painful. I lay awake at night and during the day I would fret. One night, I woke from a brief nightmare and made a hasty decision. I could sit idly no longer."

"Mother Beigler," said Edmund, "you are not one to sit idly."

"No. I packed my weathered bag and untangled the cord of my old turtle totem, hung it around my neck. Packed a few clothes, blankets and a bag of food. I set out, paying the smithy's stable boy to deliver me to the Indian camp twenty miles north.

"I met an old friend from Shamokin, Red Arrow, who told me that Logan recognizes no one."

Eleanor asked, "This is the young man whom we reacquainted several years ago? On our venture up the Beaver River with the traveling doctor dispensing fever medicine?"

"Indeed," said Maggie. "He asked why I sought him."

"I told him Logan is my brother. The young Mingo looked at me and shrugged, mumbling something about Shamokin. He asked if I would pay. I handed him a bag of coins, all I had saved, and begged to leave immediately."

"Red Arrow said little on our journey. My thoughts were full of Shamokin, like knotted bundles in heart and throat. When Red Arrow pulled the wagon into the yard of an abandoned, burned-out cabin, the knots sank into my stomach. Shredded rags and refuse were strewn about; a burned bear hide, broken glass, splintered wood and rims of a former rum barrel. 'His place,' Red Arrow said. 'Twas a clear day. The sun streamed through the high tree branches and shattered near the ground like shrouds over Logan's past. Red

Arrow told me he had returned here to his butchered family, his wife in a pool of her children's blood."

"He pointed up at the mountain above the birch-covered hills. 'He goes there.' I nodded and we continued on the creek path. The following afternoon, we heard the steady rhythm of axe on wood with a repeating echo across the valley. Red Arrow stopped the wagon and insisted we walk. He said the path had become rough, but also the approaching wagon would alarm a crazy man. I agreed and we began to walk toward the clamor. Squatting in the woods and peering through branches, I had a clear view of the woodsman's back, strong, like the man I recalled, but older. Glimpsing his face, I was struck by the likeness to old Swataney, his famous father.

"Logan had chopped down trees all around the upper part of the mountain. He had dragged them like a crown around a pile of ash at the highest peak. Stacks of green brush and small trees lay near his feet. Covered in torn rags and smeared with grey ashes, Logan stopped and looked at his work. 'He is a madman,' whispered Red Arrow. As I leaned closer, I snapped a branch with my knee and Logan swung around, spotting us. He drew his axe up in front of him, and reached for the rifle at his feet. Red Arrow bolted backwards, grabbing my arm until I jerked away. I shouted to Logan as a shot broke a branch overhead. I turned to follow Red Arrow when another shot rang out. I felt a thud on my side and my feet halted beneath me. My legs locked and I toppled forward as Red Arrow leaped into the cover of the heavy bushes. Pain shot around my middle then I scarce recall hearing any but a steady pounding, my racing heart or the sound of Logan running toward me. I felt his hand in my hair. He gripped it with his fist and threw me over on my back, leaning over me with his knife outstretched and his face twisted unrecognizably.

"I tried to call out, but sputtered. He paused and scowled, squinting at me, then I saw the flash of his knife over my head and felt a searing pain. I cried, 'Logan...do not kill me.' The last words were mostly breath, but somehow I remained conscious.

Leaning over me, still scowling, he pointed the tip of his knife at my throat, pressing down on the cord of my carved turtle totem. 'Ganyahde:,' he said. 'Turtle.' He asked in English if I stole from Turtle clan. Near choking, I sputtered, 'No! 'Twas Swataney's hand that made...gave it...'"

"He spoke his mother's Cayuga language again, tapping his forehead with his knife. I whispered that I saw the face of my brother, Tahgajut. Hearing his name, he looked closer at my face, leaning near enough that the pungent scent of streaked ashes stung my nose. He dropped down to his knees beside me.

"I saw him peering at me and said, ''Tis Maggie,' with all the strength I could muster through the throbbing pain. Wet lines darkened the ash around his eyes, making his face more frightful. I repeated his question, 'Who is this person?' He told me a dead man does not see and glanced down at the pool of blood on the side of my dress. I nodded slightly and said, ''Tis Mag-weh, old now, Logan, but I am here. I came for you. Do you see me?'

"The pause seemed an endless nightmare, the possibility of him not seeing, or knowing me, the chance he may not care. Then the hard line of his jaw eased and he asked, 'Mag-weh lives?' I lay watching as his eyes filled with the familiar. His words spilled like the water from his eyes. 'I call out my brother's name and strike with the fury Tagnehdorus can no longer aim. My brother camps with the Great Spirit, struck down like so many who were friends to the whites. My wife is sent there.' He looked at my bloody head and reached out toward it, with a shaking hand. He cried with agony, 'Ahhhh...what man kills his sister?' Quicker than I had ever seen a man move, he slashed down his arm with the knife, scraping the flesh open, and fell down next to me. 'We are finished!' he cried. 'We will finish here, together.'

"My eyes filled with tears, not of pain. I had stopped feeling pain. But of sorrow. How desperate he must have been. Blood flowed brightly over the dim grey ash on his arm, startling me more than my own wounds, no longer felt. His face leaned toward the piles of ash and tree boughs. He said, 'There I buried my family, my people.' Shaking, he held up his arm. 'No longer does my blood flow in any other human. The land thieves cast us off. In my anger, I set fire to the giant tree. When the fire finished burning and before the embers cooled, I covered myself with the ashes. Beneath those ashes I find my weapons...I avenge my family.' He choked and bowed his head. 'My sister goes to the Great Spirit,' he murmured.

"When I heard his words, I closed my eyes. I saw an image of my beautiful friend. I gasped, 'White Hawk! Surely, 'twas her restless spirit that led me here.' I begged him to tell me what became of her.

"He reminded me of Captain Cresap's attack on the old Mingos. 'My sister went to the home of her white neighbor, her friend,' he said, bitterly. 'She warned that some Indians had been drinking and had become unruly. The white woman fled to safety, but Cresap's men arrived and started shooting. Tagnehdorus was among them. When she ran to our brother's side, the soldiers shot—murdered her.'

Maggie was quiet. The cave felt more hollow and cool. Eleanor sniffed and wiped at her eyes with the hem of her skirt. Edmund looked down as the boys leaned against him. "I had often dreamed of finding White Hawk," Maggie said to her family, gathered at her feet. "Dreamed of finding my Shamokin kinfolk. Logan grudgingly told me White Hawk's infant grandchild was taken away, spared because its father is white. He, John Gibson, has the child now."

"John Gibson, the trader who lives up the river?" asked Edmund.

"Could she have been so close and we knew naught?" said Eleanor, sniffing.

Maggie said, "What followed then is like a dream, but vivid at last. I struggled to keep my eyes opened. I moaned, 'I grieve with you, Logan. Look at me...whose face do you see?' He turned to me and stared. 'Look deeply, Logan,' I pleaded.

"He moved his hand down my back to press gently on the bloody wound, stopping the flow. He moved close to my face, leaning on one elbow. 'I see the face of my wife, dying alone after watching her young ones being tortured...and cursing me for staying away so long.'

"I asked him to look again and laid my head back in the leaves. He looked at me for a quiet moment and then he lay down with his head beside mine, gazing into my eyes. 'I see the face of my wife, on the day I promised to care for her.' He cleared his dry throat. 'You, Mag-weh...whose face...do you see?'

"Tears filled my eyes and blurred my sight, but I whispered, 'My father's face. He is slipping beneath the sea, far from me, far from America.' He told me to look again. 'Yes...my father,' I repeated, 'but now he witnesses my tiny newborn face. He dreams of a grand new world he will show me...someday.'

"'Turtle Island,' Logan said. 'He knew the land waited for you to mix your blood into the soil.' He closed his eyes. 'Now our blood mixes. When we come out of this earth again, we will be the same family.'

"I reached out and took his hand. 'We are the same family, Logan.' In my blurred vision, I saw green lights and shapes, green tree boughs. Swaying over us, a massive pine tree. ''Tis not destroyed, Logan, by you, by anyone. The roots grew long before my people, or even yours.' He nodded, but did not look over his shoulder at my vision.

"He whispered, 'Mag-weh...I am sorry we came to this place.'

"He held my hand up to his streaked chin. 'I see your real face, Logan. Your deepest heart desires to see the bloodshed end. You were driven to outdo the wickedness that was done to you.' He spoke to me in Cayuga and I repeated, 'Peace, my brother.' As I said the words, a shot rang out and whistled through the air over our heads. We heard voices yelling in the woods below us.

"Logan jumped, holding his slashed arm, looking wildly about. He kneeled again and tucked a loose piece of my scalp into my hand. 'Mag-weh. Live!' He ran across the ashes and dropped out of sight over the hill. One more shot rang out before Red Arrow and another man arrived at my side.

"'She's alive!' Red Arrow called out, startled. He pulled my hand up and saw my scalp bunched in my stiff grip. The other man was already plugging my hip wound with a wad of cloth and wrapping my head with strips. I must have lost consciousness before we got to the wagon. I recall nothing until I was back at Fort Pitt with the doctor peering into my eyes. I recalled Logan asking me 'whose face.' I smiled and heard Eleanor gasp as the doctor said I would survive."

Silence hung about the cave. Eleanor let out a breath and said, "I recall that moment. You were bruised and swollen, a stitched up horror. I was never so fearful."

Morton had red streaked cheeks. He had passed a birthday in April so when Whitney whispered that he was too old to cry, Morton struck his brother and growled, "Shaddup!" He pressed his face against Edmund's chest. In a muffled voice, he said, "I thought she would die."

Whitney guffawed, "Gran was here to tell the story!"

"I mean then," snapped Morton. "When she was hurt. At the 'firmary. Mama went and we stayed home."

Edmund wrapped his arms around Morton and patted his back. He looked at Eleanor and said, "'Twas Doctor Connolly who ordered the attack on Logan's family. I shudder to consider how we entrusted Maggie into his care."

Eleanor lowered her face and covered her eyes with her hand. "A doctor. Ordering massacre. Our dear White Hawk."

"A doctor treats human beings," said Edmund. "Connolly misthinks the Indians outside that family, surely. 'Tis my conjecture."

Eleanor took Maggie's hand. "'Twas the turtle totem indeed that saved you."

Edmund nodded, "At the mission, we were shamed for using the totems. The whites could not fathom that if the Great Spirit's power could be reflected in a tiny charm, that power could be mightily reflected upon us as well."

Maggie nodded. "I feel most loved. I'm grateful for your listening." She rubbed her forehead. "As the tale came to mind, it relieved a burdensome ache."

ζ

Edmund guided Coal out of the hills, pointing out to his family that the river road winding below was highly trafficked with several wagons and a lone horseman upon the visible stretch. He brought the wagon near the road at the same time the horseman passed with a 'halloo' in their direction. Edmund waved and pulled Coal to a halt, intending to allow the horseman to ride ahead, but the man reined his horse beside them.

"Heard the news, aye?" he asked and then identified himself as an innkeeper from upriver. When Edmund said they had not, the innkeeper explained. "Lexington came under attack days ago. Massachusetts farmers loaded squirrel rifles and penned the redcoats within the confines of Boston town."

"'Tis true," breathed Edmund quietly. Leaning to Eleanor, he added, "I dreamed the fighting had begun." He called out to the man, "What more do you know?"

The broadclothed gentleman's horse sidestepped nervously when he bellowed, "Aim for Fort Pitt, er, Dunmore, in time for the town meeting. We'll learn it there." He tipped his tall hat and trotted ahead.

As the wagon lurched onto the road, Maggie realized there was nothing hanging around her neck. "My turtle," she called. "'Tis fallen."

Edmund turned around and nodded over his shoulder. "'Twas at your side on the bench. We'll return. We must get to town, post haste."

In town, there was a jubilant commotion. It seemed every person ran about the streets, some shouting and waving guns. Wagons sat empty in front of taverns and shops as the crowd gathered around a tall wooden pole freshly planted in the ground in the middle of the street. A bonfire burned in front of it and the crowd stood around in a circle, many rows deep. Boatmen filled the streets. Since the news had traveled along the river, all boats had docked and emptied their crews into the town.

"I've a mind to find that doctor," said Edmund. He called to a man nearby, "Where would we find the meetings?"

"Semple's Tavern, b'Gawd," he slurred.

"Here they be," yelled another man, pointing at the dark suited committee strolling swiftly toward them, followed by a hurried crowd in the street. The bonfire folks stood back, parting for the two men who rolled a large stump in front of the wooden pole. They secured it and used it as a rostrum, stepping up in front of the fire and calling forth the committee men as the meeting came to order. A hush fell over the street as a man began to explain the resolutions.

Edmund tied Coal to a hitching post and told the women and children to stay there while he went closer to listen. He walked into the crowd as Whitney fixed his gaze on the pole, pointed on top, a thirty foot tall tree trunk stripped of its bark and branches. "Our tree!" the boy cried, jumping over the side of the wagon and scrambling through the crowd behind his father. Eleanor caught the scruff of Morton's shirt before he followed his brother and pulled him back into the wagon.

"My God," breathed Maggie. "The boy speaks the truth." She climbed from the wagon and began to wriggle her way through the crowd.

The man on the stump was barking out names, the names of the other committeemen. He waved his hand in front of the pole, her tree, and hollered above the noise of the crowd, "We resolve to oppose those who have invaded American rights and privileges." The crowd cheered and waved their hats.

The stump man denounced the local domestic squabbles. He said, "The most important object is liberty and freedom. For this, we set aside Indian wars and border disputes. We'll man a militia, to include the Pennsylvania portion of the county."

When the cheering ceased, someone called out, "What arms shall we bear?"

The stump man said, "We'll collect and repair all arms not in service. Every person will render several shillings for a 'powder and shot' fund."

While the man read a resolution about cultivating friendship with the area Indians, Maggie saw Whitney, on all fours, climbing through the legs of the crowd to the base of the pole. He reached out to touch the smooth barkless wood with both hands, stopping at the knot where a dry lower branch had hung days ago. A soldier grabbed his collar and yanked him to his feet, spilling the papers from the buckskin pouch over his shoulder. Whitney kicked at the soldier's leg and the man slid his foot across the papers, shoving them into the fire. Whitney cried out, "No! Gran's journal."

He dove toward the soldier, head first into his stomach. The big man didn't flinch. But he lifted his hand as if to smack Whitney across the face. The boy cried out, pointing at the pole, "'Tis our tree, stolen from the yard of our cabin and stripped of its branches!"

"'Tis the liberty pole!" someone shouted. "'Tis liberty we want!"

"Liberty!" The chant was repeated through the crowd.

Edmund made his way to the front of the circle. He shouted out, "Let the boy go. He speaks justly." The crowd hushed as the soldier pushed Whitney to the ground in front of Edmund.

Edmund leaned to pull his son to his feet and brush him off. "You speak of friendly relations with area Indians," he said. "Begin with my family." A murmur rose and Edmund turned to the crowd. "'Tis true. Because I am part Indian, my family was chased from our home. The lives of my wife, mother and children were put at risk and our house stoned. This pole called 'Liberty' was a tree growing on our plot a day prior."

All eyes were upon Edmund. Then a buckskin clad trapper shouted, "Tell 'em!"

A man next to Maggie smacked his fist into his hand and said, "I sense a good fight. I ain't fought in two days!"

With that, Maggie pushed her way to the front of the circle by the well-dressed official. Cries arose from all around as the crowd became tumultuous. She pointed a bony finger at the committeeman. "Put a stop to this, or any bloodshed will be on your hands."

The plump man waved his hands from atop the stump and cried out, "Silence!" but the arguments grew louder. He signaled to one of the soldiers and a musket was fired overhead. Edmund pulled Whitney close as the crowd quieted.

The official called out, "There are complaints aplenty if we study the turmoils of past weeks."

"Past months!" someone called.

"Hear! Hear! Silence!" cried the stump man. "Witness how the local squabbles and the Indian war might distract us from our goal of liberty. We must put these complaints to rest."

"Allow Injuns in our town?" someone yelled.

"Aye, if they be fightin' for liberty alongside us," hollered another.

The man on the stump pointed in the direction of the voice. "That man has the proper spirit. We begin here and now to promote new relations with the Indians. They will be our partners in our quest for liberty."

"Liberty!" rose a cheer.

The official raised one finger. "Here's a family needs cabin repairs and windows replaced. Who shall offer a hand?" A few hands went up and the official turned to Edmund. "You come to my shop and tell me what delivery of glass you'll be needing, young man. We beg forgiveness for your suffering." Edmund put a hand on Whitney's shoulder and the soldiers led them out of the crowd.

Maggie had moved to the side of the liberty pole, and was staring up at its tallest point. "Come, Maggie," said Edmund.

She ran her hand up the shining side of the pole as the crowd's noise increased, some applause along with hearty shouts, "Liberty, liberty for all!"

Though it seemed they were headed back to their cabin, Maggie was heavy hearted as she turned to follow Edmund and Whitney. She thought she saw Doctor Connolly saunter to the rear of the committee group behind the stump and her pulse began to throb. Anger pounded at her chest.

Cries rose again from the clamorous crowd. As Maggie neared the outer edge of the circle, a drunken boatman stumbled toward her and she hopped aside. Suddenly, she saw the face of Joseph, so full and crinkled, she thought he must surely be alive. The crowd jostled around him as he held out his hand to show her the turtle totem.

"You found it." A dazed Maggie reached toward Joseph's hand. As she touched the totem, a noisy wind swept the bonnet from her head and she was overcome by a distinct odor of meat and garlic. Her head throbbed, as if she were standing in an echoing canyon with sounds rushing at her from all directions. She heard a voice behind her, saying, "Did you see that hair? Whew, ugly." Maggie spun around, dizzily, feeling as if she were falling into a deep, dark hole. She saw a face. The face of the painful words. The woman was both familiar and strange. But Maggie glared angrily, wishing to attack the woman's own head in vengeance, mutilate her brown, hatless bob. But Joseph's voice kept repeating the phrase, "Whose face do you see?" She recognized the face of ignorance. The woman knew nothing of Maggie's trials.

When Maggie thought of her own suffering, she wanted to spit and holler. She wanted to rip off her bonnet and point to Connolly, blame him for the scars on her head and the deeper scars upon the native people, but Joseph gripped her elbow. Maggie leaned closer, to hear Joseph's raspy voice.

"Ah told the doctor," the old man assured her. "Ah know his plot to cross the river to Ohio country, hire the French 'n Indians to fight against the colonies. He aims to capture Pittsburgh fer the King." Joseph pursed his lips and scowled. "Aims to enlist the very Indians he set out to murder weeks past," he sputtered. "So Ah told him. Knocked the hat off his head and leaned close to his hairy ear. Told him Ah'd more than make certain he failed. Ah'd see him dead or in prison." Joseph squeezed Maggie's elbow as she turned back to look at the committee group. Doctor Connolly had disappeared.

The crowd separated and Maggie stood across the road from the wagon. Morton sat beside white-faced Eleanor on the bench seat while Edmund and Whitney were about to climb up. Maggie pulled her bonnet back in place and looked side to side for Joseph. The only dark faces she saw belonged to younger boatmen. The sun had set and someone in the crowd tossed a log on the fire before the pole, sending sparks and the white ghosts of paper embers into the twilight. A lanky, dark-skinned boy rolled a barrel of whiskey past the wagon along the street and the crowd parted to let him pass. They cheered as he neared the pole and the barrel was uncorked.

"Old rye for the lot," someone shouted.

Maggie walked slowly to the wagon, turning nearly backwards as she scanned the crowd. Edmund jumped down to help her into the wagon and her lips parted, as if beginning to speak to him. Then she snapped them closed, looked away. What would he think if she told him she had spoken to his dead friend? She sat in the back of the wagon and watched the street chaos.

A river boatman and a woman with a bright red skirt twirled in a clumsy dance. The man began to shout, rambling words spilled in a fury: "I'm half stallion and the rest snappin' turtle. I aim to out-drink and out-fight any man from Pittsburgh to the river's end. Come on, you bargers, you milky farmers. No holds barred!" For most, the grimy mechanics of the boat yards joined with gentlemen clerks, farmers, buckskin-clad traders and uniformed soldiers as the whole town joined in a gleeful celebration. They twirled and howled around the war pole of Teutonic legend, renamed the "Liberty Pole" to suit the needs of 1775. Hunters and soldiers saluted with rifle shots, endangering all the town in praise of freedom.

Maggie tugged at Edmund's sleeve and pointed to the weary boys. "We've had our fill of excitement. Shall we venture to the weaver's cabin? Examine the damage?" The only room with unbroken windows was Maggie's in the rear, where the glass had been protected by the tree while it was still standing. Edmund lit a fire in the stove and they crowded in, the boys on the bed with Maggie. Whitney had apologized to her several times for letting her journal pages be ruined. She told him she was glad he hadn't been hurt. With their heads against her, one on either side, it was only minutes before the boys were fast asleep.

Eleanor lay on the bearskin on the floor with Edmund, gazing at the boys. "'Twas courageous to speak up in that frenzied crowd," she said.

"Whitney? Your mother?" Edmund asked.

"All of you. The cabin repairs are assured before the Emorys return and in due time, we'll be back at our farm," she said with a heavy sigh.

Maggie lifted her head. "Planting time is nigh. 'Tis the light of the moon." There was no response from Eleanor. She had quickly drifted to sleep. Maggie called to Edmund in a soft voice. When he answered, she said, "Dare I ask, would you be considering fighting with the militia?"

"I may consider," said Edmund.

Maggie snorted. "You have a great trust in this new friendship with the Indians?"

"Mother Beigler, 'tis the time for independence. We may all be called to help in ways we cannot image."

"Be certain you know who directs the orders." Her words were guarded.

"Indeed? What burden is yet untold?" He sat up and looked at her face.

She squirmed to get comfortable and moved the pillow behind her back. "You may think my right mind has made off, but I must tell you, I saw the figure of Joseph today. He spoke to me."

Edmund said, "He showed you your turtle. I saw him as well."

"You saw?" Maggie gasped.

"Did he return it to you?" Edmund asked. When Maggie shook her head, he said, "You may be in need of it no longer."

"I believe he intends to pass it on. I touched it and witnessed another face." She didn't tell him that the face was familiar—and also strange. She failed to mention the noise or the furies that passed through her or the feelings of bitterness at being ridiculed for her scarred head. She was more concerned about the issues at present and wanted Edmund to be informed before he marched off with the militia.

"Joseph has made a vow, Edmund," Maggie whispered. "He claims his spirit will not rest while the likes of Connolly are plotting to enlist innocent people in their greedy schemes." Edmund was so offended by her report, he screwed up his normally docile face and seemed apt to spit a bad taste from his mouth.

"Be wary, Edmund. 'Tis a breed of man who makes promises to benefit his own pocket."

"Where do I sign up for Joseph's militia? He aims to put a halt to the man? I pray for whatever force he musters to succeed." He lay back on the bearskin and wrapped an arm around Eleanor while Maggie pulled the candle closer to write:

My dears,

The scars I bear upon my face and head are lesser than those upon my heart. Our beloved pine tree serves as a signpost of liberty, yet to me, 'tis the sign of those cut from their roots and stripped of their lives for the sake of "progress."

When I was wounded and lying upon the ground feeling my blood run near the shadow of death, I saw a clear image of the healthy pine tree and thought how near I was to the entrance of the Great Spirit's land. The Tree of Peace cannot be destroyed. Laced and spread in all directions are the peaceful roots, through the fabric of Turtle Island.

Remember, boys. Turtle Island was created for the children of Sky Woman, the twins Sapling and Flint. Some create and some destroy. The circle goes around. But all messages float on smoke to the creator. When the tree appears absent, we people are the branches.

Logan's sole reward for his friendly proximity to the whites was the murder of all his family. He moaned, "Not a drop of my blood is in the veins of any living creature." But somewhere, there is a drop of his father's, Swataney's blood, in White Hawk's infant grandchild being raised among the whites.

The colonists hear every encouragement to call ourselves Americans. 'Tis a rallying cry to unite, an effort to reverse the hard hearts and separate minds of groups: Germans, English, Scotch-Irish, flatlanders, Dutch, on and on. We mix our blood with this soil and call ourselves Americans, joining with each other to invent a nation, we believe. But a nation was already here. America continues its invention through us. Turtle Island will always bear the soil that nourishes the roots of all our trees and every plant.

Thank you, my family, for assuring me that I am never alone. Our blood is mixed and now our thoughts are mixed as well.

Your loving Mother and Grandmother

ς

I had read Maggie's letter several times before the hospital volunteer arrived at the surgical waiting area to take me to Quinn's recovery room. The surgeon, still in his green scrubs and seeming younger than I, met me at her door to tell me he had just spoken to Quinn's parents. The procedure went as he had expected, attaching small supports to the piece of broken cheekbone and stitching her wound.

"There's massive bruising and swelling," he said. "It may look bad for some time, but there's no more danger of her eye being permanently damaged. She'll just be sore."

"When can we go back to Chicago?"

"Driving, right?" he asked. "I'd like to watch her for a couple of days. If you're doing the driving, you can head back as soon as she feels up to it, barring any complications." When I raised my eyebrows, he said, "Don't worry, I don't expect any. She doesn't even have a fever. Pretty tough," he winked. "I'd hate to see the other guy."

"I'm going to see him at the police station. I'll give him your regards," I said.

"Sorry for the trouble you two had. It's usually a pretty peaceful town."

"I believe that," I said, smiling.

He told me the nurse would get a recliner chair for me if I'd like to stay there overnight. "You've been through a lot today. I've spent more than one night here. The chairs aren't bad, if you're tired enough."

I thanked him and pushed open the door to Quinn's room. Sitting on the far side of her bed, holding her limp hand, was Joe. I stood in the doorway for a moment, hoping he wouldn't disappear. He turned and smiled.

"Sorry, darlin.' Ah surely hate to see this," he said.

I walked to the other side of the bed and sat. My body was weary. But, even more fatigued, my mind could barely move. I dreaded the idea of another colossal leap of mental aerobics. I wanted to climb into that recliner and sleep for a week with no dreams. Quinn was resting peacefully, but her face was a fright. A giant blue bruise crept from every side of the surgical bandage; she probably had a couple of inches stitched, and her eye was still badly swollen. I rested my hand on her arm.

"I feel like I got her into this," I said.

Joe shrugged. "Or she got you into it. She brought you to the turtle. What does it matter?"

"Why wasn't it me that got beat up?" I said, sniveling.

"She the one facing her power. You the one facing your heart. Everybody got a different trip down the river." He shook his head from side to side, patting Quinn's hand.

I had been in the waiting room for several hours, writing Maggie's story. I said, "I have to know, Joe. What happened to Doctor Connolly?"

"Heh," Joe said, grinning. He stood as straight as he could in front of the window. "He and all the gentlemen landowners in Pittsburgh drank a toast to

King George, a victim in their minds. They knew nothin' about the people shoutin' and dancin' in the streets. Didn' know the merrymakers considered them the hitch in their freedom. Lord Dunmore and Doc Connolly hid out durin' the war in a British man-a-war off the coast. Heh heh," Joseph chuckled. "Somehow," he leaned toward me and smiled, "Connolly's plot was revealed. None a' his men got the promised three hunderd acres. Nabbed in Maryland, went to prison as an enemy a' the country until after the war." Joseph shook his head, hands on his hips. "The man tried to waylay the American independence for years, always foiled." He smiled at me. "Ah got me a militia a' my own."

Quinn started to mumble. I leaned closer and heard her say something about her school. "Yeah, darlin,'" Joe smiled. "Ah thought you might recall." He turned to me. "She was only eight or nine, a tiny ball a fire. A coupla boys tried to pull her from the school playground, down the trail where you found me. She saw me and let out a bloody scream, put those fellas' hairs on end b'fore she gave 'em a shove right into my arms. Ah thought the shovin' was all she recalled. Little ball a fire got brighter. Them boys ne'er messed with her again."

Quinn was squinting through her good eye. "Now I remember," she whispered.

I couldn't ask Joseph about Maggie or Eleanor, didn't want to know if Edmund went to war. I understood Maggie and not wanting to know the fate of friends who probably had difficult lives. I know that brotherhood wasn't established with Native Americans, even though many fought with the colonists to win our independence from Britain. What followed for them was years of deception, oppression and genocide.

My question to Joseph was this, "Are we finished? Can we give back the turtle?" He nodded and said we could. I felt the familiar lump in my pocket, the same place it had been when we heard the humming in the woods. It had taken awhile, was almost dark by the time I had wriggled into a position where Quinn could reach the turtle and use its only sharp edge to gnaw through the rope around my hands. Fletch had disappeared and the other creep had been too cowardly to come back. Even so, the turtle had saved us from a freezing night in the woods.

"Joe, maybe I need a little more time," I said. Then I asked, "Can I think about giving back the turtle?"

"Time?" he laughed. "You have all you need."

"One thing I missed was my dad's birthday. He'll be expecting a call," I said.

"Distraction," Quinn whispered as she pointed to her cheek.

I wondered how the fracture between my dad and I would ever heal. "I'm not in any mood to listen to his disapproval," I said.

"He got his trip down the river, too," said Joe. "Keep throwin' your rope to folks afloat, all ya got is a bigger raft."

"So I have my own raft? I need to guide it myself?"

Joe nodded. "Get moving," he said. He leaned over Quinn and kissed her forehead. He laid his hand beside her bandaged cheek for a moment, then he stood in front of me and grasped both of my hands. He looked into my eyes, conveying a deep and wordless challenge to be true. To remember.

Quinn was sleeping and when I next saw her awake, her bruise had turned a deeper purple. But the swelling eased and she was okay to travel in a few days. We even worked things out with the basketball player we had missed and saw her play another game before we left. The girl's a shooter, an awesome shooter.

I drove the Beetle all the way home, so I followed my intuition and drove down the Susquehanna to hook up with the Pennsylvania Turnpike. We cruised west through the gorgeous rippling Appalachian mountains. It had turned brisk over the weekend and the straggling tree leaves had thinned to an orange shadow, ready to retire for the winter. I exited the Turnpike in Bedford and took Highway 30 past the lakes near Shanksville. I would have stopped for final directions but for the number of cars driving along Lambertsville Road. License plates showed that Americans from all the neighboring states and as far away as Nebraska were paying tribute, like us, to Pennsylvania's "Ground Zero." Thousands of people didn't die there, scarcely forty. Multibillion dollar buildings and corporations weren't damaged, not the U.S. Capitol or the White House, only fields and forests.

The giant crater where the hijacked plane hit the earth had been bulldozed, but the ground still reeked of jet fuel. I had seen newspaper photos of the blackened trees at the crater's edge. They were gone, cut down, critically damaged by the fuel and fire. Tiny pieces of debris were scattered everywhere, mostly paper from the many pounds of mail carried on the plane. I didn't know any of the travelers, but I felt somehow connected. The line of cars parked along the road told me I wasn't alone with those feelings. Our hearts broke together. This was hallowed ground. They weren't my relatives, not my ancestors, but my spirit knew to be humble, reverent.

Quinn and I sat in the car with the heater running, but I shivered when I looked out into the middle of the bulldozed field and thought I saw green flowing branches reaching high, brushing the same sky that had exploded on September 11th. Quinn was staring, too, and nodded at the forest's new edge. In the shadowy boundaries of the woods there appeared to be thousands of figures with arms crossed, heads held high. I thought of the book given by one of the nurses when Quinn had sheepishly acknowledged hearing Logan on the hillside. "People around here often talk about hearing him chanting," the nurse assured. The book had sayings from Native American chiefs, bookmarked with one from exactly one hundred years after the Indians and Moravians fled Shamokin. Tears had flowed with the tide of settlers all the way to the western shores of Turtle Island. When Chief Seattle signed the 1855 Port Elliott Treaty, surrendering his lands to the Washington governor, these words were attributed to him:

Tribe follows tribe, and nation follows nation, and regret is useless...
But when the last Red man shall have become a myth among
the White men...
when your children's children think themselves alone in the field, the store,
upon the highway, or in the silence of the pathless woods,
they will not be alone.
In all the earth there is no place dedicated to solitude.
At night when the streets of your cities are silent and
you think them deserted,
they will throng with the returning hosts that once filled them and still love
this beautiful land. The White man will never be alone.
Let him be just and deal kindly with my people,
for the dead are not powerless.
Dead - I say? There is no death. Only a change of worlds.

"Turtle Island," Logan had said. "The land waits for you to mix your blood into the soil." Deganawidah taught that the bloodshed must end, that weapons were to be put down, buried. I saw Logan's face, eyes closed, saying, "When we come out of this earth again, we will be the same family."

I reached for Quinn's cell phone as we sat at the side of the road. "Quinn," I said, "I always figured anyone I connected with was going to leave or die. So I just gave up connecting. You're the exception. And now Maggie, except I'm not sure she counts."

"She counts," said Quinn.

"I know there are some calls I need to make," I said. "Not right now, but maybe you'll help me find someone who will know how to find Tomas. I can no longer bear the idea of him being alone."

Quinn nodded. "Tomas has found his family. His tribe. There's lots of support in the gay community. You'll find him or you'll find help for your grief." She tapped on my hand that cradled the phone. "What call are you making now?"

The quirky smile curling the edges of her lips gave me confidence. She had seen the moment when I realized my mother had chosen her journey. I could let go of my image of my mother as a victim. Quinn looked at me as if she saw a powerful woman. Though the storm barometer was pressing, I knew deep down, despite my father's fears or the root of his mean-spirited words, I was loved. I punched a number and listened to the voice on the answering machine, then I said into the phone, "Dad, I'm coming home. We need to talk."

AUTHOR'S NOTE

I'm not an expert on Native American religion or culture. In researching my characters' introduction to the early inhabitants of North America, I've been privileged to have many fine tutors. In addition to my reading list, I'd like to thank the many people who continue the oral tradition and keep the stories and legends of the land alive. I'm grateful to the Huron, Cayuga, Oneida, and Lenni Lenape people who have allowed their stories to become part of the air and soil that I explored. Though my story is fiction, I have tried to convey the old legends with the dignity they deserve. I believe my sources have been trustworthy, but I apologize if I have inadvertently altered or deleted any aspects of these teachings.

I've been curious to learn about the English and European forefathers' intentions in the founding of America. One of our historical fellows, Benjamin Franklin, made a small fortune as the printer who published the records of Indian treaties and sold them in the colonies as well as in England and Europe. It was an original mass-produced form of literature. The allure was in the governing ideas displayed by the native people. Autonomous tribes with equal representation among the united whole made the Iroquois band of nations strong. Time was given to serious debates before a decision was made: 'Caucus' is a Native American word. Each member of the village had a voice in tribal decisions, an ancient tradition. In Franklin's early career, he traveled to treaty meetings for a firsthand look at how they operated. Thomas Jefferson may have been the main author of the Declaration of Independence, but he himself gave credit to Franklin for the union's principle ideas.

When I began writing A TREE ON TURTLE ISLAND, disunity seemed to be the prevailing sauce in the American melting pot. Our strides toward racial understanding and unity fell short. Religious intolerance seethed along with cultural taboos against abortion and sexual orientation. Violence was the mainstream culture for urban youth; even suburbs and rural towns contended with gangs and gun violence.

In 2001, America united against another threat—terrorism. But I had to ask if the war against our enemies differed from the war against ourselves. Someone must be right and someone else must be wrong. Someone must be good and someone else must be evil. We judge and we separate. Mediation and communication become strained or break down. My hope is simple—that we find our way back to the meeting places and continue the quest for peace.

ACKNOWLEDGMENTS

I've had rich and wonderful experiences at the libraries and historical sites and societies where my research led, among them the Newberry Library in Chicago, the Northwestern University Library in Evanston and The Webber Resource Center for Native Cultures of the Americas at Chicago's Field Museum of Natural History. I also used the Resource Center of the New York State Archives and the most valuable and rewarding Northumberland County Historical Society in Sunbury, PA, the town built on the site of the Shamokin Indian village. The State Museums of both New York and Pennsylvania were very helpful as well.

I want to thank Michele Golding, my earliest champion, as well as my first manuscript readers for their encouragement and ideas: Dr. Shelley Buntman, Lin O'Malley Butler, John McEnaney, Elena Robinson and Carole Smith. In fairness to them, they saw only the colonial draft. Susan Talmadge gave valuable assistance in language translation. Later, I had guidance from Liz Ashling, Corinne Edwards and Myrna Levy. The editing from Sandra L. Wisenberg and June Rouse was inspirational. I reserve a special level of thanks for the editorial assistance of Hawk Stone and Carol DeChant, who have been my mentors for as long as I've known them.

I met some extraordinary people as I did my research. James H. Merrell, the author of *INTO THE AMERICAN WOODS: Negotiators on the Pennsylvania Frontier*, was professor of history at Northwestern University in Evanston. I was delighted to be able to meet him and awed at the amount of time and care he offered to help me understand the significance of the historical backwoods. I'm also grateful to my teachers of the 'winkte' tradition, Gunn Hollingsworth, Myrna Levy and Michael Soto.

Whenever I wonder how I found the time and energy to complete this project, I look directly at those who have sustained me with their friendship and confidence: Kathleen Anderson, Michael Flatley, Gail Haus, Red Star, Sharon Kater and the wonderful members of my book groups and healing groups. My family has been supportive, both with reading, listening and tolerating my schedule. Thanks with all my heart to my mother, Joyce Sechler, Terry and Debra Sechler and my son, Matthew Ozmun, whom I give credit for inventing the word 'dreamality.' I saved until last my enduring gratitude for my partner, Kathy Neff, who knows how much her presence in my life means to me.

Printed in the United States
871100001B